THE COUPLES TRIP

THE COUPLES TRIP

THE COUPLES TRIP

A NOVEL

ULF KVENSLER

HANOVER
SQUARE
PRESS

ISBN-13: 978-1-335-00609-7

The Couples Trip

Originally published in Swedish in 2022 as *Sarek* by Albert Bonniers Förlag, Sweden.

This edition published in 2023.

Published in agreement with Salomonsson Agency.

Translated by Marlaine Delargy.

Hanover Square Press
22 Adelaide St. West, 41st Floor
Toronto, Ontario M5H 4E3, Canada
HanoverSqPress.com
BookClubbish.com

Printed in U.S.A.

To Adam and Olivia

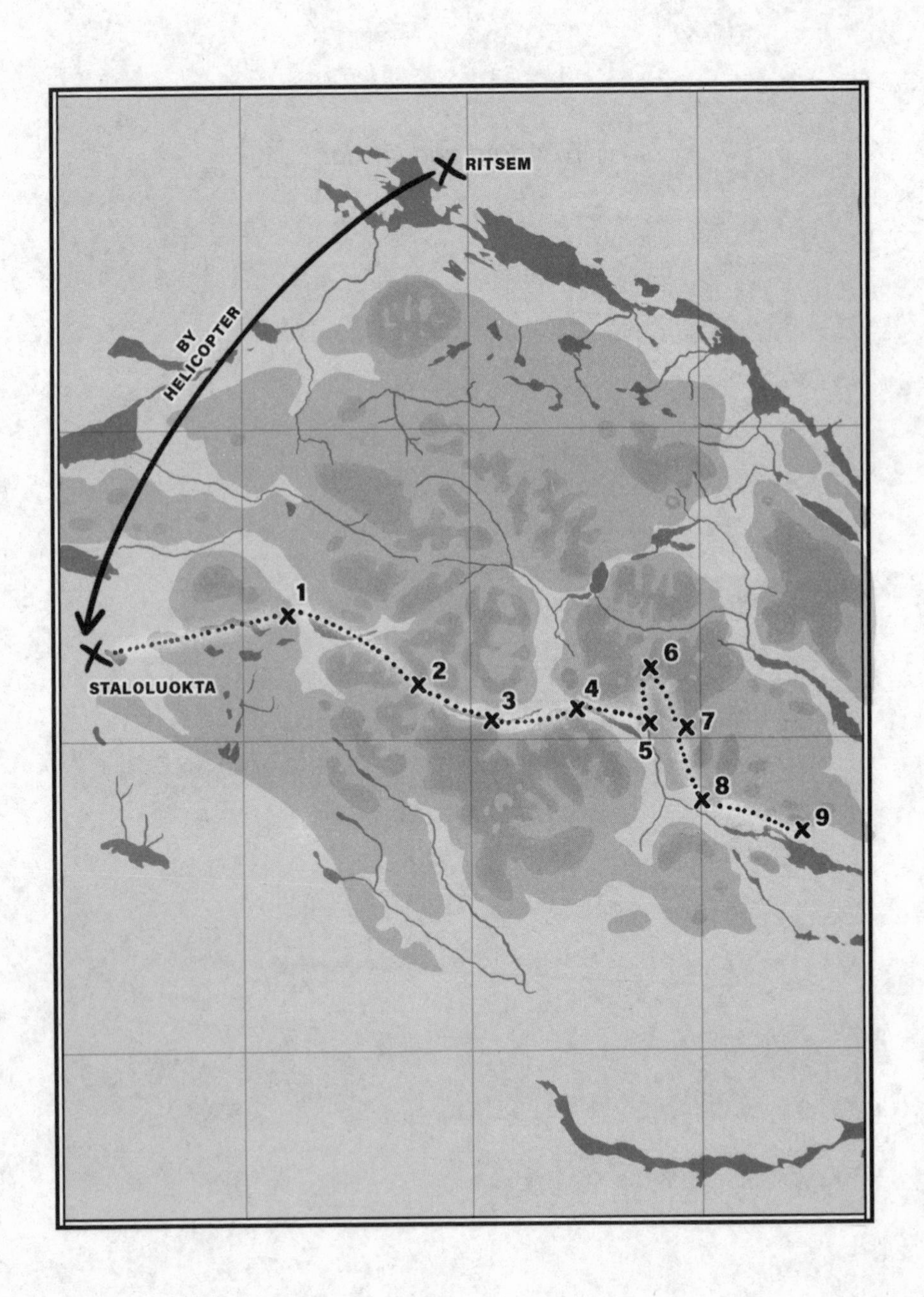
RITSEM
BY HELICOPTER
STALOLUOKTA
1
2
3
4
5
6
7
8
9

1 - Campsite Night 1

2 - Campsite Night 2

3 - Campsite Night 3

4 - "Rovdjurstorget," Predator Square. Anna sees Milena on the other side of the river.

5 - Campsite Night 4

6 - The ridge where Henrik suffers a dangerous accident.

7 - Campsite Night 5

8 - Anna leaves Milena to get help.

9 - Anna is located

To some degree, the topography has had to conform to the dramaturgic needs of the narrative. Parts of the route that the characters in this book travel do not exist in real life. In general, I would dissuade from going to Sarek if you do not have great prior experience with mountain hiking. My friends and I have hiked every year for the past twenty years, but we were still caught off guard by the difference between hiking on versus off trail. (Okay, I was caught off guard. I will not blame the others.)

Radio communication between the air ambulance and Gällivare hospital, September 15, 2019, at 2:16 a.m.

"We've just picked up the woman in Aktse."

"What's her condition?"

"She's suffering from hypothermia, and is in a pretty bad way. Conscious, but only just."

"Okay."

"She doesn't have any ID on her, but says her name is Anna."

"Noted."

"She has cuts and bruises all over her body, and her right arm is broken. We're giving her a couple of liters of a crystalloid infusion."

"Has she fallen?"

"Looks that way, but she also has marks around her neck. Possible attempted strangulation."

"Okay."

"Hard to be sure, though."

"We'll be ready for her."

"Thanks. Over and out."

STOCKHOLM, JULY 2019

I love Stockholm in the middle of July. The residents escape to Gotland, Båstad or the French Riviera, the place sinks into a summer trance. You can kind of have her to yourself.

It was a Saturday evening, the end of a very hot day. It became significantly cooler when the sun no longer reached down into the streets of the built-up city center. I had been in my office since seven in the morning, and decided to walk home in order to get some fresh air. The farther I went, the fewer tourists I saw and heard.

Vasastan was practically deserted. In a few hours, when darkness fell, the drunken, noisy weekend revelers would head for Odenplan—but by then I would be safely tucked up in bed.

I stopped and laid the palm of my hand on the ochre-colored facade of an apartment block. It was as warm as a radiator.

I thought I would pick up some food on the way, and called Henrik to ask if he wanted something. He did, so I ordered a poke bowl with salmon for him, and an eleven-piece for myself from the local Japanese place. When I picked up the dishes the man behind the counter gave me a cheerful nod, and so he should; we went there at least twice a week.

I carried on to our block and took the lift up to the fifth floor. I opened the front door and called out to Henrik.

"Hello!"

"Hi," came the muted response from the living room. I could hear the sound of the television.

In the kitchen I was confronted with a pile of dirty dishes in the sink, and a messy table. Henrik's coffee cup was still there, along with bits of kitchen paper. Crumbs everywhere.

I could have wept.

It was Saturday and I'd worked for more than twelve hours, as I had virtually every day throughout the summer. I'd called Henrik and asked what he wanted to eat, I'd ordered the food and picked it up, and he hadn't even bothered to drag himself off the sofa to tidy up after himself—let alone get out the glasses and something to drink.

He was on holiday, and spent all his time in the apartment.

This massive fucking kitchen with a table that seats ten. What's the point? We're pathetic.

The TV fell silent, and he shambled into the kitchen.

"I'm sick and tired of…" I began, my voice shaking with anger. "I've sorted the food, couldn't you at least clean up after yourself? Do you expect me to do that as well?"

Henrik said nothing, but he put his coffee cup in the sink, threw away the kitchen paper, fetched the dishcloth and began to wipe down the table. Judging by his body language, this required an almost superhuman effort.

I sighed, took a bottle of sparkling water out of the fridge and poured myself a large glass.

"I think we're going to have to postpone our trip."

Henrik looked up but said nothing. He simply carried on wiping the table. "I can't be away for a week right now," I went on.

"I see."

"The beginning of September works better for me."

"We'll have to check with Milena."

"Obviously. I'll call her."

I was too angry and upset to sit down and eat with him, so I went and took a long shower instead. The stream of hot water washed away some of my frustration, and soon I was regretting my harsh words. I was tired and had overreacted.

We made up later on. Henrik managed a wan smile when I apologized and gave him a hug. We drank a glass of wine and watched an episode of a series on HBO, cuddled up on the sofa. I fell asleep halfway through, woke up as the credits rolled at the end. I kissed Henrik and went to bed. He stayed where he was, staring blankly at the screen.

How did we end up here? Do I even know who Henrik is anymore?

Interview with Anna Samuelsson 880216-3382, September 16, 2019, Gällivare hospital, conducted by Detective Inspector Anders Suhonen.

"So… I'm recording now. Hi, Anna, my name is Anders."

"Hi."

"I'm very pleased that you're willing to talk to me—I realize you're tired and in pain, but it's good to tackle these things as soon as possible."

"Yes."

"If you start to feel too tired or in too much pain, we can take a break or stop for today and carry on tomorrow. Is that okay with you?"

"Yes."

"You promise you'll tell me?"

"Yes."

"Your pain is manageable now?"

"It's fine."

"In that case I'll just go through the formalities first… What is your full name?"

"Anna Signe Samuelsson."

"ID number?"

"880216-3382."

"Where do you live?"

"Stockholm."

"What's your profession?"

"I'm a lawyer."

"Marital status?"

Silence.

"Anna? Are you married, single…?"

"Engaged."

"To…?"

"Henrik Ljungman."

"Was he with you on the trip?"

Silence.

"Did Henrik travel into Sarek with you?"

"Yes."

"Henrik Ljungman… Do you happen to know his ID number?"

"820302-7141."

"Thank you. So we've got…"

"Have you found Milena?"

"Milena? Who's Milena?"

"Tankovic. She's… She was… When… What day is it today?"

"Monday September 16th."

"Yesterday… I think… We split up…"

Silence.

"Milena Tankovic. Was she alive when you last saw her?"

Silence. Sobbing.

"Anna? Do you know if Milena was alive when you last saw her?"

Sobbing.

"No… But you have to find her…"

"She wasn't alive?"

"No…"

Sobbing.

"Was Milena with you from the start of the trip?"

"Yes."

"Do you know her ID number?"

"No."

"Where did you leave her?"

Silence. Sobbing.

"I can't…"

"Did you… You were alone when you were found near Aktse. Can you tell me how long you'd been walking on your own?"

Silence. Sobbing.

"Do you think we might find Milena in the same area?"

"I don't know…"

"Okay… I'm going to go and fetch a map, see if you can give me an idea of where Milena could be. And Henrik. Is that okay with you?"

Silence.

"It was the three of you, right? You, Henrik and Milena?"

Inaudible.

"What did you say?"

"There was someone else."

I know exactly where and when I heard his name for the first time.

It was Friday August 30th, Milena and I were having lunch at Miss Clara on Sveavägen. It was warm and sunny but with a new freshness in the air, the sunlight was a little paler somehow, you could feel that autumn was on the way. We had met up in Naturkompaniet at twelve to update our equipment—a new supply of liquefied petroleum gas for the stove, fine woolen socks, anti-mosquito lotion and spray, and a supply of freeze-dried meals.

I'd booked a table for twelve forty-five, and by one thirty we had finished eating and were each enjoying an espresso. The bill had been paid and I really needed to head back to the office; a long lunch like this would mean working late, even though it was Friday. However Milena and I hadn't seen each other for a while and she had agreed, at very short notice, to postpone our trip until September. I didn't want to appear too stressed.

She sipped her coffee, took a deep breath. "So…there was something I wanted to ask you."

"Oh?"

I could see that whatever she was going to say was making her nervous. Milena had always blushed easily, and the color rose in her pale cheeks. She had changed her hairstyle: the dark blond hair was still shoulder-length, but she had allowed her bangs to grow out, and her face was framed by soft strands. It made her look more feminine, and still as sweet and kind as ever. As so often over the years, I felt like giving her a hug.

"The thing is..." She smiled, almost reluctantly. "I've met someone."

"Fantastic!"

"Yes, it is...fantastic." She smiled again, took another deep breath. "So who is he?"

"His name is Jacob. We met online."

"That's brilliant, Milena!" I reached out and gave her hand a quick squeeze. "How long have you been together?"

"Just over a month, so it's still pretty new."

"Tell me all about him! What does he do?"

"Well, at least he's not a lawyer, which is nice."

"Sounds like a catch."

"He's a bit older than me..."

"How much older?"

"He's thirty-eight."

"You're practically the same age," I said. Which wasn't true of course. Milena was thirty-two. I was thirty-one. But I have colleagues who are only a little older than me and who have started to panic, or realized that they're going to panic in a few years, and have got together with men in their fifties, newly divorced with kids. A guaranteed recipe for a complicated life. Jacob was the same age as Henrik.

"He's into climbing, kitesurfing, all kinds of extreme sports," Milena went on. "The two of you have something in common there."

I began to wonder if he might be someone I'd met.

"What's his surname?"

"Tessin."

"Jacob Tessin..."

"And he's spent a lot of time in the mountains, both walking and climbing. So when he heard we were going up to Abisko, he...he asked if he could join us."

The question took me by surprise; I didn't know what to say. "Right," I managed eventually.

"I know this is very last minute, so I understand if it's not okay."

"It's just...this kind of trip can be pretty intense, and Henrik and I have never even met him..."

"No, it's fine, I understand."

"Do you want him to come?"

"Of course—he's my boyfriend." Milena smiled. I smiled back.

"I'll have to ask Henrik."

"Of course."

"It's just over a week until we leave—will he be able to get the time off work at such short notice?"

"He says it's not a problem."

"What does he do?"

"He's a consultant with a company called BCG."

"I've heard of them... Sorry, but I'm really curious now—have you got a photo?"

"No," Milena said, half-heartedly digging out her phone. "It's weird, but I haven't."

She fiddled with her phone as if some forgotten image of Jacob might suddenly appear.

"It's fine, I was just thinking that if he's a climber, I might know him from somewhere."

"Sorry, no, I haven't got..." She fell silent. I smiled again.

"I'll have a chat with Henrik and give you a call. I'm so pleased you've met someone, Milena—I really am."

"Thank you."

"And I can't wait to meet him. It's just… We need to give it some thought."

"I understand—and if you and Henrik aren't cool with the idea, then tell me. It's not an issue."

"No. Great."

We left the restaurant and said our goodbyes on the pavement outside with a hug and a promise to speak on the weekend.

On the way back to the office my curiosity got the better of me. I opened up BCG's home page and searched for "Jacob Tessin." Boston Consulting Group is one of the world's largest and most prestigious consultancies. Admittedly its reputation in Sweden is somewhat tarnished due to its involvement in the New Karolinska building project, but even so. Many sought posts there, but few were chosen. Their salaries and working hours were similar to ours as corporate lawyers. Eighty-hour weeks were nothing unusual, nor was an annual salary similar to that of a company director.

However I couldn't find a Jacob Tessin. Or Jakob Tessin, or any of the other spelling variations I came up with. This didn't strike me as particularly strange; many home pages have ineffective search functions, although you might think a firm like BCG would have the ability to construct a fully operational website. Maybe Jacob wasn't based in the Stockholm office; I knew that consultants at that level were often loaned to projects in other countries.

I tried Facebook instead, and there he was.

Jacob Tessin. Tall and slim, athletic, with a muscular build that I recognized from other climbers and endurance sportsmen and women. Muscles for a specific purpose, not created in front of the mirror at the gym. His dark brown hair was cut short, and his skin was tanned; there was a warmth to his coloring. He looked like one of those fortunate people who never burn in the sun.

Almost every picture showed him in various sporting contexts: in the mountains, in a kayak riding the rapids, kitted out ready to go kitesurfing on a beach. Three guys in a forest in mountain bike gear, arms around one another's shoulders, Jacob in the middle, all three muddy and happy as little boys.

The only thing I couldn't see was his eyes. He was always wearing sporty sunglasses that wrapped tightly around his head, reflecting the world in all the colors of the rainbow.

But then I found a group of photographs that differed from the rest: Jacob and two male friends on holiday in some Mediterranean country, possibly Spain or Portugal. Surfing and sunbathing of course, plus a few taken in an ancient, crumbling town center, with narrow alleyways and shops that obviously catered to tourists. There were also several pictures from an evening at a taverna. Jacob and his friends were sitting at an outside table with the street clearly visible behind them. Colored lanterns and a warm glow from other restaurants and bars, plenty of people around. I could almost sense the warm breeze on my skin, feel the pleasant buzz of intoxication after a couple of glasses of wine, the joy of life. I longed to be there.

And Jacob had pushed his sunglasses up onto his forehead. He was smiling at the camera, his brown eyes sparkling.

Interview with Anna Samuelsson 880216-3382, September 16, 2019, Gällivare hospital, conducted by Detective Inspector Anders Suhonen.

"Okay, let's see… Could you try to show me on the map roughly where you think we should look for Henrik and Milena? And Jacob."

"I don't know…"

"Let's just try, Anna. It doesn't have to be exact. Sarek is huge, so if we can just reduce the search area a little that would be very helpful. This is where we found you."

Silence.

"I'm guessing that you'd come from the interior of the park? So you were heading east, like this?"

"Mm."

"Did you walk along this river? Do you remember? Was the river on your right?"

Silence.

"I think so."

"And you were alone? Or were any of the others with you?"

"Milena… She was with me for a while."

"So you and Milena walked together for some of the time?"

"Yes."

"Okay. Do you remember where you came from? Did the two of you pass Rovdjurstorget?"

Silence.

"Anna? Can you remember anything about the route you took?"

Silence. Sobbing.

"Well, at least we have something to go on as far as Milena is concerned, which is great. We'll leave it there for today. Get some rest, and we'll try again tomorrow if you feel up to it."

Silence.

"And you can tell your story in whatever order you like, at your own speed. I'll be listening."

"It's very late to come up with this now," Henrik said, squeezing lime juice into a bowl to make a dressing. "We leave in a week."

It was Friday evening, a few hours after I'd met up with Milena. Henrik and I were in the kitchen preparing dinner. We were expecting guests. I'd had to work late after my extended lunch break and had only just got home, but fortunately Henrik had made a start without me. He liked cooking, and the prospect of a sociable gathering seemed to have given him a burst of energy, which was much needed. He'd been back at work in Uppsala for a few weeks now, but he couldn't shake off the listlessness, the constant grayness in his attitude and appearance.

Now however a salmon on a bed of salt was baking in the oven, new potatoes with dill were bubbling away in a cast iron pan and dessert was already in the fridge—individual portions of panna cotta, along with a bowl of blueberries in lime juice and muscovado sugar. I was chopping coriander to go with the cod ceviche starter. Two bottles of Sancerre stood open and ready on the table with several more waiting in the wine cooler.

I'd told Henrik that Milena had a new boyfriend, and asked if he could join us on our trip to the mountains. I'd given the matter a lot of thought during the afternoon, and was leaning toward letting Jacob come along.

"Absolutely," I said, "but they've only just got together, which is why she didn't mention it earlier." I put the coriander leaves in a glass and snipped them into tiny pieces.

Henrik didn't reply; there was a brooding quality to his silence. He shook some pink peppercorns into the electronic mill and ground them over the dressing.

When we sold our respective flats in order to move in together, we found this four-room 120-square-meter apartment, which was unusual in that it hadn't been renovated for twenty-five years. We stripped out the whole place. I acted as project manager—except for the kitchen, which was Henrik's domain. We kept as much of the original charm as possible: the wainscoting, the stucco ceilings, the old wooden floors. And then we filled it with modern Scandinavian design. Not particularly original, but attractive and functional and not excessively personal, in case we wanted to sell up and buy a house in a few years' time.

We knocked down a wall in order to make the kitchen bigger and allow for a generous dining area. Oven, fridge, freezer, microwave, espresso machine, food processor—everything was stylish and high tech. One of the things Henrik liked most about cooking was the ability to acquire various gadgets. He used a thermometer to ensure that the eggs boiled at precisely sixty-three degrees. He loved making crème brûlée so that he could use his ridiculously oversized blowtorch, a professional tool that he'd seen the chefs wielding in a trendy concept restaurant. He was able to adjust the temperature of the oven from his mobile, wherever he might be in the apartment, while another app controlled the music that poured from tiny hidden speakers. I once counted: in the kitchen alone four different digital displays showed the exact time.

It's not that I'm unhappy in our apartment, but I have sometimes wondered whether my yearning for nature and the mountains is heightened by a need to escape from digital numbers and buttons and menus and things that beep and efficient little electric motors that hum away discreetly. I have to get back to something primordial, something that has always been there and will always be there. In some strange way, feeling small and insignificant brings me a deep sense of calm.

The mountains don't care about you. Nor do they ask anything of you.

Henrik clearly had nothing more to add, but I kept going. "I just think it's hard to say no."

"Why?"

"Milena's never objected to you coming along."

"That's different."

"Why?"

"She knows me. She knew me before you did, in fact. We haven't a clue who this new guy is."

I got Henrik's point of course. The three of us had been on many trips over the years, following well-established patterns, each with our own role to play. It was one of the few times of the year when I felt completely relaxed. No pressure to achieve anything. Letting someone we didn't know come along, even if he was really nice, would mean that none of us would be able to switch off in the same way as usual.

And if he was weird, or unpleasant, our week in the mountains might be very hard work.

"She agreed when we wanted to postpone the trip from July to September," I pointed out.

"When *you* wanted to postpone the trip."

"Okay, okay. Whatever. It just seems a bit mean if we say no now. She's never asked to bring anyone before. She must have thought about how he'd fit in. And even if he's not the nicest guy in the world, surely we can put up with him for a week. For Milena's sake."

Once again, Henrik didn't say a word. He concentrated on mixing his dressing. I sliced the fresh cod into neat little pieces, and eventually I looked at him.

"Don't you think? Henrik?"

"Fine," he said eventually. He sounded tired.

I glanced at the clock on the microwave. Our guests were due very soon. The cooker beeped to tell us that the potatoes were ready. Henrik slid the pan off the hot plate, which glowed orange beneath the ceramic hob.

Neither of us spoke again until the doorbell rang a few minutes later. It felt as if the first guests to arrive were saving us from each other.

Interview with Anna Samuelsson 880216-3382, September 17, 2019, Gällivare hospital, conducted by Detective Inspector Anders Suhonen.

"How are you feeling today?"

"Okay."

"How did you sleep?"

"Not very well."

"Were you in pain?"

"Mm."

"And now?"

"No pain, but I'm tired."

"I can understand that. We'll have a little chat, Anna, and as soon as you feel it's too much, you tell me. Is that okay with you?"

"Mm."

"I just want to check that I've got this right: you and Henrik Ljungman are engaged?"

"Yes."

"And Milena Tankovic and Jacob Tessin—are they also a couple?"

"Yes."

"And how did you all know one another?"

"Milena and I are friends from university. We both studied Law at Uppsala. Milena knows Henrik from Uppsala too. He was a lecturer in the Law Department."

"So the three of you have known one another for a long time."

"Yes. And we've spent a week in the mountains every year for ages."

"Where did you go?"

"The usual places. The Jämtland Triangle. Kungsleden from Abisko, up Kebnekaise. Norway once. Borgafjäll."

"Did you stay in cabins?"

"Usually, yes, but we always take tents so that we can spend a couple of nights out on the mountain."

"I understand. The reason I'm asking is that Sarek is a little tougher—as you've discovered. And in September…the weather can be pretty bad then."

"We always go in July, but I was working all summer so we had to postpone until September."

"I see."

"And we weren't planning to go to Sarek. We were going to follow Kungsleden again, from Abisko to Kebnekaise."

"But you changed your minds?"

"It was Jacob's idea."

Simon leaned back in his chair, stretched out his long legs under the table and emptied his wineglass.

"So when are you two going to tie the knot?" he asked in a spiteful tone of voice without looking at either me or Henrik. Everyone laughed. We'd been talking about mutual friends who were getting married later in the autumn; we were all invited to the wedding.

Henrik smiled and grimaced, as if the question were painful.

"Lovely weather we're having," he said, picking up the bottle of wine. "Anyone for a top-up?"

More laughter. The exaggerated attempt at a diversion had worked. No one could possibly believe that this was actually a sensitive issue, when Henrik could joke about it so easily.

"Good things come to those who wait and all that," I added with a smile.

"Blah blah blah," Simon said, and I realized that he was more drunk than usual.

He was co-owner of the practice where I worked, and we'd done the island-to-island swim-run race from Sandhamn to Utö together a couple of times. His wife, Jennifer, who was head of

PR at a company listed on the stock market, gave him a searching look. She'd obviously drawn the same conclusion as I had.

"Henrik?" Simon went on. "Are you the one who's dragging your heels? Do you think you might find somebody better than Anna?"

"Simon," Jennifer said.

"What?"

"Calm down."

"Absolutely, no problem, I will calm down. Sometimes you have to calm down, but on the other hand, sometimes you need to speed up, if for example, and I'm talking hypothetically here, definitely hypothetically, if for example you've been engaged for a couple of decades and..."

A chorus of protest from me, Jennifer, Erika and Olof drowned out Simon's voice. Henrik stared down at the table; he was still smiling, but there was no warmth in his expression.

Erika gave him a worried look. She was his former wingman from the Faculty of Law at Uppsala, and these days she was a professor at the University of Södertörn. She and Olof were the only couple among our friendship circle who'd had children so far.

"Simon," Jennifer said again, her tone a little sharper this time.

"Okay, okay—sorry I'm trying to get to the bottom of something we're all wondering about."

I glanced at Henrik. "Good—that's one person I can cross off the guest list," I said.

Henrik met my gaze.

"Who? What guest list?" Mark wanted to know. He and Valle had just come in after smoking a cigarette on the balcony. Mark was the fund manager at a bank we'd helped out with some major acquisitions, and Valle—a choreographer—was his husband.

"Simon's not invited to our wedding," I informed him.

"So have you set a date?" Mark asked. I simply shook my head.

Erika turned to Henrik, keen to help us change the subject. "Are you going to the mountains this year?"

"Yes, we leave in a week."

"With…what was her name again?"

"Milena. Yes."

"Did you know you can get married in the mountains?" Simon chipped in, but nobody laughed this time. He'd crossed the line from amusing to irritating. Jennifer glared at him without saying a word.

I caught Henrik's eye. "And maybe one more person," I said on the spur of the moment; I wanted to get away from the topic of our non-wedding, but I also thought it would interest everyone. Henrik scowled at me.

"Oh, who's that?" Erika asked.

"Milena's got a boyfriend."

Mark frowned. "Remind me—who's Milena?"

"You've met her here a couple of times," I reminded him. "She's an old friend of ours from Uppsala. Light brown hair, not quite as tall as me."

"I remember. Quiet, slightly mysterious."

"Was she the one you tried to pair up with Truls Kofoed?" Simon wondered.

"No, but I did sit them next to each other at dinner once."

"She's always been single, hasn't she?" Mark said.

Henrik looked annoyed. "No, she hasn't always been single."

"Hasn't she?" I said.

"No, she hasn't. She's had boyfriends."

"Anyway," I went on, "she's met this guy called Jacob. He works at BCG, and apparently he's spent a lot of time in the mountains, so she asked if he could come along."

"But you haven't met him?" Mark asked with a frown.

"No," Henrik replied.

Erika turned to Olof. "BCG—isn't that where Jossan works?"

"It is. What's this guy's surname?"

"Tessin. Jacob Tessin."

Olof thought for a moment. "I've hung out with Jossan for drinks after work a few times… Jacob sounds kind of familiar. Any idea what he looks like?"

"Tall and dark," I said. "Who's Jossan?"

"My cousin."

"A tall dark stranger," Simon said, putting on a silly voice as if he were reading from a romance novel. No one found it funny, least of all Henrik, who took a big gulp of his wine. I hadn't told him that I'd tracked down Jacob on Facebook and seen photos of him.

"I think I might have met him," Olof said. "It definitely rings a bell."

"Can you ask your cousin what he's like?" I said.

"No problem. Jacob Tessin?"

"Yes."

"So what have you decided? Are you going to let him join you?" Erika asked.

I was already regretting bringing the subject up. Henrik and I hadn't finished discussing it, and now our half-drunk friends—in Simon's case completely drunk—would be picking over the pros and cons. I realized that Henrik might easily come across as ungenerous and petty.

"We haven't made up our minds yet," I explained. "On the one hand Milena has never asked if she could bring anyone along before. I had to postpone this year's trip because I was tied up with work in the summer, and that was okay with her. So it seems a bit mean to say no. On the other hand…you're kind of thrown together in the mountains. The three of us know one another so well, and we'd have to make allowances for someone we've never met. It wouldn't be the same."

Erika nodded. "It seems a bit odd for Milena to even ask, in my opinion."

Of course you're going to agree with Henrik, I thought. *You always do.* But that wasn't fair; I hadn't mentioned who held which opinion.

"Yes, but if this guy loves the mountains... I don't think Milena would bring someone who wouldn't fit in."

"Well, we're not going to resolve the matter tonight," Henrik snapped. Everyone could tell that he was annoyed.

"You're quite right," I said, smoothing things over. "Anyone for coffee? Tea?" A murmur of voices in response. Everyone was happy to move on. Except for Simon. He knocked back the contents of his glass.

"Jacob Tessin...he sounds like a complete fucking wanker." No one laughed.

On the Saturday when we were due to leave, we got up early to pack. Everything had been bought and laid out, so all we had to do was stow it in our rucksacks.

I don't mind packing, not when we're going to the mountains. If I'd been able to focus entirely on that task, I would actually have enjoyed it. All the kit we take with us reminds me of intense experiences on previous trips. When I pick up the little bottle I use for liquid soap, I can smell the charred wood paneling in an old sauna, I can see a mountainside through a tiny window.

But of course I wasn't able to concentrate only on our packing on that particular Saturday; I had to work as well, which made the day fragmented and stressful. I was going to be away for a week, and had to take care of a number of things before I left. Those days in the mountains are the only time in the whole year when I'm not accessible; otherwise both clients and colleagues know they can call me anytime.

Right at the bottom of our rucksacks we placed changes of clothing, thermal underwear and socks, which must be kept dry at all costs. Henrik secured the tent to the bottom of his rucksack, while in return I stashed all the food in mine. We would mostly be staying overnight in cabins with a small kitchen, or at least a hot plate, but we were planning on camping out for some of the time, and we would have lunch outdoors every day unless it rained heavily or snowed. It's also nice to take a break when you find a beautiful spot on the mountainside, so I packed the Trangia stove along with gas cartridges and so on. Oats to make porridge for breakfast, packets of dried soup, quick-cook macaroni to bulk out the soup, plus several freeze-dried meals. Four different spices. Coffee, peanuts, raisins. Chocolate and a few bags of sweets.

When I'd finished with the food, I moved on to everything else that had proved necessary during our previous expeditions. Utilitarian toiletry bag, waterproofs, padded gilet, hat and gloves, Swiss Army knife. Finally I tucked the weatherproof map of Abisko and Kebnekaise in the top pocket. Job done.

I carried my rucksack into the bathroom and placed it on the scales. 12.3 kilos—good. In the first couple of years it had been around twenty kilos, and reducing the weight little by little, year over year, had become something of a challenge for me. A lighter load made walking much easier, but of course there was a cost in terms of comfort when we reached our destination. Henrik was happy to carry more in order to have a more enjoyable experience in the cabins.

One year he'd taken a bottle of wine, in spite of my repeated attempts to dissuade him. When he opened it in the cabin at Singi I refused to drink any of it on principle. Henrik and Milena had a glass each, and finished it off the following evening. I didn't give any indication that I would have loved to join them, and Henrik didn't give any indication that carrying an extra kilo had been hard work. However he had never done it again.

There was a tingle of excitement in my tummy. We were catching the overnight train to Abisko. From there we would follow Kungsleden down toward Kebnekaise, then branch off onto the route known as Durlings led. The plan was to camp there for a night or two, fit in a climb, then continue over Vierranvarri down to the Kebnekaise mountain station. We would relax there for a few days before heading home. I could venture out into the Tarfala Valley if I felt like it, or climb Kebnekaise via the more difficult eastern route. I knew I wouldn't be able to persuade Henrik or Milena to join me, but I had nothing against spending some time alone. It would allow me to set my own pace, which was faster than theirs.

By five o'clock both Henrik and I had changed into our walking clothes. I put up my blond hair in a ponytail and pulled on my trainers. My boots were draped over my rucksack, tied together by the laces. I swung the rucksack over one shoulder and slipped my other arm through the strap. Henrik did the same.

We left the apartment and locked the door behind us.

We made our way toward Central Station. The good weather had held; the air was clear and warm. The city was breathing calmly and steadily. A few passersby glanced at us curiously as we marched along with our big rucksacks. The weight on my back was familiar and pleasant, unused muscles in my legs and stomach came to life as my body adapted. I felt strong and supple and full of energy. We stopped for a double espresso at a café on Tegnérlunden—the last really good coffee we would drink for just over a week. It was delicious, and the birds chirped in the trees around Strindberg's statue.

I was looking forward to meeting Jacob Tessin.

By the time our guests had gone home the previous Friday, both Henrik and I had been in a bad mood, and said very little to each other before we went to bed. The following morning Henrik brought up the subject over breakfast and said that he agreed with me—it wasn't fair to tell Milena she couldn't bring Jacob. I was so relieved. I told him I completely understood how he felt; I would have preferred it to have been just the three of us, as usual.

"If it doesn't work, we'll go on our own next year," I promised him. On the Sunday I called Milena.

"We've had a chat and we think it would be great if Jacob came with us."

"Fantastic," Milena said, sounding less thrilled than I'd expected. She wasn't the kind of person to make big gestures or go in for emotional outpourings, but I had hoped for a little more enthusiasm. I assumed she had other things on her mind, and didn't give it another thought.

As our departure date grew closer and our preparations became more concrete, the issue of Jacob slipped into the background. After all, Milena and her new boyfriend were only a small part of the experience. Even if he was uptight or hard to talk to or a compulsive joker or just generally unpleasant, there was so much he couldn't take away from me. The experience of nature itself, the feeling in my body after walking for many hours, how delicious food tasted, the joy of a good night's sleep. He might be irritating, but he wasn't going to destroy my holiday.

Of course it would have been sensible to get together one evening before we left in order to get acquainted, but there hadn't been time. And now we were due to meet him in just a few minutes, and my curiosity was growing. Who was Jacob Tessin, the first guy my friend of ten years had introduced as her boyfriend?

We continued along Upplandsgatan, down the hill, past Norra Bantorget and on to Vasagatan. The noise of the traffic was louder here, the stream of pedestrians hurrying in all directions much busier. I longed for the mountains, where it was never necessary to step aside for another person.

We walked into Central Station's huge foyer. Footsteps and voices echoed from the vaulted ceiling high above our heads, a sound I associated with suitcases and tickets and being on the way to somewhere else.

And there they were, right in the middle of the vast open space: Milena and Jacob.

My first thought: *he's tall.* That had also been my impression when I saw the pictures of him on Facebook, but it was even clearer in reality. Milena is medium height, but she looked small next to Jacob. My next thought, which also matched my impression from Facebook: *he looks fit.* His rucksack was on the floor, he was wearing a sleeveless T-shirt, one hand in the pocket of his trousers. His arms were muscular, sinewy and tanned. His posture was also athletic: straight-backed, chest out.

He was holding Milena's hand, which was kind of sweet.

Next thought: *he must be older than thirty-eight.* His tanned face was framed by thick dark brown hair. No receding hairline, but those lines on his face, between his eyebrows, on his forehead, the skin on his throat… I would have guessed he was closer to forty-five.

Can all this really have gone through my mind in the few seconds it took us to reach them? Or have I added details I noticed later? I don't know.

I smiled and waved. Milena's face lit up and she waved back. Jacob smiled at me in return, an expectant, slightly tense smile. He let go of Milena's hand, moved his feet up and down on the spot.

"Hi, good to see you," I said when we got closer. "Anna," I added, holding out my hand to Jacob.

"Hi, hi. Jacob."

His grip was firm, the palm of his hand warm and dry. He was still smiling, eyes sparkling. I turned to Milena.

"Hi—how cool is this?"

She beamed at me, I opened my arms and we came together in a big hug. "Here we are at last," she said. Behind me I could hear Jacob greeting Henrik. "So you must be Henrik?"

"That's right."

"Hi, Jacob—nice to meet you."

★★★

There is one more thing that I know I thought back then.

I recognize him.

We made our way to the platform. I was chatting to Milena, but couldn't help listening to Henrik and Jacob with half an ear.

"I'm sorry if I've pushed my way in," Jacob said. "I can understand that you might not be happy with someone who… I mean, the three of you have been doing this for many years, haven't you?"

"It's fine," Henrik replied. "I believe you've spent a lot of time in the mountains?"

"You could say it's my second home."

"Were you born up there?"

"No, but I've visited more or less every year since I was fifteen. Skiing in the winter, climbing in the summer."

"Mm…we've been skiing in Sälen a few times, but we usually go to the Alps."

"Right… I prefer the Riksgränsen ski resort. It's my favorite place—good for paragliding too."

"Oh—is that something you're into?"

"Well, I try. But Abisko is fantastic for walking. And Kebnekaise. You've been there before?"

"Yes. It must be three years since our last trip. Maybe four."

"Being in the mountains is a kind of meditation for me. I work too hard—too many weekends, so it's nice to get away and think about something completely different for a while. Recharge the batteries, so to speak."

"Mm."

The air on the platform was still, filled with the smell of diesel and warm metal. I had worked up a sweat during our walk from home. We found our carriage and climbed aboard. The narrow corridor was cramped as fellow travelers, many with rucksacks, searched for their places. Luckily Henrik and I soon found our sleeping compartment—first-class with its own shower and toilet. We slid open the door and put our rucksacks on the floor.

"This is us," I said to Milena and Jacob. "How about you?"

"I think we must be farther along. We're not together—Jacob only booked the other day."

"Lucky there was space."

Jacob smiled at me. "Absolutely—otherwise I'd have had to hitchhike."

I glanced at Milena. She was smiling too, but at the same time there was an enquiring look in her eyes. I realized she was trying to work out what I thought of Jacob.

"Shall we meet in the restaurant car in half an hour?" I suggested.

"Fine," Milena said, continuing along the corridor. Jacob nodded to me and Henrik—but mostly to me, I thought. Then he followed Milena. Only now did I notice that he had climbing equipment attached to his rucksack—hooks and ropes and an ice ax. Was he planning to tackle Nordtoppen? Or the Tuolpagorni crater?

I slid the door closed and sank down on a folding seat. Henrik was already sitting on the sofa opposite. Eventually I said: "So what do you think?"

"He seems okay."

"He does."

"Mm."

"I have to admit I'm relieved."

"Mm."

"Imagine if we'd thought after five minutes, oh, no we're going to have spend a week in the mountains with this idiot."

Henrik didn't reply. He looked tired. "Do you recognize him?" I asked.

"What? No."

"There's something.... As soon as I saw him I felt there was something familiar about him."

"You've seen pictures of him on Facebook."

"Yes, but that's not what I mean."

"No, I don't recognize him."

The feeling that I'd seen Jacob before was elusive. As soon as I focused on the thought, tried to pin down exactly what it was that I recognized, it disappeared like breath on a pane of glass.

I sighed and looked around. Here we were in our first-class compartment with two comfortable beds and our own toilet, on our way to the mountains for a week's walking. It was a moment filled with energy and anticipation—when you're looking forward to something wonderful, but it hasn't started yet. Often those moments were better than the longed-for experience itself.

I leaned forward, placed my hand on Henrik's. "Top or bottom bunk?"

"I don't care. You choose."

"Okay, I'll take the top then."

"Although you'd really prefer the bottom."

"No, I wouldn't."

"I'll take the top."

"No, you won't—I've already bagged it."

Henrik returned my smile, then he leaned forward too and we kissed.

Everything's going to be fine.

A buzzing sound came from Henrik's pocket. He dug out his phone and opened the message he'd received. As he read it, I saw an almost imperceptible frown appear.

"Hmm."

"What is it?"

He didn't answer right away. He took a deep breath, sat up a little straighter. "Er…it's from Erika."

"What does she say?"

"She says…thanks for dinner last week, good to see you both… Olof asked his cousin, and there's no Jacob Tessin at BCG. For what it's worth. Have a wonderful time in the mountains."

Interview with Anna Samuelsson 880216-3382, September 17, 2019, Gällivare hospital, conducted by Detective Inspector Anders Suhonen.

"And how did you react when you heard this?"

Silence.

"Anna?"

"I got annoyed with Henrik."

"Did you?"

"He made such a big thing of it."

"Right."

"I mean, I couldn't find Jacob on BCG's website, but I didn't think it was that weird."

"No?"

"I might have misheard when Milena told me where he worked. Or maybe he was with a different company that was also called BCG."

"I see."

"There were plenty of possible explanations."

"Mm."

"After all, we'd met him by then, and he seemed okay. In my opinion."

"What did Henrik think?"

Silence.

"It was almost as if he wanted to call the whole thing off, go back home."

"Really?"

Silence.

"We'd… First of all he was annoyed when I wanted to postpone the trip until September, but we got over that. Then we argued about whether we should let Jacob come along or not. But we got over that."

Silence.

"Would you like some water?"

"Please."

Silence.

"There you go."

"Thanks." *Silence.*

"And then.… Then we met Jacob and he was a nice guy and I thought everything was fine, but as soon as Erika's message arrived, it all kicked off again."

"I understand."

"We started arguing."

Silence. Sobbing.

"Such stupid little things… Oh, God…"

"Would you like to take a break?"

"Mm…"

Sobbing.

When we arrived in the restaurant car, Jacob and Milena were already seated at a table. Jacob had a bottle of strong beer, Milena a glass of wine.

"Great—I see the party's already started," I said.

"Go and get what you want—we'll keep the table," Milena replied.

Henrik and I joined the queue. The restaurant car was old—possibly from the '90s—and had seen better days, but its retro design was supposed to be reminiscent of 1930s luxury. The paint was worn on some of the wooden details, and there were holes in the upholstery here and there.

The place was more or less full. The passengers were a mixed bag: plenty of mountain tourists like us, but also a family possibly going to visit relatives in Norrland and a couple of men in their fifties who had already knocked back several strong beers, judging by the noise they were making. Those who had bought their food searched for a table, carrying laden trays with their knees slightly bent in order to compensate for possible jolting as the train sped along. I saw Jacob and Milena gesture in our direction as they politely explained to two elderly ladies that the seats at their table were occupied.

The queue was growing, and now stretched almost the full length of the central aisle. I went back to Jacob and Milena and suggested that we should get their food too, otherwise it would be an eternity before we could all eat together. They gave me their orders.

Outside the windows a flat landscape swished by in the setting autumn sunlight.

Stubbly fields, groves of trees, low-growing birch along a ditch. A car drove alongside the train for a while on a road parallel with the railway line, but it couldn't keep up and eventually disappeared from view. We passed through a village with a level crossing and a closed-down station. I saw a group of teenagers gathered by a fast-food stall. Swish, swish, swish.

We returned to the table with two portions of sautéed reindeer with mashed potato, one prawn sandwich, one chicken wrap, three miniature bottles of wine and one beer, and several packets of nuts and crisps as a starter to dampen our hunger.

Jacob took out his wallet and offered me a two-hundred-kronor note to pay for his meal, but I said I didn't have any change, and no doubt things would even themselves out over the course of the week.

As we shared out the food, I was sure that Milena had picked up on the silence between me and Henrik. She must have realized that things weren't right.

Jacob opened his beer. "So how did you two meet?" he asked, smiling at Henrik and me. Had he also sensed the tension between us? Was this an attempt to get us to talk to each other?

We exchanged glances. "You or me?" I said.

"You," Henrik muttered.

UPPSALA, NOVEMBER 2009

It is Thursday evening at Stockholm's Nation, one of thirteen student societies known as "nations" at the University of Uppsala. This is party night, but before the revelry and the dancing get underway in the new extension to the building, there is a lecture in the original part, which dates from the mid-19th century. The "Thursday speaker" is an old tradition at Stockholm's, like so many other things. An invited guest gives a talk that lasts an hour or so, after which the speaker and a small group from the audience are invited to partake in pea soup and Swedish punsch.

Which is why I am setting out place cards on a long table in the "little room," which is next door to the hall where the lecture will be held. I'm actually responsible for all the arrangements, which is unusual for someone who is new to Uppsala and to the Nation. However several weeks into the term no one had expressed an interest in taking on the role, and I was approached by Carl, who is the Nation's chairman. I had already said when I enrolled that I was happy to get involved, so I couldn't really refuse.

I've been doing the job for a couple of months now, but I'm

still nervous about this evening. The speakers who attract the most attention are of course those who are known beyond the university, beyond Uppsala. So far I have managed to book a high-profile female lawyer who is actively engaged in the debate on social issues, plus a prominent company director—thanks to my father's contacts. Plus a few comedians, famous from TV, who started their careers here. But this week I haven't been quite so successful. This evening's Thursday speaker is Henrik Ljungman, a lecturer in the Law Department. I know he's something of a rising star at the university; he's won some kind of prize as the best lecturer, and he's written textbooks on law even though he's not yet thirty. He also gave a few of our early lectures when we started the course, and yes, he's good—better than most, but I can't say I was spellbound.

So this is something of a dip. In two weeks' time we have Kajsa Bergqvist, who's won Olympic gold in the high jump. Rather more appealing, I think.

I waylaid Henrik after a lecture and asked if he'd like to be our Thursday speaker. His eyes darted from side to side and he didn't say anything at first, so I suggested we should get some lunch while I told him more about it. I presume he couldn't think of a good excuse on the spot, so we had lunch. My new friend Milena was there too. I made my pitch, told him that being a Thursday speaker was one of the finest accolades anyone could receive in Uppsala, entirely comparable with being a summer speaker on the radio. He agreed, but without any great enthusiasm.

I found him kind of reserved and elusive. Formal and correct. It was hard to make eye contact with him. Is he good-looking? I don't know. He has a smooth, symmetrical face, no scars from youthful acne. His skin tone is slightly sallow, like someone who easily tans in the sun but prefers to stay in the shade. His clean-shaven cheeks and chin show the faintest shadow of dark stubble, and his thick dark hair is neatly parted on the side. I'm guessing he uses a little wax. Henrik is just below medium height, and his physique tends toward stockiness. He is wearing chinos, a shirt and jacket, with thick-soled Docksides on his feet—well-dressed but traditional, and yes, a bit boring. He looks older than he is.

I might not have fallen into a trance during his lectures, but it is clear that that is when he's at his best. His voice is deep and masculine, strong enough to be heard by the entire auditorium, and both his body and face seem to come to life when he is addressing an audience. I have to admit that his enthusiasm for his subject is infectious, so I'm expecting this evening to go reasonably well.

Carl appears as I am setting out the last of the place cards.

"Hi, Anna—you look fantastic," he says, his hand resting on my bare shoulder. We air-kiss, mwah-mwah-mwah, like they do in France. And I know he's right. I am wearing a sleeveless tight-fitting black dress that finishes just above the knee. Black stockings, black high-heeled shoes. Real pearl earrings. My long blond hair is tied back in a ponytail. I feel exclusive and feminine and gorgeous. Men will look at me tonight.

Just as Carl is doing now. He is tall and fair and muscular, a bit like a younger version of Dolph Lundgren. He is in a well-cut dark suit and a white shirt, the top buttons casually left undone. As chairman Carl has his own office. He gives an amusing speech at every party. He's going to be an economist. I know a lot of girls who want to go to bed with him.

"How's the seating plan going?"

"Very well, I think. You're here, opposite me, with Laila next to you."

Laila is the inspector responsible for monitoring the Nation's activities. She is a woman in her sixties, a professor of political science.

"Perfect. That means you and I can play footsie under the table."

"My thoughts exactly," I say with a smile, although of course the idea has never crossed my mind.

"I'll never forget the cadet ball at Karlberg Military Academy—two women played footsie with me at the same time all through dinner."

Carl looks me in the eye, expecting me to be impressed. "Wow, busy night."

"Absolutely! I almost got a cramp in my calves!"

I laugh obligingly as I put down the last card. I could have put Henrik next to Laila and myself next to Carl, but I didn't. Henrik will be sitting beside me, I'm pleased to say.

He arrives half an hour before the talk is due to begin. I am busy setting up the computer, projector and screen with one of the club assistants. Some members of the audience have already begun to take their seats; the interest seems to be greater than I had expected.

"Good evening," Henrik says behind me, and I spin around.

"Hi, welcome!" I reply warmly. He holds out his hand a little awkwardly, but I give him a brief hug. He is wearing a dark suit, I can't tell if it's gray or blue in the subdued lighting. He has a silk handkerchief in his breast pocket, and he smells really good.

I'd assumed he would show up in his usual lecturing outfit, chinos and tweed, and I'm pleased he's made the effort to dress smartly.

"How are you feeling?"

"Good."

"Shall we try out your presentation?"

"Sure." He fishes a USB stick out of his inside pocket and hands it to the assistant, who inserts it into the computer. Henrik's images appear on the screen, and he is given a little remote control with which to operate the program.

"Very high tech—I'm not used to this kind of thing."

"We do our best," I say with a smile, and Henrik smiles back.

When we've finished testing out the equipment, I ask if he'd like something to drink. He says he'd like a beer, a Hof if we have one. I lead him to the bar, and on the way we pass the room where we'll be eating later. On impulse I stop.

"Erm…it's pea soup for dinner."

"Perfect."

"I've put you next to me, but if you'd prefer I can seat you beside our inspector, Laila Westerberg."

"No, no, that's absolutely fine."

"Are you sure?"

"Yes—unless you want to swap?"

"No, I want to sit next to you."

"There you go then—in that case we have a plan." Henrik smiles at me again, his face filled with life and warmth, unlike during our lunch a couple of weeks ago. We continue toward the bar.

Why did I stop and ask him? It wasn't as if he could say *yes, I'd like to swap* without seeming rude. And I certainly didn't want to sit next to Carl. Sometimes I'm a mystery to myself.

Twenty minutes later the hall is full and the hum of conversation is almost deafening, echoing off the wood-framed mirrors and portraits of past inspectors, the chandeliers splintering the sound into descant shards. Henrik and I are in the front row. It is precisely seven o'clock. I have butterflies in my tummy, a mixture of anticipation and nerves, even though I'm not the one who's giving the talk. I place a hand on Henrik's arm.

"Shall we?"

"Whenever it suits you."

I step up onto the stage, clap my hands and ask for silence. "Good evening… Welcome, everyone…"

The noise quickly dies down. Someone coughs, there is a scraping sound as a chair is pushed back.

"Welcome to Stockholm's Nation. This evening I have the great honor of introducing one of the University of Uppsala's most sought-after speakers—" at this point I catch Henrik's eye and smile "—the youngest ever lecturer in the Faculty of Law. Ladies and gentlemen, Henrik Ljungman!"

A deafening cheer erupts and Henrik energetically takes the stage as I leave. He beams at the audience, holds up his hands in a disarming gesture.

"What an introduction! Of course I'm incredibly honored to be here. Ever since I was a little boy it has been one of my life goals to be a Thursday speaker at Stockholm's Nation."

More cheers, applause, whistling. Flattery works, even if it's delivered with a touch of irony.

Henrik holds up his hand and counts on his fingers. "I also wanted to become a fireman, and win the biggest bar of chocolate in the world at Gröna Lund. One out of three ain't bad..."

Laughter, shouts of approval. He's been on the stage for thirty seconds and he already has the entire room in the palm of his hand, like a stand-up comedian.

Henrik outdoes himself this evening. He talks about how the Freedom of the Press Act has developed in Sweden, with plenty of amusing examples along the way, including satire from the 18th century. We learn that writers back then didn't pull their punches when they chose to criticize Gustav III. He speaks for approximately forty-five minutes, less than most of our Thursday guests, which leaves his audience slightly dissatisfied. They want to hear more. Then there is a lengthy question-and-answer session, in which he engages in dialogue with a significant number of individuals. Henrik is erudite and quick-witted, with an amazing ability to think outside the box and a wonderful way of expressing himself. Mind and tongue in perfect harmony. At the same time, he comes across as someone who is genuinely interested in the questions people are asking.

He is the best speaker we have ever had by a long, long way. My nerves have disappeared—the evening has been a great success. I can't help vaguely fantasizing, without formulating the idea too clearly, that that might have had something to do with me. I put him in a good mood, made him feel comfortable. It's me he's showing off to: look what I can do!

At eight fifteen he brings proceedings to a close. I hurry onto the stage, present him with an impressive bouquet of flowers, we hug briefly, I lead the applause. Loud cheers die away noticeably quickly, drowned out by the scraping of a hundred chairs. Everyone is in a hurry to get to the bars, which have just opened.

Half an hour later we are seated in the little room. We are drinking cold beer and eating hot pea soup, the atmosphere around the table is cheerful and relaxed.

Henrik's talk provided the perfect start to the evening, and now we can all look forward to drinks, dancing, partying and maybe something more. But I am careful not to stretch out my legs.

Voices echo off the wood-panelled walls in here too, and the volume is even higher. I am sitting very close to Henrik, when we speak we have to lean even closer in order to hear what the other person is saying.

"Have you ever tried stand-up?" I ask.

"No, I haven't."

"Okay…so have you read a book about how stand-up comedians work?"

"No—should I have done?"

"Clearly not, because you seem to know how to do it anyway."

"Thank you. I'll take that as a compliment."

"Please do, otherwise I'll be annoyed. *Skål.*"

"*Skål*, Anna."

I raise my beer bottle, he raises his and we clink. "You were fantastic."

"Thanks—I'm glad you're happy."

Henrik looks at me with a different glint in his eyes, and I experience a sense of mutual satisfaction, as if we've achieved this together. We haven't of course, but that's how he makes me feel.

Maybe I'm a bit tipsy already. A tiny, tiny bit tipsy. Henrik too. Possibly.

Carl reaches across the table, wanting to clink bottles with the star of the evening. "*Skål*, Henrik! Brilliant talk!"

Laila joins in too, raising her glass. "Yes, it was very, very good. I don't suppose you've considered changing to political science?"

Everyone laughs, and we drink another toast.

"The way you started," Carl goes on, "listing your three life goals when you were little, that was so funny. When I was campaigning to be elected chair, I gave a speech where I talked about my childhood dreams, and how me and my kid brother and the other kids in the neighborhood used to play politics. I always insisted on being prime minister. It wasn't exactly a rhetorical masterpiece, but I did get elected."

Carl raises his shoulders a fraction and smiles, modesty written all over his face.

He glances from Henrik to me, ready to bask in our admiration.

"The competition wasn't exactly fierce," Laila says, taking a sip of her beer. Henrik and I are amused by her comment, and Carl realizes that he has no choice but to join in with the laughter.

"No, you're right—I guess the Nation had to make do with what was on offer," he says.

Laila pats his arm. "Sorry, Carl. You do a great job."

Carl turns back to Henrik. "Have you ever considered becoming a defense lawyer?"

"Goodness, suggestions for a career change are raining down on me—does anyone have a pen and paper?" Henrik pats his pockets, pretending to search for his notebook. I laugh and place my hand on his arm.

"I just asked him whether he'd ever tried stand-up," I explain to Carl and Laila.

Carl nods. "I think your rhetorical skills would make you a great success in court.

"And it's well-paid. My aunt is a partner with Mannheimer Swartling—she earns a fortune. She and her husband have a second home, a villa outside Juan-les-Pins, on the Riviera. I often hang out there in the summer."

Another pause to allow us to show how impressed we are.

"Well, maybe I should give it some thought," Henrik says with a smile.

"Professors earn pretty good money too," Laila points out. "And Henrik will be a professor in a few years, so I don't think you need to worry about his finances, Carl."

A chair at the head of the table is pushed back. Henning, our official song leader, gets to his feet. He is only twenty, as handsome as a prince in a fairy tale. Slicked-back dark, wavy hair, clean features, roses in his cheeks that are still visible in spite of his tan. Big blue eyes. And he sings like a god, both in the Nation choir and in a rock band that often plays at student events. He clears his throat and begins to speak, bowing his head to each person he mentions: "Madam Inspector, our distinguished speaker Henrik Ljungman, our chairman, all the other odds and sods around the table…" The sudden break from formality makes everyone laugh. Henning bestows his cherubic smile on me, then continues: "We have a long list of drinking songs to get through this evening, so we'd better make a start; I'm beginning to feel quite stressed. Let's begin with *Det var en gång jag tänkte att punschen övergiva.* Are you with me?"

He begins to sing, and we all join in. Henning's beautiful voice can be heard above the rest of us, but we croak along as best we can.

During the rest of the meal Henrik and I talk almost exclusively to each other. The conversation flows easily. We chat about law, Uppsala, our hobbies. I tell him that I love the mountains—skiing in winter, walking in summer. Henrik says that he has been skiing a few times, but hasn't tried a walking holiday. I mention that I've discussed with my friend Milena, whom Henrik has met, the idea of spending a week up in Abisko next summer—maybe he would like to join us? I am half-joking, and Henrik's response is equally lighthearted. He really should, he says, walking in the mountains is practically part of the national curriculum.

All the time I am pleasantly aware that we are at the center of the gathering, that everyone is watching us, interested in us. When Henrik chats to Laila for a little while, both Carl and Henning catch my eye. I love the attention.

Suddenly Henrik leans back and peers under the table. Carl flushes bright red and sits up a little straighter. "Sorry," he mumbles.

I bite my lower lip to stop myself from grinning.

And so we carry on talking, Henrik and I, about our backgrounds, our parents and siblings. I tell him about my beloved brothers, Erik and Gustaf, my big brother and my little brother; I spent most of my childhood and youth arguing with them and manipulating them. Henrik laughs, says it must have been tough having me as a sister.

I would like to say to him that he is totally different from my father, and that this is a good thing. But I don't; it would be too intimate.

Dinner is over and most people have already left the table. There is a sudden rumbling sound, which seems to shake the building to its very foundations. The nightclub has started up. Carl comes over, turns to Henrik.

"Do you mind if I borrow Anna for a little while?"

"Fine by me, but maybe you should ask her instead."

"Anna? May I?" Carl holds out his hand and I nod, get to my feet. "Back in a moment," I say to Henrik.

"I'm going to the bar," he replies. "Can I get you anything?"

"A G & T please," I manage before Carl drags me away, out of the little room, down the stairs and onto the dance floor, which is already packed. The concrete construction of the new part of the building is like one huge sound box, it's as if the heavy bass beat makes the walls themselves reverberate.

And I love it. Carl gazes at me with a foolish grin on his face, he has zero sense of rhythm and appears to be marching on the spot rather than dancing, but fuck him, I'm slightly drunk and I can feel the bass vibrations through my whole body, almost like a second heartbeat. I raise my arms above my head, let my hips sway from side to side, close my eyes.

God, this is amazing.

After a couple of tracks I yell in Carl's ear that I'm actually the hostess, so I leave him and go in search of Henrik. I find him in the bar, he is just turning around with a gin and tonic in each hand, and his face lights up when he sees me. We sip our drinks, find two seats at a table where some guys who heard his talk shower him with compliments. He engages with them politely, but makes sure that I am drawn into the conversation too.

The bar is too crowded, so we go back to the little room where the noise level is more bearable. We are about to sit down when Henning comes over and thanks Henrik for a fantastic talk—is it okay if he borrows Anna for a little while? He isn't wasting any time, his hand is already resting between my shoulder blades. I take a swig of my G & T, hand it to Henrik. "Hold on to this. And don't go anywhere."

"Got it." Henrik smiles but I don't smile back. Instead I stare at him to show that I am serious—he mustn't go anywhere. That's a compliment too, isn't it?

The dance floor isn't quite so busy now, and Henning takes the opportunity to jitterbug with me. Completely wrong with the heavy EDM beat, but he has enough self-confidence to ignore such a minor detail. I have only the vaguest idea of how to jitterbug, I think we tried it out in a sports lesson in junior school, but I am sensible enough to follow Henning, who knows exactly what to do. He pulls me close, lets me go, spins me around, pulls me close again but in a different way this time, with his arms wrapped around me. "You follow like a shadow," he says into my ear. I can feel his lips against my skin.

We have fun. Henning is seductive, he is elegant and he smells wonderful. It's hardly surprising that he has a reputation as the Stockholm Nation's biggest ladies' man. I have nothing against a one-night stand in principle, but with Henning? No thanks. The gossip would start before he'd even removed his cufflinks. I can't wait to get back to Henrik.

He is sitting at a table in the little room with two girls. They appear to be deep in conversation. My drink is on the table in front of him. Henrik looks very pleased to see me and immediately stands up to get me a chair, but I hold up my hand, I can do it myself. I sit down on the other side of him from his two new admirers. I greet them cheerfully, pick up my G & T and take a good swig.

"We were just saying how fantastic the talk was," the girl closest to Henrik informs me. Wavy red hair in a pageboy cut frames her sweet pretty face. Her skirt has ridden up her toned thighs.

Tell him something he hasn't already heard a thousand times this evening. And pull down your skirt for fuck's sake, everyone can see your panties.

"Wasn't it?" I say. "Are you two studying law as well? I think I recognize you."

Yes, they are studying law as well. So they can't be completely thick, and yet they can't seem to see that they are in the way, and ought to leave me and Henrik in peace. The one with the red hair seems particularly slow on the uptake, gabbling on as if she's known him for years. Eventually I grab Henrik by the hand and stand up.

"Come on—let's dance."

I pull him to his feet and drag him off to the disco before he has time to protest. I don't let go of his hand for a second, until we are in the middle of the deafening sea of noise. He moves cautiously and a little stiffly. It is clear that the dance floor isn't his natural element, but at least I have him to myself again.

I watch his face change from yellow to blue, red, green, then the light loop begins again. His eyes are fixed on me, filled with warmth and drunken devotion. I've decided that he is good-looking after all. Actually, it's not really his face that I find attractive, but his expression, so I come to the conclusion that it's his soul I am drawn to.

After a while he places his warm hand on my bare shoulder and leans forward. "I think I'm going to make a move, head home."

"Me too."

I say it without thinking. We leave the floor, pass the little room and the hall, go down the stairs to the foyer. It is quieter and cooler here. My ears are ringing from the music. There is a short queue for the cloakroom, and we wait in silence.

"I feel as if I'm half-deaf," Henrik says after a while with a wry smile, poking at one ear.

"Mm."

Why did I say I was going home too? He might think I'm clingy, intrusive. Were his eyes darting from side to side when I said it? Pathetic, but I can't change my mind now—that would look weird.

I hear a familiar voice behind me; it's one of the table hostesses who has joined the queue with a friend. She has a reputation as one of the biggest gossips in the whole of Stockholm's Nation, a walking spy center—with the key difference that she gives out more information than she takes in.

And there we are right in front of her, Henrik and I, staring at the wall and pretending we don't exist. Like two puppies who've been caught out doing something naughty. My scalp is itching like mad, but I daren't raise my hand.

Everybody will be talking about us. Shit, shit, shit.

After what seems like an eternity we retrieve our coats and

escape into the night. The city is enveloped in a bitterly cold autumn mist, the yellowish street lamps are nothing more than blurred blobs in the darkness. Up above us at the top of Drottninggatan is the majestic outline of Carolina Rediviva, the university library, an impressive colossus from the 19th century. It feels as if we have stepped straight into an old painting.

"Where are you heading?" Henrik asks.

"Studentvägen."

"I'll walk with you."

"So where do you live?"

"Eriksberg."

"I'm fine, there's no need."

"It's not a problem—it's hardly out of my way at all."

We set off up the hill. I like the chill of the night air on my face. I already feel better; I don't know why I was so stressed in the cloakroom queue.

"Did you get her number?"

"Sorry? Whose number?"

"The redhead who thought your talk was so fantastic."

"Very funny. No, I didn't."

"Bad luck."

"It's..." Henrik hesitates, tries to find the right words. "A member of staff having a relationship with a student is frowned upon."

"Is it indeed?"

We walk in silence for a while, then he says: "You were hardly short of attention either."

"Hm."

"Carl was playing footsie with me—I think his aim was a bit off."

We both laugh. "Carl is...how shall I put it...his own biggest fan."

"The song leader seems interested too, to say the least."

"Henning?"

"Yes. He looks like a member of Backstreet Boys."

"Backstreet Boys? Seriously, is that the only boy band you can come up with?"

"Sorry."

"His granddad might have been in Backstreet Boys," I say, tucking my arm through his to take the sting out of the joke, but also because I want to touch him.

He walks me to my apartment block on Studentvägen. We stop.

"This is me," I say. He puts his arms around me. I wrap mine around him. "I've had a wonderful evening," he says.

"Me too."

We stand there like that for a long time, rocking gently back and forth. Is anything else going to happen, and who will take the initiative?

"Would you like a cup of tea?" I ask eventually. Henrik sighs, doesn't speak for a moment.

"That would be lovely, but can I take a rain check?"

"Of course."

He leans back, looks deep into my eyes. "I'll see you soon. You're amazing."

He caresses my cheek and smiles, then he wanders off into the night.

"So you got together with the star of the show," Jacob said with a smile.

"You could say that. We had to keep it under wraps for quite a while." I looked at Henrik, inviting him to join in, but he remained silent and refused to meet my gaze. He picked up a handful of peanuts, stared down at the table. Milena took a crisp and munched on it for an eternity. She also kept her eyes fixed on the table, except when she glanced at Henrik. She seemed uncomfortable. The bad vibes between Henrik and me were embarrassingly clear to her.

"So how are things at work?" I asked her. "Any problem getting away for a week in September?"

We were all relieved to change the subject. Milena was a lawyer with a utility company in Stockholm, and her boss had actually been grateful when she wanted to change her week off from July to September. Jacob and Henrik gradually started exchanging experiences from different trips to the mountains. We ate and drank, and eventually everyone relaxed.

Jacob folded up his napkin and placed his cutlery in the empty cardboard container in which the sautéed reindeer had been served. He topped up his glass of beer; the second large bottle was now more or less empty. He looked at Milena.

"There's something we want to ask you," he said. Milena didn't speak, but her expression was suddenly tense. "You or me?"

"You do it," Milena said, taking a sip of her wine.

"So… We were wondering if you'd like to go to Sarek instead."

Henrik and I stared at him in silence. What was he talking about? "To Sarek? You mean now?"

"Yes. I've been there lots of times, and the way I see it—if you haven't visited Sarek, then you haven't really been in the mountains."

"Out of the question. We've booked accommodation and everything, we can't just… No."

We'd spent approximately two hours in Jacob's company, and he was suggesting a complete change of plan. A plan that Milena and I had discussed in detail, over and over again. Who the fuck did he think he was?

"A booking can be canceled," he said. "Can I explain? If you don't like it, then we forget the whole thing. Obviously."

He stood up and began to clear the table, gathered up all our packaging and empty bottles and went over to the recycling bins. I sighed. Henrik didn't say a word but I could see Milena watching him, trying to gauge his reaction. A man and a woman a few years older than us were waiting expectantly in the central aisle, trays in their hands.

"Are you leaving?" the man asked Milena just as Jacob came back with several napkins.

"No," he said without making eye contact. He started wiping the table. The woman was clearly annoyed.

"Oh, take your time," she snapped.

Jacob gave her a dirty look, but she'd already turned away, searching for a seat at another table. He went and threw away the napkins.

"If you're not keen, then of course we'll go to Kungsleden," Milena said. "No problem."

I was irritated by the fact that she was prepared to go along with Jacob. I'd suggested a trip to Sarek on a number of occasions in the past, but Henrik and Milena had always said no. And each time I'd had a feeling that Milena was the driving force. Not that they'd ganged up on me, but that there was some kind of tacit agreement where Henrik listened to Milena's point of view, then backed her rather than me. But now Jacob had come into her life, and when he mentioned Sarek, suddenly she was in.

Jacob returned, took a map out of the side pocket of his trousers and spread it out on the table. The map was of Padjelanta, the national park immediately to the west of Sarek. We'd talked about taking a trip there in the past, but it was difficult to get there and back home again. It would mean an extra day's traveling compared with other parks that offered similar walking experiences.

"This is my idea," Jacob explained. "Early tomorrow morning we get off the train in Gällivare. From there we catch a bus to Ritsem, up here. Then we fly by helicopter down to Staloluokta." He traced the route with his finger. "From Staloluokta we head into the park. We could camp here by Alajavrre. At the eastern end. This is the best way into Sarek, obviously. If you go from Kvikkjokk, for example, you have a really boring first day just getting to the park. This is a fantastic walk. It's not as flat as it looks on the map, nor is it hilly enough to be hard work. And all the time you have Sarek in front of you, you can actually see the mountains up ahead. *I'm coming for you*, you think."

He smiled at me, but I didn't smile back, nor did I say anything. I was very conscious that Milena was looking searchingly at me.

"Then—" Jacob went on, turning the map over to reveal Sarek "—we continue toward Alggajavrre, and the day after tomorrow we're in Sarek." He pointed to a lake with one shore following the border between Padjelanta and Sarek.

It was clear from a quick glance at the map that Sarek was considerably more dramatic than Padjelanta. Virtually the whole central section was covered in brown and white with blue patches and lines in between. The brown areas were the places where the contours were so close together that they couldn't be distinguished individually. The white indicated glaciers; I knew that many of Sweden's glaciers were located in Sarek. And the blue showed lakes and waterways, above all Rahpaädno, the powerful river that flowed through the Rapa Valley until it formed a delta at the northwestern end of Lajtavrre. The names of the mountains fired the imagination: Ruohtes, Tsähkok, Ålkatj, Ähpar, Skårki.

This was the real wilderness, thousands of square kilometers without tracks or cabins, difficult and unforgiving terrain. You could walk here for days without seeing a single person, especially at this time of year. An emergency telephone was marked in the middle of the park. I realized that if you were in one of the more distant corners of the park, it would take several days just to get there.

"Then we follow the northern side of the lake into Alggavagge," Jacob said. "The view over the lake is magical. Then across to Sarvesvagge, this way. We camp here—amazing view over the entire valley. Then we continue to Rovdjurstorget, where we can stay for a day or two. Climb a peak, if the weather's good." He looked at me. "I hear you're not afraid of heights."

"We haven't brought any climbing equipment."

"I've got enough kit—we can climb as roped teams. If we camp slightly to the north of Rovdjurstorget, it's possible to tackle Stortoppen in a day. You can't get any higher in Sarek."

I didn't want to admit it to myself, but the opportunity to do some climbing was…tempting.

"This is not a climbing trip," Henrik said icily. "This is a walking trip."

"I mean…" Jacob stared at the map. Henrik's tone seemed to have knocked him off balance. "There are easier climbs that don't require any equipment. You can go in via Bierikjavrre and up onto Vuojnestjåhkka." His finger traced the route again.

"We could also split up for a day," Milena suggested. "I'm happy to rest if you two want to go climbing. We've done it before."

Henrik glanced at her, but didn't say anything. Milena's words gave Jacob a new lease of life.

"Rovdjurstorget is an amazing place. You can see bears and wolves and wolverines and lynx… If you don't want to climb, you could easily spend the day watching the wildlife through your binoculars."

"You said you were once chased by a bull elk," Milena said, gazing at her boyfriend with affection.

"Yes, it was quite something. Terrifying."

"Was that near Rovdjurstorget?"

"No, farther down in the Rapa Valley, I don't remember exactly where… Did you know that Europe's largest elks live in Sarek?" Jacob said, looking at me.

"No, I didn't know that."

"We'd stopped for lunch by the river, then we lay down for a sleep. It was June, fantastic weather—really warm. After a little while I needed a pee, so I walked over to the riverbank, thought I'd piss into the river, then I see this massive elk on the other side, with huge antlers like this." Jacob held up his hands to demonstrate. "And it's standing there glaring at me, lowering its head like this. I just thought, wow, it's massive, but I'm not scared because there was a fucking great river between us." His eyes shone as he recalled the memory, and I couldn't help being drawn in by his enthusiasm.

"Suddenly it walks into the water and I'm still not scared, because the current is pretty strong in the middle of June when the snow is melting. But then the fucker starts swimming—fast! And then I realize that it's going to be on my side of the river in a few seconds. As soon as its feet touch the bottom it can break into a run, and then I'm fucked. So I turn around and head off. Unfortunately I'm so taken aback when the elk starts swimming that I forget to fasten my trousers, so after like three seconds I'm flat on my face on the rocks with my trousers around my knees. I hear this enormous bellow behind me, the elk is catching up fast… I leap to my feet and run, trying to do up my trousers at the same time and I manage to get into the undergrowth and there are like tracks and trails, it's like a maze, and the elk is still bellowing, still coming after me. So I run along the tracks and the elk is after me, it's a bit like the end of *The Shining* when he's chasing the son… Although the elk didn't have an ax."

Milena grinned, and I couldn't help smiling. "Did you get away?" I asked.

"Yes, it gave up. Fortunately. Maybe it just wanted to humiliate me. Wouldn't that be something, Anna? Being chased by a bull elk?"

"I guess so… I mean, we have talked about Sarek before, haven't we?" Milena nodded. Henrik kept his eyes fixed on the table.

"Milena told me," Jacob said.

"So another year—absolutely. But from a purely practical point of view I don't see how we can change now, just like that."

"Why not?"

"First of all, we haven't brought food for the whole week. We've got enough to last to the Kebnekaise mountain station. The plan is to buy more when we get there."

"There's a kiosk in Stalo. Parfa's kiosk. They have everything you need—freeze-dried meals, soup, bread, everything."

"And they're open now? In September?"

"Yes—I've checked."

"We don't have enough gas cartridges either."

"You can get those in Stalo too. There's a list online of all the stuff they stock."

"What about the helicopter?"

"I've made a provisional booking for tomorrow."

"You just assumed we'd go along with this?"

"As I said, it's a provisional booking," Jacob said patiently. "It's a minor expense, which of course I will bear if we don't go."

"Don't you need a satellite phone in Sarek?"

He reached into another side pocket and fished out a phone that looked as if it had been hanging around since the '90s. He held it up for us all to see.

"Emergency transmitter. If anything happens, we can send a message."

"I insisted," Milena chipped in.

"One more thing. I've checked the weather forecast, and they're promising mainly sunshine in Sarek over the next week. That's unusual for this time of year, so we really ought to take the opportunity."

I looked at the map. The blue, the brown, the white, the drama it promised, the adventure. The chance to see something I'd never seen before, somewhere I'd longed to go.

I really wanted to say yes.

"Henrik… I think we should go back to our compartment and talk this over, then we can…"

He interrupted me before I could finish my sentence.

"No. I don't want to." His tone was firm but his voice was a little shaky, a sign of suppressed rage. He'd obviously been sitting there working himself up without any of us noticing. No one spoke.

"I am sitting on this train in order to travel to Abisko and walk the Kungsleden route. I have no intention of changing my plans now. If the rest of you want to go to Sarek, then carry on. But I am not interested."

"In that case we'll forget it," Milena said quickly. "We'll stick to our original plan—Abisko it is."

Jacob scratched his chin and throat; he seemed to be struggling to deal with his disappointment.

"Can I just…" he began, but Milena jumped in.

"Drop it, Jacob."

"If I could finish." His tone was irritated. He gave Milena a sharp look and she immediately backed down. Jacob took a deep breath; he wasn't ready to give up yet. Henrik folded his arms and leaned back.

"The thing is," Jacob began afresh.

"I don't want to know," Henrik said, sounding like a stubborn child. Jacob ignored him.

"You've been up on Kebnekaise. Nowhere in Sarek is harder than that, if you don't want it to be. What can be difficult and time-consuming is finding the right route, because there are no marked trails. Should you go down into the valley or is it better to try higher up the mountainside, for example. And I know that stuff already, because I've done it several times. So it's actually no more challenging than Abisko."

"Once again: I don't want to do it. I don't know how much clearer I can be."

Jacob and Henrik stared at each other in ominous silence. The atmosphere around the table was thick with tension. Milena was uncomfortable but looked helpless, as if she didn't dare say anything after Jacob's rebuke. I realized it was up to me to try and calm things down.

"Why?" Jacob said.

"Why?"

"Yes. Give me a reason."

I spoke up. "Jacob, Henrik has said he doesn't want to do it, so you need to..." I didn't get any further before Henrik interrupted me. I'd rarely seen him so upset. His eyes were wild as he stared at Jacob.

"We've been doing this for ten years, and you pop up like some kind of jack-in-the-box a week before we're due to leave and want to come along, then you suggest a complete change of plan when we've only just left Stockholm. What the fuck is wrong with you? Who are you?"

He had raised his voice and the group on the other side of the aisle were glancing in our direction. Jacob raised his hands in a gesture of capitulation, but he didn't speak. Henrik was still staring at him.

"Henrik," I ventured, but it was no use.

"I'm serious—who are you? Anna says you work at BCG, but I have a friend who works there, he tells me there's no Jacob Tessin at BCG. So who are you?"

What are you doing, Henrik?

Milena looked taken aback. Jacob frowned.

"Let's drop it," I said. "That's enough. Henrik?" I made a move to stand up.

"BCG? What are you talking about?" Jacob's voice was deeper now, slightly hoarse. He turned to Milena. "What does he mean?" Milena didn't reply; she almost seemed frightened.

"I might have misheard," I said. "I thought you said Jacob worked at BCG—when we met up for lunch. But I might have misheard."

Milena's throat was flushed red. With calm, deliberate movements Jacob took out his wallet, removed a business card and placed it on the map in front of us.

On the card was a logo and the letters BCV. On the line below it said *Jacob Tessin*, and below that in slightly smaller print, *Senior Consultant.*

Henrik and I gazed at the card.

"There you go—I misheard. Apologies. My bad."

Silence. It lasted only a few seconds, but it felt like an eternity. Jacob turned to Milena.

"Why do you tell people I work at BCG?" She didn't answer, but her expression was one I'd never seen before. It was a mixture of hurt, anger and fear.

"Hang on, Jacob—it was my mistake. Milena isn't to blame. Once again, I apologize."

Henrik cleared his throat, sat up a little straighter. His anger had already dissipated. His voice was rough, almost broken.

"I apologize too. I don't know what came over me." No doubt he was embarrassed by his baseless accusations against Jacob, but also at having lost control in front of other people. That was so unlike him.

"I am a data consultant," Jacob said, struggling to contain his anger. Milena placed her hand on his, but he snatched his hand away and clenched his fist.

I could understand why he was mad at me and Henrik, but why Milena? What had she done wrong?

I tried again. "I really am sorry, Jacob. Honestly."

"Listen, I'm going to get us something to drink," Henrik said, getting to his feet. "I think we need it. I do, anyway. What would you like, Jacob? I noticed they have miniature bottles of brandy, whisky and so on."

Jacob didn't even look up at Henrik.

"I wouldn't mind another white wine," Milena said.

"Me too," I said.

"Okay, I'll get a mixture. I apologize, Jacob. I was… I went too far."

Henrik headed for the counter. The queue had more or less disappeared by now. Jacob turned to Milena. "Well, there's someone who didn't want me on the trip." He deliberately spoke loudly enough for me to hear.

"That's not the case." I did my best to sound sincere. "It's just that…sometimes he gets hung up on minor details."

Milena stroked Jacob's back. "He doesn't mean any harm."

Jacob grimaced, but didn't say any more. Shortly afterward Henrik came back with a tray of beer, wine and a selection of miniatures. Plus several packets of crisps and sweets. He put the tray on the table and sat down beside me.

"Okay, let's draw a line under what happened. And I've changed my mind. We're going to Sarek."

A few hours later we were spooning in Henrik's bed, and I could feel his soft, gentle breathing on the nape of my neck. The compartment was in darkness, but my eyes had got used to it, and strips of light found their way in through a gap in the blind, and a ventilation grille at the bottom of the door leading to the corridor. The carriage swayed and jolted a little. The rhythm of the wheels passing over the track was comforting, soporific. I ought to be able to sleep, but I couldn't shake off a sense of unease after the incident in the restaurant car.

We'd drunk everything on Henrik's tray, eaten the crisps and sweets. We allowed Jacob to elaborate on his travels in Sarek, sighed to show how impressed we were when he described how he and some friends had completed the mythical Sarek traverse. His mood soon improved, and after an hour or so he was feeling generous enough to go off and buy the next round. We drank more, we all got a little tipsy.

Jacob made a slightly inappropriate joke directed at me, in spite of the fact that Milena and Henrik were there. I laughed, his brown eyes sparkled.

We were the last to leave the restaurant, and parted as four friends on our way to an adventure in Sarek.

Henrik was probably the one who needed that session more than the rest of us. It was so unlike him to lose his self-control. If he'd stayed sober, he would have been consumed by shame and embarrassment, but a few drinks enabled him to look back with a certain amount of distance and humor by the time we returned to our compartment. And it actually sounded as if he was okay with the change of plan—looking forward to it, in fact.

Everything had sorted itself out in the end, so why did I still feel uneasy? There was something I couldn't quite put my finger on.

I think it was partly because the dynamic around the table felt familiar—from my own family. All too familiar. One person loses their temper and everyone else works their backside off to get him in a good mood again. Because you know if you don't do that, things will get a hundred times worse. The person in question has no boundaries, he will double the stakes. Everyone else will have to pay.

There was also a niggling concern about where Jacob worked.

I was almost one hundred percent certain that Milena had said BCG. Almost one hundred percent. If it had been a question of confusion over B and P, okay. But G and V?

And the idea that Milena would have deliberately given the wrong name in order to show off because her new boyfriend worked at a flash consultancy—no. Out of the question. She just wasn't like that.

Which left the possibility that she had misheard when Jacob told her the name of his company. Maybe.

Or.

He had said BCG and hoped that no one would see through his bluff, and printed business cards with BCV on them, just in case.

Hm.

That would make him kind of stupid, and I'd seen nothing else to indicate that.

The train slowed. The rhythm of the wheels changed, and soon it stopped with a jerk, like a small recoil. There was silence, apart from the ticking of the radiator in our compartment. Henrik slept on. Cautiously, in order not to wake him, I slipped out of his arms. I picked up my phone and sat down on the folding seat.

I went into *allabolag.se*, a website listing companies in Sweden, and searched for BCV. There were several different firms with that name, including a plumber, an electrical wholesaler and a music store in Falkenberg. Plus a consultancy—I clicked on the link.

Turnover for the last financial year: 116,000 kronor. Profit 2,750 kronor. The owner's name was Stefan Jakob Johansson.

My mouth went dry with excitement; I was wide awake now. I knew I was on the trail of something important.

Who are you really, Jacob?

Turnover 116,000, profit 2,750. Presumably the difference was made up of the company owner's salary—113,000 kronor, including national insurance contributions and so on. That was a monthly salary of around 7,000 kronor after tax—basically impossible to live on, especially in Stockholm. Stefan Jakob Johansson might well have other sources of income, but Jacob had introduced himself as a consultant with BCV, as if that were his daily bread and butter.

And hadn't he said something to Henrik about working too hard, often on the weekends as well? If he was doing that and earning 7,000 a month, then he was either Sweden's most underpaid consultant or the most inefficient.

Stefan Jakob Johansson. Is that you, Jacob?

Interview with Anna Samuelsson 880216-3382, September 27, 2019, Gällivare hospital, conducted by Detective Inspector Anders Suhonen.

"But the next morning you all got off the train in Gällivare anyway."

"Yes."

"Even though you'd started wondering what kind of person this Jacob was."

Silence.

"What was I supposed to say? *You only earn seven thousand a month, I don't want to go to Sarek with you.* I don't think so."

"No… Did you mention this to Henrik?"

Silence.

"No."

"Why not?"

Silence.

"I thought…if I tell him, he might change his mind."

"You mean he wouldn't want to go to Sarek?"

"Yes."

Silence.

"And I also thought maybe I'd gone a bit over the top. During the night."

"Googling the name of the company and so on…?"

"Yes. I tried to find pictures of Stefan Jakob Johansson to see if he was Jacob. I was at it for hours."

"I see. And in the morning you thought you'd overreacted?"

"Yes."

Silence.

"So we got off the train in Gällivare. But…something still didn't feel right."

"Okay."

"And then I remembered where I'd seen him before."

The train slowed and stopped. Jacob opened the door and we stepped down onto the platform. It was about eight o'clock in the morning, the pale gray cloud cover was dense, the air was damp and bitterly cold. I shivered. Not many people had got off; presumably most of the passengers were continuing north to Abisko.

We heaved our rucksacks onto our backs and walked the short distance to the old wooden station building, or Gällivare Travel Center as it was now known. The mountain bus was due to leave in half an hour, which gave us time to go inside and get warm. Nobody said much. Jacob was wearing sunglasses in spite of the overcast sky.

The waiting room was almost empty, but it was warm and there were wooden benches to sit on. One corner was set out like a little shop, selling local craft goods, a few clothes, maps and guidebooks. There was a guy on the till even though it was so early, and I bought a map of Sarek. There was a pump Thermos, a carton of milk, plastic cups and a box of sugar lumps on a table with a sign stating that it was self-service, a coffee cost ten kronor, cash or the app Swish. I'd had coffee with breakfast on the train, but on this gloomy morning I needed to use every trick in the book to wake me up. I Swished twenty kronor and told Henrik to help himself, then with a steaming cup in my hand I went over to the bench where I'd parked my rucksack. I sat down and opened up the map on my knee.

Henrik joined me, also carrying a cup of coffee. "Which one did you get?" he asked.

"One to fifty thousand." As I looked up at him, I saw Jacob standing by a display of handkerchiefs, and suddenly I remembered where I'd seen him before.

My heart raced, the blood pounded at my temples. I was in full-on stress mode.

I was diagonally behind him, and there was something about the angle that brought it all back. Strangely enough, you might think you'd remember a person's face more than anything, but not on this occasion. It was definitely him.

After I graduated I went to work at the court in Nacka. As a notary you prepare cases, write up draft verdicts and so on. After six months you are allowed to pass judgments in minor cases, but this was right at the beginning of my employment, and it was such a serious crime that it would never have been entrusted to a notary. It involved domestic abuse, and many ingredients were all too familiar: the couple had met online, they'd been together for about a year, the woman described how quickly she'd fallen in love, she was convinced she'd met the man of her dreams. Love made her blind to the way he gradually eroded her self-confidence, at first with innocent little comments about this or that, then with increasingly dogmatic opinions and demands about how she should dress, how she should behave when they were out in public, what she should be doing at home. He had an enormous need to be in control, and he was incredibly jealous. He took her phone, insisted on access to her bank accounts.

Boundaries shifted, the verbal abuse became a daily occurrence, sick behavior was normalized.

However she was still shocked the first time he hit her. She left him and reported him to the police. He begged for forgiveness, pleaded with her, assured her that she was the only positive thing in his life, he was terrified of losing her, he knew he had problems and he was determined to deal with them. She was still in love with him. They had moments, maybe even whole days, when things were the way they used to be at the start. She gave him another chance, withdrew her allegation to the police. A few weeks passed, then they were back in the old pattern, a destructive and increasingly violent spiral.

The medical reports that formed the basis of the case made for upsetting reading. Bleeding crush wounds to the head. A fractured jaw. Strangulation marks around the neck. A cracked elbow, a broken wrist. Huge contusions on the arms, back and thighs.

I helped the judge with the preparations, and don't recall seeing any pictures of the man during this period. I did see him in the courtroom on the first day of the trial. He was brought in with the hood of his tracksuit top pulled over his head to hide his identity. He was tall and well-built. His defense lawyer led him to his seat, and before the accused sat down he took off his top and hung it over the back of his chair. He was wearing a snow-white shirt and neatly ironed chinos. Wavy brown hair, tanned skin, perfectly groomed stubble.

Surely that was Jacob? Yes, I was certain of it. His hair was shorter now and he dressed in a completely different way, which was why I hadn't recognized him immediately. But as soon as I saw him at Central Station, I'd thought there was something familiar about him, hadn't I?

The man was sentenced to three years for violent assault, if I remember correctly. His name wasn't Jacob Tessin of course—I would have remembered that. Could he have been called Stefan

Johansson? I didn't know, but it wouldn't have been surprising if he'd changed his name during his time in prison, particularly if he wanted a fresh start when he got out.

I stared at Jacob, lost in my own thoughts. My mouth was bone-dry, and I had to make a real effort to breathe normally. Henrik could see that something was wrong.

"What is it, Anna?"

Milena was on her way over. I couldn't say anything now, I needed time to think. "Later," I murmured.

"Have you found Staloluokta?" Milena asked as she sat down next to Henrik.

"No—why don't you have a look?" I slid the map onto Henrik's knee. He gazed at me, then turned his attention to the task in hand. The map was printed on both sides, and he and Milena turned it this way and that, searching for the point where we would enter the park.

Jacob was wandering around the shop, picking up various bits and pieces, oblivious to the fact that I was watching him. I wondered if he'd been released from prison comparatively recently; that could be why the turnover for his consultancy was so low. I did a quick calculation: I started my tenure as a notary in the spring of 2015, the case in question would have been in April that year—May at the latest. The verdict gained legal force after three weeks, so Jacob could have started his sentence in early summer. Three years—that meant he would serve two, if he behaved himself and didn't commit any fresh crimes while he was inside. He would have come out in the summer of 2017. Two years ago. Okay, so he could have started a fight in the prison, or tried to escape and been given an extended sentence, but as far as I knew that kind of thing was relatively unusual. And the man who was convicted in court hadn't come across as some kind of career criminal, but rather as a relatively well-balanced individual who just happened to have a warped view of women and relationships and violence.

Suddenly Jacob turned his head in our direction. He was still wearing sunglasses, so I couldn't be sure that he was looking at me, but my stomach flipped over. I felt as if he'd caught me out, and couldn't stop my eyes from darting from side to side.

He came toward us, smiling and pushing his glasses up onto his forehead. Yes, he was definitely looking at me. I managed a half-hearted smile in return.

The bus was due to leave in fifteen minutes.

Interview with Anna Samuelsson 880216-3382, September 17, 2019, Gällivare hospital, conducted by Detective Inspector Anders Suhonen.

"It was no longer just about me."

"No."

"It was about Milena too."

"Mm."

"Henrik and I could easily drop out, but if Jacob was who I thought he was…Milena might be in real danger."

"Right."

Silence.

"But…"

"Are you in pain? Anna?"

"I…I think the tablets are wearing off."

"In that case we'll stop."

Silence.

"Anna? That's enough for today."

"I just want to say…"

Silence.

"I wasn't a hundred percent certain. If I had been, I could have told Milena…what the situation was. But…I had to…"

Silence.

"Anna? We'll leave it there for today."

"Yes."

The mountain bus was a modern double-decker with lightly tinted windows and big rearview mirrors jutting out from the sides like the antennae of a giant bee. The doors of the luggage compartment were open, and we stashed our rucksacks inside. There were five other walkers apart from us: a Swedish couple and three guys I thought were probably Italian. There were also a few pensioners with walking poles and small backpacks; maybe they were taking a day trip up to Stora Sjöfallet or Ritsem. That made a total of about fifteen passengers; there would be plenty of room on the bus.

I deliberately took my time. If Henrik and I got on first, Milena and Jacob would be able to sit next to us, and I needed to talk to Henrik without being overheard. A small queue formed to buy tickets from the driver. Jacob and Milena were in front of us; we were last on board.

"Two to Ritsem," Jacob said, taking a credit card out of his wallet. I caught a glimpse of his driver's license, and felt a tingle in my belly. If I could get his ID number I might be able to find out if he had a criminal record, but he quickly closed his wallet and I didn't see any details.

The driver, a wiry man who looked as if he had reached retirement age, tapped away on his electronic ticket machine. "That will be 860 kronor," he said in a broad Norrland accent.

Four hundred and thirty kronor per person. It wasn't exactly cheap to travel on the mountain bus.

Jacob inserted his card in the reader and entered his PIN number. After a couple of seconds the machine spat out a chit. Jacob looked confused.

"Okay…" he said.

"Try again," the driver suggested. "We might have lost contact with the bank."

"There's money in my account," Jacob said with such emphasis that he almost seemed to be contradicting himself. He removed the card, inserted it again, re-entered his PIN number and waited. His wallet was in his other hand.

The reader rattled out another chit.

"What the fuck…" Jacob muttered. The fact that Henrik and I were right behind him was no doubt contributing to his stress. Henrik politely half-turned away, while I kept my eyes fixed on the wallet. Milena took out her card.

"I'll get this," she said. The driver canceled the transaction and started again: two to Ritsem. The fact that Milena was trying to redeem the situation didn't improve Jacob's mood.

"What makes you think your card will work when mine doesn't?" he snapped. "There's money in my account, I know there is."

"We probably have different banks," Milena said. The driver gave them a sideways glance as the machine considered its options. Jacob had no intention of letting it go.

"I don't think we do. I'm with SEB, how about you?"

"SEB," Milena replied quietly. She too was painfully aware that Henrik and I were following the action from the front row. She just wanted to help Jacob resolve the matter as quickly as possible, but he seemed determined to shoot down her efforts. Henrik and I exchanged a brief glance.

"In that case it's not going to work, is it?" Jacob was staring aggressively at her now, directing his frustration at the target where it would meet the least resistance. Milena kept her eyes fixed on the reader. Jacob was still clutching his card; at some point he would put it away in his wallet, giving me another chance to glimpse his driving license.

The driver, Milena and Jacob were all fixated on the reader now, as if they were waiting for the chair of the jury to deliver the verdict in an American courtroom. Then a new text appeared on the display. I couldn't see what it said, but Milena's shoulders dropped a fraction and she transferred her weight to the other foot. The machine began to print a longer piece of paper—a receipt this time. The payment had gone through. She looked at Jacob and shrugged, as if to say that she didn't understand it either.

"That's fucking weird," Jacob muttered.

The driver beamed at them. "It happens—the line to the bank comes and goes." He tore off the receipt and gave it to Milena. Jacob shook his head and stomped off up the stairs, tucking his card back in his wallet as he went. He was holding it in front of him, so I had no chance of seeing his license. *Shit.*

I bought my ticket and followed them up the stairs. They were sitting right at the front with a panoramic view of the landscape. Jacob waved to me and pointed to the seats next to them. I gave him what I hoped was a disarming smile.

"No, I'd rather sit here," I said, choosing a row roughly in the middle of the bus. "I'm going to try and get some sleep."

I heard the doors to the luggage compartment close, and the engine began to throb. Henrik came up the stairs and sat down beside me.

"I know where I've seen him before."

He looked blank. "What?"

"Jacob—I know where I've seen him before. I told you yesterday that I recognized him."

I explained that I was sure he'd been involved in a domestic abuse case when I was working as a notary. I also told him about my nocturnal search for information about BCV and Stefan Jacob Johansson. Henrik looked increasingly bewildered. This stream of information was more than his weary morning-after brain could handle.

"Why didn't you say anything?" he asked eventually.

"I didn't think it was worth it. He doesn't earn much, he's changed his name—so what? But this is something else entirely."

Henrik sighed. "So what do you want to do? Drop out?"

"I need to be sure it's him first. I need his ID number so that I can search Lexbase."

"Okay…"

"We've still got phone coverage, we've got time to check things out during the bus journey. It's four hours to Ritsem."

Henrik rubbed his face; he seemed even more tired now. "And if it does turn out to be him?"

"Then I'll speak to Milena. If he's a convicted abuser, she needs to know."

"But you and I will drop out anyway?"

The bus began to move, pulling away from the stop and leaving the old station behind. Henrik was staring at me, demanding an answer. "Anna?"

"I don't know! If we can persuade Milena to come with us, then yes, absolutely. But if not… I'm not sure. I need to think."

We passed ugly two-story apartment blocks. On this particular morning Gällivare came across as a bitterly cold and inhospitable settlers' town. A few temporary buildings thrown together on the prairie. The sky felt like a gray lid, just above the roofs. We left the community, the bus did a ninety-degree turn and picked up speed. We drove past Dundret ski resort.

Was there any way I could find out whether Jacob had a criminal record without access to his ID number? I had a few hours, I had my smartphone, and hopefully I would have network coverage all the way to Ritsem. I had to try.

We soon left civilization behind. The road was more or less deserted, slicing through the fir tree forest in a dead straight line. The muted sound of the modern engine and the soft, gentle bounce of the suspension meant that you weren't really aware of how fast we were going.

I opened up Lexbase, a website that provides details of verdicts in the Swedish courts in a searchable online register. I'd never used it before. Like many lawyers I'm not entirely comfortable with Lexbase; I think it stretches the principle of public information further than it should. However right now I had absolutely no qualms about using it.

I hoped it would be possible to search for verdicts from a specific court during a specific time span, but that wasn't the case. You had to search by name or address. Without much hope I typed in Jacob Tessin resident in Stockholm, and left the ID field blank. No matches. Stefan Jakob Johansson—no matches. I also tried various suburbs of Stockholm combined with the two names—Nacka, Solna, Gustavsberg, Botkyrka. No matches.

"Isn't there a site that lists sex crime convictions and that kind of thing online?" I asked Henrik.

"What makes you think he was convicted of a sex crime?"

"I don't, but they might include domestic abuse convictions too."

A little while later I had found *brottsling.se*, just the kind of site I was looking for.

Pedophiles and other sex offenders were named, and in some instances there were pictures too. The whole tone of the site was unpleasant; on virtually every other line it was pointed out that perpetrators of non-Swedish origin were heavily overrepresented when it came to sexual offences. However I couldn't let that stop me now. It was possible to search within a specific geographical area. Hundreds of cases were listed, including categories such as domestic abuse. I clicked on the relevant tab, but there was no geographical listing available. There were some twenty cases spread over a number of years—in other words a tiny percentage of all convictions for domestic abuse in Sweden during that period. I scrolled through the information given, but Jacob wasn't there—nor anyone resembling him.

Another dead end. I glanced at my watch; we'd already been traveling for just over an hour. Three hours left until we reached Ritsem. At this speed I couldn't understand how it was going to take so long; we were already over halfway. I wasn't complaining though; I needed every minute I could get.

To our left I could see a long lake between the trees, lead-gray water beneath a lead-gray sky.

I was going to have to tackle this in a completely different way. I thought back to my colleagues at the court in Nacka. It was unlikely that anyone who had been a notary at the same time as me would still be there. The judges might be, but they would be difficult to get hold of and probably unwilling to help. One of the secretaries was my best bet. Several of them had been there for a very long time. I'd got along especially well with some of the younger ones who were about the same age as me, and they might well have moved on, but there wasn't the same turnover among the secretaries as the qualified lawyers. I was thinking of one person in particular.

I googled the number of the court in Nacka; my call was answered almost immediately.

"Hi, my name is Anna Samuelsson. I worked as a notary in Nacka a few years ago."

"That's nice," the receptionist replied cheerfully. She didn't appear to recognize my name; maybe the reception service was outsourced.

"I wanted to speak to Ellen Runström. She's a court secretary," I went on.

"One moment please." There was a click, followed by silence. After a few seconds the voice came back. "Did you say Ellen Runström?"

"That's right."

"I'm sorry, I can't find anyone by that name. Are you sure she's still here?"

Shit. Ellen had always helped me out.

"No, I'm not… Hang on, let me see if I can think of anyone else."

Who should I try instead? No one sprang to mind apart from Ellen. Wait…there was that slightly older woman, what was her name?

"Could you try Christina Pettersson, or maybe Persson…but I'm pretty sure it's Pettersson."

"We have a Christina Pettersson who's an assessor—is that who you're thinking of?"

Christina Pettersson—a mean-spirited, spiky career lawyer. She would never go out of her way to help me with something like this.

"No, the person I'm looking for is a court secretary."

"We have an Anneli Pettersson—could that be the right person?"

"That's it—Anneli Pettersson."

"Okay, I'll put you through. One moment please."

"Thank you." The phone rang out, over and over again. The wait seemed endless.

Eventually there was a click on the other end of the line.

"No reply, I'm afraid, but there's no message to say she's out—would you like me to try again?"

"Yes please."

The receptionist put me through to Anneli's number. The phone continued to ring out.

The bus pulled off the road, and the driver's voice came over the speaker system. "We have now reached Stora Sjöfallet, and we'll be taking a break here for approximately half an hour. The bus leaves at 10:40. I won't be counting you back on, so those of you who are traveling to Ritsem need to make sure you're on board." He switched off the engine.

This break was both unexpected and welcome. I had an extra half hour of network coverage. Hopefully that would give me time to confirm that Jacob Tessin, or whatever his real name was, had been convicted of domestic abuse.

Henrik and I stood up and made for the stairs, meeting Jacob and Milena, who were coming from the opposite direction.

"Shall we go and have a coffee?" Milena suggested.

My phone was demonstratively clamped to my ear. I nodded, pointed to the phone.

"Work."

We went into the mountain station, where we found a small shop selling most of the things you might need for an expedition. Presumably we could have bought everything we needed for Sarek here, but Jacob had assured us that the kiosk in Staloluokta would be open. And we probably wouldn't be going to Sarek at all.

If only Anneli would answer her fucking phone.

We carried on past the shop and into the spacious restaurant, newly built in a rustic style with dark unpolished wood and floor-to-ceiling windows providing fantastic views. Beyond the pines and firs Stora Lulevattnet was just visible—the long narrow lake whose seemingly endless shoreline we had been following for almost an hour. I gestured to Henrik to pay for my coffee too.

The receptionist came back on the line. "Still no answer?"

"I'm afraid not."

"As I said, there's no message to indicate that she's out. Would you like me to ask her to call you?"

I glanced over at Jacob and Milena, who were now seated at a table with coffee and cinnamon buns. Jacob met my gaze. Was there a wariness in his eyes? A hint of suspicion? Or was it just my imagination? I had no desire to join them while waiting for a call from Anneli. I was totally focused on finding out whether he was who I thought he was, and I definitely couldn't sit there making small talk.

"Thanks, but I'll try again in a little while... Could I possibly have the number for her direct line?"

The coffee was self-service. I helped myself to a take-out cup and clipped on the lid as the receptionist gave me Anneli's number, which I memorized. We ended the call, but I kept the phone pressed to my ear. I nodded to Henrik and said quietly: "I'm going outside for a few minutes."

"Have you found anything out?"

"Not yet."

He wandered over to join Jacob and Milena, and I went outside.

The sky felt somehow higher now, the lead-gray lid had lightened and the clouds were almost white. There was a fresh breeze, and over to the west I could see a patch of white. Maybe it was going to be a nice day. I wandered along a dirt track, past guest cabins and a car park down toward the water. I filled my lungs with air, Norrland air, which was completely different from downtown Stockholm. It was as if my lungs were reminded that this was how air was supposed to taste.

I sipped my coffee and tried Anneli's direct line. Surely she'd be back by now? I had a mental image of the phone ringing once, then I'd hear a click, followed by her voice.

The phone rang once. Twice. Three times. Four. Five.

No answer. I wondered whether to call reception again, ask about another secretary, but my request was so onerous, so much more than anyone could reasonably expect, that someone who didn't know me would probably say no right away. My best bet was Anneli.

Up ahead I could see what had once been the five majestic cataracts known as Stora Sjöfallet, Sweden's Niagara, but following the building of a dam at Suorva a short distance upstream in order to facilitate the generation of hydroelectric power, it was now a modest waterfall. The torrent had gushed and tumbled over its rocks for thousands of years; now they lay dry and naked for everyone to see.

I checked the time; it was already 10:30 a.m. My pulse rate increased, my stress level shot up. It was time to head back to the bus. I had hoped that this half hour break would give me the information I wanted, but that hope was draining away, minute by minute.

When I reached the mountain station the bus was waiting, its engine idling. I could see Jacob and Milena upstairs, gazing through the panorama window. Milena waved at me. I managed a half-smile and waved back. Jacob's expression was blank. I had a horrible feeling that he knew what I was up to.

I finished off my coffee, threw away my cup and climbed on board. There was no sign of the pensioners with their walking poles; it was only the serious hikers who were traveling on to Ritsem. I went upstairs; Henrik was already there. I hadn't even sat down when the bus began to move.

"How's it going?"

"Not very well," I said quietly. "I need to get hold of a particular person, and she's not answering her phone." I opened up my list of calls and clicked on the last number dialed. The phone rang out. Did I actually believe this was going to work?

The bus pulled onto the main road and accelerated.

"Listen," Henrik murmured. "I think we ought to drop out. You're probably not going to find out about Jacob, but you won't be able to let it go."

"What about Milena?"

"Talk to her, explain the situation—then she can make her own decision."

The driver changed gear and the bus sped along. The road rose, and suddenly we had a view over toward the mountains on the far side of the power station dam.

There was a brutal concrete wall several hundred meters high, extending into the distance. And far far away, snow-covered peaks glistening in the sunshine. The weather was definitely improving.

"Anneli Pettersson," a voice suddenly said in my ear. I gave a start.

Thank you, God. Thank you.

I realized I'd more or less given up. I gabbled a response, my voice sounded unnatural, I'd almost gone up to a falsetto.

"Hi, Anneli, it's Anna Samuelsson—I don't know if you remember me?" I stared at Henrik, he stared back. I gave him a thumbs-up.

"Of course I do. This is a surprise."

As she spoke, a clear picture came into my mind: a woman aged about sixty, slightly below average height, with a square face, dead-straight bangs and medium-length hair. Anneli had been at the court in Nacka for years and years. She was knowledgeable and professional, never unpleasant, but difficult to get to know well.

Anonymous. I knew nothing about her private life, and I assumed she knew nothing about mine. I wasn't at all sure that she would help me, but she was my best chance. My only chance.

We exchanged a few meaningless phrases, but Anneli was at work and I could tell from her tone that she wasn't interested in small talk. Neither was I. I took a deep breath.

"So...I was wondering if you could help me with something. I know this isn't what you normally do, but it's really important to me, and it's pretty urgent," I began, paving the way for my strange request.

"I see." Anneli was giving nothing away.

"I need to find out the identity of a man who was convicted of violent assault in a domestic abuse case I worked on not long after I started at the court—it must have been April or May 2015." I paused to let her speak, but she didn't say a word. Not a good sign. I carried on anyway.

"Like I said, I was wondering if you could help me out. And I really need to know within the next hour or so." I paused again. Still nothing.

"Anneli? Hello?"

I looked at my phone, which informed me that the call had been discontinued. It also helpfully gave me the length of the conversation. Then I looked at the top line of the menu to check the coverage. No bars out of a possible four.

"Oh, for fuck's sake..."

Henrik looked at his phone. "I haven't got any coverage either." I buried my face in my hands.

For fuck's sake!

The road wound its way alongside the lake above the dam. It was much narrower now, and the tarmac was cracked and uneven. The bus had reduced its speed; if we met a car here, someone would have to reverse. On our right the mountainside rose steeply. Small tree-covered peaks followed one after the other, and the landscape was more reminiscent of southern China or Vietnam than Norrland. On the other side of the lake, several kilometers away, we could now see the first high mountains in Sarek itself, their snowy peaks lost among the clouds.

"Leave that," Henrik said, taking my hand. "I can see how upset you are. We'll just drop out."

I snatched my hand away. "No chance," I hissed. I had no intention of giving up until every possibility, every single one, had been exhausted. I stood up, went over to Jacob and Milena and took a deep breath.

"Jacob… I don't have any network coverage, and there's a work problem I have to sort out. Could I borrow your satellite phone?"

"It's not a satellite phone, it's a tracker."

"Okay, so what…?"

"You can't use it to make calls, you can only send messages to certain prearranged contacts." My heart sank.

"I get it. And neither of you has coverage?"

"No," Milena said. "Is it something urgent?"

"I'm afraid so. I have to try..."

"I thought you were on holiday," Jacob said, his tone noticeably icier now.

"I am, but sometimes things come up that you just have to deal with."

Milena looked worried. "I'm sorry...but coverage can be tricky up here."

I nodded. "Okay, well at least I know." I turned away to go back to my seat.

"There's a mast in Ritsem," Jacob said. "You'll have coverage there—but the helicopter will be waiting for us, so you won't be able to talk for long."

"I understand—but that's fantastic. Great." I rejoined Henrik. My hope was a tiny fragile flame flickering in a gale-force wind, but it was still burning.

"There's a mast in Ritsem," I said quietly to Henrik. "Things might work out." He didn't say anything; he just looked resigned.

I tried to calculate how much time I would have. Unfortunately the range of each mast was no doubt limited up here, given the way the road twisted and turned, cutting into the mountainside. Presumably there would be coverage again as we got closer to Ritsem—maybe fifteen minutes before we arrived. If Jacob was telling the truth and the helicopter would be waiting for us, then it might take five minutes to stow our baggage and climb aboard. Once we were in the air, we would lose coverage within another five minutes, at a guess. If I was lucky.

It was going to be really, really tricky.

But all I could do was wait. Once a minute or so I checked the bars: zero out of four every single time.

The cloud cover had now properly broken up, and for a while the road was bathed in sunshine. The widening lake below us sparkled between the reflections of the clouds scudding across its surface.

Jacob was making his way down the aisle. He stopped and leaned right over me as he pointed to the mountains beyond the lake.

"That's Ähpar over there, then Sarektjåhkkå."

"Amazing," Henrik mumbled. The sky was clearing over Sarek too, and we saw impressively high jagged ridges between the drifting clouds. Jacob rested his weight on the seat in front, still leaning over me.

"You can get in from Suorva, by the dam. It's a quick route to the middle of Sarek, but it's really boring at first, and there are too many people around."

"How long until we reach Ritsem?" I asked.

Jacob smiled. "This *work thing* seems to be very important."

"It is."

"Does someone's life depend on it?"

It might well do, you fucking abuser. "Maybe not."

"Exactly." Jacob waved a hand in the direction of the mountains. "This is one of the best views in the world. Take the opportunity to enjoy it."

I didn't say a word, but I did look out the window. And yes, it was a fantastic view, but what did that matter? I was tending toward Henrik's suggestion. Perhaps we should drop out, with or without Milena.

"So do you know how long it is until we get to Ritsem?" I asked again.

"No," Jacob replied. "Half an hour, maybe. You can see Ahkka up ahead—it's directly opposite Ritsem, so we're not that far away."

I glanced at my phone again. I had one bar. I had one bar! One out of four, faint coverage, but coverage nonetheless. Maybe the game wasn't over yet. My pulse was racing, I clicked on the last number dialed and put the phone to my ear.

"Coverage?" Jacob asked. I nodded, hoping he would realize that I wanted a little privacy as I dealt with an important work call. He didn't move. "We're not going all the way up to the mountain station," he continued. "I've had a word with the driver, and he'll drop us off at the helipad."

Henrik nodded. I demonstratively covered my other ear with my hand. Jacob looked down at me, but stayed exactly where he was.

I hated him with a passion at that moment. *Go away, you fucking idiot. Back off.* "Anneli Pettersson."

"Hi, it's Anna again, Anna Samuelsson." I got to my feet and pushed past Jacob, who was blocking the aisle. I went toward the back of the bus to get away from him, and he finally seemed to understand. He ambled off to rejoin Milena, but I didn't return to my seat; I was too agitated. I paced up and down the aisle instead.

"Hi."

"Sorry, I got cut off earlier. I'm not sure how much you heard, but I really need some help." I explained once again that I was trying to find out the identity of a man convicted of assaulting his partner in a domestic abuse case in the spring of 2015.

Silence.

Oh, please not again.

Then Anneli cleared her throat. "I should be able to help you with that." At that second I loved her dry, slightly flat voice. I still had a chance.

"Thank you so much, that would be fantastic! The problem is that it's urgent—really urgent."

"Okay… I can try to sort it out by lunchtime tomorrow."

I'd worked at the court, and I knew this counted as high-speed action. A generous offer. But way too slow for me.

"I'm sorry," I replied, forcing myself to demand the unreasonable. "I need the information much sooner—within the next half hour."

Anneli's voice became even drier. "Half an hour? That's impossible."

"I realize I don't have any right to ask, but—"

Anneli interrupted me. "I have a summons that must be issued this afternoon, so I don't have time to help you at the moment." She sounded very firm; this was not up for discussion. If only Ellen had still been there; she would be on her way down to the archive by now.

However I wasn't ready to give up. The words came tumbling out of my mouth, subdued but intense.

"No, I get it, and under normal circumstances I would never ask something like this, but my best friend is about to go abroad with her new boyfriend and I recognize him." I could hear the desperation in my voice. "I'm almost sure he was the guy who was convicted in this case. So…this could actually be a matter of life and death."

Best friend, going abroad, new boyfriend. I'd changed the details to speed up the explanation, but the main gist was the same. Anneli sighed.

"Yes, but…" I heard a faint note of hesitation; she sounded slightly more defensive. Maybe it wasn't over yet. "As you know, a lot of cases go through the court in a few months; it will take quite some time to check out all of them."

"Bengt was the judge, Bengt Åkerberg, so you'd only need to focus on his cases, and only the ones involving domestic abuse, and only in April and May."

Silence.

"Anneli? I'm begging you."

"Okay, I'll go down and take a look," she said brusquely. She was clearly annoyed. "But I'm not spending any more than twenty minutes on this."

"Oh, thank you, thank you, Anneli, that's—"

"I'll pick out what I can find right away," she interrupted me. "And that's more than I should be doing."

"I know. Thank you so much. Will you give me a call?"

"I will." She ended the conversation. I returned to my seat, where Henrik looked enquiringly at me, and I took a deep breath.

"She promised to check."

"And what does that mean?"

"It means she'll go down to the archive and see what she can find. What do you think it means?"

"But what are you going to do with the information?"

"If it's Jacob, then we don't go. Simple."

"And if it isn't Jacob, then we go?" I didn't answer.

"You're going to have to make a decision in a very short time, so you'd better give it some thought in advance," Henrik continued quietly, glancing in Jacob and Milena's direction. "You already know what I think."

Before I could respond, the bus began to slow down. On the other side of the road a dirt track led down toward the water and an open grassy area with a small hut.

My stomach turned over.

No. Not yet.

The loudspeaker crackled and the driver announced: "The helipad, ladies and gentlemen."

It was time to get off the bus.

We wandered down the hill with our rucksacks. Behind us the bus continued on its journey to the mountain station. Jacob was in a good mood now, talking about the mighty Ahkka massif that now lay directly ahead of us on the far side of the lake. Back in the day you used to be able to take a boat across the lake and enter Sarek from the north, he informed us, via Ahkka, but STF had scrapped the service. When he completed the Sarek traverse, he had also climbed Ahkka.

Henrik nodded and made the right noises, but he seemed distracted. I realized that not knowing what we were going to do, whether we were going to take the helicopter flight or not, was taking its toll on his nerves. However I couldn't deal with that right now.

I said nothing. My stomach had contracted into a hard solid knot. I gazed out over the lake. Ahkka looked elegant and dignified and impregnable. It was the first time I'd seen it, and unfortunately I think I will always link the sight to a feeling of nausea. My blood was so full of stress hormones that it felt thick, viscous, and my head was pounding. I couldn't take any pleasure in Ahkka's majestic beauty.

And at that moment I heard the helicopter, first a distant sound that faded away, then it came back, louder this time as its rotors whipped through the air. I peered upward and soon spotted it, a tiny dot but clearly visible against the blue sky. The knot in my stomach tightened.

A young girl dressed in black emerged from the hut. She was chewing gum. "Are you the group traveling to Stalo?" she asked in a broad Norrland accent.

"We are," Jacob replied.

"Then you're in the right place. Have you weighed your rucksacks?" She pointed to a set of scales with a hook on a plinth.

"No—what's the allowance?"

"Twenty kilos each, so eighty altogether."

The helicopter dropped toward the ground in a wide arc. The noise was deafening now, gravel and dust whirled up from the landing area. Milena pointed to the hut and shouted: "Is there a toilet?"

The girl nodded and beckoned her to follow. I decided to tag along. We left our rucksacks with Jacob and Henrik, and the girl led the way into the hut. She pointed to the toilet door.

"I'm afraid I have to wait for a call before we leave," I said to Milena. "There won't be any coverage after this."

Milena nodded. "No problem—we're not in that much of a hurry."

She went into the toilet first, while I stared at my phone and brought up the list of my most recent calls. Twelve minutes had passed since I spoke to Anneli. And the helicopter was here, ready and waiting. Anneli had said she wouldn't spend more than twenty minutes on the search, which meant she should get back to me in eight minutes at the latest.

Eight minutes. I could delay our departure for that long, but then I would need a few more minutes to process the information I hoped Anneli would give me.

The sound of the engine died away, the rotors slowed and

stopped. Milena emerged, and I went into the toilet. I did what I had to do as quickly as possible, then sat there holding my phone up in the air. I pictured Jacob and Henrik stowing our rucksacks on board. Two minutes passed. Four. Six. Anneli didn't call.

Shit. Hurry up, Anneli. Please, please hurry up.

I heard footsteps outside the door, then a brisk knock followed by the girl's voice. "Excuse me? They're ready to leave."

"I'm coming." I got up slowly, turned on the tap, washed my hands calmly and methodically. Dried them with a paper towel. Checked the time. Seven minutes, seven and a half.

"Are you okay in there?"

I opened the door, stepped out. "I'm fine."

"You're not the only person to feel shaky before their first helicopter flight."

I gave her a stiff little smile and repeated: "I'm fine."

I went outside. Milena, Jacob and Henrik were all waiting by the helicopter along with the pilot, a young woman in dark blue dungarees, her long blond hair tied back in a ponytail beneath her cap. She too was chewing gum. There was no sign of our rucksacks, so they'd clearly been loaded already.

"Okay, let's go," Jacob said as I approached. I waved my phone and said: "I'm expecting a call at any moment." I held out my hand to the pilot. "Hi—Anna."

"Hi—Jenny."

"I'm sorry, but I just have to wait for this call."

"We're already late," Jacob interjected, "and Jenny has several more trips to do. We need to leave."

"I'm not in that much of a rush," Jenny assured him. "We can give it five minutes." I couldn't hide my relief.

"Thank you—I really appreciate that."

Jacob took a deep breath. He was clearly frustrated, more by the fact that we weren't doing as he said than by the delay itself, I suspected.

"We're going in five minutes," he snapped, "whether you've finished chatting or not."

I nodded. Henrik didn't say anything, but I could see how embarrassed he was. He knew I was prepared to make the others wait, however long it took for Anneli to get back to me.

I moved away so that no one would be able to hear the details of my conversation.

I couldn't stand still; I walked around in small circles, rocked back and forth on the spot.

The minutes ticked by. The group by the helicopter never took their eyes off me. I checked the time yet again: twenty-four minutes had passed since I spoke to Anneli. She should have called by now. I realized that she might just have said *twenty minutes* on the spur of the moment; when she was actually in the archive she may find herself absorbed in the task. It could easily be an hour before she got back to me.

Another minute. Jacob looked at his watch, then said something to Jenny. I was too far away to hear, but Jenny nodded, then clambered into the cockpit and started up the engine.

"Time to go," Jacob shouted to me, tapping his watch with his index finger. I didn't respond; I simply looked at my phone again. Should I try contacting Anneli? Was there any point? Probably not. I found it hard to believe that she would simply sit in her office when she returned from the archive; surely she would ring me right away. But I had to do something, anything, even if I knew it was hopeless, so I made the call.

The helicopter was revving up. The noise was growing louder by the second. The rotors began to spin, slowly at first, then faster and faster. Henrik came over to me.

"We can't wait any longer, Anna. We have to leave."

"I'm not boarding until I've spoken to Anneli."

"In that case we'll have to let them go without us. This is not okay."

"Bullshit—they can't be in that much of a hurry! We're no more than fifteen minutes late!"

"Yes, but…"

"It's just Jacob making a fuss!"

The engine was now operating at full throttle. The grass around the helipad was pressed flat, and dust and gravel were once more swirling up on the turning area where I was standing. Jacob came marching over.

"So what's happening?"

We had to yell to make ourselves heard. "I have to take this call!"

"And we have to go! Are the two of you coming, or not?"

"Go then!" I shouted angrily. "Just go!"

We stared at each other, Jacob and I, openly confrontational now.

Do you think I'm bluffing, Jacob? Forget it—I never bluff. It's my way or the highway. I don't care about Sarek—it will be there next year, and every year after that.

Jacob didn't flinch, but I sensed that he hadn't expected me to say they should go without us. I was about to find out how much he wanted us to accompany them to Sarek.

"She's using a hell of a lot of fuel unnecessarily if she has to wait," he yelled, as if he hadn't heard what I said. "We'll have to pay extra for this!"

"In that case why the fuck did she start the engine?" I snapped back. "Maybe someone told her to do it?"

I saw anger in his eyes, and surprise—and something else, more difficult to define. "It's probably best if you go," Henrik interjected. "This might take a while!"

Jacob ignored him. He remained where he was, staring at me. I stared right back, thinking that he was going to have to react if he didn't want to look completely ridiculous. I saw Milena climbing into the helicopter—and at that moment my phone rang.

It was Anneli's number. I answered and walked away from

Henrik and Jacob. I heard Jacob say to Henrik that he would give me a couple of minutes, then they were leaving.

"Hi, Anneli, thanks for getting back to me."

"Hi. I've found a couple of cases that fit your description." I covered my other ear with my hand so that I could hear better. She was back to normal now—calm and competent. I felt a mixture of hope and tension.

"Brilliant!"

"I can't hear you very well."

"Sorry, there's a helicopter starting up here." I moved farther away, cupped my hand over the microphone to try to reduce the noise. I glanced behind me; Jacob was just climbing on board.

"So there's a case that was concluded on May 18, 2015, with Bengt as the judge, domestic abuse, the perpetrator was Jimmy Toivonen, 870519-2737, sentenced to eighteen months."

"Sorry, did you say 870519?"

"Yes. 870519-2737."

Born in 1987, so Jimmy was now thirty-two years old. Much too young to be Jacob. "Okay... And the second case?"

"Concluded May 23, domestic abuse, Kent Stefan Jernrud, 761010-4139, sentenced to two years and six months."

"761010?"

"Yes, then 4139."

I suddenly had a strange taste in my mouth, like when you're hungry and you think of something you would really, really love to eat. It was almost the taste of blood.

Born in 1976, which made Kent Stefan Jernrud forty-three years old. Jernrud sounded unlikely. If it was him, he wouldn't be the first criminal to change his name several times. Lars-Inge Andersson. Lars-Inge Svartenbrandt. Lars Ferm. Lars Patrick Carlander. Same perpetrator, four different names.

And this guy was called Stefan. Just like Stefan Jakob Johansson. Everything fit. It had to be him.

I asked Anneli to repeat the name and spell it out for me. I made a note of the name and ID number on my phone.

"Thank you so much, Anneli—you've done me a huge favor."

"No problem." Her tone was neutral as she ended the call. Henrik had come over and was standing right beside me. He gave me an enquiring look.

"It's him," I said. "I'm sure of it."

Henrik nodded, his expression serious. "Was he called Jacob Tessin back then?"

"No—Kent Stefan Jernrud."

Henrik thought for a moment. "Okay… So shall I go and tell them we're not coming?"

"Yes—I'm just going to Google him."

"Do you want me to wait?"

"No, it must be him. You go."

But Henrik didn't move. "It's best if I hang on for a minute or two. If it is him, you need to have a chat with Milena."

At that moment Milena climbed out of the helicopter and set off toward us, her hair blowing wildly around her head. No doubt Jacob thought it was beneath his dignity to try to persuade us. I typed the name into the search box and pressed the magnifying glass. The results appeared instantly. There was a Kent Stefan Jernrud living in Flemingsberg, forty-three years old, but no phone number or any other interesting information. The other results had nothing to do with him. He seemed to be the only person in Sweden with the name Jernrud. I clicked on the Images tab and found a couple of pictures of a Kent Jerker Nilsson, plus a large number of photographs of a couple of different men called Stefan Jern, but not one single image of Kent Stefan Jernrud.

It was hard to draw any conclusions. If Jacob had changed his name from Kent Stefan Jernrud, then his former name should be on some database somewhere.

Milena reached us, asked how it was going. I barely looked up from my phone.

Henrik replied on my behalf, told her we probably couldn't come.

"It's work," he explained. "Something Anna has to deal with, unfortunately." Milena nodded but stayed put—I suppose she wanted to hear it from me.

I tried Facebook instead, and got a match. Kent Stefan Jernrud still existed—at least on Facebook. I clicked on his profile picture; it showed a mountain landscape.

Milena raised her eyebrows. "Anna? Can we go now?"

I clicked on Photos and the screen was filled with thumbnails snaps of the same person, in various surroundings and contexts.

I recognized him. But he wasn't Jacob Tessin.

Interview with Anna Samuelsson 880216-3382, September 18, 2019, Gällivare hospital, conducted by Detective Inspector Anders Suhonen.

"So what did you think at that stage?"

"I was really surprised. I was absolutely certain it would be him."

"What happened next?"

"I had a brief word with Henrik, showed him the pictures."

"But you recognized the person in those pictures?"

"Yes. I remembered the court case, but that wasn't the case Jacob was involved in."

"Right…"

"I still had a mental image of Jacob in the courtroom."

"I understand."

"But I wasn't quite so certain. I was pretty confused, actually."

"Mm."

"So…we boarded the helicopter with Milena, and we took off."

"What did Henrik say?"

"Nothing."

"I thought it sounded as if he was pretty keen to drop out?"

"He was, but when it came to the crunch I guess he thought it would be difficult to do that at the last minute. The helicopter was waiting, with its engine running."

"Mm."

"So neither of us said anything."

"Do you feel able to carry on for a little while, or would you like to rest?"

"I can carry on."

"And you're not in pain at the moment?"

"No."

"You look a bit brighter today."

"Yes."

Silence.

"Anyway… How do you feel about it now? The fact that you were mistaken about Jacob?"

"I don't think I was mistaken."

"No?"

"I saw him in court in Nacka when I was working there as a notary. I know I did."

"Right."

"It must be easy for you to check out Stefan Jakob Johansson."

"Absolutely—we're on it."

"I might have got the odd detail wrong. Maybe the judge wasn't Bengt Åkerberg. Or maybe the case was in the autumn rather than the spring."

"Could be. Obviously we'll look into that possibility."

Silence.

"We should never have boarded that helicopter."

The noise was deafening, and there was a strong smell of aviation fuel. We were all wearing a headset with a mic so that we could talk to one another in spite of the racket. The helicopter lifted into the air, then Jenny tilted it onto its side and took us out over the lake in a wide arc. The sky was now clear blue in the west, and beneath us the waves sparkled in the sunshine. The water stretched far away to the northwest, splintering into a multitude of smaller lakes. The ground looked as if it had been shredded, like a torn plastic bag.

Soon we were flying over land again, the ground rising to meet us in a series of gentle ridges and mountains. The vegetation had begun to turn yellow and red. We were now crossing Padjelanta national park, which continued south toward extensive lakes. Far, far away I could see Sulitelma, the huge massif on the border between Sweden and Norway. Immediately to our left we had Ahkka, its glaciers glinting in the sun with sharp ridges running from peak to peak. Beyond Ahkka were the peaks inside Sarek itself, still partially hidden by the clouds. Silver streams meandered along the bottoms of deep valleys.

The view took my breath away. I had never seen anything so beautiful in my entire life.

Apart from that, I felt confused and empty and exhausted. I thought back to last night's unpleasantness in the restaurant car; it was less than twenty-four hours ago, but it felt like a week. I hadn't stopped obsessing over Jacob and who he really was since then. I had slept badly. In the morning I thought I'd remembered where I'd seen him, and from then I had been totally focused on how I could confirm my suspicions. On the bus and at the helipad my stress levels had been constantly rising. I thought I'd found proof that he was the person I remembered from the trial, but I was wrong.

And now it was as if I was emerging from the thought bubble in which I'd been trapped since yesterday evening, blinking into the light and feeling disorientated. Tiredness caught up with me; I was a balloon, exhaustion was a pin, but I didn't explode with a bang. The energy simply leaked out of me with a quiet hiss, and I crumpled. I had no strength, no impetus.

I think that was one reason why I was able to appreciate the amazing view from the helicopter. Not wanting to do anything was an unusual feeling for me. Inside my head, I am almost always somewhere other than my physical location. I set goals, work out what steps I need to take in order to achieve them. But right now I was totally present in the moment. Wherever I looked, I had this magical view over the world of the mountains. I would have been content to spend the rest of my life enjoying this view. I actually believe I was happy.

Jacob was sitting next to Jenny at the front.

"So where are you off to?" she asked. She also had a Norrland accent, but a slightly softer variant compared to the girl at the helipad.

"We're starting off at Alggavagge, then in toward Skarja, and south via the Rapa Valley," Jacob informed her.

"Alggavagge—lots of bears there at this time of year."

The three of us pricked up our ears, and Henrik and I looked at each other. "I've never seen any," Jacob replied.

"Oh, yes—they go in to fatten up before the winter. They'll take whatever they can get hold of. Lots of crowberries and visitors from Stockholm." We all laughed, including Jenny.

"Good thing I'm from Huddinge," Jacob said.

"The bears aren't too fussy," Jenny countered.

I smiled at Henrik and he smiled back, but it didn't reach his eyes.

Jenny pointed out of the side window. "If you look up ahead you can just see Lake Alggajavrre. The blue-green patch. You'll have to row to get across there."

Jacob turned and looked at me. "So was it worth coming along?" I nodded and smiled wearily. He smiled back and gave me a thumbs-up. Henrik gazed out of the window; he couldn't take his eyes off Sarek's snow-clad peaks. I felt that I wanted to be close to him, so I placed my hand on his and he turned to look at me. There was love and tenderness in his eyes, and I gently caressed his cheek.

The flight to Staloluokta took about twenty minutes. It was a Sami settlement by Lake Virihaure with a long mountain along one shoreline. There was also a mountain station. Jenny slowly brought the helicopter down and landed in a small enclosure by the water. As we left we thanked her for the fantastic flight, and she wished us good luck for our trip to Sarek. We retrieved our rucksacks and set off for the mountain station. The ground was soft, covered in heather and moss.

By now it was two thirty in the afternoon. We hadn't had a decent meal since the morning, so we decided to stock up with provisions in Parfa's kiosk, then have lunch in the station.

The kiosk was a little wooden building not unlike an old-fashioned sausage stall, located among the Sami dwellings. It appeared to be closed, but as we approached a friendly looking man emerged from one of the buildings and opened up.

I had never seen so much stuff crammed into such a small space. Every square centimeter of the walls, floor and ceiling, had been used to display everything you could possibly need for a mountain hike. Preserves, powdered soups, freeze-dried meals, sweets and snacks, toilet paper and washing-up liquid and liquefied petroleum gas, local products like knitted gloves and smoked mountain char and vacuum-packed reindeer meat at a thousand kronor a kilo. We bought what we needed for lunch and the rest of the week, said thank you and left—several kilos heavier.

The mountain station kitchen was simple with LPG hot plates and big steel buckets filled with water. We heated up meatballs in a cream sauce, cooked some macaroni and sat down in the dining room with a magnificent view of the lake.

When we'd eaten and cleared away, Jacob spread out his map on the table and showed us the route. First of all there were several kilometers of a pretty steep climb until we reached the south side of the mountain known as Stuor Dijdder, then we would leave the track and zigzag between lakes in order to continue toward Alajavrre, the lake we had seen from the helicopter. It would be a long first day, a hike of about twenty kilometers, but we wanted to get into Sarek as soon as possible, didn't we?

We were full and happy and warm. We felt strong and keen to get going. We thought it sounded like an excellent plan.

I paid for the use of the kitchen, and we all took the chance to visit the outside toilets. We had a week of very primitive toilet opportunities ahead of us, and I suspected that within a couple of days we would think fondly of these smelly wooden huts as the height of civilization.

We shrugged on our rucksacks and set off. The track passed a church built as a traditional Sami dwelling, then began to climb. Jacob took the lead, and the rest of us followed in single file. After a few minutes I stopped and looked back. We were already a good way up the mountainside; the station and the Sami settlement lay below us, between the deep blue waters of Virihaure and the mountain known as Unna Dijdder. Its soft contours were clad in shades of mustard yellow and rusty red with patches of green. Beyond the lake I could see a white jagged line of peaks. It was stunning.

We hadn't done it deliberately, but I realized that we had hit the September explosion of color in the mountains of Lapland. I dug out my phone, took a picture. The sun was still high in the sky. It felt like a sunny October day in Stockholm—pleasantly warm. I put down my rucksack, took off my anorak and continued in just my top. A gentle breeze fanned my face and throat.

Milena had noticed that I'd stopped, and was waiting for me to catch up. "Isn't it amazing?" she said.

"Absolutely. I just want to keep taking photos."

"Did you sort out the work problem, by the way?"

"Yes. It was just something I had to say yes or no to."

We carried on chatting about our respective jobs, about new colleagues and mutual acquaintances who'd moved on to pastures new. Our conversation started out as small talk, but gradually became more personal. This was the first time since we left Stockholm that we'd been on our own, and soon the bond between us was restored. It had been established in Uppsala ten years ago, and it was always easy to find our way back, even if we hadn't spoken for months.

I was careful not to ask about Jacob. If she wanted to talk about him, she could do it on her own initiative. And I no longer felt that it was important for me to dig into his past. On reflection, all that research, all that phoning and Googling, seemed a little over-the-top to say the least. I was no longer afraid of Jacob, nor was I curious about him. Right now I was walking through a magnificent landscape, Milena and I were good friends again, talking to each other the way we always used to. Nothing else mattered.

The track led us down into a narrow ravine, edged with birch and willow brushwood, then up the other side. It was very steep, and we had to grab hold of branches to pull ourselves up. We were lucky that it wasn't raining, because then the muddy track would have been very difficult to negotiate. It was only a short passageway, and when we reached the next ridge, we had a clear view toward Stuor Dijdder and the small lakes at the foot of the mountain.

Jacob and Henrik were about a hundred meters ahead of us. I wondered what they were talking about. Maybe they were walking in silence. I remembered the pattern from our earlier trips: for the first few days Milena and I would chat virtually nonstop and Henrik would often walk alone, a short distance ahead of or behind us. We would talk less and less with each passing day—not because we'd grown tired of each other, but because the most important stuff had already been said, and when you spend every waking hour together, the perception that silence is uncomfortable soon disappears.

We started to discuss Henrik. Milena was worried. "He doesn't seem like himself. He looks tired."

Should I tell her that he'd hardly left the apartment all summer? That he'd turned into a couch potato? No, that would be disloyal. I replied truthfully that he was feeling pretty down about work at the moment.

"It's to do with the fact that he's never in the running for a professorship. It's taking its toll on him. He'd expected it to happen years ago, but he feels as if he's missed out."

"Does it have to be in Uppsala? Couldn't he apply for a post elsewhere?"

"I suppose so… Anyway, this is the first time he's talked about doing something else."

"Leaving university?" Milena sounded surprised.

"I don't think he's serious, but he's been in that world forever. He's never tried a different job."

Milena looked taken aback. "But what would he do? Office work?"

"I don't really know. Like I said, I don't think he's serious."

Milena was clearly more worried about this than I was. For a fleeting moment I thought of asking whether Jacob enjoyed his job, but I didn't do it.

We'd been walking for a couple of hours now, and my body had acclimatized. At first the rucksack always feels heavy and uncomfortable; the body has a new center of gravity and your knees kind of give way a little with every step because you're afraid of losing your balance. Your boots might seem hard, you're aware of the strain in a muscle at the back of your thigh. But gradually you warm up, the little cramps fade away, your whole body is working, you have a pleasantly increased pulse rate, the endorphins are fizzing in your blood and you experience a mild euphoria.

Suddenly we could no longer see Jacob and Henrik. We had left the track and were on our way down between the lakes. The ground rose and fell, crisscrossed by small ridges with puddles, dips and dense undergrowth between them. It was easy to lose the wider view here. Milena and I had stopped to discuss which way we should go when Jacob popped up a short distance ahead and waved to us. We set off in his direction.

They had found a sheltered spot with rock faces on three sides, close to one of the lakes. Henrik was already on his way back from the water's edge, having filled up the coffeepot. Jacob lit the stove and soon the water was boiling. We tipped instant coffee straight into the pot and gave it a stir, then Jacob divided the hot drink between us, while I dug out my bottle of powdered milk. We didn't have any fruit or pastries, but Henrik offered around peanuts and raisins. The ground was relatively dry, so I sat down on the moss and heather. I leaned back against a rock and sipped my coffee. I felt calm yet full of life, reveling in the peacefulness of this place, the blue sky, the sunlight.

The others were chatting about which coffee was best—espresso, filtered or freeze-dried. Jacob admitted that he actually loved instant coffee. He'd never understood the popularity of espresso. Milena and Henrik promised not to tell anyone.

After about half an hour we wiped out our drinking cups with a clump of moss and were soon on our way again. I had the map in my hand and could see that we were walking up the side of Unna Liemak. It lay next to Stuor Liemak. Unna and Stuor, just like Unna and Stuor Dijdder. Could it mean little and big? Stuor Liemak was about a hundred meters taller, so that sounded right. Both were about a thousand meters high, and I thought they were unlucky to have ended up here, just outside Sarek and with Ahkka and Sulitelma nearby. Almost anywhere else in Sweden they would have been regarded as huge mountains, but here they weren't much more than hills.

At first the four of us walked together, but meter by meter Jacob and I pulled away from Henrik and Milena. We plodded stubbornly upward. I definitely wasn't tired, but I could feel the steady rhythm of my pulse. The terrain didn't look at all as I'd expected from the map. I'd pictured a wide valley extending down to Lake Alajavrre, but instead we were constantly climbing. We came to a small brook, the first one we'd encountered, but we were virtually able to cross it without even getting our feet wet. I topped up my water bottle. Maybe the rumors about difficult crossings in Sarek were exaggerated. When we reached the fence around a reindeer enclosure we stopped and waited for Henrik and Milena. It was clear that the gradient was beginning to take its toll, especially on Henrik. He was red-faced, sweating and panting.

"Are you okay?" I asked him. "Do you want to take a break?"

"No, I'm fine," he gasped between breaths. "We'll be stopping for dinner soon, won't we?"

"We'll keep going for another hour or so," Jacob stated firmly. "That will get us to Alajavrre. It's fantastic up there." He lifted the fence, we took off our rucksacks and slid them across the ground to the other side, then wriggled under ourselves. Jacob was the last. He took out a couple of energy bars and divided them between us before we set off again.

The sun was setting now, the light falling at an angle across the landscape. The air was quickly growing cooler, and I put my anorak back on.

Eventually we were able to see the western part of Alajavrre, and from the next ridge we were looking out across the whole lake. At the far end a smaller mountain blocked the way, but the snow-capped peaks rose up beyond it, and there it was: Sarek. Just to have these amazing mountains within sight gave me butterflies in my tummy.

"That's where we're heading," Jacob said, leaning closer to me and pointing. "The far end of the lake."

"Tonight?"

"Yes, but it's an easy route from here. You just walk along the shore."

I glanced over my shoulder. Henrik and Milena had fallen a long way behind, and there was no sign of them. I felt a tiny stab of unease. I was alone with Jacob Tessin. But the feeling disappeared as quickly as it had come.

We went a little farther, out into a huge meadow of lush green grass right by the lake. I fetched some water while Jacob rigged up the stove. Dusk had fallen but it was still relatively light. The sky and mountains on the far side of Alajavrre were reflected upside down in its mirrorlike surface. I had the dizzying sensation that the ground itself was nothing more than a thin plate, the lake a gash that enabled you to see right through it. The sky was beneath our feet as well as above our heads.

"They say that the most beautiful view in the whole of Sarek is from the top of Alatjåhkkå," Jacob said, waving a hand at the mountain behind us. The minestrone soup was bubbling nicely, and I took some rye bread and a tube of shrimp-flavored cheese out of my rucksack.

"Which peak?" I wondered. "It looks as if there are several in a row."

"The farthest one, I think." He took out the map. "It's the highest—1430."

"You've never been up there?"

"No, and it's not going to happen tonight either, if we're going to get to the end of the lake."

"How many times have you been to Sarek?"

"This will be my fourth, but I've only walked this route once before."

He told me that when he first came to Sarek, between the ages of twenty-five and thirty, the main focus was climbing. He and his friends wanted to conquer the highest peaks in Sarektjåhkkå. They had challenged themselves. It was another ten years before he returned, and on that occasion he had rediscovered Sarek: the beautiful narrow valleys where you never saw another soul, the delta at the end of the Rapa Valley, the majestic elk around Rovdjurstorget.

"That was when I fell head over heels in love," he said.

A train of thought from the previous evening made its presence felt. Jacob was between twenty-five and thirty when he first came here, then ten years passed, which made him at least thirty-six. And now he was claiming to be thirty-eight. So if I asked him when he'd last been here, and if he said it was more than two years ago, then something wasn't right.

But my speculation was half-hearted, as if I were on autopilot. I didn't need to know, and I didn't ask any follow-up questions. Jacob smiled at me.

"So tell me about your trips—where have the three of you been?"

"Hasn't Milena told you?"

"A bit—Kebnekaise, she said."

We exchanged memories of our trips, compared various destinations. We both agreed that Blåhammaren had the best food in the Swedish mountains.

At long last Henrik and Milena arrived. They both looked exhausted as they undid the straps of their rucksacks and let them fall to the ground.

"Tired, sweetheart?" Jacob asked, giving Milena a hug.

"Absolutely," she gasped.

"The soup is ready," I said, smiling at Henrik. He lay down on the wet grass, took a deep breath and closed his eyes.

"I just need to rest for a minute or two."

I dropped to my knees beside him and gave him a kiss. "Of course you do. There's no rush."

I took out my mess tin and Jacob poured the soup directly from the pan. I sat down on a rock and started to eat, feeling vaguely concerned that Henrik seemed so tired after a four-hour walk. Admittedly it had been uphill most of the way, but certainly not steep, and the weather was perfect. This didn't bode well for the difficulties that might lie ahead in Sarek.

And I also felt something else, something I had touched on when I was talking about Henrik and Milena. Something I didn't really want to admit, because I was ashamed of it.

Irritation. Henrik was less fit than usual. I suspected that he'd thought our holiday would be canceled because we'd postponed it when I had to work, so he hadn't bothered training. I'd spent virtually all day every day in the office over the summer, so of course I was unable to keep an eye on what he did and didn't do when I wasn't there. He'd had a long break, seven or eight weeks, and he'd stayed in the city without doing anything special, except for a week with his brother's family on the west coast.

When I was doing the laundry, I'd noticed that his gym kit was never in the basket. On the days when I worked from home, he stayed in bed, when he wasn't reading or doing sudoku. I had trained at the gym near my office as usual, almost every day.

We hadn't had time to go on any training walks together carrying heavy rucksacks as we normally did, and he certainly hadn't undertaken any on his own.

He sat up with some difficulty, staggered over to his rucksack and dug out his mess tin.

"Some hot soup will soon perk you up," Jacob said cheerfully. Henrik managed a wan smile as he held out his tin.

We ate our soup; nobody had much to say. It was eight thirty now, and the evening was closing in. With the darkness came a chill in the air. On a sunny September day like this you could almost be fooled into thinking that it was still summer, but when the evening came that illusion was soon shattered. The temperature could easily fall close to zero tonight. That wasn't a problem, we had the appropriate sleeping bags, but before we snuggled down in our tents, there would be a certain amount of shivering and stiff fingers clutching our toothbrushes.

Jacob finished first and put on some water; he wanted a cup of coffee. Henrik ate his soup quickly and looked enquiringly at Jacob. "I assume we're camping here tonight?"

"No."

There was a brief silence. Milena looked unsure of herself. Henrik glanced at me. "But it's almost dark."

"Not quite," Jacob replied. "And your eyes will soon get used to it. No, I thought we'd carry on alongside the lake, to the far end. That means we'll be inside Sarek by lunchtime tomorrow."

Henrik's expression was skeptical. Jacob went on: "It's a really easy walk, you just follow the shoreline. One and a half, maximum two hours."

"It will be pitch-dark by then."

"We've all got head torches, haven't we? Milena and I have, anyway."

Henrik was waiting for me to respond, but I remained silent. I felt fit and alert, and to be honest I really wanted to keep going.

He turned to Milena instead. "I guess the two of us are the most tired. What do you think?"

Milena didn't answer immediately. Jacob stared at her. "I don't know… I'm happy to camp here or keep going, whatever," she said defensively.

"Right." Henrik had been hoping for support, but realized it wasn't going to happen.

A brief silence followed.

"At least it's not uphill," I said eventually. "Jacob? I'm assuming it's flat terrain?"

"Oh, yes. Completely flat. And like I said, you walk along the shore. It's really straightforward."

I nodded. "In that case I think we should go on, but we take it easy, and we stick together, all four of us. Henrik? Is that okay?"

Another silence.

"Fine." His voice was flat. Suddenly I felt a pang of guilt. I could easily have swayed the discussion, opted to camp here. Maybe I was punishing Henrik for neglecting his training.

"Great." Jacob went over to Henrik and patted his shoulder. "There'll be a good tot of Lagavulin for you when we arrive."

There was a military air about Jacob, as if he were a sergeant mustering his troops, knowing exactly how to motivate them. That was probably how he wanted to see himself, but Henrik hadn't done national service, and he hated smoky single-malt whisky—the most overrated alcoholic drink in the history of humanity, as he often referred to it.

"Thanks," he said, getting to his feet. "Shall we go, then?"

A few minutes later we were on our way, all wearing our head torches. We didn't want to switch them on until it was pitch-dark, so as not to ruin our night vision unnecessarily. We were still able to make out the black contours of the mountains against the deep blue sky and behind us, in the west, lighter strips were visible.

The shore along the waterline was no more than a meter wide, but it was indeed flat and very pleasant, after so much uphill walking during the day. Tiny waves gently lapped the shore. I made a point of staying right next to Henrik rather than forging on ahead. Jacob clearly wanted to move faster, but Milena stuck to our tempo, and in the end he stopped and waited for us. Henrik didn't have much to say at first, but when he realized that this really was an easy walk, and that I was making sure he set the pace, he cheered up.

Eventually the darkness became almost dense, and we switched on our head torches. I pictured how we would look to someone standing a few hundred meters up the mountainside: four beams of light swinging this way and that before being swallowed up by the black night. I imagined myself as a diver, walking along the seabed at the bottom of the ocean. This was an adventure, but it was cozy at the same time. I felt as if I could go on all night. There it was again, that mild euphoria.

Everything was exactly as it should be on our mountain holiday. We had a new person with us, someone neither Henrik nor I knew, but his presence hadn't affected our relationships in any way. As soon as we started walking, normality had kicked in, and I had to give Jacob the credit for that. Since we'd embarked on our trek, he had come across as extremely perceptive and relaxed. He was clearly in his element.

As we approached the end of the lake, the terrain worsened. The sand disappeared and it was no longer possible to follow the waterline. Fine gravel turned into pebbles, then bigger stones, and suddenly we were negotiating our way through a rough lunar landscape. It was difficult to work out a route when we could see only a short distance in front of us by the light of the head torches. Jacob hadn't been entirely honest about how easy the walk would be, or how long it would take. Unless of course he'd forgotten since the last time he was here.

It was almost midnight by the time we reached our goal and were able to pitch our tents. A damp chill seemed to be rising from Alajavrre, and now that we'd stopped walking we all felt the cold. The darkness and the stony ground meant it took a while to find a suitable place to camp. Henrik and Milena were too tired to help, so Jacob and I took on the task. Eventually we found a reasonable spot with room for both tents, quite close together.

We called out to the others. Henrik was utterly exhausted, shivering so much that his teeth were chattering. Neither of us said much as we erected the tent, pumped up our air beds and unrolled our sleeping bags. Henrik brushed his teeth just outside the tent, then immediately crawled into his sleeping bag. I was also dead tired by now, but there was no way I was going to go to bed in the clothes I'd sweated in all day, and which were now clinging coldly to my skin. I rummaged around in my rucksack, dug out clean, dry underwear, my towel and my toilet bag, and clambered over rocks and stones down to the water's edge.

I took off my underwear and walked out barefoot into the ice-cold lake. I splashed my body, cupped my hands and washed my face and the back of my neck. I dried myself and got dressed, loving the feeling of clean dry socks on my feet.

When I got back to the tents, Jacob and Milena's was already in darkness. The sound of the zip when I opened ours sliced through the silence like a knife. I crawled inside on all fours, slid into my sleeping bag. Henrik was fast asleep.

I remember these sounds and smells from my early childhood, when my brothers and I used to camp in the garden: the canvas flapping gently with every puff of wind, the sturdy plastic groundsheet. My body was aching, but in a good way, and now it could rest. I was warm and dry. My thoughts ran free, and soon I slipped into a deep sleep.

This could be the best walking holiday ever.

That was what I thought just before I fell asleep.

The weather gods were still with us the following morning. The sun was shining and the air was clear and chilly. The dew sparkled on the grass and rocks. Even though I had been the last to go to bed, I was first up. I had slept well all night. My body was a little stiff in places, but otherwise I felt good.

I fetched water from the lake, lit the stove and began to make porridge with dried blueberries for breakfast. As I set out rye bread with various spreads, there was movement in the other tent. After a moment Milena crawled out, stretched and yawned.

"Good morning," I said. "Did you sleep well?"

"Not really. We couldn't get the tent on even ground. I woke up like eight times with my face pressed against the canvas. God, my back is stiff."

Soon Jacob emerged, also stretching and yawning. Milena gave him a hug, but Jacob didn't say much; he probably hadn't woken up properly. However he seemed to be in a good mood—every time our eyes met, he smiled.

Our voices had woken Henrik, who came out on all fours, then stood up with some difficulty. I held out my arms for a morning hug. He came over and put one arm around my shoulders, in a half-hearted way.

"How did you sleep?"

"Okay," he said tonelessly.

Henrik didn't have much to say during breakfast either, but his aura was completely different from Jacob's. There was no sense of peace and harmony about him; he seemed to be brooding about something, his thoughts elsewhere. He could be like that from time to time, sinking into gloomy introspection. I knew there was no point in asking what was on his mind; he wouldn't tell me. After a few hours his face would lighten, so I wasn't too worried. However there was no denying that this was a side of him I struggled with, possibly because it was so alien to me. Of course I can get into a bad mood now and again, I can get really mad and yell at people, but it soon passes and I'm able to look forward again. I don't see the point of brooding over things that have happened. Okay, you can feel regret, you can analyze the situation and think *I should have acted differently there*, but then you put it behind you, move on.

I also had a feeling that Henrik had got worse. Was he really like this when we became a couple ten years ago? No. The tendency had no doubt been there from the start, but not so overtly.

Or maybe he couldn't shake off his annoyance at yesterday's decision to carry on walking even though he'd said he wanted to set up camp for the night. It was an unspoken but clear principle on our walks that whoever was the most tired decided how far we should go each day. We had gone against that principle yesterday. On the other hand he had seemed pretty cheerful when we were walking along the shore.

Maybe he'd just slept badly. We'd nearly finished breakfast.

"How are you feeling, Henrik?" Milena asked.

He shrugged. "Okay."

"Surely you're not worn out already?" Jacob asked with a smile.

"No."

"I thought you said the two of you had done a lot of walking in the mountains?"

"We have," I said, placing my hand on Henrik's. "Henrik complains a little now and again, but he's as tough as the sole of an old shoe." My tone was jokey, but I saw immediately from Henrik's expression that the comment hadn't gone down well.

Jacob didn't notice—or he did notice and didn't care.

"I don't know about the sole of a shoe, but definitely old and tough," he said with a laugh. He looked at me, eager for my approval, for it to be me and him against Henrik. I suddenly felt very uncomfortable.

"Jacob..." Milena said.

"Sorry. Just joking—sorry. Are we okay, Henrik?"

"Yes," Henrik replied in the same toneless voice.

I stood up. "Time to clear away and get going, I think."

Jacob stood up too. Milena offered to do the washing up, while Henrik and I went over to our tent, took out our sleeping bags and air beds and started to stow everything away. I took his arm and said quietly: "I'm sorry, that was a stupid remark. Henrik?"

"Mm."

"Forgive me?"

"Of course."

We finished packing in silence. I knew things were far from okay, but hoped he would feel better once we set off.

It wasn't long before we were all ready. We were at the foot of the mountain known as Nuortap Rissavarre, and decided to go a little higher to avoid the worst of the rocks. We rounded the mountain on the southern side. The sun was rising higher in the sky, and it was getting warmer by the minute. Sarek gradually revealed itself before our eyes, even more magnificent than before. The mountain dropped down toward Lake Alggajavrre in a series of terraces and ridges. The water was an almost unreal shade of blue-green. Beyond the lake, Alggavagge extended toward the middle of Sarek, a narrow U-shaped valley with steep rock faces on either side.

To the south the peaks were lined up behind one another; they reminded me of gigantic cows, standing with their heads in their troughs and drinking their fill. How far down was the lake? How far away was the farthest mountain? A long, long way, but it was impossible to judge; you lost your sense of proportion in the face of all this splendor.

On the other side of the lake, a short distance up the mountainside, I saw a small building. Jacob explained that it was a chapel where a service was held once a year in the middle of summer. I am not religious, but I realized it would be a very special experience. Nature made even someone like me feel humble and devout in this place.

Jacob and I followed a long ridge down toward the southern side of the lake, and soon we were facing our first real challenge: wading across Alep Sarvesjåhkkå. We had to do it in order to continue along Alggajavrre's southern shore. It was a relatively wide river, and the current was strong. Here and there rocks protruded above the surface, but it was impossible to tell how deep it was in the middle. From where we were standing, it didn't look as if we would be able to wade across.

We waited for Henrik and Milena, who came sauntering along after a little while.

They were deep in conversation, but fell silent as they got closer. Henrik was sweating, his hair plastered to his forehead. He and Milena sat down for a rest while I passed around a bag of nuts and raisins.

"There's more water than I expected," Jacob said. "So we'll follow the river downstream—it's usually easier to wade across where it runs into the lake."

We set off, stepping from one clump of grass to the next. In some places the ground was very boggy, and we splashed our way through terrain resembling a paddy field. However Jacob was right: where the river flowed into Alggajavrre, it divided itself into a small delta with several arms and banks of gravel. There were plenty of rocks showing above the surface, which suggested that it was shallower here. The current was still strong though, and it was hard to assess the depth of the central channel. The gushing torrent was so loud that we had to raise our voices to make ourselves heard.

Jacob took off his boots and socks and put on a pair of thin trainers.

"I'll go first and do a recce," he said, unfastening the straps securing his rucksack across his waist and chest. "Undo all your straps—if you fall you have to lose the rucksack, otherwise you could get stuck under the water, which is very dangerous. Don't try to cross via the rocks, walk along the bottom of the river, even if it's deep." He took a pair of telescopic poles out of his rucksack and looked at me and Henrik.

"Have you brought poles?" We shook our heads. "Okay, in that case you can borrow ours. I'll cross first, then I'll throw them back. Remember you must always have three points of support in the river. Foot-foot-pole, or pole-pole-foot. Never lift your foot and your pole at the same time. Got it?"

"Yep," I said. Henrik nodded and swallowed, his expression grim.

"Okay, let's go." Jacob knotted his laces together and hung his boots over his rucksack, then waded into the water.

"Shit, it's cold… You never get used to it," he complained. His feet were bare inside the trainers. He quickly crossed the first narrow arms of the river, jumping adeptly from one gravel bank to the next while using his poles for support. At one point he stood on a rock, then turned and called out to us with a grin: "I just wanted to show you what not to do!" He kept going until he reached the main channel. It was four or five meters wide, and in the middle no rocks were visible above the surface—not a good sign.

Calmly and methodically he took one step after another out into the swirling current. He was careful to follow his own advice, and always have at least three points of support. The water came over his shoes, then halfway up his calves, up to his knees, whirlpools forming around his legs where they broke the surface. Slowly, resting for a second or two after each step, he made his way to the middle. The water was now around his thighs. And Jacob was tall; I realized that when it came to the rest of us, it would almost be at waist-height.

A few more steps and he was past the worst and into shallower waters again. He turned and threw his poles onto the gravel bank on our side of the main channel, then waded a little farther. A few more arms of the river separated him from solid ground, but they looked easy, and he had obviously decided to wait for us by the channel. He cupped his hands around his mouth and yelled:

"Go for it, Milena!"

She looked scared, but reached the channel without any difficulty. Then she stopped dead, stared at the surging water and took several deep breaths.

"Come on, Milena, you can do this! Come on!" Jacob shouted.

Hesitantly she began to move forward, step by step. I could see the current tugging at her legs. She was up to her knees now, and her courage deserted her. She looked over at Jacob and spread her hands in a gesture of resignation.

"You can do it, Milena—just keep going!"

"I can't!" She sounded very upset. "It's too strong, my foot keeps slipping!"

Jacob did his best to reassure her. "It'll be fine. Use your body weight, push your foot against the current. Feel the support of the poles."

She tried several times, lifting one foot and attempting to move forward, but the power of the water frightened her. "I can't…" Jacob, without poles, waded back in. He wobbled, but kept his balance. Soon he was standing right in the middle with the ice-cold water swirling around his thighs, holding one hand out to Milena. Still she hesitated.

"Come on, for fuck's sake!" Jacob shouted eventually. "It's

freezing in here!" Milena took one more deep breath, then stepped forward and grabbed his hand. The water came up to her waist and she let out a scream. They stood there motionless for a moment, then began to move to the other side, one step at a time.

Milena's relief when she finally reached the gravel bank was immense. Her face broke into a big smile, then she and Jacob hugged and kissed and said something to each other.

I had also changed into trainers, and as Henrik was still busy unlacing his boots, I decided to go next.

Jesus that's cold.

Glacier water poured over my feet, and Jacob had been absolutely right—there was no way of getting used to the shock of cold like this. You can take a dip in the sea in the spring and it feels cold, but your body soon grows accustomed to it and you can manage to swim for a little while. The sensation stabilizes at a certain level. But wading through a mountain stream is something quite different. Instead of abating after a few seconds, the coldness translates into pure pain. It is agonizing, penetrating your very bone marrow. Soon after that your body begins to stiffen and grow numb. You wear the cold like a suit that is too small, pulling and straining everywhere and making it impossible to move normally.

I reached the main channel and picked up Jacob's poles. I adjusted the length, then stepped out into the water. I had already lost some of the feeling in my feet. I focused on getting my center of gravity exactly right before I moved again, so that I could edge my way forward. If I stood on a rock and twisted my ankle, that would be it—I would definitely end up on my back. The water was swirling around my thighs now, and I understood why Milena had been so hesitant. The current was powerful, tugging at my legs, wanting to knock me over. Deeper and deeper… I was now standing with both feet and both poles on the riverbed; would I ever dare to lift my foot again? Jacob and

Milena were watching me carefully, and Jacob took a couple of steps forward, ready to come and help me too.

Oh, no, you don't.

I took a deep breath, bent my knees a fraction and tensed my muscles. Three determined steps later and I was in shallower waters. I had done it. The final step onto the gravel bank was child's play. Jacob and Milena smiled and applauded.

"Nice one, Anna!"

Jacob held his hand up to give me a high five, and I couldn't help grinning and returning the gesture. Milena gave me a high five too, but her attention was already on Henrik. He had just put on his second trainer and was holding a boot in each hand.

"You can do this, Henrik!" Milena yelled.

"Tie your boots together and hang them over your rucksack!" Jacob shouted.

But Henrik didn't listen to Jacob's advice—in fact he didn't even look up. He set off across the shallower reaches of the river, slowly and cautiously.

"Looking good, sweetheart!" I called out.

He reached the main channel. Jacob picked up his poles, which I had dropped on the ground. He waded out into the water and threw them in Henrik's direction. "Throw me your boots!" This time Henrik listened and did as Jacob said. The boots came flying through the air and landed on the gravel bank where we were standing. Then he began to wade, steadily and tentatively like the rest of us.

Just before he reached the middle, he stopped dead. He seemed very unsure of himself, looking both upstream and downstream as if he were looking for an easier route that none of us had discovered. There wasn't one of course.

I could see from both his posture and his facial expression that he was frightened.

His hands were gripping the poles so tightly that his knuckles were white. Milena, who knew him almost as well as I did, could see it too.

"I think you're going to have to help him," she said quietly to Jacob.

"Hang on—I'm coming!" Jacob began to move toward Henrik. I'm certain that Henrik must have seen him out of the corner of his eye, even though he didn't look up. The humiliation of needing assistance from Jacob was too much, so instead of waiting, Henrik took a long stride forward, then another and another, and I don't know whether he stood on a wobbly rock or whether the current was simply too strong, but he lost his balance and fell.

Milena let out a scream and I ran into the river.

For a few seconds both Henrik and his rucksack disappeared beneath the surface.

He half stood up, his mouth gaping with shock from the icy water, but the current caught him again and he tumbled backward. In seconds he was carried ten or fifteen meters downstream. He managed to find a foothold and tried to stand up, but fell again. Fortunately he was in shallower waters now, and wasn't washed any farther along.

I made my way over to him as quickly as I could and grabbed hold of his collar with one hand and his rucksack with the other. I dragged and heaved, and together we struggled onto the gravel bank. Henrik was still clutching Jacob's poles in a viselike grip. I let him catch his breath for a minute or so, then we made our way across the narrow arms to the safety of the other side. We had made it.

Henrik shrugged off his sodden rucksack and collapsed onto the grass. He kicked off his trainers, lay down on his back and started to remove his trousers. Milena helped by tugging at the legs. I was busy stripping off my own clothes—I too was soaked to the skin.

Thank goodness the sun was still shining down from a cloudless sky. At least we had a chance of getting warm and dry again. If the weather had been less kind, we might have been condemned to shiver for the rest of the week.

"You should have waited—I was coming to help you," Jacob said. Henrik didn't reply.

"You can borrow some of my clothes for the time being," I said, also ignoring Jacob. Henrik nodded.

"Didn't you undo the straps of your rucksack?" Jacob persisted.

"I did," Henrik said tersely before turning back to me. "I guess we should have lunch now—maybe that will give our clothes a chance to dry."

But Jacob hadn't finished.

"That could have gone really badly. What if you'd broken your foot, or banged your head? We might have had to abandon the whole trip. So unnecessary."

"Well, it didn't." Henrik stood up.

"Perhaps you could lend him some clothes?" Milena said to Jacob, who simply looked away.

Henrik went through his rucksack and quickly established that the only dry items he had were the boots he'd thrown to Jacob. If he'd had a more modern rucksack it might not have been so bad, but his had seen many years of service. The worst thing was that his phone refused to start. Admittedly there was no coverage in Sarek, but he'd been planning to take photographs and do some filming. He'd also bought a digital map of the park and downloaded it onto his phone. Now it was gone.

Once again I felt a stab of irritation. I'd reminded him about putting his phone in a waterproof bag—I'd even given him a special bag for that very purpose, but he'd forgotten.

Milena took out the stove and started to prepare lunch. It was earlier than Jacob had planned, but after the challenges of the morning we were all in need of hot food. We opted for freeze-dried meals. Jacob didn't protest, but he looked less than happy.

Henrik and I spread out our wet clothes on rocks and low-growing bushes. I put on my dry clothes and Henrik tried one of my vests, but it was far too tight and looked quite comical. Even Jacob couldn't help smiling. He lent Henrik one of his vests, which in contrast was much too big.

As we ate our lunch, the tension and ill humor gradually eased. Jacob joked that Henrik must be very clean by nature, since he'd decided to take a bath before lunch. We all laughed, including Henrik.

Afterward we lay down on the grass for a rest. It was the middle of the day, and the sun was pleasantly warm. The odd blackfly buzzed around in the air above me, black dots darting to and fro against the blue sky, but they didn't bother me.

Jacob propped himself up on one elbow. "Do you mind if I point something out?"

"What?" Milena replied sleepily. She was lying on her stomach with her eyes closed, her cheek resting on one arm.

"Ladies and gentlemen, we are now in Sarek."

We allowed this to sink in. Then I said, in a slightly worried tone of voice: "I'm not sure… I think we should have gone to Abisko after all."

It took a couple of seconds for Jacob to realize that I was joking. When I caught his eye and smiled, he looked lost for a moment, almost hurt, like a child that has been told off. Milena came to his rescue.

"Yeah, right," she said with a big grin.

I sat up and pointed toward Alggavagge, the dramatic U-shaped valley that lay ahead.

"I think that looks pretty flat and boring."

Jacob relaxed. "I guess some people are just kind of picky."

I stood up and went over to the stove. As I passed him, I gave him a quick pat on the shoulder. "Just joking—it looks perfectly okay." He glanced up at me; the sparkle was back in his brown eyes.

"Time for a coffee before we set off?" I asked, picking up the coffeepot.

Our entry into Sarek had been eventful, but I was sure that everything would be better from now on.

We continued along the southern shore of Alggajavrre. Thickets of low-growing willow extended quite a distance from the water's edge and up the side of the mountain, and in many places it reached as high as our faces. There were tracks through the vegetation, presumably made by reindeer, but they meandered here and there and were crisscrossed by roots and branches. It felt as if we were fighting our way through a hedge that was several meters thick, growing on a steeply sloping mountainside. Here and there a narrow stream had cut deep into the mountain, and we had to climb down for a meter or two, then up the other side. Sarek seemed keen to protect its secrets.

After an hour or so the bushes thinned out, and we were able to make better progress. Alggavagge lay before us like a gigantic piece of guttering. In the distance we could see the impressive almost perpendicular face of Härrabakte stretching up into the sky. Nine hundred meters from the bottom of the valley to the top.

When we reached the opening to Niejdariehpvagge, a narrow valley descending from the mountain to our right, we took a break to eat an energy bar and fill up our water bottles from a stream. The steepest climb so far lay ahead.

Jacob and I took the lead as usual. I soon got my heart rate up, but we maintained a steady pace.

After half an hour I stopped and gazed out over the valley. I could see diagonally across Alggavagge, all the way to the snow-covered peaks on the other side. Henrik and Milena had already dropped far behind, but neither Jacob nor I felt like waiting for them. Our bodies were warmed up and we had found a tempo that suited us.

They would just have to catch up with us later.

"I hear you and Milena met online," I said as we set off again.

"Yes." Jacob didn't seem keen to discuss the matter, but I kept digging.

"I've been with Henrik for almost ten years, so I've been out there. Well, I did some online dating when I was in my twenties, but nothing serious."

"I…I've had lots of girlfriends, lots of relationships," Jacob began. "I've often met someone in a bar, or through climbing or other interests."

"Mm. But they say dating apps are the most common way of meeting people now."

"Maybe—I don't know. I just felt I wanted to try something new, find something a little deeper, so I thought I'd give it a go."

"And it worked out well."

"Milena is a top girl."

There was something about the way he said it that sounded slightly condescending. *A top girl*—that's what a guy might say about a girl after he's finished with her. A girl he likes and respects, but isn't in love with.

"She really is. You won't find anyone better."

"We'll have to see where it goes. We're very different in some ways."

"It's good to be different. Complementing each other rather than competing."

"Maybe. In some ways."

"Have you…have you ever been married? Had kids?"

"Fuck, no. No, no."

"You haven't got three kids to support in Helsingborg?"

"Not as far as I know," Jacob said with a smile. "Although I was involved in a paternity case once—a DNA test, the whole thing. But it wasn't mine."

"A close call though?"

"It certainly was." His expression was more serous now. "But I wouldn't… I mean, if I find the right woman, then I'm ready to settle down. Obviously. With the right person I want the kids and the house and the dog. The whole package."

"Seriously?" Now he'd started talking about himself I didn't want to interrupt.

"That's the way I am—whatever I do, I go for it one hundred percent. There's no middle ground. If I'm climbing, I'm climbing—to the max. If I'm traveling then I'll go to the end of the fucking world. You get it."

"I get it."

"And if I'm building a family, then I'm building a family. I'll be there for my nearest and dearest for the rest of my life. My children will have a completely different upbringing from the one I had."

Jacob was talking as if he were taking part in a TV reality show. Suddenly I wished that Henrik had heard what he had to say; I knew we would have exchanged a covert glance and thought the same thing.

And there's your problem, Jacob.

"So what makes a good father?" I asked.

He didn't answer immediately. For a few seconds the only sounds were our breathing, the creak of our rucksacks, our boots hitting the ground. Was he reluctant to tell me any more? Had I got too personal?

"To be honest, I don't know," he said at last. "My father left before I was even born."

"That's awful."

"My mother had a whole series of boyfriends, some were pretty good, but the relationships never lasted long. They couldn't cope with her, so they disappeared."

"Right."

"So that just left me for her to take it out on."

"Sounds tough," I said as sympathetically as I could.

"She was mentally ill. I realized that when I was quite young—she just wasn't the way people are supposed to be. I know I spent some time with foster parents when I was seven or eight years old; I assume it was the school that sounded the alarm."

"But your mother managed to get you back?"

"Yes. It was kind of up and down—sometimes she pulled herself together. But she was…among other things she was a hoarder. So at home there were old newspapers and all kinds of crap piled up everywhere. There were like narrow corridors from room to room. I never invited a friend over. Never. Not in nine years at school. My worst fear was that she'd find out there was a parents' evening and come along. She once got a letter asking her to come in and see my teacher, but I told her the meeting had been postponed because he had the flu. Fortunately she believed me."

When Jacob was talking, his self-confidence was nowhere to be seen. He sounded sad, and I couldn't help but feel for the little boy who was ashamed of his mentally ill mother.

"That must have been terrible."

"It was tough."

"Wasn't there an adult you could turn to?"

"I had a good teacher in junior school—Tony. He knew some of what was going on, but not everything. I hung out with him and his family on the weekends now and again—we'd go fishing, that kind of thing. It was fantastic. And he got social services involved again. At least I thought afterward that it must have been him. But my mother got her act together, tidied the apartment. I guess they didn't think there was anything to worry about."

"God, Jacob..."

"I remember once when I was about six. I got really cross about something and said *cock*. My mother dragged me into the bathroom and squirted Toilet Duck in my mouth. She tried to get the toilet brush into my mouth to scrub it clean, but it wouldn't fit, so she started hitting me instead."

"That sounds horrific."

Jacob gave a wry smile. "It was pretty crazy at times."

We walked on in silence for a while, then I asked: "Are you still in contact with her?"

"She's dead. I don't exactly lay flowers on her grave. When I feel a bit down, I..."

"What?"

"I'm sure this sounds stupid, but I think I've done pretty well in life in spite of my childhood. And I don't owe anybody anything."

"I get that."

"Listen to me, going on and on," he said apologetically. "Now you know a lot more about me than Milena does."

"Really? I didn't mean to pry."

"It's fine—it feels good to get it off my chest. I can talk to you." He gave me a long intense look, and I nodded and smiled, but felt a little uncomfortable. He was getting a bit too close. I wanted to know more about him, but I hadn't expected him to go into so much detail.

"So how was your upbringing? I assume you were born with a silver spoon in your mouth?"

I started to tell him about my childhood in Stocksund. It felt good to change the subject, to get away from the sudden intimacy that had sprung up between us. There was also a vague compulsion to share some of my difficult memories in return for Jacob's description of his dreadful background.

"Superficially everything was good, financially and so on. My father had set up companies, then sold them and made a fortune, so when I was a child he was mainly a professional board member. And a friend of former politicians, company chairmen and so on. My mother is a qualified art teacher, but she stayed home and ran the household."

"Mm."

"And I don't think there's anything wrong with being a housewife—you can divide responsibilities as you wish, as long as both parties are in agreement."

"Of course."

"But my father is a very dominant character, so I'm pretty sure my mother didn't have any choice. She didn't dare go against him—none of us did. The whole family was constantly on edge, trying to read him. *Great, he's in a good mood—we can relax this evening.* But if you made the tiniest mistake, or if you didn't get straight A's, for example, he'd be furious. Or else something had happened at work, and he'd take it out on us. Often we had no idea why. And it was always worse when he drank."

"He sounds like hard work."

"Yes—he really knew how to hurt us when he was in that humor. He wouldn't stop until his target was completely crushed. He might have a go at Mum because the food wasn't good enough, or because she'd put on weight, or because she hadn't been firm enough with the cleaner—anything, really. He would keep on and on until she was in tears."

Just talking about my father made the old grief and rage bubble up in my chest.

Jacob remained silent, waiting for me to continue.

"And if you complained, it was twice as bad. You just had to keep your mouth shut, deal with it. But whenever we had guests, he would be incredibly charming and generous—everyone loved him. *If only you knew*, I often thought."

"Was he violent?"

"Yes. He'd give us a slap, or when we were little he would grab us by the arm, drag us through the living room—that kind of thing. I didn't suffer too much—it was worse for my brothers."

There was a brief silence as we continued upward. Eventually Jacob asked: "What's your family situation now? Do you all celebrate Christmas together?"

"Er…no," I said, hesitating.

How much shall I tell him? Shall I tell him everything?

STOCKHOLM, JUNE 2010

"By the way, where's my bicycle?" Dad says without looking up from his bowl of pasta.

We are at our summerhouse on the island of Värmdö; we have been here since Friday and now it is Sunday. It has been a cold early summer weekend with lots of rain and wind. We haven't been able to eat outdoors at all, to Mum's great disappointment. However, apart from that, things have exceeded expectations. My older brother, Erik, is home from France, so Mum has invited about twenty people over to see him during a weekend by the sea: me and Henrik, my younger brother, Gustaf, and his girlfriend, Ninne, plus relatives and close friends.

But now there are only four of us left—me and Erik, Mum and Dad. The relatives and friends left after breakfast yesterday, Gustaf and Ninne in the afternoon because they were going to a party in town. Henrik went back to Uppsala after breakfast this morning; he had work to do.

We are having dinner in the open-plan living room/kitchen. Painted white, wood-paneled walls, Carl Hansen wishbone chairs and table. Mum was given a free hand to decorate the cottage, but she knew that this freedom came with responsibility.

Dad would never have accepted sandblasted concrete or any other newfangled idea; he wanted to feel real wood beneath his feet.

Outside the panorama windows the pine trees sway in the wind. I can see the inlet beyond the decking and the rocks. The gray waves are tipped with white.

Mum has made Dad's favorite dish, spaghetti carbonara with genuine pancetta and masses of grated Parmesan and black pepper, just the way he wants it. Red wine in big generous glasses.

When Mum told me about her plans a few weeks ago, I felt a stab of anxiety in my belly. Erik hasn't been back to Stockholm for several years, and it's even longer since he saw Dad. And now they were going to spend an entire weekend together.

Erik is probably the member of the family who has suffered most from Dad's darker side. As the eldest son he carried certain expectations, but he found school difficult, struggling with both dyslexia and an inability to concentrate. Mum wanted to have him properly assessed, but Dad said a flat no. We don't do that kind of thing in our family. Instead he delivered his own diagnosis: Erik was spoiled and bone idle. He needed a firm hand, not mollycoddling.

"Erik? Where's my bicycle?" Dad says in his deep, rasping voice, which seems to be made for addressing hundreds of people. When he tries to speak in a normal conversational tone, it doesn't really work.

He bought a Ferrari when he sold his companies ten years ago and suddenly found himself with half a billion in the bank. When the engine is ticking over, it rattles unevenly like an old moped. It's not until you get above a hundred kilometers an hour that it sounds the way it should—a soft almost beautiful hum.

Dad's voice is like that Ferrari engine.

He looks up and fixes his gaze on Erik. Dad has just turned sixty, his eyes are bloodshot and a little watery behind his glasses. His complexion is darker than it used to be, more red, while his nose and cheeks are almost purple. He has put on weight, the roll of fat around his neck is exposed by his unbuttoned white shirt, and his waist has thickened. His double-breasted dark blue cardigan cannot hide it.

He drinks too much. That's a fact. But his hair is still thick and wavy, the silver threads barely visible among the blond. He never stints on his heavy expensive fragrance; it surrounds him like an aura, as does his financial and social success. Dad is still a powerful character, the kind of person who is the center of any gathering. He can captivate people. He is both charming and amusing when he is in the right mood.

This weekend he has definitely been in the right mood, and I realize that it was clever of Mum to organize a big gathering, to make sure Dad and Erik met in the company of others, out here on the island where guests stay in various cabins and cottages on the estate. This has given them the opportunity to get away from each other when necessary, to avoid being pushed together. And Dad is perfectly capable of controlling himself in social settings, both when it comes to how much he drinks and how vile he is to his nearest and dearest.

Mum looks tired now, which is hardly surprising. She must have been on tenterhooks all weekend. She is fifty, and the same weight as when she was twenty. Her straight hair is still shoulder-length, but I think she looks old; I've never felt that way before. Something has happened to her face, her neck, her hands. She is wearing a thin nondescript cream-colored cotton sweater, which was probably a lot more expensive than it looks. Gold necklace, gold bracelets. One day she will be an old lady.

It's a long time since we were together for three days in a row like this; maybe that's the difference. When we're on top of one another all the time, she can't hide how worn down she is.

Dad is staring at Erik, waiting for an answer. "Where is my bicycle?"

I want to run away, I don't want to be here, but of course I stay where I am, my body completely rigid.

What does Dad see when he contemplates Erik?

His eldest son, twenty-five years old. Tanned skin after many salt-sprayed hours in the sun, a skin color you often see in construction workers who spend all summer bare-chested. He had his medium-length hair bleached at some point a while ago, but now it is growing out. The dark roots are showing and it needs cutting. A small hoop in one ear. A hoodie that looks as if it's made of some South American possibly Peruvian fabric, the kind you buy at a street stall in Majorca when you're twenty and don't have much money. Orange dungarees with lots of pockets. Black socks with holes in them.

Does Dad see the dark circles beneath Erik's eyes? Does he hear how sad Erik sounds, even when he's laughing?

Erik never rebelled as a teenager; he simply left the battlefield as soon as the opportunity arose. He has earned a living as a ski-and-surf bum all over Europe since he finished high school, and for the last few years he has been working in a bar in Biarritz. At least that's the official version, but we've talked for hours over the weekend, and it appears that he has several other enterprises on the go, some more shady than others. He often crosses the French-Spanish border, and sometimes he travels to North Africa.

When Erik arrived on Friday and I saw that he hadn't made any effort to dress up for dinner, but looked exactly the same as he does now, I felt two things simultaneously: anxiety over how Dad would react and joy, because I took it as a sign that Erik simply didn't care what Dad thought, and had finally broken free. That's what Erik needs most in the whole wide world, I'm sure of it—to stop seeing himself through Dad's eyes.

Two days later and I'm no longer quite so sure. It might mean that he just couldn't be bothered—or that he doesn't own any other clothes.

"You borrowed the bicycle on Friday," Dad says, glaring at him now. "Where is it?"

"I assume it's in the garage. I put it back."

Dad has kept a lid on his nastiness, both on Friday when we had many guests and yesterday when only Henrik, Gustaf and Ninne remained. More or less. I heard him say to an old friend on Friday, in a jocular tone, that when you have a big family, there is always a black sheep in every generation—that even applies to the Wallenbergs. In fact it's the size of the family that makes the color of the renegade so visible; in an ordinary small family the actions of the black sheep wouldn't make a negative impression.

Erik was standing only about a meter away and heard the whole thing, but didn't react.

Dad is capable of saying worse things than that. Much, much worse. And that's where we're heading now, we can all feel it. He's suppressed his anger and frustration all weekend, but this evening it's just us, no outsiders to see or hear. He has drunk a lot for several days in a row, he's already emptied the big red wineglass once, refilled it and almost emptied it again, and all the blackness inside him needs to come out.

We cower around the table. This scene is all too familiar. It's as if we have been on our way to this point since Friday. We arrived at the summerhouse as free people, Erik and I. Like the individuals we have chosen to be. A surf bum, a law student. But forty-eight hours later and we are sitting here playing our old roles. Son, daughter, brother, sister. A little world of our own where Dad has absolute power.

"No, it isn't in the garage," he says.

"But I put it back there," Erik says quietly. "Honestly, Dad, I did." He sounds as if he is fourteen again.

"That bicycle cost 75,000 kronor."

In recent years Dad has opted into the cycling trend. Needless to say he bought a top-of-the-line model, a bicycle so light that it can't be used in any competition. I once saw him setting off in his cycling gear—shiny Spandex straining over his belly, two spindly legs sticking out underneath. The metal clips on his cycling shoes clattered against the tarmac. The final touches were a helmet and wraparound rainbow-colored shades.

I almost burst out laughing.

But Dad loves that bicycle, it means almost as much as the Ferrari, and now it's gone.

"I don't know what else to say…" Erik mumbles.

"Have you sold it on the quiet?"

"Jan, please…" Mum tries to intervene.

"What?" Dan turns his bloodshot gaze on her instead. "Am I not allowed to ask a simple question? He just needs to answer yes or no."

"But I think I saw him putting the bicycle in the garage on Friday."

"You *think*?" Dad says scornfully.

I am finding it hard to breathe, my heart is pounding. I need to defend my brother, come to his rescue. But I don't say a word.

You're not thirteen anymore! You're an adult, for fuck's sake! Pull yourself together!

Dad focuses on Erik again. "Answer the question. Have you sold my bicycle?"

"No, of course I haven't."

"How can I be sure of that, Erik? How the fuck can I be sure of that?" He raises his voice, the storm is about to break. "You look like a junkie, you sound like a junkie. You've stolen money from us before, so how the fuck am I supposed to believe a single word you say!"

He is bellowing now, his voice has come into its own—this is what it was made for, to shout and show off.

Mum tries again: "Jan, please…"

"Do you think I don't know that you paid for his ticket to get here?"

"Dad, calm down," I venture.

"This is all your fault!" he yells at Mum. "It's your fucking fault! He's never been made to face the consequences of his decisions! He learned, before he could even walk, that it's fine not to give a shit about anything—it will all work out fine in the end. You worthless fucking cunt!"

"Stop it, Dad!" Erik shouts with despair in his voice, and almost at the same second Dad's arm flies out as if he is hitting a backhand stroke in tennis. He catches Erik across the mouth.

"Jaaan!" Mum screams.

I am shocked, paralyzed, I can't breathe, I try to speak but no words emerge.

Erik touches his lip; there is blood on his fingers. He makes a move to stand up but Dad grabs his arm, forces him to sit down again.

"You fucking stay where you are! This is my house, my rules apply! We're having dinner, we sit at the table until everyone has finished!"

Erik gives in. He remains seated. He is twenty-five years old, but dares not leave the table until his daddy gives permission. He wipes his mouth with his napkin, his lower lip begins to tremble, he fights to keep control but his face crumples and soon we hear a sound that could be a sigh—but we know it isn't.

Dad has taken another forkful of his food. He looks up at Erik as he chomps on his spaghetti; he seems surprised.

"Are you…crying?"

He leans forward, peers closely at Erik as if he really can't believe his eyes. It is all an act of course; this is part of the humiliation.

"Jesus Christ," he says with a sigh. He wipes his mouth, leans back on his chair. Mum reaches out and takes Erik's hand; she too has tears in her eyes. Dad catches my eye, looking amused.

"Who are these people?" he says in disbelief, gesturing at

Mum and Erik. "Are we really related to them? Where does this come from?"

And I know what I ought to say. I really do try, but my tongue refuses to cooperate. I sit there in silence, as stiff as a broom handle. My body is stuck in a slightly hunched position, ready to defend myself. I open my mouth, but once again no words come out.

I am thirteen years old again, I am Daddy's girl and I don't want him to direct his anger at me.

I utterly despise myself in that moment. But I remain silent.

A few hours later Erik and I are alone in the kitchen. We wash the wineglasses by hand, empty the dishwasher, refill it. We can hear the distant sound of Dad's snoring coming from the bedroom. Mum has gone for a long walk. Maybe she's talking on the phone to one of her old friends, those who have always been there for her.

Maybe she is opening up to them. Maybe they are telling her that she must leave her husband, and maybe this time she will listen. I hope so anyway.

When we have finished I go and pack my things, get ready to go back to Uppsala. I am too angry with Dad to say goodbye to him, nor do I intend to wait for Mum to return from her walk. To be honest, I can't get away from here fast enough. Away from my betrayal of Erik.

My family makes me a worse person. I want to go back to my ordinary life, my ordinary self.

Erik walks me out of the house. The wind is howling in the tops of the pine trees. They are swaying back and forth so violently that you almost expect them to come down. Cold salty drizzle is gusting in off the sea. I put down my suitcase, open my arms and give Erik a big hug. We hold each other for a long time. I don't want to let go, as if a hug from me can make him happy, give him a good life.

He lets go first.

"Bye then, sis," he says. He smiles, but his eyes are sad and weary.

"Bye, Erik—speak soon." I pick up my case and set off up the steep hill toward the main road. The bus stop is a few hundred meters away.

Halfway up the hill I turn and see him gazing out across the sea. I continue toward the bus stop.

I never see Erik again.

How much shall I tell him? Shall I tell him everything?

It took me only a fraction of a second to decide how to answer Jacob's question.

No. Of course not.

"Er...no, not exactly. I don't speak to my dad anymore."

Jacob gently placed his hand on my arm. It didn't seem calculated; it was probably just a spontaneous gesture of sympathy, and at that moment it felt good. However I realized that I had told him far more than I had intended, even though I had kept the most important part to myself. No doubt Jacob thought I needed to *open up*, to have someone listen to me. What had begun as a diversionary tactic had actually made the atmosphere between us more intimate.

Neither of us said anything for a while. We had been walking steadily uphill for several hours with only a brief pause to drink some water. The terrain was flattening out now, as the valley narrowed between two high rock faces. We were approaching the pass. I looked around. Just like yesterday Henrik and Milena were so far behind that they were out of sight.

Soon we had a long level snowfield before us. Jacob told me that it had been exactly the same the last time he was here; it seemed as if the snow never went away. I dug down past the crust with my boots, stood still and slowly felt the cold reach my overheated feet. It was very pleasant. Jacob smiled at me.

"Let's go," he said. "Once we get over the brow of this hill we'll be able to see into the next valley. And the next, and the next. It's the most amazing view."

I had another drink of water and we set off again. The sun had softened the snow, and it was much heavier going than on bare ground. The sparkling whiteness was too much, and I put on my sunglasses. We walked in silence, and slowly the promised panorama revealed itself: I could see into the next valley, Sarvesvagge, also framed by high mountains, and far beyond these there were even higher mountains with jagged, pointed peaks. It looked more like the Himalayas than northern Sweden. Jacob stopped and turned to me, beaming with delight.

"Fantastic, isn't it?"

"It's quite something." I carried on past him without breaking my stride. The thought of standing close together gazing at the view felt somehow uncomfortable.

I guess that's what they call a warning bell. Or instinct.

The ground began to slope downward, and the end of the snowfield wasn't far ahead. The view really was spectacular, but I had no intention of stopping to admire it. I needed to top up my water bottle, and made my way to bare ground, where a stream gushed out from beneath the snow. Just as on the other side of the pass, it had cut into the rock face and formed a small canyon. I followed its course until I found a spot where it was relatively easy to get to the water. I knelt down and let the ice-cold water pour over my bottle and forearm. I stood up and clambered out of the canyon, then looked out across the vista and had a drink. The water was so cold that it made my teeth and cheeks ache, and that was when Jacob put his arms around me.

A tight embrace from behind.

I froze.

I shouldn't have been shocked, I knew he was somewhere behind me, but the rushing of the stream meant I hadn't heard his approach.

I couldn't move.

When I think back, my first feeling is one of shame. Shame that I froze, shame that I didn't immediately push him away, or slap his face, shame that I was unable to defend my physical integrity. I know that this is a normal reaction in both men and women who are assaulted, but I never thought it would apply to me.

My second feeling is anger because of the shame. It was Jacob who crossed a line; he was the one who should have been ashamed, not me.

Then he bent his head and tried to kiss my neck, and that was when the spell broke. I pulled away, gave him a hard shove and yelled: "What the fuck do you think you're doing?"

Interview with Anna Samuelsson 880216-3382, September 18, 2019, Gällivare hospital, conducted by Detective Inspector Anders Suhonen.

"And did he let go?"

"Yes."

"How did he react afterward?"

"He…he apologized, but then he said he had strong feelings for me. He believed that we belonged together, which was completely insane—we'd only known each other for two days."

"Mm."

"And he was with Milena, one of my closest friends. So I said I don't know what you're talking about, you're imagining something that doesn't exist. But he didn't want to hear that."

"He didn't?"

"No. He said…he'd noticed that I felt something for him too, that things weren't good between me and Henrik… He said a whole lot of weird stuff."

"I see."

"And he wouldn't give up. He…he thought we had such a lot

in common—walking, climbing, and… Oh, this is so stupid, I can hardly bring myself to say it."

Silence.

"He…said we were the good-looking ones. That he and I belonged together because we were more attractive than Henrik and Milena."

"Right."

"And fitter."

"Mm."

"I mean, I'd been wondering who he really was, but in a social context there was nothing that stood out. On the contrary, he was very nice. Now I realized how fucked up he actually was. I tried to stop his harangue, but he wasn't listening. He kept saying *wait, wait, let me finish.*"

"How long did this go on?"

"I don't know. Ages."

"And where were Henrik and Milena?"

"They were so far behind—it must have been an hour before they caught up with us."

"Was Jacob's behavior threatening?"

"Not at first. But eventually it began to sink in, the fact that what he'd been fantasizing about wasn't going to happen. And that's when his tone changed."

Jacob and I, the valley below us, the stream rushing by. The snowfield above us. No sign of Henrik and Milena.

I considered retracing my steps, going to meet them; the thought of being alone with Jacob was almost unbearable. However, if I did that, Henrik and Milena would immediately realize that something had happened. I would have to answer questions, and my gut reaction was to pretend that everything was normal. Jacob hadn't put his arms around me, he hadn't tried to kiss my neck, and he hadn't spent half an hour trying to persuade me that we should be together.

Eventually he had given up. He moved away, sat down on a rock and stared out over the valley. He had his back to me, so I was able to observe him secretly. He looked as if he'd just received a piece of news that had turned his whole world upside down. He was struggling to take in the fact that I didn't feel the same way about him as he did about me.

I wasn't afraid of him—not then. Only later did it occur to me that he could have physically attacked me. Why didn't I see that from the start? Admittedly it would have been totally irrational, given that Henrik and Milena could appear at any second, but by this time I knew that all was not well inside Jacob's head. How could I be sure that my rejection wouldn't provoke him into an assault?

It soon became apparent that I couldn't.

There was a horrible moment, just when it became clear to him that he was wrong about my feelings for him. The damaged child I had glimpsed earlier was suddenly there again. Shame was written all over his face, along with self-loathing and a sense of smallness. He knew he had messed up, and he looked completely lost. I couldn't help linking this expression with what he had told me about his childhood. It was as if he had become a vulnerable, defenseless six-year-old all over again.

He turned away, went and sat on the rock. Maybe that was why he kept his back to me: he didn't want me to see his face. He stayed there for a while; I watched him, glancing up at the snowfield from time to time.

Jesus, how slowly are they walking? Surely they must be here soon!

But they didn't come.

Gradually I began to reconcile myself to the idea that Jacob and I were going to be here for quite a while, with him sitting on the rock and me by the stream, looking out for Henrik and Milena. I felt calmer. This was bearable.

Then he stood up, sighed deeply and slowly came toward me. His eyes were fixed on the ground and he was rubbing his chin and the corners of his mouth with one hand. The damaged child was no longer visible. He had regained control of his features and now looked closed down, hard. Instinctively I tensed my body, felt my heart pounding. He stopped a short distance away.

"We don't need to mention this, do we?" His voice was rough.

"No. Let's just forget it."

Neither of us said anything else for a while, but I could tell that he wasn't done. He was searching for the right words. Eventually he took a deep breath.

"There's one thing I don't understand. And I would like an explanation."

"I don't think there's any point, Jacob. We're not going to get anywhere."

"You were flirting with me in the restaurant car yesterday evening. Why did you do that?"

I didn't respond at first; there was nothing to be gained by entering into a discussion, so I tried to kill off his question with silence. Of course he wasn't having that.

"Why were you flirting with me?"

"I wasn't. I'm sorry if you interpreted it that way, but I really wasn't."

"Yes, you were."

"No."

I looked up at the snowfield.

Where the fuck are you?

"You were checking me out in a particular way."

"There's absolutely no point in talking about this."

"And you've taken every opportunity to make sure that you and I were doing things on our own, without Henrik and Milena."

"Seriously, Jacob..." I was finding it difficult to grasp exactly how distorted his perception of reality was.

"We've been walking on our own most of the time—nearly all day yesterday, and all day today. More or less."

"Yes, because we're faster—don't you get that? Do you think that means I'm flirting with you? That's just…"

"You're sending out signals, Anna."

"When Henrik, Milena and I go away together, I always go on ahead. I want to walk faster, that's all there is to it. Why can't you understand?"

"And today you made me tell you a whole load of stuff that I haven't even shared with Milena."

I sighed. I wanted to challenge him, but I stopped myself. I realized that everything I said was simply adding fuel to the fire, and would lead to more absurd accusations. I remained silent.

"I felt as if you were interested in getting to know me properly, but you just wanted to dig the dirt."

Still I didn't speak.

"Do you think that was a nice thing to do?" Out of the corner of my eye I could see Jacob staring at me, but I had no intention of answering.

He moved closer. "Do you?"

"This is a waste of time," I said as calmly as I could and without looking at him. "I don't want to talk about it anymore."

Jacob took another step toward me.

"In that case I have to assume you agree, since you're not contradicting me. You've flirted with me, and toyed with my emotions." Once again, I chose not to answer.

"Haven't you?"

He took a few more steps, he was very close to me now, I could feel his breath. I stayed perfectly still, but not because I was paralyzed. Every muscle in my body was tensed, I knew exactly where my center of gravity was, and I was ready to hit back if necessary, to fight him off. I had taken self-defense classes. I would go for the eyes first. I knew more or less how it would feel, like digging my finger into a ripe cherry tomato, the skin being pushed in before it gives way, the liquid spurting out. My heart was pounding even harder now, and my mouth was dry.

"Hello?" Jacob clicked his fingers right in front of my face and I exploded. I knocked his hand aside, stared at him and yelled:

"Back off! Don't touch me!"

"I didn't..." he protested, but I cut him off.

"Stay away from me, or I'll go and meet Henrik and Milena and when they ask why, I'll tell them exactly what's happened! This is your last chance—fuck off!"

Jacob took a step backward and laughed. It was an unnatural, a little whinny, so fake that he could hardly expect me to believe it. That didn't really matter though; the intention was to oppress me, to highlight the fact that he was pleased to have provoked me.

The mask was gone. Jacob was showing who he really was.

"Why are you so angry, Anna? We're just having a little chat, aren't we? Anna?"

I stood my ground, and said in a calmer tone of voice: "I'm warning you. If you want this to stay between us, don't come near me."

I had my back to the snowfield now, and I saw Jacob glance over my shoulder. I turned and saw them at long last—two figures in the distance, highlighted against the blue sky. Henrik and Milena. I waved; they didn't seem to see me, but I felt an enormous wave of relief. Jacob, on the other hand, suddenly looked a lot less self-assured. I couldn't help rubbing it in.

"Aren't you going to wave, Jacob? Otherwise they might think something's wrong."

"I'm warning you too," he said. "You have your version of what's happened—I have a different one."

"A different version?"

"My version. My truth. You don't know who they'll believe."

"My truth? What does that mean?"

"Exactly what I say."

"Are you going to make up a pack of lies—say I was the one who jumped on you?"

"I don't need to lie. I'll just tell it like it is. You've been flirting with me ever since we met up at the station in Stockholm. I didn't realize what the fuck you were doing, because I've got a girlfriend, Milena, whom I love very much, and you're engaged..."

Henrik and Milena were approaching at a steady pace; they were halfway across the snowfield now.

"Seriously, Jacob. Milena and Henrik were there. They'll know that what you're saying is a lie."

"That's right—they were there. In the restaurant car. They saw and heard exactly how you were behaving."

This was a desperate attempt on Jacob's side to establish some kind of balance of terror, but I wasn't buying it. Okay, so maybe I'd been extra-nice to him the previous evening, but that was in order to calm him down, to restore his good mood. Henrik and Milena had done more or less the same thing. Jacob had nothing with which to counter my threat to tell Milena what had happened. I was holding all the cards, and he knew it.

"Who do you think they'll believe, Jacob? Me, whom both of them have known for over ten years, or you, whom Milena has been dating for a month?"

"Milena will believe me," he said with a conviction that sounded entirely false. "I'm her boyfriend, she's in love with me, I've got something she needs."

"No, you haven't got anything that Milena needs. Nothing at all. You're the last person she needs."

Jacob smiled and waved to Henrik and Milena. I turned and saw that they were close now, only a couple of hundred meters away. We stood there side by side, waiting for them.

"You don't know her," Jacob said without looking at me. I didn't look at him either. Milena stopped and Henrik went on ahead. Maybe she was going to take a picture. "How close are the two of you anyway?"

"I know her considerably better than you do, Jacob."

"She'll believe me, and she'll do whatever I say. You'll see." He sounded alarmingly confident. I smiled and called out to Henrik.

"Hello!"

"Hi there," he replied wearily. We put our arms around each other and exchanged a dutiful kiss. His throat and the back of his neck were wet with sweat.

"That took a while," I said.

"It was hard work. We stopped for ages."

Jacob went to meet Milena, opening his arms to his girlfriend. He gave her a big hug. "Was it tough going, sweetheart?"

They kissed, more passionately than Henrik and I had done. "Kind of," she panted.

"Have you been waiting long?" Henrik asked me.

"I'm not sure—an hour maybe." I kept my tone as neutral as possible. "I'll make some coffee."

Jacob still had his arms wrapped around Milena, and he was gazing down at her with warmth and love. Jacob, who had recently spent some considerable time trying to convince me that we were soul mates who ought to spend the rest of our lives together.

I despised him. Actually I think I hated him at that moment.

Interview with Anna Samuelsson 880216-3382, September 18, 2019, Gällivare hospital, conducted by Detective Inspector Anders Suhonen.

"So what time was this? Approximately?"

"I think it was about four, four thirty."

"Mm."

"We had a cup of coffee before we set off. The atmosphere was…pretty bad."

"Go on."

"Henrik soon realized that something had happened. He could see it in my face, yet at the same time Jacob was pretending to be in such a good mood, smiling and laughing and talking a lot. He kept on hugging Milena, but she's not stupid—she could also tell by looking at me that there was something wrong. And I think she knew that what Jacob was doing was just some kind of game."

"I understand."

"So before we left, she asked me how I was feeling."

"And what did you say?"

"I told her I was okay, that maybe I hadn't drunk enough water. Something along those lines—I don't remember exactly."

"Mm."

"And Jacob stayed close to me all the time—during the afternoon and the evening."

"Did he?"

"He was terrified of leaving me alone with either Henrik or Milena for a second."

"Because he thought you'd tell them what he'd done?"

"Yes. And he did it very discreetly—I don't think Henrik or Milena noticed. But it was very unpleasant for me."

"It must have been."

"When we set off, I stuck close to Henrik and Milena, of course. And Jacob stayed with us too, so the four of us were together for the rest of the day. We walked for a couple of hours more, down into the next valley."

Silence.

"And I...I kept on wondering how I ought to handle this. Whether I should tell someone, and if so, who—just Henrik, or Milena too. Whether I should stop the whole trip, or whether I could pretend it hadn't happened."

"You had a lot to think about."

"I did. Absolutely."

Silence.

"I came to the conclusion pretty quickly that I couldn't carry on. Being around Jacob was just too uncomfortable. Seeing him made me feel almost physically sick. Plus we were entering Sarek now. It's huge, almost as big as Gotland, and there's one emergency telephone right in the middle of the park. You can go weeks without seeing a single person. Did I really want to set off into this wilderness with someone as disturbed as him? I kept thinking...this could be more than unpleasant. It could be dangerous."

"Mm."

"So I decided that next morning I would say I wasn't feeling well, that I'd picked up a chill and I had to go back to Staloluokta. And then of course Henrik would go with me."

"Right."

"And I thought it might not arouse Milena's suspicions, because she'd already asked how I was feeling, and I'd told her I probably hadn't drunk enough water, so she might think *that's why she didn't look right yesterday.* Hopefully."

"I understand. So you'd decided not to say anything to her about you and Jacob?"

"That's right. Maybe I was being a coward, but I was intending to tell her when we got back to Stockholm. At the time I just wanted to end the trip as easily and quickly as possible. I had no intention of telling Henrik either, not until we were away from Jacob. There was no point. By the time we found a place to camp for the night, I was happy with my decision."

"But it didn't go according to plan?"

"No. That evening everything became more…critical."

"What happened?"

Silence.

"Anna?"

"I don't know if I…"

"Are you tired?"

"Yes."

"In that case we'll stop for the time being. Get some rest."

We didn't go all the way to the bottom of Sarvesvagge; instead we found a little plateau partway up the mountain where we pitched our tents for the night. We'd walked for a couple of hours more after finishing our coffee, and it was early evening. The sun no longer reached down to us, and the mild autumn warmth of the day had quickly given way to a chill in the air. However the snow-clad peak of Rijddatjåhkkå, the closest mountain to the east, still lay bathed in sunshine, glowing like gold. The whole valley was on fire with the colors of autumn.

I was surrounded by all this fantastic natural beauty, but I couldn't enjoy it. When I recall those images now, I realize they will always be connected to the emotions I was experiencing when we arrived: anger, agitation, anxiety, impatience. I had decided not to break off the trip until the following morning; that would be the easiest solution. But once the decision was made, I just wanted to get away from Jacob as quickly as possible.

One aspect that I couldn't stop thinking about was my responsibility toward Milena. If I felt that it was too dangerous to enter Sarek with Jacob, then shouldn't I try to persuade my friend to abandon the trip too? I couldn't do that without telling her what had happened, and Jacob would know that I'd told her. This was bound to provoke him, and who could predict how he would react? My feeling was also that Milena had less to fear from Jacob than Henrik and me. She was so submissive, she allowed him to dictate what they did, which was why I thought that the risk of him losing his temper or his judgment and doing something really stupid when they were alone was minimal.

Plus Milena was a grown woman; she was the one who chose to ignore all the warning signs when it came to Jacob, so she was going to have to take responsibility for herself.

Henrik and I picked a spot and began to put up our tent. The previous evening Jacob and Milena had started to erect their tent first; we had chosen a spot a short distance away so that we could have a quiet conversation inside without being overheard. A bit of space after a long intense day in one another's company.

Tonight however Jacob had waited until we made our choice, then selected his place right next to us. The guy lines were no more than a meter apart. It was almost comical: the view was endless, there wasn't a soul in sight in any direction, and there were these two tents squashed together on the same little plateau, as if they were on a campsite on the island of Öland at midsummer.

Henrik discovered that everything in his rucksack was still damp, or in some cases wet. Spreading the contents on the ground now, when the warmth of the sun had gone, wouldn't help at all—quite the reverse in fact. He was facing a chilly night.

When we had put up the tent and laid out our air beds and sleeping bags, we crawled in and lay down for a while with our arms around each other. Henrik looked deep into my eyes and asked: "Did something happen?"

I shook my head reassuringly and was about to reply when we heard footsteps outside, followed by Jacob's voice.

"Hi, guys!"

"Hi," Henrik said, half getting up. There was the familiar sound of the zip, and Jacob stuck his head through the gap, grinning broadly.

"This looks cozy!"

"Yes. Can't complain."

"We didn't have much luck with our pegs," Jacob went on. "There's solid rock beneath the ground, so we couldn't get them in. If you hear someone messing around out here, it's me."

"So why don't you try a different spot," I suggested. "Farther away."

"No, it's nice and level, so I think we'll stay put," Jacob said cheerily. "Shall we eat in half an hour or so?"

"Great," Henrik said, yawning.

"Excellent." Jacob withdrew and did up the zip behind him. We heard him start playing about with the pegs. Judging by the noise, it was only the ones on our side that were a problem. It sounded as if he was right next to the canvas. Henrik and I exchanged glances. I could see that Jacob's behavior had aroused Henrik's suspicions, which was bound to reinforce his feeling that something must have happened between the two of us during the walk.

"I'll tell you tomorrow," I whispered. "It's fine. Don't give it another thought." I gave him a kiss, but he didn't respond. And he looked even more worried.

It was Milena and Jacob's turn to cook dinner, and a little while later Milena called out to tell us it was ready. She had heated up some chicken soup with added macaroni for energy. It tasted good, and for dessert Jacob shared out a bar of chocolate. The relaxed atmosphere from lunchtime wasn't there though. Neither Henrik nor I had much to say, and Milena was quiet too, wondering what was wrong with us. Jacob was the only one who talked, prattling away with forced jollity. I couldn't help but admire his perseverance; he had decided even before Henrik and Milena caught up with us that he was going to maintain a cheerful facade, and he was stubbornly sticking to that decision. Unfortunately his behavior came across as increasingly odd, since the rest of us were so subdued.

Eventually the weirdness got too much for Milena. She suggested that we should play MIG, a question-and-answer game similar to Trivial Pursuit, but with a deck of cards. It had become a regular feature of our holidays in the past, and no doubt she hoped it would put me and Henrik in a better mood. I couldn't face it; I was tired and had no desire to spend any longer than necessary in Jacob's company. I also saw an opportunity to lay the foundations for the story I was going to tell the next morning.

"You guys carry on, but I'll pass. I'm tired and I don't feel too good." Milena was concerned.

"Are you coming down with something?"

"I don't know—maybe. I'm a bit stiff and sore."

Jacob looked searchingly at me, but didn't say anything. Perhaps he had an inkling of where this was going. I went on: "I'm going to call it a night, see how I feel in the morning. Good night."

"Good night," Milena replied. I bent down and kissed Henrik, then headed for the tent.

"Good night—hope you soon feel better," Jacob said. I kept on walking.

"But you two are in, right?" Milena said.

"Fine by me," Henrik replied.

"I don't know what it is." Jacob sounded petulant. "Is it like Uno or something?" I assumed that Milena had taken out the cards.

"No, it's questions and answers. You'll soon get it—it's very straightforward."

"I'll just fetch the whisky."

I collected my towel and toilet bag and headed toward a stream gurgling down the mountainside not far away. It wasn't exactly a gushing torrent, and it hadn't cut into the rock, but it was a decent depth, and the water was clear and icy. I removed my boots and socks and washed my feet, the unfathomable cold once again gripping my ankles like a vise. I took off my top and splashed my face and under my arms, which made me feel much fresher and brighter. I gazed out across Sarvesvagge while brushing my teeth. Now that I was away from the tents and the others, I was able to appreciate the magnificence of nature. This stunningly beautiful valley had been here for thousands of years, through all the seasons, all kinds of weather. Sometimes a human being would pass by and enjoy the sight, but the valley would still be here, looking more or less the same, when I was long gone. The thought gave me a strange sense of calm.

I went back to the tent, crawled inside and fastened the zip. I wriggled into my sleeping bag, then lay there listening to the others' voices as they played MIG.

"What was the name of the woman who danced with bananas, and was named a *Chevalier of the Légion d'Honneur* for her contributions to the French Resistance movement?"

"Er... Josephine Baker."

"Well done! Henrik knows more than anyone should."

"What have I got so far...five?"

"Yes."

"My turn to read the question. Are you going to throw?"

"What?"

"You need to throw the dice, Jacob."

"Right."

"Red or blue. And MIG chance."

"I'll take blue. But I don't get the other thing—what's MIG chance?"

"If you get the answer right, you tick off that color. The first person to tick off all the colors is the winner."

"Okay. Go."

"How many lines of longitude are there in total: 24, 180 or 360?"

"How many lines of longitude?"

"Yes. 24, 180 or 360."

"Er... How the fuck should I know? I'll have to take a guess..."

"It's one out of three."

"In that case I'll say... God this is hard... 24."

"Sorry, that's wrong. 360."

"Three fucking sixty?"

"Yes."

"I would never have guessed that. This is hard."

"Your turn to throw."

I heard a glugging noise, which I assumed came from Jacob's hip flask. "Anyone want some?"

"I'm fine, thanks."

"No thanks."

"Sweetheart, if we're going to be together, you'll have to learn to appreciate a fine smoky whisky. Try some."

"Just a drop then."

The voices blended as I dozed off. I felt tired and calm and pleased with my decision to break off the trip in the morning. The last thing I heard was Henrik:

"Heat. Bikram yoga is practiced in a room heated to almost forty degrees."

I woke with a start and sat up. My heart was racing and at first I didn't know where I was, but it soon came back: the walk, the tent, the others playing MIG outside.

For a second I thought I'd been dreaming, but then I heard voices, mainly Jacob's—loud and aggressive.

"Did I ask for your help? Did I?"

"No, sorry." Milena's tone was submissive, defensive.

"No I fucking didn't."

"I'm sorry, Jacob. I just... It doesn't seem fair, you've had five really hard questions in a row—"

Jacob interrupted her. "Pack it in! Shut the fuck up!"

"I'm sorry. You—"

"Stop treating me like a fucking child!"

Suddenly I was wide awake. I held my breath and listened, all my senses on full alert. Jacob sounded as if he was on the verge of losing control. When Henrik spoke, he too seemed defensive, almost afraid, and like Milena he tried to calm the situation.

"Listen, Jacob, why don't you throw again and have a new question. We'll forget that one."

Jacob ignored him. "I might have known the answer, but now you've sabotaged my chances," he shouted at Milena. "Are you satisfied? Are you *satisfied*?"

"No."

Henrik tried again; he was clearly stressed, searching for the right words.

"What if we… Why don't we assume you got that question right, and you can carry on."

"What do you mean? I didn't get it right, I didn't fucking answer it."

"No, but…"

"Why would we assume I got it right when I didn't answer it? Henrik?"

I heard Henrik take a deep breath. "I don't know, I just…"

"Shall we just carry on anyway? I can…" Milena ventured, but to no avail.

"The two of you keep talking over each other, I can't fucking think. I asked Henrik a question. I'd like to hear his answer, without you piping up. Can you keep your mouth shut for three seconds? Do you think you can manage that?"

Milena didn't speak.

Jacob mumbled something, but I couldn't quite make it out.

Fucking cunt? Did he really say that?

I couldn't listen to this anymore. I unzipped the flap and crawled out of the tent. Dusk had fallen since I went to bed, but it wasn't yet pitch-dark. Jacob turned his attention back to Henrik.

"Why should I get a point when I haven't even answered the question?"

"I don't know… Let's just forget it."

"You don't know? But it was your suggestion!"

I went over to join them. My heart was racing, but I kept my voice as neutral and relaxed as possible. "What's going on, guys?"

Milena and Henrik looked up at me; there was no mistaking their discomfort. Jacob ignored me and continued to stare at Henrik. His eyes were wild—I wasn't even sure he'd heard me.

"Things have got a bit…out of hand," Milena said.

"I thought I told you to keep your mouth shut?"

I felt a surge of rage. "That's enough, Jacob—calm down."

Only now did he register my presence. He switched his gaze to me, pointed his index finger at me. "This has nothing to do with you. Go back to your tent."

"Go back to my tent? You think you can tell me what to do? Are you out of your mind?"

My intention had been to defuse the situation, but I was furious and couldn't stop myself. Jacob got to his feet.

"This has nothing to do with you!" he yelled.

Milena stood up as well. "Jacob…"

"Calm down," Henrik said with a new firmness in his tone. Suddenly everything happened very fast. Jacob took a couple of rapid steps toward Henrik as he was getting up. Henrik was caught off balance as Jacob gave him a hard shove.

He landed on his back, and the next second Jacob was standing over him, screaming in his face: "ANSWER THE FUCKING QUESTION! I ASKED YOU A SIMPLE QUESTION—GIVE ME THE FUCKING ANSWER!"

"Jacob!" Milena was in despair. I grabbed hold of Jacob's arm and pulled him away from Henrik, and Milena stepped between the two men. Jacob tore himself free and walked off, breathing heavily and making weird grunting noises. He disappeared into the darkness. Henrik struggled to his feet, looking shocked and frightened.

"Are you okay?" Milena asked.

"I'm fine." He was clearly shaken, but didn't seem to have injured himself.

Milena couldn't hold back the tears. "I'm sorry. I'm so sorry…"

"You're not the one who should be apologizing," I said. "He's crazy." Milena headed away from the tent, but not in the same direction as Jacob.

Henrik and I sat outside our tent for some time, gathering our thoughts. There was no sign of the other two. After a while Henrik's entire body started shaking; he was shivering as if he were suffering from exposure. I suggest that we should go inside and get into our sleeping bags so that he could warm up, but he wanted to carry on talking.

I told him what had happened earlier; there was no point in keeping quiet about it now. He listened and shook his head, then repeated the words I had said to Milena.

"He's crazy. He's fucking crazy."

I put my arm around him, rubbed his back to get his circulation going. He was still shaking.

"We have to put a stop to this trip," I said.

Henrik nodded immediately. "Yes." And so the decision was made; there was nothing more to say.

We went inside and got into our sleeping bags, but instead of zipping them up we shuffled together and put our arms around each other. I couldn't help feeling uneasy; what if Jacob rushed at the tent during the night and started wielding his ice ax? I remembered that Thomas Quick had confessed to the murder of two Dutch tourists at some point in the '80s using exactly that method, although his confession had later turned out to be false.

I heard footsteps outside and immediately propped myself up on one elbow, my nerves on full alert. Henrik raised his eyebrows, but didn't look afraid. It sounded as if both Jacob and Milena were there.

"Hello?" Jacob's voice was dull and flat, quieter than usual. "Are you awake?"

Henrik and I looked at each other. "Yes."

Jacob cleared his throat. "Sorry. About before." He paused for long enough to allow one of us to tell him it was fine, but we lay there as quiet as mice. Eventually he went on: "I lost my temper. I shouldn't have drunk so much whisky either. Sorry."

Silence. I pictured the two of them standing out there in the darkness, waiting for a reaction. I was absolutely certain that Milena had persuaded him to apologize. The subdued voice, the reticence suggested that it wasn't his idea. Maybe she did have some influence over him after all, or maybe he'd realized that an apology was the only way to try to prevent this Sarek trip from coming to an end first thing in the morning.

Still we didn't say anything. A gust of wind caught the tent flap. Outside the tent we heard someone shifting from foot to foot.

"It's fine," I said, my tone making it clear that it was anything but.

"See you in the morning," Milena said, sounding tired and upset. I couldn't help feeling sorry for her. She was such a good friend—she deserved so much better than this.

"Yes—sleep well," I replied, a little more warmly.

After a few moments we heard them getting into their tent. Henrik and I exchanged a look and I silently shook my head before zipping up my sleeping bag. I soon fell into an uneasy sleep.

I was woken by noises from the other tent. At first I couldn't work out what it was, but then I realized it was Milena, sobbing and whimpering. I could also hear a rhythmic pounding, the rustle of fabric, groaning and grunting.

They were having sex.

I sat up and listened. Henrik was still asleep.

Yes, they were having sex, but it seemed more like abuse. The sounds Milena was making were muted, as if Jacob had his hand over her mouth. And they were sounds indicating pain, not pleasure. She was shouting and screaming through his hand, pleading and sobbing. Jacob's activities seemed to become more violent.

You fucking monster.

I shook Henrik awake. He too appeared to have been in some kind of subconscious defense mode, because he immediately sat bolt upright, gazed around and whispered hoarsely: “What is it? What’s wrong?”

“Listen,” I whispered back.

We both sat there holding our breath. I could still hear Jacob grunting and groaning, but Milena’s sobs had diminished in strength to little more than shallow panting. Henrik gave me an enquiring look.

“Wait.”

Soon everything went quiet next door.

“Before I woke you… It sounded as if she was crying and screaming, but with his hand over her mouth.”

We listened for a while longer. After a brief silence we heard the rustle of fabric, the zip was opened and someone went out of the tent and walked away. I couldn’t be sure, but I thought it was Jacob.

“Milena?” I called out in a low voice. No response. I tried again, a little louder this time. “Milena?”

“Yes?” She seemed to be speaking from far, far away. Her tone was strangely distracted.

“Is everything okay?”

“Yes. Everything’s fine.”

“Are you sure?”

“Yes. Good night.”

Little raindrops were tiptoeing cautiously across the tent when I woke up. I was warm and dry in my sleeping bag, but the air felt damp and cold against my face. It was already light. Henrik was still asleep. I wondered what his night had been like. Damp underwear in a damp sleeping bag.

I crawled outside. The sky was overcast, the gray lid that had pressed down on us in Gällivare was back; the peaks of the mountains surrounding us were hidden by the clouds. It was drizzling, and the temperature had fallen by several degrees. I shivered and shuffled back under the awning to dig out my waterproofs. Our boots and rucksacks were protected from the rain, but the moisture had crept along the ground, and nothing felt properly dry.

I felt both calm and not calm at all. The question of whether or not we should travel to the mountains with Jacob had nagged away at me ever since the first time Milena suggested it, and now it was resolved, once and for all. Henrik and I were going to end our involvement in the trip. It felt good.

What worried me was Milena. As I lay there thinking things

over during the night, I had concluded that I had a responsibility to try to persuade her to come with us.

However I was by no means certain that I would succeed.

I had woken Henrik with my poking about; I could hear him moving. "Morning," I said quietly. "How did you sleep?"

"Not too well. Is it raining?"

"Yes. I'm going to make some breakfast, then have a word with Milena as soon as she wakes up."

"Okay."

I went and fetched some water, then we set up the stove and began to prepare breakfast in silence. Soon the stove's blue ring of fire was hissing reassuringly.

When the sun is shining, meals are easy in the mountains. You can simply spread out the contents of a rucksack on the ground or on a groundsheet, everything is immediately accessible and it takes no time at all.

When it's raining, as much as possible must be kept under the awning. You're on your knees rooting about in the rucksack, the orderly packing you are trying to maintain is gone in seconds. And then there's the cold. Your fingers stiffen as soon as you take off your gloves, having discovered that it's impossible to get a match out of a box while wearing them.

We must have been making enough noise to wake someone in the other tent; I could hear movement.

Please let it be Milena who wakes first.

Someone rummaged in their rucksack. Someone pulled on their boots. The zip opened.

"Jesus it's cold," Milena said as she emerged clutching her waterproofs. I nodded, relieved to see her.

"We're making enough porridge for all of us. But… I need to talk to you."

She looked confused, but followed me down to the little stream. Bearing in mind how Jacob had behaved the previous day, I was under no illusions that he would leave us alone once he woke up. I had to put across my point quickly and efficiently.

It also occurred to me that the babbling of the stream would help to drown out our voices.

Before Milena managed to pull on her anorak, I had noticed red marks around her neck.

They looked like strangulation marks.

You fucking monster.

"The thing is," I began as I stopped and turned around. Milena stopped too, her expression wary. Of course she realized that what I was going to say had something to do with last night's quarrel.

"Henrik and I have decided to drop out. We're going to head back to Staloluokta."

Milena gazed out across Sarvesvagge, the valley that had stretched for many kilometers before us yesterday. Now it vanished into the drizzle's gray mist. She stood in silence, letting my words sink in. I could see that she hadn't expected this.

In the end she simply said: "Right." Her voice sounded thin, brittle, sad.

"We're not happy about spending any more time with Jacob. After the way he behaved yesterday evening."

"No…" There was an enquiring note in her voice now.

"The fact that he attacked Henrik. And he was horrible to you."

"Yes, but…" Milena paused, searching for the right words. "I mean, none of that was okay, but he did apologize."

"Milena, he physically attacked Henrik."

She stared at the ground. What the hell was going on? "Milena?"

"I'm not defending what Jacob did, but… I just…"

"What?"

"As far as I could see, he didn't actually touch Henrik. Yes, he was angry and he did go…"

A bolt of fury shot up from my belly, and I interrupted her. "He pushed him over. Jacob pushed Henrik!"

"I think you'll find that Henrik tripped and fell over backward, but maybe that's irrelev—"

I cut her off again—I just couldn't help myself.

"Milena, Jacob pushed Henrik over. That's what happened. He was physically threatening. I'm surprised you're defending his actions."

"I'm not, but… Whatever." She took a deep breath, and we stood in silence for a short while. We were both wet and frozen, hungry because we hadn't had any breakfast yet, and now we'd fallen out. Why had we come to Sarek? Why hadn't we stuck to our original plan and gone to Abisko, just me, Milena and Henrik, walking from one cabin to the next, like we'd done for years?

"Henrik and I want you to come with us."

"No, I'm staying with Jacob," Milena answered instantly. Her voice shook a little, almost as if she were on the verge of tears, but I could tell that she was angry rather than upset. It wasn't an emotion I'd heard her express on many occasions in the past, but there could be no mistaking how she felt.

"But…"

"And I think you're making a ridiculous fuss about what happened yesterday." She was speaking quickly now, as if the words were pushing and shoving, elbowing their way out. "Jacob lost his temper when we were playing a game—you've done the same plenty of times. When we've played cards, or Trivial Pursuit—lots and lots of times. And Jacob apologized—I don't think you ever have."

"Hang on…" That was all I managed to say before Milena went on.

"He's a crap loser, but he said sorry. And he didn't push Henrik. He really didn't."

"Okay…" I tried to gather my thoughts, play for time. Milena's insistence that Jacob hadn't pushed Henrik infuriated me. They must have talked about it last night, Jacob denying the whole thing, making Milena doubt the evidence of her own eyes, getting her on his side. However bickering about it now would get us nowhere. I took a deep breath, tried to stay calm.

It was time to put all my cards on the table.

Out of the corner of my eye I saw Jacob crawling out of the tent. My pulse rate increased and my stomach turned over.

"There's something else," I said.

"Oh?"

"I don't know if you noticed an awkward atmosphere when you and Henrik caught up with me and Jacob yesterday."

"No." Milena looked completely bewildered.

Over by the tent Jacob stood up and put on his anorak. His posture showed that he was cold. He saw Henrik preparing breakfast, and even though I was thirty meters away I could tell exactly what was going through his mind. *Where are Milena and Anna?* His body stiffened, he looked around. It only took a second for him to spot us.

He reminded me of a dog, a German shepherd—eyes fixed on a certain point, ears pricked, body motionless.

I was running out of time.

Milena had her back to the tents and hadn't seen Jacob. I took a deep breath. "He tried it on with me. Jacob tried it on with me." Milena didn't say a word. She stared at the ground.

Jacob began to walk rapidly toward us.

"You know I would never make up something like this, Milena. You've known me long enough to—"

"Good morning!" Jacob called out cheerily. Milena turned and looked at him, but didn't say anything.

"And I heard you last night," I continued quietly, time was of the essence, I was almost gabbling now. "I can see the marks on your neck. Please, please come with us."

Milena stared at me with an expression I found hard to interpret. There was anger in her eyes, and sorrow, and also something else I couldn't quite put my finger on. Was it…contempt?

A second later, and Jacob was there.

"Hi, sweetheart." He put his arm around her shoulders and kissed her, or rather pressed his lips to hers. She didn't respond in any way to these affectionate gestures. He kept his arm where it was, held her close. He bestowed his fake smile on me.

"Did you sleep well, Anna?"

"Yes."

There was a brief silence, then Milena said: "Henrik and Anna are dropping out of the trip." She turned and headed back to the tents, leaving Jacob and me staring at each other.

Interview with Anna Samuelsson 880216-3382, September 18, 2019, Gällivare hospital, conducted by Detective Inspector Anders Suhonen.

"So how did Jacob react to the news that you and Henrik wanted to drop out?"

"He didn't say much. I think he was very nervous about what I might tell Milena, so he was probably relieved in a way."

"You'd already told her, hadn't you?"

"Yes, but he didn't know that. I couldn't bring myself to discuss it with him. I just wanted to get away, I didn't want to see him anymore."

"I can understand that."

"And to be honest I was… I was pretty angry with Milena too."

"Mm."

"I thought, *are you really going to stick up for that bastard? What the fuck are you doing? Well, in that case I can't help you. If you want to go into Sarek with a psychopath, then be my guest.*"

"You're saying she'd been brainwashed?"

"Yes…"

"I thought she and Jacob had only been together for a month or so?"

"Maybe brainwashed is a bit too strong."

Silence.

"The thing with Milena is…"

Silence.

"It doesn't feel right, talking about this."

"Why not?"

"I feel as if I'm letting her down. Betraying her."

"I get that."

"We've known each other for a long time, and she's always been a fantastic friend. The best you could imagine. I haven't got a bad word to say about her. But she was… She'd never had a boyfriend."

"Right."

"At least nothing long-term. And I think she really, really wanted that. She was desperate to find someone. And when she met Jacob… I believe she just kind of blanked out all the stuff about him that was weird or bad."

"I understand."

"I guess that's how it works. You have an image of the way you'd like reality to be, and you suppress anything that doesn't fit with that image, so that you can carry on living with your… your skewed version of reality."

"Mm."

"That was the situation with Milena and Jacob. She didn't want to accept who he really was."

"Okay. So if we can move on… I assume you and Henrik packed up your things and set off back to Staloluokta."

"Yes. Henrik tried to speak to Milena as well, to see if he could persuade her to come with us, but of course Jacob wouldn't leave them alone, so it didn't happen."

"I see."

"We set off up toward the pass, the same way we'd come."

"And what did Milena and Jacob do?"

"They carried on into Sarek, just as we'd planned."

"So you split up at that point?"

"Yes. And I really thought we'd seen the last of Jacob."

"But that turned out not to be the case?"

"Definitely not."

Henrik gave Milena a brief hug and they mumbled their goodbyes. I was still angry with her and hadn't intended to say anything, but when she turned, nodded and said goodbye to me too, I couldn't ignore her.

"Bye," I said tonelessly.

Jacob was busy taking down their tent. He walked around pulling out the pegs without even glancing at us. Fine by me—I never wanted to exchange another word with Jacob Tessin.

Henrik and I set off uphill. The pass above us was hidden by clouds and veils of misty rain; I couldn't even see the beginning of the snowfield. My body was stiff and uncooperative. My rucksack, with its dark green waterproof cover, felt heavier today. I don't think it was my imagination; everything was wet or at least damp, and all in all I was probably carrying an extra kilo.

The gentle drizzle from earlier had now turned into a steady rainfall, the drops pattering on the hood of my anorak. My coat was of very good quality, but it was the kind of fabric that breathes, so it wasn't one hundred percent waterproof. Constant rain like this meant that it eventually began to feel damp on the inside, sticking to my clothes. And the rain was cold. I was wearing my thin gloves but they didn't help; my fingers were already seizing up.

I was still angry and upset after the argument with Milena. Was this the end of our friendship? I couldn't remember us ever having an exchange of words like the one we'd had about Jacob. In fact we'd never really fallen out, but Jacob had changed her, she was no longer herself. The future would show whether the change was long-term, or whether they would split up and she would go back to the way she used to be. It made me sad to think that we wouldn't be spending time together anymore, but it wasn't the end of the world.

When you are faced with the end of a relationship, you realize how much it really means. I could see now that my association with Milena was mostly based on habit. Maybe nostalgia too. Every time we met up, we were reliving our student days to a certain extent, renewing our contact with the people we used to be, harking back to a simpler, more carefree existence. But how much did we really have in common anymore?

It was up to her whether we continued to see each other or whether it was over, I thought grimly.

I looked back and saw that I was way ahead of Henrik. I stopped and waited for him. At least my speedy ascent had warmed me up. Far below, through the mist, I could just see the plateau where we had camped. Jacob, Milena and the tent were gone.

Henrik caught up with me. He already looked worn out, and paused to catch his breath.

"How are you feeling?" I asked.

"This is tough," he panted, shrugging off his rucksack and flopping down onto a rock. "I can't seem to get warm, even though I'm sweating."

"Shall we carry on a bit farther, as far as the edge of the snow cover? Then we can stop for coffee."

"Okay. I just need to sit here for a minute or two."

We stayed where we were with the persistent rain pouring down. The temperature seemed to have dropped since this morning. We couldn't see much of either the mountains or the valley now; the rain had drawn a curtain across it all.

What an inhospitable place this is.

Now our destination—crossing Sarek—was gone, I couldn't get away from here fast enough. The magic spell had been broken. I wanted to get back to Staloluokta, be indoors, have a sauna, sleep in a bed, feel warm and dry. We ought to be able to do it with only one overnight stop en route, as we had on the way into the park. If Henrik was up to it—he looked alarmingly tired.

I was keen to leave; the rain had already destroyed the little warmth I had generated, and I was beginning to feel stiff and chilled to the bone again. Henrik was right; in weather like this you're never properly warm. However the difference between being on the move and sitting or standing still was enormous.

At long last Henrik laboriously got to his feet, picked up his rucksack and we set off. I let him go first, and matched his pace. We didn't exchange many words; the rain and the gradient took their toll on our mood.

We walked for half an hour. Forty-five minutes. An hour. Grassy slopes gave way to rocks, treacherous underfoot. Henrik slipped and almost lost his balance. We still couldn't see the beginning of the snow cover.

He stopped, let out a long breath. "I need a break."

"I thought we were aiming for the edge of the snow cover?"

"I'm tired. We've been walking for an hour." He sounded resolute, bordering on irritated. He took off his rucksack.

"We can't have far to go now," I ventured in a positive tone of voice. "It's probably just that we can't see it because of that ridge."

"I think we should take a look at the map," Henrik mumbled.

He took off the waterproof cover and started rummaging in his rucksack for the stove.

"Fine, but we're following that stream over there. It was on our left all the way down, so we can't go wrong."

"Even so," he said without looking at me as he began to assemble the stove.

The map was in the breast pocket of my anorak, neatly folded. I'd looked at it a couple of times during the past hour. I took it out and demonstratively handed it to Henrik.

"Thanks. Can you go and fetch some water?"

"Why don't we just have an energy bar? We'll have to stop for lunch soon anyway."

"No—I want a hot drink." He picked up the coffeepot and marched off in the direction of the stream babbling away nearby. His passive-aggressive reproach worked—I hurried after him.

"Give it to me—I'll go."

He handed me the pot without a word, and went back to the stove.

I lowered the pot into the ice-cold water. Yesterday it had been a shock; today my hand was already so cold that I barely reacted. I rejoined Henrik and placed the pot on the ring, and before long Henrik tipped instant coffee straight into the boiling water. We filled our cups and sat down on a rock. I wrapped both hands around my cup, as if it were a baby bird in need of protection. My frozen fingers began to thaw.

We drank our coffee in silence, but Henrik had been right; we needed something hot inside us. I felt a bit more cheerful.

"I think the rain is easing off," I said. It seemed to me that the sky above us was a lighter shade of gray. Henrik didn't answer. He sat in silence, sipping his coffee and staring blankly at the pot. After a while he said: "What were you and Milena talking about this morning?"

"What were we talking about?"

"Yes."

"But you know that. I asked her if she wanted to come back with us."

"It sounded as though you were arguing." He gave me a quick glance, then turned his attention back to the pot.

"I wouldn't say that, but she was trivializing what happened yesterday. Okay, I was annoyed."

"What do you mean, trivializing?"

"Well, she claimed that Jacob hadn't pushed you. For example."

I had hoped that Henrik would back me up—sigh, groan or mumble something along the lines of *unbelievable*. Anything, really. I'd expected his support, but instead he lapsed into silence again. He took another sip of coffee, stared into space. So I went on: "It wasn't just that, it was her whole attitude. She said that I often lost my temper when we played games—as if that was comparable! I mean, I might be a bad loser, but I've never called anyone a *fucking cunt* or attacked them physically."

Henrik frowned, looked at me. "Fucking cunt? When did he say that?"

"He mumbled something just before I came out of the tent."

"I didn't hear him."

"So are you saying it is comparable? Have I ever behaved the way he did yesterday?"

"No, of course not."

"I thought we agreed that the whole thing was very unpleasant."

"We did."

"You kept saying *he's crazy*."

"I'm not defending Jacob…"

"That's exactly what Milena said, but you are—both of you."

Henrik suddenly flared up. "So the fact that I said I didn't hear Jacob say those words—that means I'm defending him? Is that what you're claiming?"

I sighed. "I don't know why we're arguing about that idiot." I couldn't help sounding defensive.

"You're always the same, Anna. You get your teeth into something, and if I don't agree with you down to the last tiny detail, it means I'm against you, and you just have to keep pushing until you win. You overinterpret and misinterpret and you get like this… So fucking aggressive."

He was angry and upset. He'd raised his voice, and his cheeks were flushed. The strength of his reaction surprised me.

"Okay, okay. Sorry."

"I hate it."

The icy rain was still pouring down on us, we were wet and cold and we had at least forty kilometers of walking before we would have a roof over our heads. And now we'd started quarreling.

What an inhospitable place this is.

Henrik hadn't said he hated me, but he hated one aspect of my behavior, and my behavior was a part of who I was, therefore he hated a part of me. Strong words.

He'd never said anything like that before.

We remained silent for a little while, then Henrik took a deep breath and went on: "The thing is… Breaking off the trip was absolutely the right thing to do. What happened yesterday was completely unacceptable. So we're actually on the same page, but…" He sighed.

"But what?"

"Nothing. That's it. But he actually didn't touch me—Milena was right about that. It doesn't matter overall. He came at me in a very threatening way as if he was going to punch me, but I stumbled and fell. If I hadn't, then maybe he would have attacked me. So it's…irrelevant really."

I nodded slowly. The rain was falling into my cup, cooling and diluting my coffee, but I took another sip anyway.

My anger wasn't hot and burning; it was as ice-cold as the rain.

"What do you mean when you say *what happened yesterday*?" I asked.

"The argument last night."

"Because what also happened yesterday was that Jacob came on to me."

"I know, and that's terrible."

"Which is why I look at him a little differently from the way you do."

"Anna, I realize that Jacob is sick in the head. He might even be a psychopath. I get that." Henrik's voice was softer now, and he was actually looking at me while he was talking. He was beginning to regret the stance he had taken.

"I can tell you some of what he said when he came on to me."

"I'm sorry I snapped at you just now. You have every right to be angry. Forgive me." He was almost pleading with me.

"He said that he and I belonged together, because we were more attractive than you and Milena. More attractive and fitter."

There was a silence as Henrik allowed this to sink in. His shoulders were hunched, against the rain and what I was telling him. He shook his head.

"He's crazy," he said quietly.

"Now do you understand what I mean?"

"Yes. Yes, I do."

We packed away the stove. My anger had dissipated, and I tried to make a few encouraging comments. Henrik nodded and made noises of agreement, but he seemed distracted. We set off once more.

This time, and this time only, I was right about the ridge and the snowfield. After half an hour we saw the snow, and fifteen minutes later we had reached it. The terrain was flatter now, the walking easier. We stopped to fill up our water bottles, and I smiled at Henrik.

"Didn't I tell you the snowfield couldn't be far away? Didn't I?"

He gave me a wan smile. "Maybe you did."

I moved closer, gave him a hug and a kiss. "You know I'm always right, sweetheart."

"Mm."

"Let's walk for another hour until we start going downhill, then we'll stop for lunch."

Henrik nodded, but seemed reluctant to meet my gaze. He was breathless and red-faced from the exertion.

"Then, once we've passed the peak, it will be easy to get back down into Alggavagge. We'll be looking into Padjelanta, and do you know what's in Padjelanta?"

"No."

"Staloluokta. And in Staloluokta there are beds, and stoves, and a wood-fired sauna." I took Henrik's face between my hands and gave him a big kiss, right on the lips.

We set off across the snow with Henrik in front and me behind. Progress was instantly more difficult, as we sank down a centimeter or so with each step. And visibility quickly deteriorated too; the rain had almost stopped, but instead we were enveloped in a bitterly cold fog, or maybe low drifting clouds, which made the contours of the world around us even more blurred.

In silence we slowly plodded upward. I don't think either of us spoke for half an hour. The only sounds were our breathing and the crunching of our footsteps in the snow. I focused on the day ahead, tried to plan our breaks, predict where we might be at different times, worked out strategies and ruses to keep Henrik's spirits up.

This morning I had vaguely hoped that we might cover some distance inside Padjelanta today, but given the state Henrik was in, I thought we should probably camp for the night at the far end of Alggajavrre, on the border between Sarek and Padjelanta. Even that would be a real test of stamina for him. I was beginning to accept the idea that we might not make it to Staloluokta with just one overnight stay; we might need two.

You're not like you used to be, Henrik. Five years ago you would never have neglected your training.

I had no idea what he was brooding about as we trudged along.

I was expecting the snowfield to flatten out as we approached the peak, but it didn't happen, even though we'd been walking uphill for an hour. If anything, it…

No, that's not possible.

Neither of us said a word.

It actually felt as if…the terrain was getting steeper. But that was impossible.

It must be my imagination. Or was it?

Yesterday, walking in the other direction, I had been with Jacob. Maybe I'd been so shocked by his embrace that I hadn't noticed the shifting landscape?

No.

The incident with Jacob had happened at the end of the snowfield. Henrik and I had been walking on snow for an hour. A little longer, in fact.

We should be at the top now, the ground should be flat, or sloping downward. It was definitely getting steeper. It couldn't be my imagination.

My stomach turned over, and even though I was already cold, I felt a shudder run through me.

Could we have gone the wrong way? How?

Get a grip, Anna. You need to stay calm. You mustn't worry Henrik unnecessarily.

Henrik stopped dead, breathing heavily. He pointed to the rock face diagonally to our left.

"What's that?"

A hundred meters farther on I saw a darker outline in the snow, a slash in the sea of white, half-hidden by the fog.

"I don't know," I said, but I had a horrible suspicion about what it might be. I passed Henrik, moved closer to the dark patch, heard Henrik following me. The outline became clearer with each step we took.

Now I could see that the color was actually bluish-green. It was a crevasse—a deep crack in a glacier.

We had definitely gone wrong.

The snowfield was not a glacier. A crevasse like this couldn't possibly be there. Henrik caught up with me, still breathless.

"Is it a crevasse?" he asked. I felt rather than saw the way he was looking at me. "We need to check the map," I said, making an effort to sound calm and composed.

"Absolutely."

There was a brief pause. Henrik moved from foot to foot, took out his water bottle, had a drink. He gazed up at the crevasse, as if he were waiting for me to do something.

"The map?" I said.

He looked at me blankly.

Interview with Anna Samuelsson 880216-3382, September 18, 2019, Gällivare hospital, conducted by Detective Inspector Anders Suhonen.

"So the map was gone?"

"Yes."

"How come?"

"I gave it to Henrik when we stopped for coffee. He must have put it down.

Presumably."

"Right."

"It was… Like I said, we argued a bit while we were having coffee, so we were both a bit shaken up. I didn't give the map a thought."

"That's understandable."

"And Henrik refused to admit that he was the one who'd lost it—he insisted he'd given it back to me. Which wasn't true."

"So you fell out again?"

"No. I didn't think we could afford to waste any energy discussing whose fault it was, so I said *it doesn't matter, it is what it is*. And I decided that I would try to go back down and look for it. After all, we knew where we'd last had it."

"And Henrik would stay where he was?"

"Henrik would stay put, yes. He was too tired to walk even a meter unnecessarily."

"I see."

"It wasn't that late in the day. I thought I'd be able to find the map, get us on the right route, then we could manage a few hours' walking before we camped for the night."

"And?"

"That was the wrong decision. We should have gone straight back down together.

"But it's easy to be wise after the event."

I jog across the snow with light, well-balanced steps, keeping up a steady rhythm and following my own footprints. I am carrying my water bottle, but I have left my rucksack with Henrik. My pulse rate is high, but not too high, and I feel agile and free without the rucksack; I am used to moving like this from my endurance running.

Body and soul. My soul is disappointed, anxious and frustrated because we've gone wrong, because the map is missing, because Henrik blames me. I am relying on my body to rebalance my soul. My hormones will do the job.

We have walked for about two hours since we had coffee. Going in the opposite direction and setting my own pace, I should be able to get back to the same spot in half an hour. Forty minutes max. Then an hour to get back up to Henrik, without having overdone it. If I can find the map, it's definitely worth it.

And why shouldn't I find the map? It's got to be there somewhere.

It isn't just about the map though. I need this time for myself. I need to be away from Henrik to regain my equilibrium. I know I have to be the stronger one now. I have to plan and drive forward. I have to give him energy, lift him up. I almost lost patience with him when he blamed me for losing the map; I managed to stay calm, but it was a close call.

Patience isn't really my thing. Maybe I can learn something important from this.

I keep following our footprints. The fog seems to be thinning as the wind picks up. Maybe it will blow the clouds away and the sun will shine from a clear blue sky again in an hour or so. Once we have that panoramic view, it will be easy to orientate ourselves and find our way to the pass. Tonight we will camp at Alggavagge and talk about the adventure we have had, when Sarek showed its predator's teeth. We will begin to shape a narrative, a good story with which to entertain our friends around the dinner table back home in our apartment on a cold autumn night. Erika and Olof, Simon and Jennifer, Mark and Valle. We will eat game casserole and drink Amarone and laugh about the time when Henrik and I lost the map and took a wrong turning in Sarek.

Yes. That's how it will be.

I can see the end of the snowfield now. Soon I am jogging on bare ground, completely focused on not twisting my ankle on the scree. The rocks are wet and slippery, so I do my best to avoid jumping from one to the next.

It is harder to follow our route now that I don't have footprints in the snow to guide me, but here and there I see the imprint of the sole of a boot in a patch of mud, confirming that I am on the right track. And there are markers I recognize—a big rock here, a tangle of undergrowth that has somehow managed to take root high up on the mountainside there. I can hear the stream on my left the whole time.

The wind is stronger now, and it is raining heavily again. It is as if it had merely paused for breath, gathering its strength to attack me again. It lashes my face from the side. I tighten the cord around my hood so that only a small oval is exposed, from my eyebrows to my lower lip.

Suddenly I reach the place where we had coffee. I see the rocks we sat on, I even see a faint impression on the ground where the stove stood. Optimistically I look around, the bright colors and orange edging on the map ought to make it easy to spot among all the muted shades of green and brown and gray.

I quickly establish that it isn't exactly where we sat. I peer behind all the rocks, look into the small crevices on the ground where a layer of earth and moss and grass covers the scree. If Henrik put it down when he was setting up the stove, it should still be here—but of course it might have blown away, or maybe he dropped it over by the stream when he was rinsing out his cup before we set off again.

I widen my search area, go over to the stream and look around, follow it for twenty meters in each direction. My brain is fixated on finding something orange and blue and white, like when you're looking for a jigsaw puzzle piece with a particular shape among hundreds of others. I walk around in ever-increasing circles, carefully scanning the terrain, but I can't find the map.

The rain is still lashing my face and hammering against my hood, every drop that lands next to my ear seems to send a clap of thunder straight into my head.

I am constantly moving, looking first here, then there, but trying to maintain some kind of system. Ever-increasing circles. Ten meters from the spot where we rested, twenty meters, thirty, forty.

I have been searching for a while now. At least fifteen minutes, maybe twenty, perhaps even a little more.

I came back to this place full of hope, and I have no intention of giving up yet, but an element of doubt has begun to gnaw at me. I might not find the map. Not here, at any rate. What if Henrik pushed it into a pocket and forgot to close the zip?

In that case it could have fallen out somewhere on the way up. Why didn't I look for it on my way down?

You're never going to find it.

For a few brief seconds my brain runs amok, gives the doubt free rein, and is overwhelmed by a tidal wave of fear in its wake.

Map gone. Lost in Sarek. Worst-case scenario.

I regain control, force myself to focus. Consider less likely hypotheses that are still worthy of consideration. For example, the map could have been blown into the stream and carried away by the current, ending up some distance from my starting point. It's a long shot, but I go back to the stream and follow it much farther than last time. One hundred meters, two hundred meters.

Come on, you must realize you're never going to find the map. How much time are you going to spend on this? Wasted time? Okay, so you're being systematic and investigating every possibility in order to exclude it, but who do you think you're fooling? You just don't want to accept that it's gone.

I am almost ready to give up on the stream when I raise my head and see a strip of orange glowing next to something white and blue, by a rock just at the water's edge.

It's the map. Fuck me, it really is the map.

Thank you, God!

My heart slows then beats double time before relief floods my body. I hadn't realized until now to what extent I had actually given up hope. I take a deep breath, feel that my shoulders have dropped.

Yes. Yes, yes, yes.

I break into a jog, anxious to reach the map before it blows away again. The wind is stronger now, and the rain feels different, almost as if…

Yes, it's turning to sleet.

I have to take my eyes off the map for a second now and again just to see where I'm putting my feet, it would be a disaster if my eagerness made me careless and I twisted my ankle.

It is the map, isn't it?

I slow down. Stop. Breathe. Stare at it from a distance of five meters. The map, which is not a map at all.

The orange is a kind of lichen that I have seen in many places in the mountains. The white is a different lichen. And the blue is not blue, but a shading of the gray rock on which the lichens are growing.

Disappointment floods my body, just as relief did a moment ago. The map is gone—I have no choice but to accept that now. The worst-case scenario is no longer a scenario, it is reality.

Shit. Shit, shit, shit, shit.

And all around me the sleet has turned to snow, cold heavy flakes landing on my face. I can't believe it.

Snow in September? What is wrong with this fucking place?

I am in the middle of a proper snowstorm now, some of the flakes seem to be whirling upward into the sky where they came from. Others have already begun to settle on the ground. I am facing a white veil, like a thin curtain—still transparent, but not for much longer.

The footprints in the snow. Our footprints. My only chance of finding my way back to Henrik.

I begin to run uphill. I am not jogging now—I am running. Suddenly the map is irrelevant, my disappointment already forgotten. Because now I am afraid in a different way—I am terrified. What if I can't find my way back to Henrik…

I have to find my way back to Henrik.

I run with full concentration, focused on not making a misstep, on following the footprints and markers that will lead me back to Henrik. I quickly realize that I might as well forget most of the markers; the snowfall is too heavy, visibility is down to ten meters. At one point I lose my bearings completely; I have to retrace my steps and set off again from the previous footprint. I stay a little farther to the right this time, and find the route.

I am running uphill, but I am not racing along. However

fit you are, you can easily start producing lactic acid when you run uphill. I don't want to be tired when I get to the edge of the snowfield, because it will be harder to make progress from then on.

I try to work out how long it will take for me to reach Henrik at my current speed. To the edge of the snowfield, maybe five or ten minutes. From there we walked for about an hour, maybe an hour and fifteen minutes. So at least half an hour on my own, running.

Can I keep up this pace for another forty minutes? Doubtful. I am breathing heavily, drawing the ice-cold, damp air deep into my lungs. I am sweating from the inside, swathed in cold from the outside, warm and cold moisture meet somewhere along the way between skin and clothing. I ought to slow down to make sure I don't hit the wall.

And yet…the snow is beginning to settle. The sheer voile curtain on the ground is beginning to resemble thick densely woven wool. Will our footprints still be visible in forty minutes from now?

Not a chance.

Will I even be able to see them in five minutes? Will I find the first prints in the snowfield in time?

I can't possibly slow down. On the contrary, I need to speed up, run like I've never run before. And if I hit the wall, then I will have to run right through it. I will find the strength from somewhere.

I increase my pace, race up the last few meters to the snowfield, and yes, I get there in time. When we were walking up, I followed in Henrik's footsteps, so the impressions they left were quite deep. I even hit some of them again on the way down, so I can still see them clearly. However the blanket of fresh snow is already at least a centimeter deep, and the flakes are falling fast.

As soon as I set foot on the snowfield, it becomes much harder to make progress. I am concentrating, my technical control is good, I am making sure that I synchronize the movement of my legs and upper body. However the pace and the terrain underfoot soon begin to take their toll. I feel the first signs of lactic acid in my thigh muscles. A persistent pain. The ice-cold air hurts my lungs.

Visibility was ten meters; now it's down to five. Some of the shallower footprints begin to disappear. The storm is mercilessly eradicating the traces we left behind.

I loosen the cord around my hood, it is too tight, I feel as if I can't breathe. The wind immediately grabs hold of the flapping hood and whips it off my head. I am running straight into a blizzard. I know I ought to stop and pull up my hood, but the cold wet snowflakes feel good on my sweaty skin.

How long have I been running? Only a few minutes. I have at least half an hour to go before I reach Henrik.

This is never going to work. I'm not going to make it.

The storm sweeps across the mountain like a sponge across a whiteboard. Our footprints are inky marks, erased in a second.

My thighs are burning with lactic acid. My lungs are screaming. The footprints are no longer an unbroken chain; they disappear for a meter or so, then I spot a couple more. Only the deepest impressions are visible now, and they will soon be gone.

Henrik is sitting up there on the mountain, all alone in a snowstorm, and I'm not going to be able to find my way back to him. We could die out here—both of us.

This seems to be as good a moment as any to panic.

A wild, uncontrollable feeling takes hold of me, as if a monster is snapping at my heels and I have to escape at this very second, my life depends on it, and I forget everything I know about an efficient and energy-saving running style and simply flee, hell for leather. The pain in my thighs and my lungs is gone.

Maybe this is the extra reserve of strength that I need? The strength that will enable me to run straight through the wall?

Better than all the energy drinks in the world: mortal fear. "Henrik!" I yell into the curtain of snow. "Henrik!"

I ought to slow down so that I don't miss the increasingly rare footprints, but I can't. I have no control over myself. I am simply rushing blindly on. Is that a footprint? I think so, but I can't be sure. I keep on running, meter after meter, second after second without seeing any more prints, until eventually I think I see one. I slow down and stop. Yes, there is the faint outline of a boot sole in the snow. I can still see it… I think… The snowflakes whirl before my eyes, into my eyes. I stare at the ground as if I am looking at a three-dimensional picture, waiting for the hidden image to reveal itself.

My brain is groping for a pattern, but fails to find one. The footprint is gone.

I raise my head and all I can see is an even, thick layer of fresh snow. The mountain has forgotten us.

"HENRIK!" I roar at the top of my voice. "HENRIK! HEEENRIIIIK!"

I am in a perfectly soundproofed world. No echo. It is as if my roar is only happening inside my head; the world stifles it immediately.

"HEEEENRIIIIK!"

There is no answer of course.

The world is silent and cold and white, like oblivion. Like death.

"HEEENRIIIK!"

I don't know how many times I yelled, but my throat started to hurt. And there wasn't a sound in response. I was alone and marooned in the snowstorm.

The tsunami of panic had knocked me off my feet, but it was gradually beginning to recede. I was able to stand up on wobbly legs.

It was the realization that I might actually die that had brought me up short. Once I got used to the idea, grasped that it was a realistic outcome, I also understood that it wasn't an inevitable outcome.

I stood still for a little while, allowed my pulse to slow down. I wiped the snowflakes off my head, pulled up my hood and fastened the cord, leaving only my face exposed once more.

My breathing was under control, which meant my brain could start working again. It was still up to me to determine how well or how badly this was going to go.

The first decision was the most critical: Should I leave Henrik in the lurch and save myself? Or try to find him?

Even as I formulated the question, I knew the answer. It would be unthinkable to leave Henrik on the mountain.

Which of course removed the opportunity of assuring my own safety with relative simplicity, because I didn't doubt for a second that I'd make it if I turned around and went back down on my own. When the storm abated, which I reckoned it would do pretty soon, it shouldn't be too difficult for me to find my way to Staloluokta. If the storm continued, I could carry on into Sarvesvagge, catch up with Milena and Jacob and accompany them through Sarek, as per our original plan. It wasn't an appealing option, but it was achievable.

However, if I continued uphill, I increased my risk factor significantly. The chances of finding Henrik weren't great in the current weather conditions. And he was the one who had the tent. Spending the night outdoors with no protection in a snowstorm was something to be avoided at all costs.

At the same time I wasn't sure that he had the presence of mind or the strength to cope with a night on his own. Just putting up the tent when the wind was so strong was a challenge in itself.

So I made my decision: I would go on searching for Henrik for a few more hours, until dusk began to fall. If I hadn't found him by then, I would head down into the valley where it would be a few degrees warmer, and hopefully it wouldn't be snowing. I would find a sheltered spot under a rocky outcrop or something similar. It wouldn't be the best night I'd ever had, but I should be safe.

But where should I go now to look for Henrik? In which direction?

So far I had followed our footprints from earlier in the day. My fresh prints were still visible behind me, even though the weather was working hard to erase them. They formed a faint but discernible line.

I should of course carry on up the mountain, taking that same line. What was the easiest approach? I had to avoid going off course.

I decided to walk backward, so that I could make sure my footprints stayed in line.

I realized that it would also be useful to create a track leading down into the valley, hopefully for me and Henrik. Maybe I should pile up some big snowballs at regular intervals, as if I were building a snowman. Then again, that would take up too much time and energy. A quicker and simpler solution would be to retrace my own footsteps from time to time, making the impressions fresher and deeper. That would at least lead me in the right direction.

I set off backward up the mountain. Working out the smartest and most rational course of action under the circumstances had a calming effect on me. I had a plan, and it kept the panic at bay.

After a few hundred meters I stopped and shouted Henrik's name. Still no response. I carefully retraced my footsteps, turned and went up again, then continued walking backward.

I thought I was probably moving at about the same pace as Henrik and I had maintained when we were together. My headlong dash across the snow hadn't lasted very long—no more than five minutes, which might correspond to fifteen or twenty minutes' walking at my current rate of progress. Therefore, I should be between forty-five minutes and an hour away from Henrik.

Hardly surprising that he couldn't hear me yet.

I stopped and shouted again, even though I had little hope of getting an answer. It was important to stick to the plan—my security blanket, my vaccine against the panic. I didn't want my blood to start boiling again.

I drank some water, kept going. Even, rhythmical, purposeful steps, my eyes firmly fixed on keeping the line straight.

Wasn't there an old TV program called *Linus on the Line*? An angry little man, gesticulating and pulling faces at the person who had drawn him. I think I'd seen a few clips on YouTube.

I was *Anna on the Line*, although I was drawing my own line in the snow. Plus I was calm and focused. *Anna on the Line* wouldn't make much of a TV show—a woman walking backward at a steady pace, stopping occasionally to shout "Henrik," retracing her steps, turning and going back up, turning and continuing backward.

Repeat.

It might have been my imagination, but I thought the snowstorm was abating slightly. I knew that snow in Sarek in September was a possibility, but I'd never heard of it snowing for days on end, like in the middle of winter.

Stubbornly I stuck to my plan, my voice growing more and more hoarse from shouting, and my calves beginning to ache. I checked the time: I'd been walking for half an hour.

The snow was definitely less heavy now. I thought I could see my footsteps for a little bit longer.

I kept going. Fifteen minutes, twenty.

This is never going to work. You're never going to find Henrik.

After an hour I stopped, drank some water, cleared my throat and yelled as loudly as I could: "HEEENRIIIIK! HEEEEN-RIIIIK!" I roared at the snowflakes drifting to the ground.

"HEEEENRIIIK!"

The same lack of an echo, the same feeling of being in the world's biggest soft playroom. No echo, no response.

If he was still where I had left him, and if I had gone in the right direction, which I should have done because I had followed THE PLAN precisely, he ought to be able to hear me now.

But maybe THE PLAN hadn't worked. Maybe it was a crap PLAN.

This is never going to work. You're never going to find Henrik.

The doubt set in now, like the first tickle in your throat before a cold breaks out in earnest. The sense of calm, just like the panic, was a wave breaking on the shore, then ebbing away.

I realized there were elements of uncertainty. I might not have been walking at the same pace as Henrik and I had maintained earlier in the day. In fact I might still have another thirty minutes to go before I was anywhere near him. I took a deep breath, refocused.

There's nothing wrong with the plan. It's a good plan. The worst thing you can do when you have a good plan is to abandon it too soon.

So I kept on going, walking backward for another ten minutes, my eyes fixed on the footprints I was leaving behind. I was concentrating so hard that at first I didn't notice the narrow dark line running parallel with my footprints, a few meters to the right. It was six or seven meters long, maybe twenty centimeters across at its widest point, narrowing like a salmon filleting knife at both ends. It was covered in fresh snow, but I could see that it was lower than the surrounding terrain.

There was only one thing it could be, but I went over to take a closer look anyway. Yes, it was a crevasse. Snow had been blown into it so I couldn't see the bottom, but it had to be pretty deep.

I turned around and looked uphill, and my jaw dropped.

About fifteen meters ahead there was a deep gash in the landscape, cutting diagonally across my route. It was several meters wide, and at least fifty meters from one end to the other.

Cautiously I approached the edge and looked down, taking care to keep my center of gravity on my back foot. The turquoise luster of the ice was partly hidden by the fresh snow and disappeared into the darkness. The crevasse was curved and I couldn't see the bottom. Maybe I would be able to if I leaned forward, but I chose not to.

I had seen enough.

It must be at least thirty meters deep. If I'd walked backward over the edge, I probably wouldn't have had any idea what was happening until my body was torn asunder on the jagged ice far below. If I had survived the fall, against all the odds, I would have had no chance of getting out of the crevasse under my own steam.

The realization of how close I had been to death made my heart pound.

What an inhospitable place this is.

I must be farther up the mountain than I thought. Perhaps I had in fact gone faster backward than Henrik and I had gone forward. Or my fantastic PLAN to find the right route, my genius METHOD, was somehow flawed.

Maybe I hadn't kept to a straight line after all.

I had moved a few meters away from the crevasse, but it was

as if its turquoise gloom seeped over the edge, making the world a darker place.

I checked the time; it couldn't be twilight yet, it was too early. The cloud cover must have thickened, taken on a darker shade of gray.

But it *felt* like twilight.

I could of course go around the crevasse and continue upward, but I had a strong feeling that I had already come too far up. I needed to head back down. I could go off to the side every so often to look for Henrik, but this was treacherous terrain. How could I be sure that there wasn't another crevasse hidden beneath the drifting fresh snow, waiting to swallow me up?

I heard a strange noise, almost like a wailing voice. It must be the ice, moving. I didn't know anything about how a crevasse was formed; perhaps sudden drops in the temperature in the autumn cause tensions in the ice and made it crack?

There it was again.

Aaa.

A tiny flame of sound that flared up, only to be extinguished by the wind and snow.

Aaann…

I stood stock still, held my breath. The gentle patter of snowflakes on my hood bothered me. I yanked at the cord and pushed back the hood. My mouth was hanging open, as if that might help. I instinctively turned my head into the wind.

I listened for a long time, holding my breath, until my chest began to hurt and the muscles in my throat were working to get some air and I let go and breathed out, then filled my lungs with fresh air in one single deep breath and then I heard it again.

Aaannaaa!

"HEEENRIIIK!" I roared.

Aaaannaa!

I ran toward Henrik's voice, still calling out, keeping my eyes on the ground in order to avoid catching my foot in some hidden crevasse. In no more than a minute I saw a darker shape through the whirling snow, and then I was with him. We hugged each other, a cold and wet embrace, cheek to cheek. Henrik was so cold he was shaking.

"Oh, Henrik, thank God…" My eyes filled with tears of relief. I had started to believe that I would never find him. Now at least part of the nightmare was over. Whatever trials awaited us, we would face them together.

Henrik's teeth were chattering and he could hardly talk. "You came back," he gasped. "You came back."

I kept on hugging him. I never wanted to let go of him again. I rubbed his back with both hands, firm rapid movements to generate some warmth for both of us. Only now did I realize that I was shivering too. I had worked up a real sweat when I raced up the mountain in a panic, but then I had walked at a steady pace for over an hour.

Now I felt as if I had a film of ice-cold moisture next to my body. In addition the heavy wet snow had begun to find its way down the back of my neck.

At least I had been on the move; Henrik had remained in the same spot for almost two hours, in the middle of a snowstorm. His body was shaking violently now, and he kept repeating:

"You came back… You came back…"

"Of course I came back. Now we have to get down off this mountain."

"I tried…to put up the tent…but…"

Only now did I look around. My rucksack was where I had left it, partially covered in snow; I don't think Henrik had touched it. The waterproof cover was still on, so the contents should be fairly dry.

His rucksack however was sitting there with the top flap wide open, gaping up at the sky like a child trying to catch snowflakes on its tongue. Clothes and items of equipment lay strewn across the ground, and the tent had been spread out. Pegs everywhere. He had made a start with a couple of the metal supports, but got no further.

This wasn't good. All his stuff was now soaking wet again, plus things could easily disappear in the snow. It wasn't as windy as it had been, but who knew what had already gone whirling away. I let go of him and said: "We need to gather all this up and get down into the valley as quickly as possible."

He nodded. "I'm sorry, I thought I needed some kind of protection…"

"It's fine, let's gather it all up and leave."

"It was stupid… I'm so sorry…"

We worked quickly and efficiently, brushing the snow off each item and stuffing everything into Henrik's rucksack. I wondered how he could have left it with the top open in the middle of a blizzard; he must have lost the plot completely.

Look who's talking. You went into a complete panic back there for a while.

There was no sign of his waterproof cover, but it didn't really matter now that everything was wet anyway. We pulled out the ridgepoles and spent some time searching for the nylon bag in which they belonged, but we couldn't find them. It was no great loss; we could pull the poles apart and lay them on the tent when we rolled it up, but Henrik didn't want to stop looking.

"I must have put it here somewhere..."

"Leave it, we can manage without it."

"Maybe it blew away... It was very windy when I started..."

"Tent."

I grabbed hold of one end and nodded to him to grab the other. We lifted it and shook it to get rid of as much snow as possible.

"Did you find the map?" Henrik asked.

"No."

"You were right, I was the one who lost it..."

"Forget it. That doesn't matter now."

"I remember now, you gave it to me, then I put it down when I went to light the stove..."

"Hold your end up and give it another shake."

"Or it might have fallen out of my pocket on the way..."

We laid the tent down on the ground. Henrik straightened his side and placed his knee on the edge to secure it. I rolled up the fabric, brushing off the snow as I went.

"Otherwise you would have found it where we stopped for coffee... You did go back to the right place, didn't you?"

"Mm."

"Unless it blew away too..."

When I'd finished, I fetched the tent bag, which we'd found when we were looking for the other bag. Henrik held up the rolled tent and I slipped the bag over it. We secured it under my rucksack, and at last we could set off down the mountain.

Together. Frozen, tired and hungry, but together.

I had run to the right in order to reach Henrik, so now I kept slightly to the left in the hope of finding the line of footprints. If that didn't work, it wouldn't be a catastrophe; as long as we were moving downhill, we were going in the right direction to get to the valley.

The snowstorm was definitely abating now, and visibility was improving all the time. Soon we could make out the contours of the mountains around us.

I realized that my PLAN had actually worked pretty well. Okay, so I hadn't found my way directly to Henrik, but I had only missed him by a hundred meters or so. And he had heard my voice—and I his—at roughly the place where I'd expected that to happen.

Henrik said that the storm had suddenly hurled itself at him as if it had been lying in wait, and his first thought was more or less the same as mine: How is Anna going to find me when the footprints disappear? He began walking downhill, but soon realized that carrying two rucksacks was too much for him. He had to stop and rest every twenty meters. The snow came down more heavily, and he got colder and wetter. He tried to put up the tent, but things vanished in the snow and it was too windy for him to secure it and he was shivering, shivering so much…

There was something feverish about his account; he was almost gabbling.

"And then suddenly I heard you shouting and I shouted back but it was ages before you answered… I could hear you but you couldn't hear me…"

"No."

"When you shouted again, it sounded as if you were closer and I started to think that maybe it's going to be okay…maybe I'm going to survive this…"

"Of course we're going to survive."

I could hear how terse I sounded. I hoped he wouldn't realize it was because I'd had the same fear as him, but had felt that I couldn't give way to that fear even for a second, or even acknowledge its presence, because doubt weakens us. However Henrik had no problem acknowledging the doubt and talking about it at some length.

"I actually thought I was going to die up there. I thought, *I'm going to freeze to death.*"

"Mm."

He kept on and on about what he'd thought and how he'd felt when he was alone in the snowstorm on the mountain, while I said very little. This agitated babbling wasn't like him at all. Presumably it was down to relief: the nightmare was over, we had found each other again and we were on our way to safety.

In which case he was more optimistic than me. I was by no means certain that the worst was over.

We had been walking briskly for fifteen minutes, but Henrik was still shivering so much that his speech was affected. I could hear his teeth chattering. He was clearly frozen, but was he on the verge of hypothermia?

Probably not—under the circumstances the signs were positive. I knew that when someone is suffering from severe hypothermia, he or she loses the ability to shiver, which is the body's way of generating heat. However I needed to keep a close eye on him.

He had a theory about how we had ended up on the wrong route. We'd crossed a small stream quite late on the previous day, hadn't we? Yes, we had. And after that we had continued along the mountainside at an oblique angle for a short distance until we found the plateau where we camped for the night. But this morning, when we left Milena and Jacob, we had gone straight up the mountainside, then followed a different stream.

"Maybe," I muttered. I felt a growing irritation over the fact that he was brooding about everything we'd done wrong instead of focusing on what we needed to do from now on. However I had to admit that he was probably right.

"It's hardly surprising—we were both pretty upset this morning," Henrik went on.

We couldn't find our old tracks, but we were soon off the glacier. The bare ground was now hidden beneath several centimeters of fresh snow, but I still thought we should take a break.

I boiled water and made hot chocolate. Henrik borrowed some dry thermals from me, and he also dug out a fleecy top from the bottom of his own rucksack that was still damp rather than soaking wet. Meanwhile I put on several more layers—a merino wool and polyamide top, a padded gilet and a thin woolen hat—in an attempt to conserve the body heat I'd managed to generate.

The wind had almost dropped completely, but snowflakes were still drifting to the ground.

We slurped the chocolate with our hands cupped around our hot steaming cups. It almost hurt our stiff frozen fingers, but we needed every scrap of extra warmth we could get.

Henrik said: "You should always carry two maps in the mountains."

"Mm."

"At least if you're walking with me."

I didn't answer.

"It's strange though… Because I've kind of designated this breast pocket here, the one on the left, as my map pocket. That's where the map always goes when I'm carrying it. It's the same as when I fly. I always put the tickets—and my passport—in the outside pocket of my bag. And yet…when I've got two things on my mind at the same time, I just drop it on the ground… It's crazy…"

"More chocolate?" I went over to the stove and picked up the pan. I didn't get a response, but topped up his cup anyway.

"Do you think we should have another look for the map on the way down? I mean, since we're passing the spot anyway?"

"No."

"If we camp nearby, I can search for it."

Stop talking about the fucking map.

"I think we should go farther down before we stop for the night. Try to find a sheltered spot."

"Right."

"If the wind gets up again when everything is damp, it's going to be a very cold night."

"Okay, let's do that."

Henrik managed a smile, wan and submissive, then took another sip of chocolate.

He was still shivering.

A few hours later we had continued our descent and found a place with huge rocks that should provide shelter from the wind coming from two directions. The ground was sloping and uneven, but we had to compromise somewhere. It had stopped snowing, but an icy cold lingered in the air, and the sky was gray. There was nothing to suggest that we would be able to get warm and dry in the foreseeable future.

We put up the tent, which wasn't just damp—it was soaking wet, inside and out. So were the air beds and the bedrolls. My sleeping bag was dry, and I decided to leave it in its bag until it was time to sleep.

We heated water on the stove and ate our freeze-dried meal—an Indian chicken and rice stew. It was no culinary masterpiece, but it was good to get some hot food in our bellies. We had some more hot chocolate as the darkness began to close in over Sarvesvagge.

Henrik had grown quieter as the day went on, and while we were eating, he hardly spoke at all. He seemed bone-weary. After his babbling when we were first reunited it was almost a relief when he reverted to his familiar brooding silence, but I wondered if he had it in him to make a fresh attempt at finding the pass the following day. Perhaps he wasn't just tired but also slightly traumatized by the hours he had spent alone on the mountain in the snowstorm, thinking he was going to die.

Personally I had suppressed the memory of the brief burst of panic when I raced blindly up the mountain, but my body remembered. I only had to nudge at the recollection of those moments for my blood to run cold and my heart to start racing.

If it snowed again tomorrow morning, or looked as if there was any risk of another storm, then…no. We would stay here for a day, gather our strength.

I was brushing my teeth. Darkness had fallen, and ice-cold rain began to fall. The world was dark and silent, apart from the raindrops pattering over my jacket. There were no smells in the air, no tastes. It was as if Sarek had decided to exclude all sensory impressions, apart from physical sensation, in order to hammer home its point once and for all.

Welcome to Sarek. But be prepared to feel colder than you have ever felt before.

According to my usual bedtime routine, I ought to have a good wash and put on fresh clothes to help me sleep better. The problem was that I had given Henrik my last dry change of clothing. Stripping off in the cold rain and splashing my body in the even colder stream, only to put on the same damp, chilly underwear again would be pointless, so this evening I made an exception.

What an inhospitable place this is.

I crept into the tent and zipped the flap behind me. I took my sleeping bag out of its protective cover and spread it out on the air bed. It was dry, but that was a small consolation, given how cold and miserable I felt.

Henrik was already in his sleeping bag beside me, staring blankly at the roof of the tent. I got in and wrapped the sleeping bag tightly around my legs. The ground was sloping, and I rolled over toward him. I leaned across and kissed him lightly on the lips.

"Good night."

"Good night," he mumbled.

An automatic gesture, lacking any real emotion. No tenderness, no longing for intimacy. But even an automatic gesture has some value. Without it there is definitely something wrong.

I settled down, listening to the rain pattering on the tent. I was still freezing, and knew that I would be freezing for several days, every hour and every minute, until we reached the sanctuary of Staloluokta.

Henrik suddenly unzipped his sleeping bag and sat up. He reached for his head torch, got onto all fours and crawled into the area covered by the awning. The torch came on, the beam swept from side to side, played across the fabric of the tent, across my face. I could hear him rummaging among his stuff. Endlessly.

"What are you doing? What are you looking for?"

"I think I..."

"What?"

"I might have put the map in one of the outside pockets of my waterproof trousers..."

I sighed. Henrik carried on rummaging. "Henrik? Leave it, please."

He didn't reply, he simply continued rooting among his things. Opening and closing zips. Opening and closing snap fasteners. Digging into rucksacks.

"Seriously, Henrik—can't you find your waterproof trousers?"

"I found them."

"So you've checked the pocket—was the map there?"

"No."

"Come back to bed then."

"I'm just going to check my jacket too..."

"Haven't you already done that, like five times?"

No reply. More rummaging. There was something manic about the whole thing.

How long was it going to go on? I was struck by a sudden

suspicion. I propped myself up on one elbow and peered out through the tent flap.

"You're not checking my stuff too, are you?"

He looked at me blankly, a little offended. "Of course not."

"Come back to bed then—I've had enough of this."

Eventually he gave up, came back in and crawled into his sleeping bag. Turned off the head torch and put it away. Silence descended. For a while. Until I heard his voice in the darkness:

"Maybe Jacob was right. Maybe we don't belong together." His voice was flat and sad, somehow resigned.

I felt a spurt of rage.

"I don't want to hear that!" My voice shook with anger. "Don't give me that crap!" He didn't speak, so I went on:

"We're still fighting for survival here—don't you get that? We're in the middle of the wilderness without a map. We're in real danger, for fuck's sake!"

I had kept the lid on it for too long—my frustration at the fact that he'd lost the map, his constant picking over our mistakes instead of focusing on the way forward, the feeling that he was forcing me to carry both of us mentally. The lid flew off, my anger boiled over.

"If we get out of here alive, we can talk about whatever you like—but not now!"

"So you think we're going to die?"

"No, not if we focus and keep a cool head. But we can't… brood on things that have already happened. Don't you understand that?"

"Everyone wonders why we're not married," Henrik went on in that same flat tone of voice.

"Oh, for God's sake."

"Why do you never want to talk about children?"

"SHUT UP!" I yelled, and punched him on the arm. Hard. I just wanted to make him stop. It can't have hurt, his upper arm was protected by the sleeping bag and several layers of clothing, but I shouldn't have done it. This was something completely new in our relationship. Neither of us had ever resorted to physical violence during a quarrel.

He was stunned into silence, and I was so ashamed. I immediately apologized. We hugged and kissed, lay cocooned in our sleeping bags with our faces close together, and soon Henrik's breathing slowed. He had fallen asleep.

But I lay awake for a long time.

Why do you never want to talk about children?

I thought about that spring seven years ago, when we went to Florence. How warm it was during the daytime, even though it was only April. Like Sweden in July. How short the twilight was—darkness fell like a curtain, bringing with it a surprising chill in the air.

Almost two years had passed since that dreadful midsummer and everything that followed, shattering my family. I no longer spoke to my father. Henrik had become my new fixed point, my safe harbor in life.

He had just been appointed to a permanent post as a lecturer at the university, and we went away to celebrate. After two and a half years we no longer felt it necessary to keep our relationship a secret. Not that it had bothered me; on the contrary it had added a certain spice. Arranging to meet at a mediocre pizzeria in a remote part of Uppsala where no one from the university would ever go. Taking the commuter train to Knivsta, walking a hundred meters from the station and being scooped up by Henrik in a hire car before speeding off for a weekend at a luxury manor house hotel in Sörmland.

Maybe it was just a game we played because it amused us. Henrik once mentioned that he thought his colleagues were aware of the situation.

But now we were in Florence. Henrik had been there on several occasions and knew the city well. We spent our days wandering between galleries and churches. He was an entertaining guide, but I didn't have his ability to become absorbed in a painting or a sculpture, apparently oblivious to the passage of time. I often left the venue before him and headed to the nearest pavement café. I would sip a latte in the spring sunshine, watching the stream of people passing by. Chinese, Japanese, Americans. The super-elegant Italians, the Florentine upper class I assume, with gleaming black hair, pomaded and perfectly swept back, olive skin, sunglasses, pink shirt with casually rolled-up sleeves, barefoot in dark blue suede loafers.

After a while Henrik would emerge and I would wave to him. He would join me and order a latte for himself. We always sat very close together, our bodies entwined.

In the evenings we ate fantastic food in local bars off the tourist beat, surrounded by noisy Italians, big groups, sometimes families with small children even though the hour was late. When we got back to the hotel, we would make love—or if we had drunk too much wine and were too tired, we would do it in the morning when we woke.

We hired a car and spent a few nights at an *agriturismo*, a farm that had been converted into a hotel, a few kilometers from the city. It was on a hill with an avenue of cypress trees leading up to the old buildings. From a distance they looked as if they were about to collapse, but in fact the interiors had been renovated to the highest standard. The view over the rolling Tuscan landscape was magical.

One evening Henrik borrowed a Vespa from the owner and we drove to a beautiful spot on the other side of the valley. I sat behind him, my arms wrapped around his waist. The wind felt soft against my face as we sped along. We parked and walked a short distance to a grove of pine trees. The countryside shone like gold in the low evening sunlight.

Henrik went down on one knee and proposed.

And I thought: *Life can be like this. Peaceful, pleasant, secure, like drifting along on a raft along a wide beautiful river. Enfolded in goodwill, in love.*

I said yes.

He looked happy, maybe also a little relieved. We both shed a few tears. And then?

The months pass by, months turn into years, life with Henrik becomes routine, something I take for granted, a backdrop against which the rest of my existence plays out. I focus on achieving top grades. I focus on getting a good position as a notary. I focus on gaining employment with a prestigious practice. I focus on becoming a lawyer as quickly as possible.

So much focus. Perhaps I'm trying to avoid listening to that voice inside my head.

This isn't enough, Anna.

This isn't what you dreamed of.

A feeling of being secure and peaceful and surrounded by love—it's not enough.

Life has to be more than that.

On other days it *is* enough. Everything is fine. I curse myself for always wanting more, for never being satisfied.

Henrik caught me when I fell. He loves me. Why can't that be enough?

Why do you never want to talk about children?

I lay awake for a long time.

And I hoped that Henrik would feel better in the morning, and that the weather would improve so that we could get over the pass and set off toward Staloluokta. I had a horrible sense of being trapped, a feeling that Sarek had closed in around us and that we were now banging on the door in vain, begging to be let out.

Interview with Anna Samuelsson 880216-3382, September 18, 2019, Gällivare hospital, conducted by Detective Inspector Anders Suhonen.

"So the plan was to make a fresh attempt to find your way back to Staloluokta the next day?"

"Yes."

"What made you change your minds?"

"Henrik had a panic attack. On the way up."

"Oh?"

"I noticed in the morning that he was very tired, but I still thought it was the best option."

"Right."

"The rain hadn't stopped, but visibility was better than the previous day. We set off after breakfast… I thought we could stop often, have plenty of hot drinks along the way. Take our time. We headed up the mountain at an angle in order to find the original stream, which we did after a while, so we were on the right track."

"And you were sure about that?"

"Yes. I was sure. I recognized...the place where Jacob came onto me, among other things. We definitely passed it."

"I understand."

"So before we went up onto the snow, we stopped and made coffee, had an energy bar each. Everything felt good."

"Okay."

"Then we began to walk up the snowfield, but before long Henrik stopped, and he... He put his hand on his heart, as if... as if he thought it was going to stop or something. He kind of collapsed...dropped to his knees first, then onto his side. His face was contorted."

"Did you know what was happening?"

"At first I thought it was something physical, that he couldn't get enough air. I knelt down beside him, unbuttoned his jacket, unzipped his top and so on, but he...he still couldn't breathe..."

"Go on."

"He couldn't speak, so I tried mouth-to-mouth resuscitation. Eventually whatever it was began to pass. And that's when I thought maybe it was a panic attack."

"Right."

"Henrik had never suffered from anything like that before, so..."

Silence.

"Anna, do you think it was to do with what had happened the previous day?"

"Yes, of course. He thought he was going to die out there in the snowstorm, so as we headed up the mountain across the snow, it all came flooding back."

"Mm... And that's when you gave up the idea of getting through the pass?"

"Not right away."

"No?"

Silence.

"I took out the stove and heated some fruit soup. I was hoping that when he'd recovered a little more, we'd be able to carry on—but there was no chance."

"Really?"

"He couldn't even look up the mountain without feeling bad again."

"No?"

"The peaks were hidden behind rain mist and fog, so you couldn't see... Visibility wasn't great. I guess it was the sensation of being lost. Again."

"That's understandable."

"Mm. So we sat for a while longer, then we set off downhill. He had to lean on me for support. When we left the snowfield, the terrain was flatter, and it became easier. We stopped for lunch, and decided to go for Plan B instead."

"Which was?"

"To continue toward the center of Sarek, as Milena and Jacob had done."

"Were you expecting to catch up with them?"

"No—they had a twenty-four-hour head start."

"You didn't consider resting for a day and then making a fresh attempt?"

"I considered all kinds of things."

"But?"

"But Henrik was absolutely certain that he wouldn't make it through the pass. *I just can't do it*, he kept saying. *I can't do it, I can't.* I didn't want to push him too hard."

"No."

"The other option..."

Silence.

"How are you feeling, Anna? Are you tired? Would you like to stop?"

Silence.

"No, it's fine."

"Are you sure?"

"Yes."

"We'll be stopping soon anyway, but it would be very helpful if you could carry on for a little longer."

"So…the other option was to go in the opposite direction into Sarvesvagge. Come out somewhere in Padjelanta. I knew there were marked trails and cabins and so on."

"Yes."

"But it can be a considerable distance from one cabin to the next, and I didn't have a clear idea of the trails. There was a significant risk that we could end up wandering around for days on end."

"Absolutely."

"I'd spent a lot of time studying the map of Sarek, so I had a picture in my mind of how Sarvesvagge leads in toward Rovdjurstorget, then it's the Rapa Valley and so on. I also thought the chances of meeting other hikers in central Sarek were pretty high, which meant we would be able to photograph their map with my phone. So we chose Sarek, but I wasn't entirely comfortable with the decision. I had a bad feeling in my stomach."

"Mm."

"The thought of setting off into this vast wilderness without a map, it… I knew how easy it was to get lost, because that was exactly what we'd done the previous day. So like I said, I had a bad feeling in my stomach. I almost felt faint, to be honest."

"Mm… You know what, Anna—I think that's enough for today. Try and get some rest."

Here comes a man who was hungry and cold, but triumphed after all.

One of Evert Taube's songs about Fritiof Andersson. I had sung it at student parties in Uppsala, and I could still remember that line. It popped into my head as Henrik and I made our way down. Both the valley before us and the surrounding mountains were lost in ice-cold rain mist.

A man who was hungry and cold.

I had never thought about what that really meant; being cold and hungry is no longer a real threat in our part of the world, but not very long ago it was. The struggle against cold and hunger had been a battle for life and death through thousands of years until comparatively recently. Like half a second ago. And straight away there are a couple of idiots who voluntarily leave a safe place and once again expose themselves to the forces of nature.

Our ancestors would have thought we'd lost it completely.

The first few hours were fine. We ambled across soft grassy fells. Maybe Henrik should have gone first, because he was considerably more tired than I was and I needed to adapt my pace to his—but even simple walking like this required constant decisions about the route, because we weren't following a designated trail. We passed small brooks, then suddenly the terrain was wet underfoot and we had to jump from one clump of grass to the next until we reached solid ground. Henrik was too exhausted to raise his head and pick out the best way through, so I went first, keeping to a very modest tempo, while he followed on behind, lost in a world of his own.

Gradually the mountains loomed higher and higher on either side of us; we could just make them out through the clouds. I tried to convince myself that we hadn't lost the map, we knew exactly where we were going, Jacob hadn't put his arms around me, Milena and I hadn't quarreled—how would my experience of this walk have been under those circumstances? Fantastic. The landscape was beautiful and magnificent. The veils of rain only made it more mystical and fascinating. The red-and-yellow shades of autumn didn't glow the way they did in the sunshine, but some of the bushes almost seemed to be lit from within at close quarters.

Sarvesjåhkkå, the river in the middle of the valley, had cut its way into the bedrock, and we were now walking through a canyon about five meters deep. It was about a meter wide, maybe a little more, and I realized that this was a place where we could cross the torrent with comparative ease—if you were brave enough to risk the leap. The ground was covered in brushwood rather than grass, and we followed narrow, winding reindeer tracks through the bushes. There was no snow left; it had all been washed away by the persistent rain. We were trudging through mud. I looked for footprints left by boots, but couldn't see any. Milena and Jacob must have passed this way, but there were thousands of similar tracks to choose from. The mud seized hold of our boots, slowing our progress, and it was tempting to step on rocks or the bare roots protruding above ground. However they were as slippery as soap thanks to the rain. Behind me I heard Henrik trip and almost fall several times.

We kept on going, squelching and stumbling. I slowed down even more, but still I had to keep waiting for Henrik. We stopped, boiled some water and drank our fruit soup, but we didn't stop shivering until we set off again. This time I let Henrik go first. A high mountain towered above us on the right, its peak lost in the mist, but slowly we drew closer to its massive rock face.

An hour or so later I found a grassy plateau near the stream that was big enough for our tent. A short distance away there was a slope that became steeper and steeper until it turned into a bare perpendicular rock face. It was hard to say whether its presence was benign or malign.

I suggested that we should stop for the day. Henrik nodded, too tired to speak. We worked together to erect the tent and inflate our air beds. We peeled off our wet, stinking clothes and crawled into our sleeping bags, still wearing our slightly less stinking, but still cold and damp, underwear. I kept on a layer of merino wool and polyamide; it helped, but I shivered for quite a while. The sleeping bag itself was far from dry; the wet had got in everywhere. The rain had won in the end.

Henrik fell asleep almost immediately, but I wasn't all that tired; it was warmth I wanted, not rest. Eventually I stopped shaking. I was still cold though; chills ran across my skin as I twisted and turned. They only stopped when I lay completely motionless. I reached down and took off my socks, squeezed one foot in the palm of my hand. Ice against ice. I pinched the pad below my big toe and didn't feel a thing. It was like pinching a piece of meat you've taken out of the freezer and left to defrost for a few hours.

I didn't get warm; I was just a tiny, tiny bit less cold. And I realized that all the warmth to which we had access inside Sarek was our own body heat, whatever we could generate by cooking and eating hot food, and that we would have to conserve that body heat as early man conserved the first fire in his cave. Nothing must go to waste.

What an inhospitable place this is.

We ate our supper inside the tent, propped up on our air beds. Afterward we made a quick dash outside to pee and brush our teeth. Dusk was falling and the world was losing its colors, everything was the same dark gray as the sky above us, and the rain continued to fall. The immense, rough rock face rose up a short distance away, unmoved by our presence. In fact it was neither benign nor malign. It simply didn't care. That was obvious, but it made me uncomfortable. Whether we lived or died at its feet like a pointless sacrifice made no difference whatsoever to the mountain. It had every intention of remaining here for a few million years more, silent and immutable.

I woke several times during the night with increasing frequency toward morning. The rain seemed to ease off, then come down harder, then ease off again. Henrik was snoring away beside me, which was a good thing; he needed an unbroken night's sleep more than I did. Every time I woke up, I was a little colder. The cold was like an army, retaking lost ground.

It was beginning to grow light. I checked the time: seven fifteen. I was too cold to go back to sleep, so I crept outside, taking care not to disturb Henrik. I stood up and stretched my stiff limbs. Yesterday's icy downpour had been replaced by a soft drizzle that almost felt agreeable in comparison. The sky was a paler shade of gray. The mountain was still there, and for the first time I could just make out its conical peak.

I retrieved my waterproofs and the pot and went down to the stream to fetch some water. I longed for the feeling of fullness, the warmth in my belly from a big portion of porridge. We had left the stove safe in the shelter of the awning; I brought it out and put it on the same spot where I had cooked our meal last night. I took the matches out of their protective plastic bag and turned the tap on the LPG cylinder.

I couldn't hear anything.

I turned the tap a little more. Why wasn't it hissing?

I turned the tap a little more. Still nothing.

The cylinder was empty.

I was on my knees under the awning, emptying my rucksack completely. Clothes, food, various bits and pieces—I piled them all on top of Henrik's rucksack and my boots and his boots, and when I ran out of space I placed them directly on the damp, muddy ground. I had to find what I was looking for.

The other LPG cylinder.

I was absolutely certain that we'd brought two from Stockholm.

I emptied the side pockets and the compartment right at the bottom, where I normally stowed only my sleeping bag and the rucksack's waterproof cover. I even opened the top compartment to check, although I knew perfectly well that the cylinder wouldn't fit in there.

Right. So it must have ended up in Henrik's rucksack.

I stuffed everything back in my rucksack any old how and attacked Henrik's with the same desperate energy. I heard sounds from inside the tent; not surprisingly, I'd woken him.

"What did you say?" he asked sleepily.

Only then did I realize that I'd been mumbling to myself, a long meandering harangue, *Shit* and *How can it possibly have?* and *Please, please, please* and *Where the fuck has it gone?*

"Er…nothing," I replied, trying to sound composed.

"Have you lost something?"

"Mm."

By now I had emptied the main compartment of Henrik's rucksack. No cylinder. He unzipped his sleeping bag, wriggled out. Muttered: "Jesus I'm cold…"

We crouched inside the tent, eating rye bread with shrimp-flavored cheese and drinking ice-cold water. We were out of the rain, which was something, but our teeth were chattering.

And this was how it was going to be until we found our way out of Sarek, or came across other walkers. No gas meant no hot food, no hot drinks, nothing to raise our body heat even temporarily, no defense whatsoever against the cold and the wet.

All we could hope for was a change in the weather, for the sun to return. That would help us during the daytime, but at night we would still shiver like stray dogs in our damp clothes and sleeping bags.

In my head I went through the food we had. Powdered soup, macaroni, freeze-dried meals. And the drinks: instant coffee, tea, packets of hot chocolate. Every single thing needed boiling water. Apart from that we could make sandwiches, plus we had sweets and seasonings like salami, parmesan and some dried mushrooms. How long would our supplies last?

"Here comes a man who was hungry and cold, but triumphed after all."

We would be hungry and cold, but we would triumph after all. Wouldn't we?

There it was, raising its ugly head again: panic. My mood took a dive, like a burning plane plummeting toward the ground in a death spiral.

No, no, no. You can't allow yourself to think like that. You will get out of this alive.

You will triumph after all. Pull yourself together.

We chomped on our rye bread and talked about the cylinders. Or rather: I talked about the cylinders and Henrik listened.

"I know we had two. I checked the one we had at home and it wasn't full, so I bought another at Naturkompaniet when I was there with Milena. To be on the safe side."

Henrik chewed mechanically, staring blankly into space. A shiver passed through his body, then he said: "Are you sure you packed both? Not just the new one?"

"I'm absolutely certain. I don't get it—could Milena and Jacob have taken one?"

"Possibly."

I realized now that that was exactly what could have happened. Jacob and I had prepared the meal together on the first evening, but who had provided the cylinder? I had, but I didn't recall getting it back from him.

Henrik could barely keep his voice steady when he went on: "I want to know…how bad it is."

"Well, it's not good."

"Okay, but how bad? Are we going to die?"

Are we going to die? How the fuck should I know? We're in the middle of the wilderness, the temperature could easily drop below freezing overnight and we can't cook anything or make a hot drink. Yes, we might die.

I looked him in the eye and said as resolutely as I could: "No. We are not going to die."

His eyes darted from side to side—I could see that he didn't trust me. "Henrik. Henrik, look at me. We are not going to die."

"No. Absolutely."

"We're going to be bloody cold, and we're going to be hungry, but we are not going to die."

"Sorry—it was a stupid question."

"No, it wasn't."

"Yes, it was—obviously you can't know for sure."

"I should think we'll reach the Rapa River today—and Rovdjurstorget, which is right in the middle of Sarek. And I would be very surprised if we don't bump into some other walkers there."

"Right."

"Plus that's where the emergency telephone is. And I'm sure it's inside some kind of hut, rather than being exposed to the elements."

"Mm."

"So we have a good chance of finding that little hut and the telephone. I suggest that we…make for the river, and if we see a building of any kind, we try to get there. And on the way I expect we'll meet other walkers. Does that sound like a plan?"

"Mm."

"As for the food…we've got plenty of crispbread and sweets and so on, easily enough for three or four days. And after that we can survive without food for another week. At least. So we are not going to die."

Henrik said nothing, refused to meet my gaze. We rolled up our sleeping bags and deflated our air beds, emptied the tent and took it down. Soon everything was packed away, and the only evidence of human activity was a rectangle of flattened grass where the tent had stood. Within a day or so that too would be obliterated.

I looked around. The massive rock face, silent and brooding as before. The valley, stretching far into the distance in both directions, leading to more peaks. And beyond those, yet more peaks.

Sarek was so terrifyingly vast, and so terrifyingly silent. And now we were about to head into the wilderness. Once again I felt slightly faint, and I set off so that Henrik wouldn't notice.

The rain was coming down harder now, just like yesterday. The terrain also gradually changed for the worse with more dense thickets of undergrowth to be negotiated. There were reindeer tracks, but they were crisscrossed by tough crooked branches that caught our feet and legs. I assumed that the undergrowth couldn't get a grip on the reindeer's slender ankles and hard hooves, while our bulky boots provided an easy target. Nature had developed a perfect method of making life difficult for those hiking in the mountains.

We stopped by a little stream to refill our water bottles, and to eat some nuts and raisins. The water felt like a bolt of ice as it flowed through our bodies, from our mouths and down into our throats, chilling the area behind our lungs before arriving in our bellies. We'd thought we were cold the previous day when we stopped, even though we'd been able to make a hot drink. However that had been like a gentle zephyr compared to today. After a couple of minutes our whole bodies were shaking uncontrollably. We could barely reach into the plastic bag to fish out a few more nuts and raisins.

"At least the fact that we're shivering means we're not suffering from hypothermia," I said. "When things get really bad, that reflex stops working." I spoke with extreme care; I was afraid that my chattering teeth would damage my tongue.

"Fucking hell," Henrik muttered.

"It's probably best if we stop as infrequently as possible, try to keep up a steady pace instead. Let's go."

A couple of hours passed, and I walked along, lost in my own thoughts. Suddenly I realized that Henrik had dropped a long way behind me. I waited for him, then we stopped for lunch on a low ridge. There was a flat grassy area, and I suggested putting up the tent so that we could shelter from the rain and wind for an hour or so after we'd eaten. Unfortunately Henrik couldn't help. Getting up onto the ridge seemed to have taken the last of his strength. He lay down on the ground, too exhausted to care about the damp and cold beneath him or the rain hammering on his face. I managed to erect the tent on my own and rolled out the groundsheet, but then I ran out of energy. I needed food.

I checked our store of bread. We had four double rye rolls left—eight sandwiches, plus half a packet of Wasa Sport crispbread. A half-full tube of shrimp-flavored cheese, and the same of smoked fish roe spread.

This would be our main diet from now on. Breakfast, lunch and dinner. If we ate until we were full at every meal, we would run out of food by lunchtime tomorrow. We were going to have to start rationing our intake immediately. We'd had rye rolls for breakfast, so now we had two pieces of crispbread each with spread. I had the idea that we could sprinkle powdered soup on top for extra nutrition, and Henrik didn't object when I tipped half a packet of minestrone over his lunch. We munched our fiber-rich meal in grim silence. The powdered soup meant that every mouthful swelled as we chewed.

Afterward we crawled into the tent and lay down. We had chased the hunger away, temporarily at least. The cold and the wet followed us inside. Henrik stared blankly at the roof of the tent; a violent shiver passed through his body at regular intervals. I moved closer to him, we held each other. I was shaking too, but not at the same time as him. Our bodies were singing the same song in a chilly rondo.

We set off again, accompanied by the cold. It never left our sides, but when we were on the move, it simply talked loudly. When we stopped, it bellowed right in our ears.

After our sparse lunch it wasn't long before the hunger came back. I began to feel hollow and weary, but I kept on picking my way through the undergrowth. One step at a time.

Slowly the landscape ahead of us began to change. The panorama widened, more and more peaks appeared. I realized that we were approaching the end of Sarvesvagge, which should have cheered me up—it meant that we would soon reach the Rapa Valley. But I was colder than I had ever been in my entire life, and I was hungry, and I was tired.

"Here comes a man who was hungry and cold, but triumphed after all."

Another fast-flowing stream joined Sarvesjåhkkå, and it took us just over an hour to get across. We rested on the other side, ate an energy bar and shared a packet of Tutti Frutti. I knew that we shouldn't have eaten so much. Rationing required discipline.

We stopped talking to each other. Staggered on toward the Rapa Valley, two zombies in activewear. I stopped at regular intervals to let Henrik catch up.

I felt as if my bones and joints had turned to ice. The permafrost had found its way deep inside my body. I knew I would never be warm again.

The undergrowth was replaced by dense thickets of birch taller than us. The landscape was hidden and I lost my bearings. There were tracks here too, but they meandered this way and that, and would suddenly disappear. In some places we simply had to force our way through, the branches tugging and tearing at our clothes.

Sarek doesn't want us to reach the Rapa Valley. Sarek wants us to die here.

But I didn't want to die. I battled on, and at some point I discovered that Henrik was no longer with me, but I didn't stop. I couldn't get trapped here. Couldn't let Sarek win.

What an inhospitable place this is.

I was lost in the birch thickets. Nothing but green and yellow leaves. No idea what the right direction might be. Weak. Alone. Afraid.

"Here comes a man who was hungry and cold, but triumphed after all."

I pressed on, caught a glimpse of a rock face through the foliage, kept going, the branches became less dense, and suddenly I was out. I tottered onto a patch of grass at the edge of the Rapa River. Dropped to my knees, shrugged off my rucksack. Rolled over onto my back.

Completely shattered. I had reached the Rapa Valley. Sarek's main artery.

I took some time to catch my breath, lying on my back with my eyes closed. The effort of fighting through the birch thickets had chased away the cold for a little while, and for the first time in many, many hours I wasn't shivering. I was warm—in fact my back was a little sweaty.

I sat up, took in the surrounding scenery. Everything we had seen of Sarek so far had been magnificent and awe-inspiring, but what I was looking at now was something else. Three huge valleys came together at this point, framed by high snow-clad mountains. Sarvesjåhkkå flowed into the wild, wide Rapa River, which formed a bewildering delta of streams and sandbanks. The sound of the rushing water was deafening. Wherever I looked, I saw more mountains, more valleys joining the Rapa Valley, glaciers and waterfalls, sheer rock faces, impenetrable undergrowth and birch thickets. Like an Arctic rainforest.

This must be Rovdjurstorget. I was in the heart of Sarek. And for a short while, a very short while, I was able to forget my situation and rejoice in the fact that I had made it, that I was experiencing this unique sight.

I had been afraid to venture deeper into the wilderness, the very thought had made me feel faint and dizzy, but here I was in the middle of Sarek. Whichever way I went, I would be moving closer to the edge, closer to civilization. I felt as if I had solid ground beneath my feet again.

I looked around, my gaze systematically following the river, close by at first, then farther and farther away along the valleys in all directions, up the mountains toward high plateaus and glaciers.

No sign of anything man-made. I assumed the hut housing the emergency telephone was somewhere nearby, but I couldn't see it from where I was. It must be hidden behind a protruding rock face or down among the vegetation by the river. Or else I was mistaken, and the telephone was nowhere near Rovdjurstorget.

Which way should we go? We. Henrik and I.

I was going to have to go back and search for him. Back into the birch thicket. A labyrinth the size of several football pitches.

There wasn't a soul in sight. There were no walkers in Rovdjurstorget or on the surrounding mountains today.

Before me the mighty Rapa River rushed toward lower

ground. I could see how many tributaries fed into it in the valley upstream. The influx must be huge after the rain and snow of the past few days.

How deep was it? Would we be able to cross it?

And which way should we go to find the shortest way out? Obviously we could follow the valley in either direction, but that probably wasn't the shortest route. And given the vegetation lining the banks, we wouldn't have the strength to get very far before we ran out of food. We would collapse, freezing and starving, exposed to the elements. We might not even survive one night if the temperature plummeted.

Maybe there was a shortcut out of Sarek across the mountains in front of me, but heading up there without a map would be madness. Henrik wouldn't even make it halfway up.

What if I can't find him?

I felt a stab of panic, not unlike the one I had felt during the snowstorm, but this time my body didn't respond. I remained as weak and cold and hungry as before. The panic tried to kickstart a moped with wet spark plugs and an empty tank. Of course nothing happened. I had no reserves left.

Laboriously I got to my feet; it was time to search for Henrik.

Suddenly I stopped dead. I had seen something odd out of the corner of my eye, partway up the mountain on the other side of the river. It looked like a bush, swaying wildly in the wind—but there was virtually no wind.

Where exactly was it? I scanned the mountainside. There.

A bright spring-green bush that stood out against the darker tones. It started waving its arms.

Interview with Anna Samuelsson 880216-3382, September 19, 2019, Gällivare hospital, conducted by Detective Inspector Anders Suhonen.

"And it was Milena?"

"Yes. Apparently she'd been standing there waving for ages, but I hadn't seen her."

"And Jacob… Was he…?"

"Jacob was there too."

"So contact was re-established."

"Yes."

"I imagine you must have been relieved."

"Yes, it felt as if… I almost burst into tears. I'd worked so hard to suppress the thought that we might die, that we might not make it. So when I realized it was Milena… I think I did cry, actually."

"Hardly surprising."

"The fact that Milena and I had quarreled, and that Jacob had come on to me—I just didn't care about any of that. I was just so pleased to see them."

"I can understand that. So what happened next?"

"Jacob came over to my side. Of the river. Then we went to look for Henrik."

"And how did it go?"

"We split the terrain between us so that we each had a patch of about a hundred meters, then we went back through the birch thicket, calling out his name. And after a while he answered."

"And had he… What had happened to Henrik?"

"He'd simply fallen behind. He was very, very tired, but it wasn't as if he was incapable of walking any farther. We headed back to the river together."

"Right."

"And of course that was the next problem—crossing the river. Apparently this ford is well known… What was it called…."

"Tielmavadet?"

"That's it. You go via an… There's an island in the middle of the river with some trees on it, so you go via that. You can also jump from one sandbank to the next, but it was still horrible. Really deep. Above my waist. And the current was very strong."

"Mm."

"I don't think it's something people would normally tackle—not after so much rain.

"But Henrik and I… We didn't have any choice. In that particular situation."

"No."

"We had to do what Jacob said."

"How did Henrik cope? It sounds as if he was pretty weak."

"He was. But he got across somehow."

"Okay."

"I didn't see… When I got to the other side I hugged Milena, and she hugged me, then I told her what had happened, so I didn't actually see how Henrik got across."

"Right."

"But now… When I think back… In the light of subsequent events… I think maybe Jacob didn't believe Henrik would make it. Maybe that was what he was hoping for."

"What makes you think that?"

"Jacob must have realized how dangerous it was for us—especially for Henrik, given how weak he was. It would have been better to continue along our side of the river."

"You mean for Milena to join the three of you?"

"Yes, but that was never in the cards. Jacob insisted that we had to cross that fast-flowing river. And of course he had a map and a compass and a stove, everything we needed to make it out of Sarek alive, so we had to do what he wanted."

"Okay, but when you say he hoped Henrik wouldn't make it…?"

"If Henrik got swept away and drowned, then Jacob would be shot of him."

"And why would he want that?"

"Because he'd have the chance to gain absolute power—over me and Milena, but above all over me."

"Go on."

"Jacob was some kind of psychopath. I don't know what the clinical definition of a psychopath is, but as far as I'm aware they're often quite intelligent, they know how to play the game socially, they're manipulative."

"Right."

"And incredibly narcissistic and easily offended. And of course I'd really offended Jacob when I rejected him."

"Mm."

"That was probably the worst thing you could do to him. So when we came back and needed his help, that gave him the perfect opportunity to take his revenge."

"I understand."

"I could see it in his face when he crossed the river—he felt absolutely triumphant, because we'd come crawling back."

"Surely there was bound to be an element of *I told you so*, wasn't there?"

"Exactly."

"But to go from that to wanting to kill someone is a bit of a leap, wouldn't you say?"

"For a normal person, yes. But..."

Silence.

"Listen, put yourself in Jacob's situation. He's maladjusted, finds it hard to fit in to normal society. No proper job, no family. Incredibly disturbed upbringing, if what he told me is true. He's always felt like an outsider, a failure. And now here he is in the wilderness, where suddenly...society no longer exists."

"No."

"There's no one to hear if you call for help. There's only the four of us, and it's the strongest person who counts. And Jacob is the strongest. All at once he's the one who sets the rules. He can rape, he can kill, he can do whatever he wants. For a few days."

"Right."

"He'd probably been fantasizing about this his whole life."

"Yes... But even if he killed all three of you, there was a considerable risk that someone would ask questions afterward."

"Absolutely."

"As I'm doing now. I'd say it was pretty much inevitable."

"He'd have to make sure he did it in the right way. Don't forget the margins are smaller in Sarek. You're at the mercy of nature, and there are plenty of ways to die that look natural. You can drown in a river, fall from a mountain, freeze to death..."

"Let me just check if I've understood you correctly, Anna. Are you saying that he'd planned this from the start?"

"No. But when Henrik and I came back, I think Jacob realized what position he was in. How much power he had over us. He had the chance to play God, and I can definitely imagine that he hoped Henrik would drown in the river."

"Mm."

"But Henrik made it, against all the odds."

"Did Jacob seem disappointed?"

"No, I wouldn't say that. He knew he'd have more opportunities. Maybe he even enjoyed making the process a little more long-drawn-out."

"Okay," Jacob said, slurping his coffee. "You need to get out of Sarek as quickly as possible, so we're going to alter the route."

It was the following morning. At the moment the rain had stopped completely, but the sky was still overcast and there was a chilly breeze. Jacob, Milena and I were sitting on rocks around the stove, finishing our breakfast. Henrik was still out for the count in the tent. Milena had lent him her dry sleeping bag in spite of our protests, and he had also borrowed a pair of thermals that were far too big from Jacob. It wasn't actually Jacob who'd handed them over, but Milena. I'm sure it wasn't his idea. He was generally taciturn and sour-faced.

The view was magnificent. We had made good progress up the mountain, and could see Sarvesjåhkkå flowing into the Rapa River about ten kilometers away, far below us. I had a good idea of where I had been standing the previous day when I caught sight of Milena on the other side of the river. Impressive mountains towered above us in all directions.

It had been hard going to reach this spot yesterday, but when Milena had tentatively suggested that we should stop and put up our tents, Jacob had resolutely shaken his head.

"It's the most beautiful place to camp in the whole of Sarek. That's where I'm going. The rest of you can please yourselves."

He stomped off, and we stomped after him.

I was in pretty good shape, to be honest. Milena had heated some soup for me and Henrik when we got across the river, which improved both our body temperatures and our moods. We still shivered if we were standing still, but the soup thawed us out from the inside. The relief at being rescued—because that's how it felt—also gave us a burst of energy.

Milena explained that she and Jacob had stopped for a day to climb Nåite, a mountain in Sarvesvagge. From her description I realized that we had camped at the foot of that very mountain. The previous day Jacob had had to spend a lot of time finding a place where it was possible to wade across the Rapa River.

"He was already pretty annoyed when I saw you," Milena confided quietly when we'd set off again. "Because we were behind schedule. That's why he's a bit… Well, you know."

Jacob was walking on his own, a considerable distance ahead of the rest of us. "Of course, it's fine," I replied.

Henrik had already fallen behind me and Milena, in spite of the fact that I'd promised myself that I would stay at the back. I had lost concentration when I was talking to Milena, and in no time at all we were twenty meters ahead of him. We stopped and waited. Henrik was staring at the ground with dead eyes, and simply staggered past us as if he hadn't even noticed we were there. Milena glanced anxiously at me. I met her gaze, but didn't say anything. I started walking and gently placed a hand on Henrik's shoulder.

"We'll take another break soon." No response.

Twilight began to fall before we reached the campsite, making our way up from the river to the small plateau with the amazing view. Milena and I had transferred some of the contents of Henrik's rucksack to our own in order to make it lighter, but he was still on the point of collapse. We had to keep stopping. Milena shouted to Jacob, asked him to wait for us.

"What?" he yelled back from several hundred meters higher up the mountain.

Milena shouted again, louder this time:

"I think we ought to camp for the night!"

"Here? How the fuck do we do that?"

Jacob turned and continued on his way. He was absolutely right—it was impossible to put up a tent here; it was much too steep.

I suggested we should take a final break, make some hot fruit soup before we tackled the final section. It couldn't be far now; we wouldn't be able to walk in complete darkness. However as I spoke, I realized that Jacob had the gas cylinder.

"It would be good if we had a gas cylinder," I said. "This way we can stop and have something hot whenever we need it." Milena nodded and muttered something vague.

We had a drink of water, ate some nuts and continued to plod over patches of grass, scree and low-growing scrub. For a while I put my hand on Henrik's rucksack and helped to push him along. Suddenly he swung around, his eyes like two dried-up wells.

"Don't," he said in that flat, toneless voice, then he turned and kept on walking.

Before long we heard Jacob calling out from the semidarkness above us, and as the last of the evening light died away we put up our tents and crashed into a dreamless sleep.

So here we were the next morning, sipping coffee around the stove. Jacob took a deep breath, ready to explain the new route. He was right—we needed to get out of Sarek as quickly as possible. The question was which would be the best option, given how exhausted Henrik was.

"We go over this mountain," Jacob began, pointing over his shoulder. "Over Skårki, down into Bastavagge, then out to Suorva."

I looked up. Above the plateau the terrain quickly became

steeper again. Grass and bushes gave way to stony ground, rocks and patches of snow. Then there was a ridge, and beyond that what I assumed was Skårki—jagged, snow-clad peaks that disappeared into the clouds.

I shook my head.

"Henrik isn't capable of going over any mountains."

The tent was only a few meters away, and I kept my voice down so as not to wake Henrik. He needed all the sleep he could get.

Jacob didn't say anything at first. He stared down into his cup, and his frozen expression told me everything I needed to know. It was as if I could read his thoughts, word for word.

This is your fucking fault. You had to go off on your own, but you couldn't make it.

And you're still making trouble. You worthless fucking cunt.

After a long pause, he went on: "We'll save at least a day by taking that route."

"But that involves climbing," I said, nodding in the direction of the peaks. "It's not… No."

"It's not climbing. I've done it several times. It's not difficult."

"I'm sorry, but Henrik is too weak." I looked at Milena. "You've seen him—do you think he's capable of getting over a mountain?"

She hesitated, then Jacob raised his head and fixed his eyes on her. "I…" she began, then fell silent.

"Milena? Seriously?" I stared at her, and Jacob broke in.

"We climbed four hundred meters yesterday evening. He managed that, even though the two of you had already walked a fair distance."

I turned my attention to him.

"But if we're going over a mountain, that has to be an altitude of a lot more than four hundred meters, right?"

"We do as I say," Jacob snapped. There was anger in his eyes, and agitation; I caught a glimpse of that damaged child again.

His desire for me had metamorphosed into its opposite. It was the same energy, but a negative instead of a positive. Or maybe the desire was still there, alongside the anger and contempt. Whatever—he seemed alarmingly close to exploding again, as he had done during the game of MIG.

I responded in my calmest tone of voice: "Okay. Just because I'm curious—what route had you originally planned?"

"That's irrelevant."

"I realize that, but...what were you thinking?" Jacob didn't answer.

"We were going to carry on into the Rapa Valley, down to... What was the name of the place?" Milena said.

"Aktse," Jacob spat out eventually.

"Can I have a look at the map?" I asked sweetly. I felt like a submissive sixteen-year-old.

"It's thirty kilometers from Aktse out to Salto," Jacob said. "At least another day."

"Okay, but can you show me on the map what you're planning to do instead?" Slowly and reluctantly he produced the map and spread it out.

"We're here. That river there is Alep Vassjajågåsj. So we go up here, over the ridge...and down into Bastavagge. Then out here, to Suorva."

The route Jacob traced with his finger certainly looked like the shortest way to Suorva; it was almost as the crow flies. But it meant that we would have to pass through Skårki, a massif with peaks of over eighteen hundred meters, crisscross between glaciers and follow a ridge that looked as if it had a sheer drop on both sides.

This was a significantly tougher challenge than anything he had outlined when we were sitting in the restaurant car on the train. And he wanted us to tackle it now, when Henrik was already in a very bad way.

And why was Jacob suddenly so willing to change the route

for our sake? He was angry because we'd turned around, come back and caused more problems for him and Milena. He knew that we were entirely dependent on him and his goodwill, and yet he was prepared to alter his plans, *because it was the best thing for us.*

Something didn't fit here. Something was definitely wrong. I stared at the map, my mind racing.

Cautiously, tentatively, I said: "I'm just thinking… There's a cabin in Aktse. And an emergency telephone, according to the map."

"That's not true anymore, it's been removed," Jacob snapped, glaring at me. Every objection had to be stamped out immediately, like glowing flakes of ash in dry grass. "There is one, but it's by Skarja."

"Well, we can still make our way there so that we have a roof over our heads. And contact Mountain Rescue."

Jacob looked surprised, then his face broke into a big smile, as if he could hardly believe his ears. He hadn't realized quite how stupid I was. He turned to Milena.

"Who is this woman? Where does she get all this crap from?"

I'm not particularly interested in football, but some of my colleagues once dragged me along to a sports bar after work. It was a Saturday night toward the end of May, the Champions League Final. Ronaldo was playing, and every time a decision went against him, he gave a big smile and shook his head, as if to say *this is so ridiculous, you just have have to laugh.*

Jacob was demonstrating that exact same smile now. It looked theatrical and totally false, master suppression technique at a rudimentary but effective level. He turned back to me.

"Sweetheart, Mountain Rescue won't come and pick someone up just because they're a little bit tired."

Keep calm, Anna. Don't walk into his trap.

"Henrik isn't a little bit tired, he's exhausted."

"There's absolutely no chance that they'll come out if we've got a roof over our heads in Aktse."

"Okay, then maybe we can book a helicopter. We'll pay."

"No."

"Why not?"

"Because they're fully occupied herding reindeer."

"But we flew to Staloluokta in a helicopter the other day."

"Yes, because I'd booked in advance."

"So you're seriously telling me that if I phone up and say *I'll pay you ten thousand kronor if you come and pick us up in Aktse*, they won't do it?"

"How are you going to phone them?"

"How am I going to phone them?"

"Yes."

"Well… You've got a—"

Jacob didn't let me finish. "It's a tracker. I've told you a thousand times, it's not an emergency phone. You can't use it to make calls!"

"But surely you can send a mess—"

He interrupted again, raised his voice, his eyes wide and staring.

"It's not going to happen! What the fuck is it you don't understand? I'm the one who makes the rules!"

And there it was, the line. I had pushed Jacob until he ran out of his nonsensical objections, forced him to show his hand. This wasn't about what was best for me and Henrik—this was about power.

Maybe there was no point in arguing with him, but at least I had shown Milena what a house of cards Jacob's reasoning was. I had a feeling that it might be important to get her on my side.

My heart was pounding; I felt Jacob's aggression like hot breath on my skin. The latent violence was like a strong headwind, determined to make me change direction. He could easily raise his fist, in a second I could be sitting here with a split lip or a broken nose. It went against the grain to keep going, but I had no intention of giving in. I tried to speak calmly.

"Can I take a picture of the map?"

"Why would you want to take a picture of the map?"

"Because I think it's good to have a backup. This is the only map we've got."

"But this is my map. It's not going to disappear."

"Why?" I asked, meeting his wild eyes. "Why is it a problem if I take a picture of the map?"

I glanced at Milena, who was watching Jacob somewhat warily. I don't think she realized to what extent this discussion was actually about her. It was like a court case where Milena was the judge whom both sides were trying to influence. As long as Jacob had her support, he could exercise his power through her. It was easier for him—he didn't have to use threats or violence in order to get his own way.

He stared back at me for a long time, then eventually said: "It's not a problem. Did I say it was a problem?"

"No, that's great." I held out my hand for the map.

"I didn't say you could have the map, I said you could take a picture of it."

"So I can't carry it over to the tent, three meters away, and take a picture?"

"No, you can't."

I smiled and tried to catch Milena's eye, but she was focused on the map. "Because…?"

"You've already been careless enough to lose one map."

"It's probably best if you photograph it here," Milena said quietly. "I can hold it still for you." She wouldn't look at me.

Was she on my side, or Jacob's? She was certainly supporting his refusal to lend me the map, even for one minute. On the other hand maybe she just wanted to make sure I got a good picture.

And maybe she also realized instinctively that our lives might depend on the existence of a copy of the map.

So I went over to the tent and rummaged in my rucksack for my phone. Henrik was waking up, stretching and yawning. I could hear the rustle of the nylon sleeping bag as he turned over. I opened the zip and peeped in. He peered at me with tired, swollen eyes.

"Hi—did you sleep well?"

He nodded. "I feel a bit better," he said and yawned again.

"There's breakfast out here—porridge."

"What's going on with the map? What are you all talking about?"

"I'm just going to take a photo." I removed my phone from its waterproof bag, switched it on, saw the display light up.

Jacob kept a firm hold on the map with both hands while I took the photographs. Milena helped by keeping the corners flat, in spite of the gusts of wind.

"Thanks," I said when I had pictures of both sides. Jacob glowered silently at me as he folded up the map and tucked it in his breast pocket. Contempt. Suspicion.

"Is Henrik getting up?" Milena asked.

"He's on his way."

"Maybe we should reheat the water," she said, lifting the lid of the coffeepot. A few curls of steam found their way over the edge.

Jacob wasn't having that. "It'll do. We can't afford to waste gas."

I took a deep breath, steeled myself. Might as well get this out of the way. "Actually, we need to talk about the gas."

Both Jacob and Milena were looking at me now, Jacob with open hostility, Milena with a certain wariness. They waited for me to go on.

"The thing is… Henrik can't possibly get over the mountain, so we'll be going off on our own. Again."

"But..." Milena began, then sighed deeply.

"I know, maybe it sounds strange, and it's not necessarily what I'd choose to do. However this—" I gestured toward the peaks towering over us "—just isn't an option. Not for someone in his condition. Sorry—it's out of the question."

Jacob's eyes were fixed on the ground between his feet, elbows resting on his knees, one hand clenched into a fist, the other frantically rubbing the back of the fist with his fingertips. The anger gave him an energy that had to find an outlet. His whole body looked tense, as if he were crouching ready to pounce.

"So there's the business of the gas cylinders," I went on.

My breathing was a little irregular, knowing that what I was about to say would go down badly, although I didn't know how badly. The pressure in my chest, the words stuck in my throat.

Come on, for fuck's sake. You're not thirteen anymore.

"We brought two cylinders with us, but when Henrik and I were on our own, I could only find one. And it ran out. Which means you two must have taken the other cylinder."

Jacob stared at me. "Are you out of your fucking mind?"

"Jacob..." Milena ventured.

Keep calm. Breathe. Steady voice.

"This is what I think must have happened. On the first evening we cooked using my cylinder, and then I think you must have—" I didn't get to the end of the sentence.

Jacob leaped to his feet, he threw his cup to the ground; his entire body seemed to be involved in the movement. The cup hit a rock with full force, ricocheted into the air and landed five meters away.

"Seriously! Are you OUT OF YOUR FUCKING MIND?"

He was shouting at the top of his voice. He took a couple of steps toward me, looming over me like the mountains behind me, almost two meters of pulsating blood and adrenaline and muscle that wanted to fight, to crush.

And I was terrified.

It was a purely instinctive reaction. I fell silent, I cowered from the expected blow, trembling like a little rabbit.

Milena was on her feet too, tugging at Jacob's arm. "Jacob," she pleaded. "Jacob, calm down…"

"What the fuck—she's saying I've stolen her fucking gas cylinder!"

"No, I didn't mean—"

"Absolute fucking bullshit! I brought three cylinders with me, and I've still got them!"

"That's actually true, Anna," Milena added quickly. "We brought three cylinders. We haven't taken any of yours."

"Absolute fucking bullshit," Jacob repeated. He was too agitated to stand still; he was moving his feet up and down on the spot. "Absolute fucking bullshit."

Zziiiip. Henrik emerged from the tent on all fours. He looked uneasily from Jacob to me, to Milena. "What's going on?"

"Ask your fucking girlfriend!" Jacob's voice was rough, trembling with rage.

"We're talking about the gas cylinder," I said.

"But before that—something about going over the mountain?"

"Yes—Jacob wants to change the route."

"For your sake!" Jacob spat. "For your fucking sake!" Milena stroked his arm but didn't speak.

"I can take a different route if necessary," Henrik said. "I think we should stick together from now on."

Jesus, Henrik—you have no idea what you're getting into. Just shut up.

His words knocked my legs from under me. Was he giving in to Jacob without a fight as well? Was I going to have to conduct this battle all alone?

"Henrik," I began, as calmly as I could manage. "Going over the mountain isn't a good idea."

"It's the quickest way out of Sarek," Jacob said. He spoke rapidly, firing off the words in a staccato pattern. "And the two of you need to get out of here as soon as possible." He glared at me. "Including you—you're losing your fucking mind."

"Why is going over the mountain not a good idea?" Henrik asked me.

"Because it's too difficult. For you."

He remained silent for a moment. "I feel better today."

"Really, Henrik, it's—"

"I do. I've slept well, and I—"

"We're talking about an altitude of twelve hundred meters, Henrik. Yesterday you were so tired you could hardly speak."

"We didn't have any hot food. Until the evening."

"We'd be walking along a ridge with a sheer drop on both sides, crossing a glacier... You do remember what happened the other day? When we were about to set off across the snowfield?"

I stared at him, and eventually he answered quietly: "That was a unique set of circumstances."

I explained to the others: "He had a panic attack. We had to turn back. That's why we're here."

The expression on Henrik's face was painful to see. He looked tired and resigned, but above all hurt because I was obviously blaming him for the situation in which we now found ourselves. Hurt, not because I was lying but because I was telling the truth.

I felt disloyal, hanging him out to dry in front of Jacob and Milena, but I had to try and make him understand why we couldn't take the route across the mountains.

After a moment he shook his head and said to the others: "I still think we should stick together."

Is that how it's going to be from now on, Henrik? You're siding with Jacob instead of with me? Okay, at least I know. Let's do that.

Jacob had calmed down. The unexpected support from Henrik had cooled his anger, enabling him to regain his equilibrium.

"You two must do exactly as you wish, of course," he said in quite a pleasant tone. "But the gas cylinders stay with me. And we're leaving in thirty minutes."

I am walking uphill at a steady pace, focusing on not going fast enough to catch up with the others, letting my whole body help out with deliberate and well-chosen arm movements. It involves only moderate exertion; I can keep going like this forever. My body has work to do, and it feels good.

The clouds are breaking up above us, occasionally letting the sun shine through. There is a breeze and the air is fresh.

The vegetation is becoming increasingly sparse. It is a while since I saw the dew sparkling on the last patch of grass. We are now walking on scree dotted with green, russet and brown lichen. The odd burst of orange here and there. The few flowers that can survive at this altitude are as low growing as moss.

Jacob is leading the way, but he is taking care to set a pace that means we all stay together. Milena and Henrik are on his side at the moment, and naturally he doesn't want to give me the opportunity to speak to either of them in private. I am bringing up the rear, keeping my distance.

Yes, I'm furious.

Our only chance—mine, Henrik's and Milena's—to stand up

to Jacob is to stick together, to form a unit. But when it came to the crunch, they gave way.

That's how violence works as an instrument of power. It doesn't even need to happen—the threat is enough to influence people's behavior. Jacob becomes aggressive, and both Milena and Henrik immediately take on the responsibility of calming things down by doing what he wants.

Milena's attitude hurts me, but it doesn't surprise me. Ever since we met at the station in Stockholm Jacob's power over her has been clear to me. She has made his view of her into her own self-image.

Henrik's weakness is even more painful.

He was trapped in a snowstorm, and I went and found him, putting my own life at risk. He was incapable of going over the mountain toward Staloluokta, and I turned back with him because I knew it was my responsibility to make sure he got out of Sarek alive. I let him rest and I prepared food for us, even though I was bone-weary. I made sure we caught up with Milena and Jacob so that he could have hot food and sleep in dry clothes in a dry sleeping bag.

I saved Henrik's life, for fuck's sake.

But as soon as things get a little tricky, as soon as Jacob bares his predator's teeth, none of that counts. There is no loyalty, no trust in my judgment—all that matters is to placate Jacob.

Which is very shortsighted. Okay, so Jacob calmed down, he didn't push anyone over, he didn't punch anyone on the nose. The strategy worked. On the other hand we are now heading up into an environment where the margins are even smaller, where the difference between life and death can be a careless step on an unstable stone, a second when you lose your balance, then it's all over.

And our guide on this expedition is a person with clear psychopathic tendencies.

Who clearly enjoys having us in his power.

So therefore I am focusing only on myself now. I am not responsible for anyone else.

I am walking uphill at a steady pace, letting my whole body help out, with deliberate and well-chosen arm movements. My body has work to do, and it feels good.

After a few hours Jacob stops and shrugs off his rucksack. It is time for a snack, and he takes out the stove to heat some water. The rest of us dig out instant coffee, bread and spreads, and sit down on the ground. Henrik asks me how I'm feeling.

"I'm absolutely fine," I answer a little snippily.

Don't you worry about me.

He is out of breath and takes several gulps of water. "Me too. Better than yesterday."

I realize that, like me, he is still smarting from this morning's unpleasantness. Fine, so be it. I am not going to make the first move to reconciliation.

I turn around and gaze out over the valley. The terrain has flattened out recently, and beyond the ridge a few hundred meters below I can see nothing of the mountainside we have just walked up, only the massif on the other side of the Rapa Valley, many kilometers away.

The sky is more blue than gray now. The sun actually provides a little warmth, even though we are so high up.

There is no vegetation here, just scree and gravel as far as the eye can see with snow-covered areas farther up the slopes and a glacier protruding between the mountains to the northwest. Directly in front of me, and a considerable distance on either side, a very steep rock face bars the way. I'd estimate that it's a three to four hundred meter almost perpendicular climb to the ridge at the top. We can't get up there, so how is Jacob planning for us to continue? I take out my phone and look at the picture of the map. As I recall, he drew a virtually straight line from our campsite to Suorva in the north. The only possibility I can see is that we follow the foot of the mountain to the west, then turn north along a ridge that runs just this side of the glacier known as Alep Vassjajiegna. That would also involve a steep climb, but slightly less daunting.

Then the real problems begin.

If we go around the edge of the glacier and pass a peak with an altitude of about eighteen hundred meters, we will have climbed about seven hundred meters since this morning. Will Henrik be able to manage that? Or will he collapse, incapable of taking one more step? From there a sharp ridge runs to the north with a sheer drop on either side—a free fall of hundreds of meters on the right and on the left.

How tall is the Kaknäs Tower? About a hundred and fifty meters, maybe? Imagine placing two Kaknäs Towers one on top of the other. And then you fall from the very top.

How wide is the ridge? As far as I'm concerned, that's the critical issue. Five meters—no problem. The drop isn't constantly in your eyeline, and if you happen to stumble, it's not dangerous.

One meter or less—hm. Even I would feel the pull of the drop, and I'm not really afraid of heights.

It's not hard to walk along a meter-wide track in the mountains. You do it automatically without thinking about how you're doing it. But every day, once or twice, you will catch your foot on a stone that's sticking up from the ground, you trip and have to take a couple of steps to the side to regain your balance, or perhaps you actually fall and use your hands to save yourself.

Twenty thousand steps in a day; you misjudge two or three of them and stumble. If you're walking along a ridge that is a meter wide, you're going to have a problem. If it's half a meter wide, you're going to die.

So now you start thinking about every step you take, and suddenly it's not so straightforward, the thing that you are used to doing automatically becomes much more difficult when you try to focus on it. How do you actually raise your foot, how do you set it down? Your heart beats faster, your muscles feel soft and weak, your knees are like spaghetti. You feel the pull of the precipice, like when you're standing on a platform and the train comes hurtling along and you have to fight against the impulse to throw yourself in front of it, that same feeling but much, much stronger.

The precipice is tempting you, wanting you to have the courage to jump. And in order to resist you have to stand still. Not move a single centimeter. You are paralyzed.

I've been there. I've felt it. The fear of heights is irrational, and it is impossible to defend yourself against it when it sinks its claws into you.

What you do next is vitally important. You need to control your breathing. Look at yourself from a distance. Think that you are experiencing a feeling. Think that you are thinking that you are experiencing a feeling. Let the wave wash over you, and ebb away. Then you begin to walk again. One step at a time.

In my case the fear has always let go comparatively quickly. Henrik, on the other hand… I remember one occasion in the Sylan mountains in Norway when we were standing at the bottom of the steepest section. Just looking up at the rock face in front of us made him feel sick and dizzy, and he had to go back to the mountain station.

What is before us is on the same level. At least.

I don't think Henrik has realized that. But he soon will.

We follow the rock face in a westerly direction, along a stretch of slightly flatter terrain. The ground is strewn with substantial rocks; at some point there has been a landslip. Impossible to say when—a million years ago? A thousand years ago? Last Tuesday? Some of them are remarkably symmetrical, meter-long rectangles with smooth sides.

It is very difficult terrain; you constantly lose and gain height. Most of the rocks are at an angle and you hardly ever put your foot on a flat surface, your ankles twist this way and that. Some of the rocks tip as soon as you stand on them. This is a hike that requires total concentration.

And I love it.

It's as if we are on another planet, in a dead, sterile world. If a little space rover equipped with cameras and thick rubber tires came trundling along, I wouldn't be surprised. There is nothing here but rocks and mountains and ice beneath a clear blue sky. The climb ahead of us gives me a tingle of anticipation, a challenge that will demand mental acuity and focus. And the view from the ridge must be fantastic on a day like this. We really are lucky with the weather.

As we draw closer to the glacier, the slope becomes significantly steeper. Henrik is a few meters in front of me, and I can see from his posture that he finds it unpleasant. His body is leaning into the mountain, and he is using one hand for support with every step. And he is tense, which increases the physical pressure. We have walked for almost an hour in this terrain, and it has taken its toll. When he pauses with one boot on a sharp edge, his heel begins to jiggle uncontrollably up and down, his calf muscle can't keep his foot still. He reaches out with both hands and falls onto a rock. He takes a deep breath, exhales slowly. He is red-faced and dripping with sweat as he struggles to take off his rucksack.

"This is no fucking fun," he mumbles, taking out his water bottle.

"It's not far to the glacier now," I reassure him. "Then we won't have to walk on scree. It's better to be heading upward."

I look at Jacob and Milena, who continued to scramble over the rocks. Jacob has already reached the edge of the glacier. He stretches his back, drinks some water. Milena isn't far behind.

I remain standing next to Henrik; it's too much effort to sit down and take off my rucksack. He has a drink and stares gloomily out across Sarek, magnificent and terrifying, beautiful and ice-cold and as hard as stone.

We don't say anything else. I wait until he is ready, and after ten minutes he puts away his water bottle and prepares to go on. I suggest that I should go first, pick out a route over the rocks. He nods and accepts; he seems grateful.

I know. I am not responsible for Henrik. But my bad mood after the confrontation with Jacob has dissipated, without my noticing how it happened. The few days I have spent in Sarek have taught me that a person's mood changes as quickly as the weather. All emotions are on the surface, all the time. From the deepest misery to euphoria in half an hour. I assume it's because of the mental and physical exertion; it strips away self-control as efficiently as a plane strips away a coat of old veneer.

We soon join Jacob and Milena by the glacier, where Milena is preparing lunch. I immediately start helping her. Henrik catches his breath for a few minutes, then he helps too. Jacob, on the other hand, makes a point of sitting alone a short distance away, resting with his face turned up to the sun. None of us would dream of asking him to lend a hand.

Aggression, physical or verbal, makes people walk on eggshells, makes them close in on themselves in order to avoid exposure. I know this very well from my own family.

We have lunch, and Milena and I chat about all kinds of things. Like me, she seems to be in a good mood, while Jacob keeps his distance, taciturn and grim. Henrik also has nothing to say. He looks uncomfortable, puts out one hand to keep his balance as soon as he takes a few steps, even though the spot we are in now isn't steep.

The passage over the rocks seems to have given him a real fright.

We set off again in the same order as before: Jacob, Milena, Henrik, me. Jacob sets a rapid pace, while the rest of us pause frequently to breathe and lower our pulse rate. The sun shines down from a cloudless sky, and we are sweating as we walk. Every time I turn around and look down, I am delighted at how far up the mountain we have come. We might be halfway to the top by now.

Jacob is like a mountain goat, skipping along well ahead of the rest of us. And yes, I would love to be moving at the same speed.

The climb is really taking its toll on Milena and Henrik. They are red-faced and breathless, and we have to stop for longer each time in order to bring their pulse rates down to normal levels. Milena has a drink of water and gasps:

"It feels as if there's no end to this slope!"

Henrik nods in agreement, puffing and blowing, incapable of saying anything.

"I hate the fact that there's no end in sight," she goes on. "You think *that must be the peak*, but it never is."

"Four hundred meters is quite a height," I say. "But we're more than halfway."

"Hallelujah," Milena mumbles.

"Shall we make a move?" I suggest.

"I need to rest for a bit longer," Henrik says. "Just a little while."

His gaze is fixed on the mountainside the whole time, at eye level. He never looks up toward the peak or down toward the valley. Milena is clearly concerned.

"How are you feeling, Henrik? Is the height bothering you?"

"A bit."

She touches his arm, an expression of empathy. Henrik sets off when he is ready with Milena behind and me bringing up the rear as usual.

Milena has come between us, but that doesn't bother me.

The terrain levels out as the ridge narrows; on our right the drop is almost sheer. And at last we can see the peak. Because surely that must be the peak? There is a small plateau about a hundred meters ahead of us, and beyond it we can see only blue sky.

The problem is that before we reach the plateau, the ridge tapers even more, and the last section will involve a steep scramble over scree.

Jacob is already there. He reminds me of Spider-Man, or someone climbing the stairs to the Fun House at the Gröna Lund amusement park who doesn't quite know what to do. One long leg outstretched, the other folded against the chest, hands wide apart. Step by step he heaves himself up the slope.

We all stop to watch.

He moves his foot one last time, then hauls himself onto the plateau on all fours. He immediately stands up and turns to face us, raises his hands in the air and yells:

"WOOO-HOOO! AAOOOOUU!"

He howls like a wolf. Someone is in a better mood now. And someone is not.

Henrik looks up at the plateau and swallows hard.

Henrik, Milena and I stand in silence beside one another on this glorious autumn day in Sarek's barren lunar landscape, watching Jacob perform his dance of victory on the plateau. Henrik looks thoughtful, takes a few gulps of his water.

"So we're going up there?" he says eventually. His gaze follows the ridge we are on all the way to the plateau, sees that it becomes a sharp edge. There's really no other way of describing it. On one side is a sheer drop to the glacier; if you slip there, you might not die, but you can look forward to a helter-skelter of a kilometer or so. If you hit an ice crack or a protruding rock when you have picked up speed, you're done for.

The drop on the other side is very steep, maybe not free-fall-for-hundreds-of-meters-instant-death steep, but steeper than anything we have encountered so far.

"Maybe it looks worse from here than it actually is," Milena says.

Henrik doesn't answer. He is frozen to the spot, seems unable to move forward. "Okay, let's go," I say.

Milena sets off, but Henrik still doesn't move. I wait for a moment. Nothing happens.

"We'll go and take a look. One step at a time." I follow Milena, but I can't hear any footsteps behind me.

Enough. I stop, turn around.

"Henrik, come on! We can't stay here."

My tone is a little harsher than I'd intended, a little sharper, but it has the desired effect. At last Henrik begins to move.

"You go ahead," I say.

He passes me, and I follow on behind.

You wanted to take the route Jacob had chosen. Even though I warned you. So take it.

In minutes we reach the steep section where the ridge has narrowed and become a sharp edge, much too dangerous to walk on. The best option is to go down a few meters and lean in toward the mountain.

Milena waits for us, and she was right—it's not quite as bad as it looked from a distance. Okay, so it is steep, and I feel the pull of the drop to our right, but it doesn't involve actual climbing, which was the impression Jacob gave when we watched him go up. We need to lean into the rock face and hold on with both hands, but to be honest it doesn't seem that difficult.

Jacob calls out to us, tells us which is the easiest route up onto the plateau. Milena goes first—cautiously, step by step, making sure to move only one foot or one hand at a time, always three points of support against the rock face.

Henrik sinks down onto a rock where he is standing, but he is facing outward with the drop right in front of him. He squeezes his eyes tight shut; he daren't look. Clings on with both hands even though he's sitting down. His body is tense and he is breathing in short intense gasps.

The fear of heights has him in its grip.

I place a hand on his shoulder, speak softly and kindly, I know that it's up to me whether he is going to manage this. "Henrik, listen to me. First of all, you need to breathe from your stomach. Can you hear me?"

He nods, eyes still tight shut.

"Take a deep breath, feel the air go all the way down into your stomach." He tries, does the best he can.

"And again. Close your mouth and breathe through your nose. A long deep breath. Down into your stomach. There's no hurry, just take it easy. We can sit here for an hour if necessary."

He inhales through his nose, fills his lungs, and I put my hand on his stomach. "Breathe out, calmly and deliberately, then take another breath. You need to feel it down here."

He does as I say, and this time I feel his stomach expand a little when he inhales. "Good. Again."

I am standing very close to Henrik, bent over him, one arm around his shoulders and one hand on his stomach. He inhales again.

"You don't need to worry about holding your stomach in. I know you've got a bit of a beer belly, but I love you anyway."

He smiles and covers my hand with his. I run the fingers of my other hand through his hair, feel the curve of his skull.

And at last he relaxes. The tension eases in his neck and shoulders. He takes another deep breath, and this time his whole body is involved. His muscles are no longer rigid, fighting against him; this time they let the air through, and it seems to flow all the way down to his toes.

He makes a strangled sound, and I realize that he is crying.

I shouldn't be surprised. This is Sarek. All emotions on the surface. All the time. I hold him, kiss him gently on the cheek. "Sweetheart? What's wrong?"

Another deep breath. He snuffles, wipes one nostril with his thumb. "Nothing. I just… I don't know."

"Maybe it's the thin air."

"I'm sorry I lost the map."

"Forget it."

I give him a hug and he hugs me back. Puts his arms around my waist and pulls me close. We stay like that for a while as his breathing returns to normal.

I glance up at the plateau. Milena has made it, and is looking down at us. Jacob is pacing restlessly back and forth, his frustration at the fact that we are stuck again is very clear.

My intention is to let Henrik take all the time he needs, but I can't do it. In the end I say, as warmly as I can, "Shall we give it a go?"

"Mm." One more deep breath, then he straightens his shoulders and nods resolutely. "Let's do it."

"Don't look down. Look at the rock face. Focus on each step. Don't think about anything else. Make sure you move only one hand, or one foot, at a time. Always three points of support."

Henrik nods again, then he stands up and turns away from the drop. He holds on with both hands, moves his right foot. Then his right hand. Then his left hand. Shifts his center of gravity. Left foot. Calmly and methodically.

I can see that he's feeling much better now. His body is no longer rigid. He is using his hands for support rather than clinging on for dear life as he was doing before.

We scramble up toward the plateau, executing something between a hike and a climb. The angle is more or less like that of a ladder propped up close to the wall of a house. I can't resist the temptation to look down. I want to test my resistance. The rough rock face is a concave bowl that changes into a more level block terrain far below. Would I survive a fall? Maybe. With a bit of luck. It's not inevitable that I would tumble all the way to the bottom; it's not that steep.

Henrik is approaching the edge. Milena is shouting encouragement. She holds out her hand to help him up the last part, but he doesn't take it. He has found a way of making progress that works for him, and he has no intention of trying anything else at this point. He isn't going to take any risks.

His upper body is on the plateau now, he pushes off with his right leg, and he's there. Milena claps her hands.

"Well done, Henrik!"

I am right behind him. He crawls a short distance on all fours, away from the edge, then he rolls over onto his back. Lets out a long deep breath. Milena bends down and gives him a hug.

"Well done!"

"This feels so good. Oh, my God..."

Jacob is staring at them with his arms folded; I don't like the look on his face, but he doesn't say anything.

I heave myself up onto the plateau and stand up. We have seen incredible views over and over again during our time in Sarek, but this takes my breath away.

Suddenly I can see to the north and the west majestic snow-clad massifs in all directions.

We learned in school that the Swedish mountains were eroded by inland ice recession, which is why they are not so high—stubby hills in comparison with the Alps. However the inland ice seems to have forgotten Sarek. When I look around, it seems to me that I could be in the Himalayas. Black jagged ridges are highlighted against the intensely blue sky. Far below the Rapa Valley's impressive delta sparkles in the autumn sunshine. A gigantic rock stands guard along where the river divides; I bring up the map on my phone and realize this must be Tjahkkelij. Beyond it there are huge lakes and more mountains, then hills, the landscape calms down and settles, and the endless forests take over. I fill my lungs with intoxicating fresh air.

Mild euphoria. Again. We did it. We made it.

My main feeling is one of relief. I actually thought we were going to have to turn back because Henrik couldn't do it. Back down to the valley, having lost an entire day—but here we are, and it seems as if the worst is behind us. The plateau on which we are standing is the start of the ridge we are going to follow northeast, and it doesn't look anywhere near as narrow as I feared. The mountain resembles a gigantic dragon resting on the ground, Godzilla having an afternoon nap in the middle of Sarek, its barbed tail curving down into the next valley. The drop on either side of the ridge is pretty much perpendicular, but as far as I can see the ridge itself is at least three or four meters wide. That shouldn't cause a problem for any of us, and the view will be magical—all the way.

Henrik and Milena are now lying close together on the ground, smiling at each other, laughing and chatting. She places her hand on his arm.

It looks intimate.

Maybe a little too intimate.

The thought flits through my mind, and at that same moment Jacob takes a few steps toward them.

"Time to get going," he says impatiently.

Henrik slowly turns his head and looks up at him. "I just need five minutes to catch my breath." Then he looks back at Milena, as if Jacob will just have to like it or lump it.

You're playing with fire, Henrik.

"We have to get off this mountain before dark," Jacob goes on, taking a step closer. "Come on, up!"

"Just five minutes, Jacob. Seriously, what's your problem?" Henrik stares at Jacob, challenging his authority, and suddenly I am on full alert; this could go badly wrong.

"All you do is catch your fucking breath! Up!"

Jacob bends down and grabs Milena's arm. His body language shows how angry he is. He drags her to her feet and she lets out a little whimper.

"Ouch… Don't…"

"What the fuck are you doing? Let go of her!" Henrik raises his voice as I move toward them.

"Everybody needs to calm—" I say before Jacob interrupts me.

"On your fucking feet!" he yells at Henrik, who raises his chin defiantly and remains lying on the ground.

"Like I said, what's your problem, Jacob? Are you jealous?"

No. No, no, no, no. For fuck's sake, Henrik.

Milena looks frightened.

"Please, Henrik—we have to go," she says quickly, taking Jacob's arm.

I join in: "She's right—stop messing around, Henrik."

We are both trying to appease Jacob, who is looking down at Henrik with hatred in his eyes. He is breathing heavily, and I can see that he is on the verge of losing control.

Yes, Jacob is jealous. And now Henrik has said it, the word has been spoken, and we all know it's true. Including Jacob. He has lost face in front of everyone.

"Please, Jacob," Milena says, stroking his cheek. "Calm down."

After a few seconds he shakes his head and says in a rough voice: "Waste of fucking space."

He turns and walks away. Milena hurries after him, while I remain where I am, staring at Henrik.

So what was the point of that, Henrik?

But Henrik refuses to meet my gaze.

I dig out my last packet of Tutti Frutti, open it and go over to Jacob and Milena. Hold it out to Jacob as a gesture of reconciliation.

"Sorry about that. He's not himself."

Jacob doesn't look at me, but eventually he glances at the packet, fishes out some colorful sweets and stuffs them in his mouth without saying anything.

"Amazing view," I venture.

"Absolutely amazing," Milena agrees, helping herself to a few sweets.

"I didn't think we'd manage this," I go on, "but I'm so glad I was wrong." Operation Get-Jacob-in-a-Good-Mood trundles on.

"Mm."

"I'm looking forward to the next part," I say, pointing to the ridge. "It looks exciting."

I smile at Jacob, he smiles back, and his smile looks totally genuine, as if I've just said something funny. He quickly looks away.

Why do I feel uneasy?

Jacob's expression was one of cunning, as if he knows something I don't know.

You haven't a clue, bitch. Not a fucking clue.

Suddenly I'm no longer quite so sure that the worst is behind us.

We are walking along the dragon's back.

In my imagination I see it wake and rise. Shake us off like tiny insects, rear up on its hind legs and roar to the heavens. What a sight that would be.

The terrain on either side of us is getting steeper, but it doesn't bother any of us—including Henrik apparently. The passage up to the plateau has provided him with a method—and self-confidence above all.

The atmosphere is strained after the unpleasant exchange on the plateau. We walk in silence.

We are heading downhill at the moment, which is less strenuous, but it isn't an even slope. First of all we lose quite a lot of height, then the ridge begins to climb again. After a fresh peak halfway along, lower than the plateau, the land drops away toward the valley once more, but beyond the peak is a part of the ridge that we can't yet see.

It takes us just over an hour to reach the second peak. It is late afternoon by now, and the sun no longer provides as much warmth. In a few hours darkness will start to fall and we should be down in the valley by then. The ridge may be comparatively wide, but it wouldn't be any fun to walk in the twilight with a sheer drop on either side.

We stop for a quick snack of fruit soup, crispbread and cheese spread flavored with bacon. Jacob busies himself with the stove. He is still taciturn, giving only monosyllabic responses when Milena speaks to him.

I secretly study his expressions, follow every little change. I don't think he looks quite as grim now; he is more distant somehow, as if his thoughts are elsewhere.

Perhaps it's just my imagination, but the bad feeling I had on the plateau has grown stronger.

What are you thinking about, Jacob?

A hundred kronor for your thoughts. Or ten thousand.

Milena asks me to take a photo of her and Jacob together. He cooperates reluctantly, dutifully draping his arm around her. Jagged peaks and glaciers form a stunning background. Then Milena wants to take a photo of me and Henrik.

"A kiss," I say, turning to face him. He presses his lips to mine, but there is no emotion. Henrik also seems distant. Milena presses the button.

Good friends on holiday in the mountains. Frozen moments to talk about over cozy dinners back home in Stockholm.

Oh, yes, that was the year you brought that weird guy along, what was his name...Jacob? Do you remember, Milena? Oh, my God...

Will I recall the unease I felt, the anxiety that cast its shadow over this walk along the ridge? Unlikely, I think, because on an intellectual level I realize that it's probably just my demons that are affecting me. There is no objective basis for the way I feel. A sly smile from Jacob and my brain gets carried away.

I don't believe in intuition—it's just preconceptions and imagination in a destructive union. Subconsciously we are constantly attempting to have our view of the world validated.

I make an effort to be in the moment instead of speculating about what is going on inside Jacob's head. For a while I almost succeed. As he packs away the stove and I wash my cup by licking it clean, I think that by this time tomorrow we will be out of Sarek.

We set off, downhill once more, and I can't see the ridge because I have Henrik, Milena and Jacob in front of me. I stop and move to the side, toward the edge.

No, it's impossible to see the whole ridge; a long section is still hidden. Which can only mean that it is much, much steeper there.

Henrik hasn't noticed yet, or has failed to draw the right conclusions. He doesn't know what is coming. The slope we are on is dropping all the time.

Jacob stops, turns to face us.

"Okay, guys, so…the next part is a bit tricky."

A bit tricky?

We all stop. The ridge continues in a steep downward slope for ten meters or so, then…vanishes.

What the fuck?

Jacob takes a few steps, then turns sideways and begins to climb down, step by step he disappears from view. Milena walks forward, goes over to the edge and lets out a cry.

"No! Jacob, seriously…"

She backs away. Her face is ashen. "What's wrong, sweetheart?"

Jacob's voice is warm and cheerful as he calls from the abyss. Milena doesn't reply, and Henrik looks anxiously at her. Her expression gives him an idea of the drop that is concealed beyond the edge.

I shrug off my rucksack; I want to see with my own eyes. Even I feel dizzy when I look down.

As the ridge plunges steeply down it also narrows and becomes an edge, as sharp as a razor blade. It is impossible to walk along it. Jacob is now climbing sideways along the edge. Beneath his feet, a free fall of hundreds of meters. Fifteen to twenty meters farther ahead the edge both rises and widens, and the ridge continues from there.

A little way down from where Jacob is, maybe five or six meters, there is a small shelf, an outcrop that it should be possible to stand on. I have a sudden compulsive urge to try and jump from where Jacob is standing to that shelf. I think that it would be almost impossible. That the risk of plunging to almost certain death would be huge.

I feel a physical pull from the drop below, as if I am going to fall forward into the air. Instinctively I take a few steps backward.

Jacob smiles up at me, a triumphant smile. This was what he wanted to put us through; this was the whole point of changing the route.

You thought the worst was over. I found it very difficult not to laugh, let me tell you.

He is as happy as a child, and as cruel as a child. He revels in pulling off the spider's legs, one by one, then watching the legless body twitch and wriggle, unable to move from the spot.

"We need to rope up," I say to him.

"No, no," he answers dismissively, continuing to move sideways.

"But you've got ropes and belay devices with you?"

No reply.

"Aren't we going to use them? That's insane!"

"This isn't difficult," Jacob assures me. He has already reached the other side, where the edge becomes a ridge. He scrambles up and waves to us.

"Fuck off!" I yell at him.

"If we're going to mess around with ropes and belaying, it will take hours," he shouts back. "It'll be dark, and then this really will be dangerous."

"In that case we're going back," I snap. I am furious. I go over to Henrik, who has taken off his rucksack and slumped to the ground.

"Stop being such a wimp," Jacob calls across the abyss.

"He's fucking crazy," I say to Henrik, loud enough for Milena to hear.

Jacob shouts again: "Milena! Come on!" His tone is authoritative, brooking no disagreement, but Milena doesn't say anything. She stands there motionless, hesitating.

Is this the moment when she changes sides? Is this when she realizes that Jacob isn't right in the head?

"Honestly, Milena—we can't get over there without roping up," I say to her quietly—I don't want Jacob to hear. "It would be madness."

Please, Milena, break the spell now. Please, please.

Jacob is now climbing back along the edge at some speed. He has realized that he might not be able to persuade Milena to join him, which worries him.

"I'll take your rucksack," he calls to her. "I'll tell you exactly where to put your hands and feet. It's not difficult, I promise."

Still she hesitates.

He clambers up and strides over to her with a menacing energy. He is seething; his authority has been challenged yet again, the rebellion must be crushed at birth.

"Give me your rucksack," he hisses, hardly moving his lips, and Milena obeys automatically. As soon as Jacob looms over her it as if she is a radio-controlled robot. He puts on her rucksack and goes back to the edge.

But Milena doesn't move.

"You don't have to do this, Milena," I say quietly.

Jacob swings around, stares at her, his eyes wild. "Milena! Now!"

At last she obeys, and my heart sinks. She follows Jacob, who has already clambered down.

"Turn around and move sideways. Hold on with your hands, and put your right foot here. Don't look down."

Jacob issues instructions for every single step. I can see that Milena is terrified, but she does exactly as she is told. She dare not do anything else. Her head slowly disappears below the edge.

I am too agitated and angry to stand still, I pace around Henrik in circles. "This is completely fucking… It's insane."

A couple of minutes pass. There is no sign of Jacob and Milena. Have they fallen?

Of course not. One of them would have screamed. I haven't heard anything. Henrik looks anxiously toward the edge.

"How far is it? Shouldn't we be able to see them by now?"

"Yes." I walk over to the edge and see Jacob scrambling up onto the ridge. He holds out his hand to Milena and helps her up.

They have done it.

They both stand up. Jacob has a drink of water. Milena looks relieved. She even smiles at me and shouts: "It wasn't too bad, actually!" I do not return her smile.

Bullshit, Milena. You were fucking terrified, but Jacob forced you to do it. Don't stand there and tell me it wasn't too bad.

I hear footsteps behind me, then Henrik is by my side. He sees the abyss for the first time and lets out a deep groan, as if he is in terrible pain. He puts out his hands and slowly drops to his knees, like an old man who is afraid of breaking something if he makes a sudden movement. From a kneeling position he rolls sideways onto his bottom, then lies down flat on the ground. One leg is sticking out at an odd angle.

He is hyperventilating and his face is chalk-white. Beads of sweat break out on his forehead. He closes his eyes, then opens them. He is utterly panic-stricken, incapable of focusing on anything. He closes his eyes again.

"I can't see," he gasps.

"What?"

"I can't see! It's… I can't see a thing!"

"Lie back and breathe, Henrik. Keep your eyes shut." I adjust his leg, straighten it out.

Milena and Jacob are watching us. "What's going on?" Milena shouts anxiously.

"Fear of heights," I shout back.

My insides are a maelstrom of emotions, all of them bad. Anger, frustration, fear, weariness. I am angry with Jacob, who lured us into a trap. I am angry with Milena, who is incapable of standing up to Jacob. I am angry with Henrik, who has put us in this hopeless situation.

That's right—the anger I felt toward Henrik earlier comes surging back. His fear of heights has already fucked things up once, and now it's happening again. I know that I am perfectly capable of following Jacob and Milena across the edge, but I doubt if Henrik can do it. In which case, what's the alternative?

Maybe we can persuade Jacob to help him with ropes and belaying devices.

Maybe. But that will take time, and Henrik has to recover before we can even make a start.

I look down at him. He is making a sort of snoring noise. His head has fallen to one side and his mouth is open. He looks as if he is sleeping. His face is still chalk-white, covered in a sheen of perspiration.

I realize that he has fainted. His fear of heights has become so acute that his brain has shut down. Perhaps it's just as well; hopefully he will recover more quickly.

If we'd done as I wanted this morning, we might have had a day left before reaching Aktse by this stage. It would have been awful to manage without hot food and drink again, to feel the night cold creeping into our bones. But we wouldn't have lost any time, and we wouldn't have been dependent on Jacob's goodwill.

"Henrik? How are you feeling?" Milena calls out.

"He's fainted." At that moment Henrik opens his eyes and peers at the sun. He looks confused. He rests his head on the ground and closes his eyes again.

"What happened?" he asks in a flat voice.

"You fainted."

"Was I out for long?"

"No. Can you see now?"

"Yes. I can see."

He rubs his face with the palm of one hand, wonders what

the strange dampness he can feel might be. He is still pale, but the color is coming back to his cheeks.

Henrik fainted. Because of fear.

I think of an image from a 19th-century novel, or maybe it was a TV series. A noble lady sees a horse in a paddock, and the horse defecates, and the delicate little lady faints out of pure fear.

Or *swoons* as they probably said back then.

I begin to giggle at the picture in my mind, and I know it's entirely inappropriate at this point, but I can't stop myself. I am too tired and I have been too angry and too frustrated for too long. It's as if my brain is desperate for a change, and hurls itself at this opportunity.

This is Sarek. All emotions on the surface. All the time.

It's just so funny that Henrik has fainted out of fear. I clamp my lips tight shut, determined not to let the giggles escape. I grimace and turn away. But the suppressed giggles make my body shake.

"What's wrong?" Henrik says, placing a hand on my arm. He probably thinks I'm crying.

Shall I pretend I'm crying? Can I get away with it?

"Anna? What's wrong?"

I imagine him in 19th-century clothes, a floor-length empire-line gown, a bonnet on his head, the bow neatly tied beneath his chin. He has fainted in a ditch, one hand dramatically resting on his forehead, palm upward.

And now the dam bursts; I can't hold it in any longer. The giggles force their way past my lips with a snorting noise, then turn into silent laughter.

"Sorry..." I blurt out, "I just..." I am clutching my stomach as if I'm in pain.

Henrik sits up, hands flat on the ground behind his back. He looks bewildered, and unhappy, but he doesn't say anything. He takes out his water bottle and has a drink.

I gasp for air with a weird rasping sound; that's what happens when I can't stop laughing.

"Sorry," I manage again, then I keel over sideways on the grass and carry on laughing.

Henrik vaguely realizes that I am laughing at him, at the fact that he fainted, but I decide to spare him the details. At least I can do that for him.

"What's going on? Is it because I fainted?"

I don't answer. I simply lie there staring up at the blue sky, almost sobbing with laughter. I'm no longer trying to fight it, that would be pointless, I just let it flow. It feels as if it will never end; it could go on for hours. The laughter is feeding itself now. I've already forgotten the original trigger.

The body takes over in Sarek. Henrik needed to faint. I need to laugh. Neither of us has anything to be ashamed of.

Eventually Henrik gets to his feet, and my very personal little laughter hurricane begins to abate. A final gust or two, and it's over. Tears have run down my cheeks and stomach muscles I haven't used for a long time are aching, but I feel liberated. Energized.

So I stand up too and go over to Henrik, who is putting on his rucksack. I touch his arm and ask gently: "What do you want to do?"

"Go across."

"We don't have to."

"Yes, we do."

"No. We can go back down."

He looks at me as he adjusts his rucksack, fastens the shoulder straps and the belt around his waist.

"Well, let's ask Jacob to rope us up," I suggest.

"Not for my sake."

I have rarely heard him use that tone of voice—dull but resolute. He is determined to make it to the other side. That is nonnegotiable.

Perhaps my laughter made him so angry that he is able to rise above his fear of heights. Or perhaps the fainting episode has somehow rebooted his whole system. He thought he suffered from vertigo, but maybe that is no longer true.

I am surprised. And uneasy. And impressed.

He goes over to the edge, and Milena calls from the other side: "What's happening? Are you coming?"

He doesn't answer. He turns and kneels down in order to begin the descent, toward the edge and the abyss. I follow him.

"Take it easy, Henrik!" Milena shouts. She sounds worried now. "Jacob can rope you up!"

Henrik doesn't seem to hear her. He presses his body against the rock face, his right foot waving around in the air. He finds a foothold, shifts his center of gravity, allows himself to move down. Left hand, right hand, left foot. Down, a little bit farther.

"Henrik! Take—your—time!" I stress each syllable.

He is going too fast. He doesn't look as if he always has three points of support, he is moving hand and foot almost simultaneously. Okay, so it's not really a difficult climb, but he's not used to this kind of thing, and the consequences if you lose your hold are definitive. A fall of hundreds of meters.

Milena seems to see the same thing.

"Wait, Henrik! Stay where you are! Jacob is coming to help you!" There is a note of panic in her voice.

Jacob is already on his way down toward the edge, climbing quickly and nimbly.

Henrik pays no attention to either me or Milena. He keeps going, and he has already reached the edge. It strikes me how relaxed he looks; there is no tension or fear. He displays the same easy confidence as if he were coming down a ladder from an apple tree. Well-considered actions, sound balance.

Jacob is approaching him from the other side. Henrik pauses, catches his breath. I call out to him:

"You're doing brilliantly! That was fantastic!"

He glances up at me, our eyes meet and we smile at each other. "But please slow down—I'm having a heart attack up here!"

He looks almost happy. Jacob is only a few meters away from him now. "Hang on, let me help you," he says.

Henrik and I are still looking at each other, him down there above the abyss, me up here.

"You're climbing like a champ, sweetheart," I tell him. We smile at each other again, a slightly melancholy smile this time. We stay like that for a few more seconds, and it feels good to know that we are friends again.

Henrik takes a deep breath, gets ready to continue. He looks down into the abyss beneath his feet. Hundreds of meters of air.

Don't do that, Henrik. Don't get overconfident. You don't have to challenge yourself.

He leans in toward the rock face, closes his eyes. Time passes. Is he going to have another panic attack? Is this when he loses it? Jacob takes a step closer, holds out his hand.

"Here. Take my hand."

Henrik looks at Jacob. I can't see any sign of panic in his body language, none of the rigidity from before. He moves his right foot in Jacob's direction, then his right hand, left foot, left hand.

Jacob still has his hand outstretched. He is smiling—a warm, inviting smile. Henrik doesn't need Jacob's help, but he reaches out his hand anyway, presumably because he doesn't want to leave the friendly gesture unanswered.

Jacob takes it.

And there is something about Jacob's posture that suddenly looks completely wrong, he tenses his body and seems to take a firm grip on the rock face with his other hand, as if he is thinking.

I open my mouth but I don't have time to scream. Jacob pulls Henrik toward him with a powerful jerk.

Henrik loses his balance and his other hand waves in the air. Jacob lets go of his hand.

Henrik falls.

Interview with Anna Samuelsson 880216-3382, September 19, 2019, Gällivare hospital, conducted by Detective Inspector Anders Suhonen.

Silence. Sobs.

"Do you want to stop for today?"

Silence. Sobs.

"No. It's fine."

"Would you like a glass of water?"

"No."

Silence. Deep breaths.

"I'd rather keep going now. So I don't have to… I don't want to come back to this again."

"I understand."

Silence.

"It's not often that…you experience something that you know will change the rest of your life."

"No."

"So you can't quite believe it. When it happens. I mean, I know it happened, but it feels unreal."

"Yes."

"Sometimes I focus on something else for a little while... maybe only a minute or so...and then when I remember that Henrik is dead, that Jacob killed him, there's a second or two when I think what a nightmare it would be if Henrik fell from a mountain and died. And then my brain catches up, and I know that...it isn't a nightmare. It happened."

"Mm."

Silence.

"I'd like to ask you a few more questions about the incident itself, if that's okay."

"Fine."

"What would you say was Jacob's motive?"

"What was his motive?"

"Yes."

"Well...he was insulted. And his authority had been challenged."

"By Henrik?"

"Yes. When he asked Jacob if he was jealous. I immediately thought *yes, that's it exactly. Henrik and Milena are lying here chatting, and Jacob feels like an outsider.*"

"Mm."

"If you're a narcissist and a psychopath, you just can't take an insult like that."

"No... But from there to killing someone is a pretty big step."

"For a normal person, yes. Like I said before."

"Mm."

"Even if you find the body, you will never be able to prove that Jacob killed him, will you?"

"Probably not, which is why your witness statement is so important."

"If Jacob had been the sole survivor, which was his intention, then of course he would have said that Henrik stumbled. You wouldn't have been able to disprove it."

"No. Okay, let's move on. So after Jacob had caused Henrik to fall—what happened next?"

"I was in shock. I screamed. And on the other side, beyond the steep section, Milena started screaming too. I saw Henrik fall, but then… I looked away. Instinctively. So I didn't see him hit the ground."

"Right."

"Then I just ran. Away from Jacob. There was no hesitation; he was going to have to kill me too."

"So you ran…?"

"Back the way we'd come."

"What did Jacob do? Did he come after you?"

"Yes, and I panicked. I think maybe…if I'd taken it a little easier, I could have got away. But I fell and hurt my knee. I tried to get up and keep running, but by that time Jacob had already caught up with me. And then everything went black."

I wake up in the tent and I don't know how I got here. Or how many hours have passed since Henrik fell and I ran.

It's not dark yet. I guess that it's dusk, because the inside of the tent has a particular nuance that I'm not used to.

Run for your life.

Back at the abyss Henrik has just fallen, I have screamed. My mouth is a gaping hole of horror, and I look at Jacob and his expression tells me that I need to run for my life.

I back away, then I turn and run. Jacob yells at me to stop, but I ignore him. I leave my rucksack behind. Right now it's about surviving the next ten minutes—to start with.

Run like you've never run before.

I don't know how far I run. Eyes fixed on the ground. Then the fall, pain shooting up from my knee through my body like a burning spear. Have I fractured my kneecap? I try to get to my feet but my leg gives way and I pitch forward. I can hear Jacob's rapid heavy footsteps approaching from behind, I can hear his breathing, then everything goes black.

I try to feel at my knee and discover that I am in a sleeping bag. How did that happen? It doesn't matter right now. I unzip the bag, reach down with my hand. My kneecap seems to be in one piece, but it's very sore.

Rewind. Play.

My brain is like a media player on a tablet in the hands of a two-year-old. The child presses the buttons at random and tiny fragments appear from my memory bank, are interrupted halfway through, fast-forward, repeat. Without any chronological order.

Fast-forward. Play. Rewind. Play.

Jacob reaches out his hand to Henrik; Henrik takes it; Jacob pulls Henrik toward him. Henrik loses his grip on the rock face with his other hand, tries to grab hold again with a wild, panicky movement, but it is no use. A second later the hand is waving in thin air.

What does he feel at that moment? Standing there with hundreds of meters of air below him, his balance begins to tip outward. He tries to grab the rock face again, but his fingers scrabble fruitlessly. The shift in his body weight is already too great for him to be able to correct it with the tiny amount of purchase he can gain with his fingertips.

I have nearly lost my balance lots of times, but just managed to pull it back. It is as if a shudder runs through your body and lands in your belly. Then when you realize what almost happened, there is a prickling sensation all over your scalp. You can feel your heartbeat pounding at your temples, in your chest. You take a deep breath. Regain control of yourself.

What did Henrik experience?

I absolutely should not dwell on this. It is completely pointless. It can't lead to anything positive. But I can't help it.

What did Henrik experience?

Surprise, certainly. He looks into Jacob's smiling face and at the same time he feels the tug on his hand that runs up into his arm, into his body.

What are you doing?

Then the shudder when he realizes that he is losing his balance.

No-no-no-no.

The same feeling I have experienced many times.

This could go very badly.

Jacob lets go of his hand and Henrik falls backward, instinctively waves both arms in the air to try to get back on an even keel. Now his whole body in is the air apart from one foot that is still in contact with the rock face, and his brain tries to process the fact that the incomprehensible is happening.

Wow. I know it's happening, but is it really happening?

He can't do it. Henrik is falling backward, and as he picks up speed, he slowly rotates around his own axis, now he is falling head first.

Does he have time to see the ground rushing toward him? And when he rotates another half turn so that his head is at the top again, does he catch a glimpse of Jacob fifty or a hundred meters above him?

The airspeed. The acceleration must be brutal when you're in free fall. After a few seconds you must reach a hundred kilometers an hour or more. How does it feel when you stick your head out the side window when you're traveling along a motorway? Your skin tightens over your cheekbones, any loose skin flaps and flutters, your hair flies in all directions at once. A loud rushing that drowns out every other sound.

I saw Henrik fall, followed him with my gaze before I looked away; at that point he still had quite some distance to go. The fall must have lasted five, six seconds.

Just stop this, Anna. Stop it, stop it, stop it.

What goes through your mind in six seconds? Or do you instinctively keep trying to regain your balance, pointlessly floundering in the air until you hit the ground?

The mountainside isn't perpendicular; it curves outward the closer you get to the bottom. Presumably you bounce off the rock face a few times before you land. Your body is torn apart, splits open like a ripe watermelon. Suddenly one leg and half your belly is gone. It happens in a second. You leave a cascade of blood in the air, an elegant arc. Intestines and other internal organs spill out, but they are still attached to the rest of your body by sinews and membranes, everything flaps in the wind during those last seconds. Your stomach is a little balloon, sparkling in the sunshine.

There's someone outside the tent.

Now I am one hundred percent back in the present. My heart starts pounding.

Someone opens the awning—I hear the zip—but it is not a strong, resolute movement, but quite cautious. As if the person in question doesn't want to wake me.

I hear them crawl in. Carefully, quietly.

There is something about the sounds. I can't put my finger on exactly what it is, but it gives me a clear picture of who the person is.

Jacob.

Fear kicks in, my heart pumping adrenaline to every muscle. I tense my body, ready for fight-or-flight.

Flight? How the fuck is that going to work? I am in a sleeping bag, inside a tent. I am trapped.

Shall I call out to Milena?

Do I even know that Milena is alive?

I swallow hard, my eyes fixed on the fabric of the tent. I breathe silently through my open mouth.

If I call out, I will reveal that I am awake and lose what is perhaps my only advantage—the element of surprise. And there is no point in calling to Milena if he has already killed her.

Where is my Swiss Army knife?

I am lying on my side and I feel, as quietly as possible, in the trouser pocket that is uppermost. No knife.

Now someone slowly begins to unzip the inner flap.

The other pocket? The one I am lying on? I push down my hand and feel the long curved outline of the knife.

The slider slowly and discreetly separates the teeth of the zip. The person will be inside the tent very soon, and at that point I need to lie perfectly still. I have to get the knife out before then.

As quietly as I can, I shift my position so that I can reach the flap of the pocket.

Why the hell does activewear and sleeping bags have to be made of fabric that rustles so loudly.

And of course the flap is fastened with a sturdy metal snap fastener, one of those that often requires the use of both hands to get it open.

The slider continues its journey along the curved line of the zip. The noise it makes separates into its constituent parts. I can almost hear the teeth opening one by one.

With grim, desperate energy I insert my thumbnail between the two sections of the snap fastener and pull at the flap with one hand, pushing down with the other and eventually I hear a *plack* as the snap fastener opens; the noise is deafening. I lie motionless and hold my breath. Jacob must have heard it.

But the measured progress of the slider continues.

Quickly I reach into my pocket and fish out the knife, settle down with it resting on my stomach. In this position I will be able to flick open the blade without anyone noticing. I think.

There is silence now. Apart from the breathing. The person is breathing through their nose, but it is not calm, regular breathing. It seems as if it's an effort not to breathe through the mouth. A lot of air needs to go in and out. The pulse rate is heightened.

It has to be Jacob. I am absolutely certain now.

He sounds as if he has just completed some kind of physically demanding task. Or maybe he's excited.

My face is turned away from the tent flap, but I can see him in my mind's eye; he is on his knees looking down at me. He is wondering how to go about this.

I run my fingers over the knife. Turn it around with the other hand. Where is the main blade?

Jacob enters the tent, and now I can smell him too. Damp clothes, layers of fresh and stale sweat, an odor that is sour and acrid and bitter at the same time. And something else, his own unique bodily smell.

Protected by my posture I open up one blade, feel at it with my thumb. Yes, that's the right one. It's about ten centimeters long. I open it all the way.

There is total silence in the tent now, which must mean that Jacob is sitting perfectly still and holding his breath.

Has he seen something? Did my elbow move when I opened the blade?

Fear sinks its claws into me, and involuntarily I hold my breath too, until I remember that I have to breathe as if I am sleeping. My breathing sounds unnatural and I curse myself for being such an amateur. I am just waiting for the moment when he hurls himself at me, twists the knife out of my hand and holds it to my throat.

Stupid little bitch, did you think I hadn't noticed anything?

I feel weak, I can't do this, but then he starts breathing again, he moves, and to my surprise I realize that it's not over yet. He hasn't noticed anything. It sounds as if he is stretching out on the mattress beside me.

I adjust the position of the knife in my right hand. Clutch it tightly. Place my left hand on the ground. When it is time, I intend to push myself up as fast as I can, then whirl around and stab with my right hand.

Aim for the face, which should be exposed. Stab, stab, stab.

I feel Jacob's body touch mine, his breathing is even closer now, tickling my ear. I take a deep breath. *Now.*

At that moment I hear a voice from outside. "Jacob?"

He freezes, holds his breath again. "Jacob?"

It is Milena.

"Jacob?"

Milena sounds afraid, almost pleading.

You're alive. Thank God.

Jacob remains motionless for a little while, then he sighs in frustration, gets up off the mattress and crawls out through the flap. His movements are no longer slow and cautious, but exaggeratedly loud and frantic. He is annoyed.

Oh, Milena. Thank God.

Jacob zips the flap behind him with a single long aggressive swipe.

"What?" he snaps. He somehow manages to shout and whisper at the same time.

He wriggles outside, gets to his feet, and I hear a muted conversation. "I was just wondering where you—"

Jacob interrupts aggressively. "I'm looking for the lighter!"

Looking for the lighter. Yeah, sure.

They walk away, presumably because they don't want to wake me. I can't hear what they're saying, but the tone is unmistakable: Jacob angry and domineering, Milena defensive and imploring.

I take a deep breath, then exhale.

The immediate danger has passed. I won't have to fight for my life just yet. And Milena is alive, which improves my odds significantly. I have to put all my energy into getting her on my side. We have to form a pact. And she has to be on her guard, just like me.

I close the knife and put it away, then change my mind, take it out and open the blade again. From now on it must be ready for use at all times. If I have to fight for my life, I don't want to waste valuable seconds opening it up. I put it back in my pocket.

My knee is really painful. I unfasten my trousers, reach down and feel it with my hand. It is badly grazed, but it doesn't seem too serious. My fingertips are damp, but nothing more. It has stopped bleeding.

I crawl outside and stand up. There is a stabbing pain in the side of my right knee, but I am on my feet. I put on my hard-shell jacket and zip it up.

Twilight is falling over Sarek; it will be dark in half an hour or so. We are high up on the side of the mountain. Far below the Rapa River flows toward lower terrain. In the distance I can hear the rushing of a stream.

Jacob and Milena are sitting a short distance away, preparing a meal. I can see the blue flame of the stove clearly through the dusk. Milena notices me.

"Anna!" She stands up and comes over. "How are you feeling?"

As she gets closer I see how worried she looks, how tired and unhappy, how lost.

Of course Henrik's death must have been a terrible shock for her too. Plus the realization that her boyfriend is a psychopath. That both she and I are in mortal danger.

Surely she must have realized that by now?

She puts her arms around me, hugs me and begins to weep silently. I put my arms around her too, but I don't say a word. Jacob is watching us.

I've got my eye on both of you. Don't forget it.

We stand there holding each other for quite a while. Nothing is said, nothing needs to be said. Or rather, a lot needs to be said, but now is not the right time. Milena cries.

We eat by the light of our head torches. It is almost completely dark now. No one has much to say. Eventually I ask the question that has been bothering me for some time.

"How did I get down?"

Jacob and Milena look at each other, but don't reply. They look slightly bewildered. "I remember falling when I was running up there. On the ridge. Then everything went black. I woke up in the tent."

Jacob stares down at his plate, pushes his food around, takes another mouthful, but still doesn't say a word. His face is closed. It is Milena who answers.

"You ran again."

"What do you mean?"

"You came to after a while, and we helped you to your feet. But then you took off again."

"I took off again?"

"Yes."

"How far did I go?"

"To the top. To the plateau. And then when you tried to climb down on this side, you fell again."

Milena glances at Jacob, and I have a strong feeling that something about this story isn't right. She goes on: "You were completely out of it. We carried you here, then we put up the tent."

There is something about the way she is telling the story. She keeps looking at Jacob, as if she is seeking his approval.

Am I getting it right? This is what we agreed, isn't it?

As if she is reciting a piece of homework that she has learned by heart.

What are they hiding? What actually happened during the gap in my memory? I continue eating in silence, feverishly trying to think of possible scenarios.

Maybe Jacob tried to murder me too, and Milena managed to stop him. Now she is concentrating on keeping him calm, demonstrating submissiveness, defusing his aggression. She might be making this story up as she goes along, which suggests that she knows how dangerous Jacob is, and that she understands the importance of making him feel secure.

However I have a feeling that this scenario doesn't ring true either. There are bits of information that don't fit, although I can't work out which ones. They are lurking on the edge of my consciousness, but when I reach for them, they slip away.

Maybe I am just too tired to solve the puzzle.

We have sat in silence, concentrating on our food for quite some time, when Jacob clears his throat. He is preparing to speak, and I listen attentively. After a brief pause he utters five words: "I tried to save him."

Those words hang in the air, and I know that with each second they remain unchallenged, it will be more difficult to distinguish Jacob's lie from the truth. But it would be a huge tactical error to point out that he is lying, to face up to him, before I have spoken to Milena. We have to form a pact, strike when he is least expecting it.

So I don't say anything. Now I know: this is what Jacob is going to present as his truth.

I tried to save him.

Both Milena and I know what happened, but if we hear this message over and over again, *I tried to save him*, then perhaps eventually we will begin to doubt the evidence of our own eyes. Is it possible to interpret what we saw in a different way? Uncertainty will come creeping in.

One of the insignia of power, like the orb and scepter: the ability to blur the line between truth and lies.

Milena begins to cry quietly and switches off her head torch. For some unknown reason I switch mine off too. A vague gesture of solidarity, I suppose. The last strip of light in the sky above the mountains in the west dies away.

It is almost pitch black now. Only Jacob's head torch sends out its beam into the darkness. The cold is sneaking up on us, a hungry wolf padding around the edges of our camp.

"Milena, can you help me with something?" I say. "I've scraped my knee, but I can't see it properly."

I am leaning against a rock a short distance from where we were sitting. I have rolled up my right trouser leg. There is a gash on the side of my knee, and a nasty graze.

Milena is crouching down in front of me, cutting off a strip of dressing from a roll by the light of her head torch. I tear up an antibacterial wipe and clean the wound and the skin around it. It stings, but it's not too bad. Milena removes the backing strip, I straighten my leg and she presses the dressing in place. As she rubs her thumbs over the sticky parts, I look over at Jacob. He has switched off his torch; I think I can make out the shape of him, but I'm not sure. Has he crept closer so that he can watch us under cover of darkness?

Milena looks up at me with a wan smile. "There you go."

"Thanks."

She rolls down my trouser leg and gets to her feet. I hesitate briefly. What if Jacob comes rushing from an unexpected direction? Am I going to do this? I take her hands in mine, look deep into her eyes and whisper: "Milena… We need to stick together. He wants to kill us."

She stares at me, her eyes widening. She looks frightened. Terrified, actually.

Interview with Anna Samuelsson 880216-3382, September 19, 2019, Gällivare hospital, conducted by Detective Inspector Anders Suhonen.

"What did you think about the fact that she looked frightened?"

Silence.

"I… I'd hoped that she would look me in the eye and nod, show that she'd understood. That she'd come to the same conclusion. But she didn't."

"No."

"And at the time, I didn't know if it was because she was so scared of Jacob that she didn't dare stand up to him, even if it was our only chance of survival, or if she was still so brainwashed that she'd bought into his lie. It's just occurred to me that she might not have seen what happened when Jacob pulled Henrik off the mountain."

"No."

"I mean, I know she screamed, but that could have been a second later—when Henrik was already falling."

"Right."

"Anyway, whatever… It was a negative outcome for me. I knew that. Our only chance was to stick together against Jacob."

I am lying in the tent again and Milena is lying beside me. She thinks I have fallen asleep, and she is trying to hide the fact that she is crying. Judging by the sound, she has buried her face in the pillow or the sleeping bag, but I can hear her muffled sobs.

Henrik is dead.

I know that, and that's why Milena is crying, but the realization hasn't hit me yet. Henrik is dead—it's simply a fact. My name is Anna—that is also a fact. I am still alive—another fact.

All my resources are focused on staying alive and getting out of Sarek. If I manage to do that, then I can grieve for Henrik later.

I really need to sleep in order to regain some strength, but my body has declared a critical incident. At the slightest noise from outside I raise my head a fraction, hold my breath and listen intently. Is Jacob coming, is he going to slash his way through the side of the tent and massacre both of us?

I do understand that this is unlikely. Jacob isn't crazy in that way—he's not insane. He has us in his power, and I'm sure he wants to make the most of it. Plus he must also be tired after today. No doubt he is fast asleep in his tent.

While I have been lying here thinking, Milena has fallen silent. She is sleeping now, quiet as a mouse. Milena is one of those rare individuals who doesn't make a sound when she sleeps. Her sleeping bag rises and falls in a calm, steady rhythm.

I still don't quite know where I stand with her, but at least we are in the same tent, which must be a positive. I have made my point and hope it has begun to take effect, like the red pill in *The Matrix*.

During the rest of the evening we were never more than a few meters apart. That's my tactic now, to make things more difficult for Jacob. Here we are, side by side, and that's good.

However there is a problem: I need to pee.

I was so focused on staying close to Milena that when she brushed her teeth and went to bed, I did the same. I didn't need a pee then, but that was several hours ago. I've started thinking about it, and now I can't stop.

Can I force myself to forget it? No. I might drop off for a few minutes, but there is no chance of a longer sleep.

The alternative is not appealing—sneaking out of the tent on my own, into the cold and darkness. What if Jacob is awake? Maybe he's lying there waiting for this to happen.

Should I wake Milena, ask her to come with me? It's definitely a possibility. I prop myself up on one elbow and look at her, or rather in her direction; it's pitch-dark and I can't see a thing. I think about her crying, and I realize that she needs a good night's rest at least as much as I do. She is exhausted, mentally and physically. The more she can recover, the greater the chance that she will recognize the reality of the situation.

We need to stick together if we are going to survive Sarek.

Didn't I think just a little while ago that Jacob must be tired, and is probably fast asleep in his tent? I did. And I haven't heard a thing from his direction since he went to bed straight after us, even though I've been lying here on full alert. The only sound disturbing the silence is the rushing of the river a short distance away.

Once I have begun to accept that going outside for a pee is a real possibility, my body buys into the idea and I need a pee even more. In the end I have no choice. My body has made the decision.

Creeping out of a tent without anyone hearing is above all a question of one thing: doing it slowly. I tell myself that it can take thirty minutes, forty-five if necessary. I need to be patient.

Slowly, slowly I pull down the zip of my sleeping bag. Extract my legs. Like a sloth I roll over on the air bed and shuffle a little closer to the tent flap. I don't want to lie with my arms outstretched as I unzip it; the maneuver will be a long-drawn-out process and I don't want to get a cramp.

I start edging the slider along in slow motion, much slower than Jacob a few hours ago. I need to be sure that Milena won't wake and that Jacob won't hear a thing from his tent. I have to keep changing position, which also takes time, but eventually the flap is open and the chilly air comes pouring in.

I hadn't thought about that. The icy draught might wake Milena, but there's nothing I can do about it now. If she does stir, I can put my finger to my lips, show her that she has to keep quiet, or ask if she wants to come with me.

I crawl along on all fours, placing one hand or foot at a time with the utmost care. My knee hurts with every movement. I grope my way to my boots and flop down on the ground while I put them on.

It's hard work, doing everything so slowly. I am out of breath, and I am still only halfway out of the tent. I adopt the same position as before, crawl to the next flap and start to open the zip with the same agonizing slowness. It is even more important to be silent now, because it will be easier for Jacob to hear this zip.

Milena still seems to be fast asleep. She hasn't stirred or made a sound.

I wonder if I ought to zip up the flaps behind me. I quickly decide to leave the inner flap open, but to close the outside one. If I don't, there is a risk that it will be caught by the wind and make a noise.

Should I dig out some toilet paper? I know where my rucksack is, but I'm not sure exactly where the toilet roll is. I would have to search through lots of pockets, undoing snap fasteners and cord locks. And the need for silence means it would take forever.

No. I'll manage without paper tonight.

I can see the night sky through the growing gap as the zip opens, tooth by tooth. It is filled with stars—I have never seen anything like it. In fact it is hard to find a patch of sky that is completely black. Stars everywhere, near and far, stars shining brightly like a hundred-watt bulb, stars twinkling shyly. The Milky Way is an opalescent streak, like fish roe in the cosmos. Billions of stars in billions of galaxies.

It is so beautiful, so extraordinary, that for a little while I forget that I am in mortal danger. I let go of the slider, gaze up at the stars and feel humble in the face of infinity.

This was what Sarek was supposed to be like. We came here to experience moments like this. But that's not how it turned out.

I return to my task, and soon the opening is big enough to allow me to crawl out.

With the same endless patience I zip it up again, not quite all the way, but enough to make sure it doesn't start flapping in the wind.

Outside at last.

I get to my feet, stretch my back. The clicking of several vertebrae is probably the loudest noise I have made since leaving my sleeping bag, but I feel relieved. The trickiest part is over.

I tiptoe away from the tent. My eyes have got used to the darkness, and the stars are like a misty night-light. I see black outlines to my right, angular shapes hiding the sky. Skårki and the other peaks. The glaciers glow faintly, as if they were fluorescent.

I go behind a rock, undo my trousers and crouch down, legs apart. *Finally.*

Then I hear something from the direction of the tents. A zip opening. My body reacts immediately—my heart is pounding, the hairs on the back of my neck are standing on end.

I straighten up cautiously, pull up my pants and thermals and trousers. Hold my breath and listen. The silence whines in my ear canal. I can't hear a second zip.

And then I do.

I have heard two zips, and now I can hear footsteps approaching. I reach into my pocket and take out the knife.

The footsteps stop, I hear a click, then I see the beam of a head torch a short distance away. Lighter, darker, lighter again. Jacob—because surely it must be him—is turning his head this way and that, looking around, checking out the terrain.

"Anna?" It is a whisper, but a loud whisper, a compromise between two irreconcilable goals—to be heard by me, but without waking Milena.

Yes, it's Jacob.

How the fuck can he have heard me leaving the tent? I didn't make a sound. It's not possible. He must have been lying there waiting for me to get up.

Jacob wants me to himself, without Milena as a distraction. And I realize that I have given him a golden opportunity, but what was I supposed to do?

Maybe I should have wet myself, stayed with Milena.

The footsteps come closer and the beam of light passes over the rock behind which I am hiding. I raise the knife, get ready to stab, my legs are trembling with stress and fear and I just manage to suppress a sob that is on its way up through my throat.

Dear God, please don't let him find me.

I am so frightened. I am terrified. The footsteps stop.

"Anna?" Another intense loud whisper, much closer. He sounds as if he is on the other side of the rock. I am finding it difficult to control my breathing; I am sure he must be able to hear me.

I can't do this anymore.

I run.

In full panic mode—again—I rush blindly straight ahead

with no thought of keeping quiet. Gravel flies in all directions, I stumble, and my sudden burst of speed takes Jacob by surprise.

"What the fuck…" I hear him hiss angrily behind me.

I run as fast as I can, as fast as I dare, but my knee is killing me. I am limping along; the pain is taking its toll. The beam from Jacob's head torch pierces a hole in the darkness to my left, then to my right, and then he has found his target and I feel the beam burning my back like a tongue of fire.

Fuck-fuck-fuck.

Heavy steps behind me as he takes up the chase. "Anna, for fuck's sake! Stop!"

I try to run in a zigzag pattern in order to escape the light. I am like a hare with a fox after me, but an injured hare that doesn't really have a chance.

Jacob is catching up with me fast.

The rushing of the stream is much louder now. I must be running toward it. I had imagined it as a relatively small watercourse, quite near the tent, but when I still don't see it and the sound continues to grow, I realize that it must be much bigger and farther away.

Much bigger.

I give up the zigzag pattern. Jacob is so close that he must be able to see my outline in the darkness, plus of course he has the head torch. Instead I run in a straight line as best I can. My knee is less painful now; I assume the adrenaline has knocked out the pain signals.

The stream is a possibility. I will try to reach it before he catches me. The bigger and more powerful it is, the more it will even out the odds between Jacob and me. Maybe I can get to the other side. Maybe he will be washed away.

The knife is in my hand. With each step I stab a fresh hole in the air.

"Stop!" Jacob yells. No doubt he assumes that the rushing of the stream will drown out his cry. Milena won't be able to hear him.

But he is close now. Very close.

I try to increase my speed, the risk of stumbling and falling is considerable, but I have to take a risk. I can hear his heavy breathing; the effort has taken its toll on him too. He is only seconds away from me. He finds an extra burst of energy to cover the last few meters.

The stream is louder now. It sounds like a powerful torrent; I think I feel a hint of dampness on my face. And just as the ground begins to slope downward in front of me, Jacob's fingers grasp the back of my top.

No-no-no.

I twist myself free, but he trips and falls forward onto my legs, making me lose my balance too, and we tumble down the slope. I use my hands to slow myself. I graze my palms but I hardly notice because Jacob has managed to get one arm around my legs, I desperately try to pull away but my leg is stuck. We are no longer falling but fighting, a life-or-death struggle. I realize that I dropped the knife when I fell.

Shit, shit, shit.

Jacob's other arm is around my waist now. It is as if I am in the grip of an octopus or ten boa constrictors, but I sense his head to my right and draw my arm as far to the left as I can, then elbow him in the temple with every bit of strength I can muster.

Ooohhhhh.

I hear myself groan, it's as if my arm has cracked in the middle, stars dance before my eyes, I feel weak and sick, but Jacob's hold loosens for a second, enough for me to scramble to my feet and stagger toward the river.

Because it is actually a raging river, seven or eight meters wide. The torrent is deafening now, surging over the rocks with brutal power. I can't judge the depth in the darkness, but I realize it would be suicidal to attempt a crossing.

I hesitate. How would I prefer to die? Drown in the river, or be beaten to death by Jacob?

He is on his feet behind me.

Drown, definitely. I step out into the water, protected by several large rocks at first, so there is no current, but then I walk on into the main body of the river and it is difficult to place my feet on the bottom, because the current is so strong.

Jacob comes staggering after me.

I keep going. The water is over the top of my boots now. There is an ice-cold vise around each ankle. It gets deeper and deeper and the current pulls and tugs at my legs, and every instinct tells me *turn back, you're going to die*, but my fear of Jacob is greater. I force myself to keep going, one step at a time, without making sure of my balance between steps. I totter forward, and of course my attempt is bound to fail.

I fall over.

I am carried away as easily as an autumn storm whisks away a dry leaf from the ground. The cold shocks my body, attacking me simultaneously from all directions. I stop breathing. I tumble around beneath the surface, completely disorientated. I have no idea which way is up or down. The mass of water rushes me along. My body accelerates until *boooom*.

The sound of a dull, heavy thud that reverberates through my body and into my eardrums. My back has struck a huge rock underwater, stopping me dead. Fresh, agonizing pain radiates from my spine.

I consist only of pain now. My elbow, my back, the cold. It saps my strength.

The river pins me to the rock, but at the same time it is trying to drag me away. I am pressed against the rock, spun around, and suddenly my head is above the surface and my feet are on the bottom.

I open my mouth, but don't perceive any difference. My lungs are still screaming for air. I am surprised. Isn't this how you breathe? You simply open your mouth, don't you? Or is there something else, something I've forgotten? Then the shock passes and at last I am able to fill my lungs.

Breathe in, breathe out, breathe in, breathe out, breathe in, breathe out.

I gulp down the air, gorge on oxygen without chewing, but gradually I begin to breathe more calmly.

Breathe in. Breathe out. Breathe in. Breathe…

Out of the corner of my eye I see something coming and I recoil, but it is too late. Jacob grabs hold of me with both hands, drags me away from the rock and pushes me under the water.

I give up.

No one can say that I didn't try. I gave him a good fight, but the odds were against me.

I have earned the right to rest. I relax, stop struggling against the cold and the pain, and guess what?

It's nice, so nice.

Jacob holds me down and I feel weightless, as if I am floating free. His grip suddenly feels almost tender, like a father holding his baby daughter in his arms and spinning around and around, letting her experience the sensation of flight.

No fear, no hatred, no battle. Why did it take me so long to realize that life can be like this? Going with the flow. Why didn't I live my life this way? Why the constant striving for something better, the constant need to achieve, to maximize.

Who knows. I might even have been happy. I think about Henrik, about Erik, about Dad.

Dad is pushing me under the water. He is trying to hold me down, just like he's done all my life, and the old anger floods my body. I know he intends to drown me.

Fuck you, you bastard.

I grope with my hand, find a knee. Push one arm between Dad's legs, wrap it around his calf. Put one foot against the rock. Brace myself.

I manage to tip Dad over. He roars like an angry bear as he disappears under the water, and it isn't Dad's voice, it is someone else's. What was his name again? He loses his grip on me, whoever he is, and I am carried away by the current.

But I don't resist. I have realized that the river wishes me well. It is a slightly clumsy friend who might hurt me by mistake, but still a friend. Like Frankenstein's monster.

Jacob. That's his name.

I allow the river to carry me along, I even attempt a few swimming strokes to increase my speed. When Jacob's head pops up I want to be as far away as possible. Protruding rocks slow me down, hit me, try to cut me. At one point I come to a complete halt and have to take a few steps out into the deep central channel in order to be carried farther. I have grazed my face, I might be bleeding, but I couldn't care less. A few steps and then I relax, let the current do its job.

It is a game with Death that could save my life. And I no longer feel any fear—none at all. Quite the reverse—I am strangely elated. I have accepted that I am going to die, so every extra minute of life is a bonus. I might as well have some fun before it's all over.

I tumble downstream, I have no idea for how long, but I am enjoying it. Maybe this isn't an *activity* anymore but a *lifestyle*. Then suddenly the ground and the water vanish from beneath me, and I just have time to think that this is a new sensation. I feel as if I am hovering in the air, then I realize that that is precisely what I am doing.

A waterfall, only about a meter high. Enough to smash me.

To pieces.

I land on my shoulder and bang my head, scrape one side of my body, then I am lying motionless against a huge rock, halfway out of the water.

I catch my breath for a while, or fifteen minutes, or an hour. I have lost track of both time and space. I peer up into the darkness, try to work out if I can hear anything unusual above the roar of the torrent. I am half-prepared to see Jacob come flying over the top of the waterfall like I just did, a black outline against the starlit sky.

But there is no sign of Jacob.

I realize that I have been lucky. I could easily have broken an arm or a leg when I landed. Been knocked unconscious, ended up with my head under the water. I am freezing cold and black and blue and bleeding here and there, but I am alive.

My only real problem is my shoulder. Not that it hurts—nothing really hurts. But I can't move it, or my arm. I seem to have dislocated it.

I have had enough of the river for the time being, so I crawl ashore and get to my feet. When I look down at myself, see the torn clothes and grazes and bruises, feel the bleeding wound on my head, warm blood on numb fingertips, I am surprised at the absence of pain. There is still that sense of elation. I feel totally invincible. It's the best feeling ever.

I set off upstream. One arm is dangling by my side, but I

hardly notice it. My plan is to follow the river until I find the spot where Jacob and I fought on the ground, and from there to retrace my footsteps back to the tent. And then? Hard to say. I can't think that far ahead.

Is Jacob still alive? I stare down into the water as I go, hoping to see a lifeless arm or leg sticking up by the bank. Jacob's body slumped over a rock in an unnatural position, his head bashed in. But I also gaze out into the darkness by the side of the river, up the mountain and at the surrounding terrain. He might have got out of the water. He might be sitting quietly somewhere, just waiting for me.

My sodden clothes are beginning to stiffen in the night air. It is becoming increasingly difficult to walk, but strangely enough I don't feel cold at all. On the contrary I am warm. I am almost sweating.

I have no idea how long I have been walking, but I should soon reach the place where we fought. Shouldn't I? I have only the starlight to guide me, and I realize it might be hard to find the exact spot. I would like the dawn to break now.

I look to the east—and see a strip of light on the horizon, still so faint that there is no sign in the rest of the sky, but still a strip.

I asked for the dawn, and I got the dawn.

I am the creator of the universe, mistress of the sun, the earth and the moon.

You shall have no other gods before me.

The sky in the east turns blackish-blue, dark blue, deep blue, cobalt blue. The dawn eats up the stars; they fade away one by one. I keep on going, moving more slowly now, my eyes fixed on the ground. Was it here? Was it over there?

Darkness and starlight are replaced by a blue half-light. The landscape appears before my eyes.

Suddenly I stop. I know where I am. This is where the river cuts a little deeper into the mountainside, the ground drops more sharply down toward the water. Could it have been here? I head up the slope, away from the rushing river, pause and look around.

Yes. Maybe. I can't say for sure. This slope reaches about a hundred meters up the mountainside, along the water's edge. The ground is completely covered in scree, so my struggle with Jacob hasn't left a trace. Not here, nor anywhere else.

I set off again, but then I see something red, standing out against the black and gray sea of stones. The blue light of dawn is just enough to enable me to see the difference in color. If it had been a little darker, the red would have looked black too.

It's the knife. The Swiss Army knife.

Everything falls into place. It is almost unbelievable. The fading stars are perfectly aligned on this clear cold morning that could be my last in this life. At least Sarek seems to want to make sure that I have a decent chance against Jacob. Even out the odds. Sarek helped me out of the river, and now Sarek has shown me the knife.

Maybe Sarek just wants to see a fair fight.

I go over and retrieve the knife. When I straighten up, I feel dizzy and weak at the knees. The steady march upstream seems to have taken its toll. I sink down on the ground for a little while. One arm is completely numb, as if I have slept on it for a whole night. When I use my other hand to lift the forearm onto my lap, it feels like a piece of meat that has nothing to do with me. I vaguely register that this can't be a good sign, but the arm doesn't hurt, so I decide not to worry about it.

No one is going to tell me that I'm not living for the moment.

I am still sweating, sitting there on the cold stones. I'd really like to take off my ripped, bloodstained trousers; they are flapping around my legs and serving no useful purpose. But that would mean taking off my boots first, and I just don't have the energy.

I would love to lie back and rest. Maybe even have a little

sleep, but of course that would make me a sitting target for Jacob, so I fight the urge and remain sitting up.

After some considerable time I think that I will get up and head for the tent.

However my body refuses to obey. It seems to be staging some kind of mutiny; my brain has been demoted to an organ among all the rest. I now have a completely flat organizational structure. My thigh muscles are every bit as important as my brain.

Get up and start walking, or die here.

I head away from the river at a ninety-degree angle. Totter along on wobbly legs, so exhausted that I can barely lift my feet. It has been a tough night. The same applies to Jacob though. He can't be in top form either—if he's even alive.

After only a few minutes I see the tents a few hundred meters away, huddling in the dawn light. They are so close together, almost as if they are clinging to each other for protection against the merciless mountain. There is no sign of Jacob or Milena.

I keep going until I can hide behind a large rock. I take several deep breaths, try to focus my thoughts. Work through the various alternatives so that I will know what to do depending on what happens when I reach the tents. Any hesitation could cost me my life.

Okay. Let's do this.

I creep toward the tents. Should I try to wake Milena, get her on my side? Which tent is she in?

What if Jacob wakes up?

Is Jacob in either of the tents?

Too many options. I start again, attempt to flesh out the various scenarios: I creep toward the tents. I need to find my things. Where is my rucksack?

I peer around the side of the rock. I can't see my rucksack from where I am standing. Have they moved it into one of the tents? If so, which one?

I have a vague memory of me and Milena lying in one tent before I crept out for a pee. Then again, the other tent looks like mine and Henrik's.

So where is my rucksack? And where is Jacob?

Pull yourself together, Anna. Focus.

I try again: I creep toward the tents. I creep toward the tents. I creep toward the tents.

I can't get any farther, it's impossible, I am too tired. White dots dance in front of my eyes even though I am leaning against the rock and I begin to weep silently because I know I'm finished. I just can't do any more.

I creep toward the tents. That is my entire plan. And of course it's not enough. Jacob will rush at me and kill me, but that's fine. I can't do any more.

I snivel, wipe the tears from my cheeks with the back of my hand, realize I'm holding something, and that something is the knife. I had forgotten about it. I don't think I could loosen my grip even if I tried.

I set off toward the tents. Fear conquers my exhaustion, at least a little bit, at least temporarily. Clearly there was a tiny amount of adrenaline left to be squeezed out into my bloodstream. My knees don't feel quite so weak. Meter by meter I draw closer to the tents, my eyes firmly fixed on them, watching for the slightest movement. I am listening for the slightest sound, but I neither see nor hear any sign of life.

Either Milena and Jacob are asleep, or they're not there.

I make my way to the tent that I think is mine and Henrik's. Stop in front of the closed flap, the knife raised, ready to strike. My heart is pounding, I am breathing through my open mouth.

I can't see any indication that someone is lying inside the tent, no bulges at the sides.

I lean forward, listen hard. Silence. Shouldn't I be able to hear breathing? It seems as if no one is there.

I creep around the tent—no bulges at the back either. I bend down, put my ear close to the fabric, but I still can't hear anything.

I go back to the front. The flap is firmly closed, the zip pulled right down. I have to open it to see if my rucksack is there. I know it's almost impossible to do this silently, but I have no choice—I have to try.

I am more or less convinced that the tent is empty, but if I'm wrong, I could find myself in a fight to the death with Jacob in thirty seconds.

I take hold of the slider with the same hand in which I am clutching the knife.

Somehow I manage it without losing my grip on the shaft. I start to pull slowly, but the flap buckles, it is not taut enough for me to unzip it with one hand. I will have to try to hold the bottom with my other hand.

Quietly, cautiously I drop to my knees, and my right kneecap lands on a sharp little stone.

Aaaahh…shit…

I can't suppress a groan as the pain shoots up my leg and makes me a little dizzy. I almost fall over sideways but just keep my balance. If there is anyone inside the tent, they are bound to have woken up now. Which means I might as well go for it. I use my good hand to move the useless hand to the bottom edge of the flap and insert the fabric between my thumb and forefinger. I open the zip without paying any attention to whether anyone can hear me or not, one single long arc-shaped movement.

The porch is empty.

The inner flap is also open, and I can see that there is no one inside.

My rucksack, containing everything I need to survive alone, must be in the other tent.

At that same moment I hear the sound of the zip opening from the other tent.

Jacob is coming to get you.

I struggle to my feet with a desperate burst of energy, just in time to see Milena scramble out. She stands up and stares at me, her eyes wild and terrified.

Oh, thank God, it's Milena.

I stagger over to her.

"Where's Jacob?" I hiss, but she doesn't answer. She still looks petrified.

"He tried to kill me," I go on, trying to sound calm and composed, but it's difficult because I am agitated and out of breath. "Hasn't he come back? Do you know if he's dead?"

Milena is still staring at me, and at the knife in my hand. Slowly she shakes her head.

"Listen to me, Milena." I take a deep breath so that I can speak more clearly, but I don't think I succeed particularly well. "Jacob tried to kill me last night, you and I need to stick together now, otherwise we haven't got a chance, understand? We need to stick together if he comes back, but first of all we need to gather up everything we need and get out of here, as fast as we..."

I fall silent.

Because now I hear noises from the tent.

A wild boar, or a bear, is making its way out, so clumsily and violently that the whole tent is shaking, on the point of collapse. A second later Jacob emerges through the opening, doubled over, and one shoulder catches. He drags the tent with him as he straightens up, but he simply shakes it off and then he is coming toward me at full speed. All this in one single movement, in seconds.

Two meters tall, weighing maybe one hundred kilos, Jacob is rushing at me with the intention of killing me.

I raise the knife, and as he hurls himself at me I thrust it into the side of his chest.

His own impetus drives the whole blade in.

We tumble over and I land with his heavy body on top of me. The useless arm has swung back and ended up underneath me, and I hear a distinct *crack* as the arm snaps like a dry branch. I am trapped beneath Jacob and it feels as if my chest is completely crushed.

no air

can't breathe

There are only fragments left of my ribs. I manage to pull the knife out of Jacob's side and stab at the back of his neck instead, but the blow is too weak, or maybe his muscles are too tough and strong. The blade slips and I have achieved nothing.

God give me air, air

Milena is standing over us, trying to pull Jacob off me, but he is too heavy, too powerful. I make another attempt with the knife.

can't do it, too weak

with an equal lack of success, but it must have hurt because he raises his hand to the nape of his neck and twists to the side, and somehow I push him off me.

at last, air

I roll over and fill my lungs, coughing violently, I put one foot on the ground to heave myself up.

have to get away from here

but then I feel Jacob's hand around my shinbone, he yanks at my leg, I crash down face first and the knife flies out of my hand.

no no no

"Help me," I gasp, looking up at Milena. "Help me."

And now Jacob is on top of me again, heavy, strong and bloody. He grabs my hair and bangs my head on the ground once, twice, three times. My skull explodes with pain and I can't see anything anymore, everything is red and yellow and throbbing, but I feel him turn me over so that I am lying on my back, then he straddles me. His big hands find my throat. My vision returns and I see Milena upside down. She is looking at me, paralyzed with fear.

"Help me," I whisper again, and then Jacob tightens his grip. And squeezes. With all his might.

It's not just that I can't breathe.

I can hear crunching and cracking inside my neck. I think he's broken something.

He looks down at me, his face bright red, the veins on his forearms distended. My good hand scrabbles uselessly at one of his, tries to get a grip or at least insert a finger to loosen his iron grasp, but in vain. I might as well be trying to break open a padlock with my bare hands.

There is a murderous intent in his eyes. It isn't even hatred, hatred would be human, no, this is something animalistic, primal.

Now, Anna. Now you're going to die.

We are staggering down the mountain toward the Rapa River on this clear cold morning. It is going to be a beautiful day. Beautiful and merciless, like Sarek itself.

I have a splitting headache. Probably concussion. My throat still feels constricted, when I swallow, it hurts like an open wound. My skin is grazed, punctured, torn in a hundred different places. My shoulder is dislocated and my arm is broken. The bones have snapped somewhere around the elbow.

But I am alive. I didn't think I was going to make it.

Milena is staggering along behind me. She isn't as badly injured as I am, but she has a nasty cut on the side of her neck.

In the end Milena decided where her loyalties lay. My God, did she decide…

Everything went black. I was unconscious for a while. When I came round Jacob's weight was no longer pressing down on me. I sat up and saw him lying motionless on the ground a short distance away.

A weird kind of stick was protruding from his head.

Everything was blurred. I found it difficult to focus. Laboriously I got to my feet and took a few steps toward the body.

The thing protruding from Jacob's head was a shaft. The ice ax.

And Milena hadn't just stabbed him once. In fact half his head was a mess of brain tissue, blood, hair and fragments of bone. His face was intact, wearing a bizarrely peaceful expression. A screen hiding the chaos behind.

Milena was wandering around in tiny, tiny circles, incapable of standing still. Her entire body was shaking. I went over to her, tried to put my arm around her, but she kept sliding away, as if her life depended on constant motion. Blood was welling out of a wound on her neck, and I made her press her hand against it while I fetched a dressing and surgical tape. She let me dress the wound, but was still shaking uncontrollably.

I didn't want to stay in this place for one minute longer than necessary. Obviously I realized that Jacob was dead, but a small part of me—not that small, actually—hardly dared take my eyes off his body. I was afraid that he would get up, against all the odds, and attack me once more with brain matter trickling out of his skull.

We had to collect everything we needed and get out of here. As soon as possible.

My priority was fresh clothes. My top, trousers and underwear were in shreds. I asked Milena to help me, and this concrete task seemed to bring her back to reality. She opened my rucksack, dug out the necessary items, unlaced my boots and removed them and my trousers.

I wasn't much help in getting dressed. My upper body was a particular problem because of my broken arm, but with care and concentration Milena managed to get me into my underwear, trousers, top and hardshell jacket. She also helped me with my cap. I smiled gratefully at her, and she gave me a wan smile in return.

My head was still caught up in what seemed to be a never-ending explosion.

We packed up the tent, mine and Henrik's. Once again I wasn't much use. I gave the instructions and Milena carried them out. I took anything that wasn't absolutely necessary out of my rucksack, because I was going to have to carry it looped over my good shoulder. Milena dismantled Jacob's stove and stowed it in her rucksack.

We moved back and forth across our campsite, gathering together our bits and pieces. I didn't want to look directly at Jacob, but I kept him in my peripheral vision all the time. I wanted to be certain that he wasn't moving.

Finally we were ready to go. We left behind a tent, a dead body and an ice ax.

We are staggering down the mountain. We are walking on grass now, and there is tangled undergrowth, and the odd gnarled birch with its rheumatic branches. The sun is shining from a cloudless sky, but it provides no warmth at all. The chill of autumn is in the air.

I have begun to shiver. Here it comes. In addition to the headache and the pain in my throat, I am now aware of a dull ache from my shoulder and my broken arm, an ache that is bound to grow and grow into an unbearable crescendo.

We stop and I take out the plastic bag of medication. I fill my cup with water from a little stream and dissolve two Treo painkillers in it. I take an Ipren as well, to be on the safe side. I have no idea whether the combination will be more effective or less, or if I might be risking kidney damage or whatever, but I don't care. I'll settle for minor kidney damage if the pills can avert the tsunami of pain I can see rushing toward me.

Neither of us is hungry. I know we ought to eat something, get something warm inside us, especially me, but we're much too tired to rig up the stove right now. Later.

I dig out an energy bar and offer half to Milena, but she doesn't want it. She mumbles that she feels sick. Then she bends forward and throws up in the grass—nothing but viscous, transparent strings of mucus. She must have emptied her stomach several times without my seeing her—maybe when I was out of the game up by the campsite, after she'd hacked Jacob to death.

She really does look exhausted. I force her to drink a little water, then she lies down on her back and closes her eyes. We ought to go a bit farther before we take a longer break, but I sit down—it looks so appealing. Milena seems to have fallen asleep immediately. I slide my rucksack off my shoulder.

I know I shouldn't lie down. There is a real risk that I will fall asleep too, and we must make progress. I have absolutely no intention of lying down.

Maybe I could lie down without closing my eyes. That would be a good compromise—but I promise myself that I definitely won't close my eyes.

Carefully I lower myself onto the grass. Every movement, every tiny impact on my arm and shoulder as I lie down on my back is sheer agony, like flashes of lightning from the storm clouds of pain.

But eventually I am settled, staring up at the clear blue sky. I take a deep breath, but cautiously—I don't want to move my arm or shoulder even one millimeter. I can't even begin to think about how I'm going to get up again. For now the pain has abated slightly, my headache is less sharp. I am freezing cold, but that's a good thing—it means I am less likely to fall asleep. I lie there motionless.

Now all I have to do is make sure I don't close my eyes. That can't happen.

When I wake up, it is already afternoon. The pale autumn sun is in a different place in the sky from when I fell asleep. I am shivering.

I am in full defense mode from the first second. I try to sit up quickly, but my broken arm protests, and I sink back down with a protracted groan. At least I can raise my head, look around. Milena doesn't seem to have moved.

Good. My pulse rate slows. Maybe the fact that we've had a few hours' sleep is no bad thing, given the night we've both had. And the previous day...

Henrik is dead.

Over the past twelve hours I have been so totally focused on my own survival that I have been able to keep that thought at bay, but now the realization hits me with full force. Henrik, my fiancé and best friend for almost ten years, is dead.

The shock is almost as overwhelming as when he fell from the mountain. Henrik, murdered by Jacob.

I begin to cry because I am cold and my arm hurts so much and Henrik is dead. I sob loudly and uncontrollably. I feel utterly abandoned and defenseless. Suddenly it's all too much for me.

I've always said that it's no good feeling sorry for yourself—either do something about the situation or accept that it is what it is. But right now I do feel sorry for myself, and I think I deserve to.

I lie there sniveling for quite a while, until it occurs to me that Milena might be able to hear me. As before with Henrik, I know that it's down to me to make sure that Milena and I get out of here alive, so I pull myself together. I don't want her to see me losing faith. I raise my head again, look over at her. She still hasn't moved; she almost looks lifeless.

I have always been the strong one, the active one, the optimistic one in our relationship, and that role still has power over me. It's as if it marches off on its own and forces me to follow on behind.

Perhaps it's just vanity, but if so, it is a vanity that can help us get through this.

Slowly, laboriously I drag myself into a sitting position and turn to face her. “Milena?”

No reaction.

Now I’m worried. I roll onto my knees and consider crawling over to her on all fours, but realize that will mean dragging my broken arm along the ground. The pain would probably make me faint. So on trembling, unsteady legs I stand up and totter toward her.

“Milena?”

She is very pale. The dressing on the side of her neck is red and sodden, and one corner has come away. Her neck is red too, and the grass beneath her head is wet and dark.

“Milena!”

I drop to my knees beside her, lift up the dressing. The wound is open, but it is no longer bleeding. I put my hand on her chalk-white forehead. She is very cold.

“Milena! Milena!”

I place my fingers on the uninjured side of her neck to check for a pulse. For a moment I think I can feel a faint rhythm, and I start CPR, I bend over her as if to kiss her back to life, blow air into her mouth.

“Wake up, Milena! Please… Wake up!”

No reaction. She remains in exactly the same position, pale and cold and unreachable. I repeat the procedure several times, but to no avail. I check for a pulse again, but this time I can’t feel anything. I try her wrist, moving my fingertips around desperately, seeking the tiniest movement, the tiniest vibration.

Nothing.

I try chest compressions, place my good hand on her rib cage and use my body weight to push down. But there is no strength behind it; my broken arm is hindering me. It is nothing more than a useless dabbing, and my shoulder is screaming in protest.

You can’t leave me, Milena.

I try mouth-to-mouth again. Then chest compressions.

Twilight is falling in Sarek, and I don't know how long I have been trying to revive Milena, but I do know that I haven't yet given up hope that she is in some sense alive. When I give up, that is when Milena will die. Then there will be no going back, then we will never text each other again, never get together for lunch to plan the summer's mountain hike, never meet at Stockholm's central station to catch the train, heading for our adventure. Never share a pan of minestrone soup bulked out with macaroni at the foot of a majestic mountain. Never laugh in mutual understanding at some comment made by Henrik, proving how gadget-obsessed he really is.

At that moment Milena, my wonderful friend, will become a part of my past. And that is unbearable.

You can't leave me.

In the end I run out of energy. I have been kneeling by her side for several hours, trying to blow life into her, but now I roll onto my bottom—with considerable difficulty. My head is spinning. I close my eyes and take a deep breath. I think I'm going to faint, but the dizziness passes.

I open my eyes and gaze out over Sarek. The Rapa Valley lies in shadow below me, but some of the peaks on the other side are still lit by the evening sun, their snow-clad slopes shining like gold.

Beautiful, and merciless.

I take Milena's hand. It is ice-cold in mine, yet it still feels as if we are experiencing this together. A final moment of friendship. She looks so peaceful lying there.

"Milena..." I begin, but my voice gives way. I squeeze her hand, try to suppress my sobs. It is a while before I am able to go on.

"I have to leave you now—I'm going to fetch help. But I'll be back. I promise I'll be back. So you can't die. Promise me you'll keep fighting."

A final act of self-deception so that I can cope with leaving her behind. Sometimes the instinct for self-preservation takes a strange route.

Only now does a thought strike me: Jacob's tracker, the emergency phone. Why didn't we bring it with us?

How stupid.

I could have stayed here, called for help.

We wanted to get away from Jacob's dead body, from his smashed-up skull, as quickly as possible. We didn't stop to think. We forgot the tracker.

I consider going back to fetch it, but…no. That would involve walking uphill, and I need to conserve my strength. Would I even be able to find the way in my confused state? Plus there is the totally irrational fear that…

What if the fucker is still alive?

No. I don't want to do that.

Better to head for the river and follow it eastward, toward Aktse.

It takes forever just to put on my rucksack. And when I've succeeded, I realize that I should have taken more painkillers. I have had so much pain from my shoulder and arm, and a hundred other places, that I doubted if they'd served any purpose.

However as the effect begins to wear off, I realize they had in fact taken the edge off. My head is about to explode. Every time I jar my broken arm, I feel as if my knees are about to give way.

I can't take off the rucksack to find my pills—I'd be stuck here for another hour.

Maybe forever. I have to get going.

One last look at Milena, then I stagger on toward the Rapa River.

Interview with Anna Samuelsson 880216-3382, September 19, 2019, Gällivare hospital, conducted by Detective Inspector Anders Suhonen.

"How far did you get on that day?"

"I don't know."

"Because that must have been the day before you were found, if I've got it right."

"Yes. I suppose I got down to... I almost made it to the river."

"And you slept out in the open?"

"In my sleeping bag, yes. But I was in a bad way."

"Of course."

"Plus I'd forgotten to bring the stove when I left Milena, so I couldn't cook anything.

"But I wouldn't have had the strength anyway, so I ate a few nuts and some bread, and drank water."

"And you were in pain?"

"Terrible pain, yes. I didn't get much sleep. Like I said, I was in a bad way."

"Mm."

"I find it difficult to... I think I dreamed that I was walking along by the river and bumped into some walkers, so when it actually happened the next day, it felt like a reprise."

"Déjà vu."

"Yes...although not really. It was like two versions of the same event. They were similar, but they weren't exactly the same."

"Right."

"I can't explain."

"It's okay, it's not important. So the next day you set off again, and just before Nammasj you come across a German couple, Robert and Steffi Zimmer, who use their tracker to request help. And about an hour later the air ambulance picks you up."

"Yes. I have vague memories of the helicopter."

"Mm. The thing is, I'm wondering..."

Silence.

"Is there anything you've told me that you're now thinking *maybe I didn't get that quite right*?"

"No."

"I understand. Just give it some thought."

Silence.

"Yes... No, I don't know what you mean."

"It's fine, I just wanted to check. We've been talking for a few days now, and I've noticed that you've got better and better. Your physical recovery has been amazing, I have to say. You're incredibly strong."

"Maybe."

"Which makes me think, maybe there's something you told me at the beginning that has gradually become clearer, maybe... maybe your memory has come back, or you remember something in a different way. Nothing like that?"

"No."

"No?"

Silence.

"Are we done here?"

"Not quite. I'd like to go back to the morning Jacob died, to make sure I've understood correctly."

"No problem."

"You said you had a blackout."

"Yes, because he was trying to strangle me."

"That's what I'm wondering about. You've described other occasions during those few days, where you've said you were unsure about exactly what happened, and in which order and so on, and you've said there were gaps in your memory."

"No."

"Yes… If I…"

"That was only on the last night. Not any other time."

Silence.

"You also mentioned that you didn't remember how you got down from the mountain. After Henrik had fallen."

"I…no. That's not the same thing."

"Isn't it?"

"No. I fell over and hurt my knee and I fainted because it was so painful. That's not the same as a gap in my memory."

"Mm…"

"That's not what's meant by a gap in someone's memory, surely? Fainting doesn't count."

"No, but this is exactly why I think it would be good if we could go back, go over a few points again so that I'm perfectly clear about what you mean."

"We can do that."

"Good. Okay, so like I said, I want to go back to the morning when Jacob died. You had a blackout, or a memory gap or whatever you want to call it… Is there any other chain of events that could explain what happened? Anything you can think of?"

Silence.

"Take all the time you want."

Silence.

"Anna?"

"No. What I've already told you—that's what happened."

"Mm, but the main issue for me is that Milena killed Jacob while you were having a blackout. So your story is a hypothesis."

"But it can't have happened any other way."

Silence.

"I assume that means you have nothing more to add?"

"No."

"In that case I can tell you that we've found Milena. And she's alive."

Silence.

"Milena's alive?"

"Yes."

Silence.

"And her story differs from yours. In a number of key points."

TWO DAYS EARLIER

Interview with Milena Tankovic 871121-01410, September 17, 2019, Gällivare hospital, conducted by Detective Inspector Anders Suhonen.

"Hi, Milena—my name is Anders."

Silence.

"I just have a couple of questions, then you can rest."

"Have you found Anna?"

"Yes. She's alive."

Silence.

"Is it true that you were with Anna Samuelsson, Henrik Ljungman and Jacob Tessin?"

Sobbing.

"Milena?"

Sobbing.

"Yes."

"And you and Anna have known each other for a long time, ever since you were students—is that correct?"

"Yes."

"And you've also known Henrik for a long time?"

Sobbing. Silence.

"Milena? You've known Henrik for a long time?"

Silence.

"I knew Henrik before Anna."

UPPSALA, OCTOBER 2009

It is the first really wet, cold autumn day since I arrived in Uppsala in August. The warm summer continued for a few days into September, and since then the weather has been clear, but increasingly chilly. The rain started last night, and this morning it is pouring down. The trees have begun to lose their yellowing leaves, which cling to the sodden pavement. The sky is dark gray, and I think it's going to be one of those days when it never gets properly light.

I usually cycle to my lectures at the Faculty of Economics. It's quite a way from Norby, but it's been enjoyable on those beautiful autumn days. Today I am catching the bus for the first time. I am wearing my bright yellow raincoat. I loved the color in the shop, but whenever I put it on, I feel a little self-conscious, as if it draws too much attention to me. That's probably just my imagination though.

It is warm on the bus, and the windows are covered in condensation thanks to the passengers' steaming clothes. I can smell damp wool and heaters. It is some distance into the center, and there are still spare seats. As the bus pulls away from the stop,

I sit down by a window and take out my textbook on constitutional law.

Today's lecture is about the fundamental law on freedom of expression. I find the right chapter and start to skim read.

The lecture will be given by a young doctor, Henrik Ljungman—I'd heard about him even before his initial session with us. Rumor had it that some of the lectures by older members of staff were so boring that the clocks actually stopped, but that Henrik Ljungman wasn't to be missed. His lecture on the Freedom of the Press regulations was brilliant.

When he stepped up to the podium in front of a hundred or so expectant law students crammed into the steeply sloping banks of seats in the lecture hall, I was disappointed. Was this really the much talked about Henrik Ljungman? Apparently he was only twenty-seven, but he looked older. Okay, I was some distance away, but I could easily have assumed he was middle-aged. His face was unremarkable and his expression was kind of closed, almost bored, as he opened his briefcase and took out his laptop. But then he began to speak. His features came to life, and his enthusiasm for the subject made his face light up. His voice was deep, melodious and beautiful. He moved across the floor with confidence and ease, and now he looked younger than his age, if anything. The way he spoke, the words he used—a rich, lively language with an almost childish joy in the phraseology he chose. He had a dry, self-mocking humor that could make the whole room burst out laughing.

Henrik is one of the authors of the book I am reading on the bus. I am looking forward to today's lecture.

The bus pulls over at a stop in Eriksberg, and several more passengers board. It is filling up now, people are standing in the central aisle, but the seat next to me is still empty. I am absorbed in the book and don't look up when someone sits down beside me. I am vaguely aware of a pair of dark trousers on the edge of my peripheral vision, and I hear the person shaking the rain off his umbrella. The bus sets off and continues its journey to the city center. The warmth, the smell of wool and the fact that I am reading have combined to make me feel slightly nauseous, and I glance up in the hope that it will pass. I steal a quick glance at my neighbor.

It's him, isn't it? It's Henrik Ljungman!

Yes, I think it is. He's half-turned away from me, so I can't be completely certain. I don't want to stare, but I think it is Henrik.

And I'm sitting here with his book open on my lap. He probably saw it when he sat down. Is that why he's turned away—because he doesn't want to be dragged into a conversation with a stranger?

I consider closing the book and putting it away, but that would also reveal that I have recognized him and find the situation embarrassing. It might even seem like an unpleasant thing to do. So I sit there with the book open, eyes forward so that I won't feel sick again, irresolute. And the person beside me turns so that he is also facing forward. I glance at him again; it is definitely Henrik Ljungman. He gives me a quick look, accompanied by a shy smile. I smile back.

"It's a good book," I say after what seems like a very long minute. So much thinking time—was that really the best I could come up with? *It's a good book*. My face burns with embarrassment. He doesn't say anything for ages; I wonder if he's actually going to reply.

"Thanks," he says eventually. Another lengthy pause. Henrik seems to be having just as much difficulty in finding something witty to say.

"Are we going to the same lecture?"

And so we begin to chat—about the terrible weather, about the bus and about where we live. Henrik has just moved to Uppsala from Stockholm, and has an apartment in Eriksberg. I tell him that I come from Norrköping and am lodging with a retired couple in Norby. The rain is still hammering down when we change buses at Slottsbacken, and Henrik offers me shelter under his umbrella. I say no because I'm wearing my raincoat, but I appreciate the gesture. As we hurry into the department and go our separate ways outside the auditorium, I say that I am looking forward to the lecture; the previous one was excellent. Henrik beams, and now he looks younger than his age again.

I am buzzing when I sit down next to my new friend Anna, waiting for Henrik to appear. I tell her that I met him on the bus, and that we chatted nearly all the way. She doesn't seem to be particularly interested or impressed.

Anna and I ended up next to each other during registration, and since then we have hung out quite a bit. We are part of the same base group and prepare for seminars together. Anna is fun to be with, always positive and energetic. She is my first real friend in Uppsala.

The rain continues relentlessly for several days, and I catch the bus every morning. I spend time studying in the huge bunkers down in the basement.

I often meet Henrik on the bus. It feels as if we have already become friends. I no longer think about the fact that he is a lecturer and I am a student. We are both newcomers in Uppsala—that makes us equals and gives us a lot to talk about. The constant biting wind that sweeps in from the surrounding plains. Which Nation has the best coffee and cake on Sundays. How to find your way around Carolina Rediviva, the prestigious university library.

I tell him about growing up in Norrköping with parents who fled from the Balkan conflict, and always took it for granted that I would make the most of the opportunities for higher education that were on offer in my new homeland.

Henrik tells me that he is aware of an aversion toward him from some of his older colleagues; they feel that he is an upstart who has had everything served up to him on a silver platter, and somehow gained his doctorate. I console him with the assurance that as far as the students are concerned, he is the only one they talk about. I can see that he is pleased to hear this, even though he pretends to hide it.

One morning I don't change buses as usual at Slottsbacken. I explain that I am going to prepare a seminar with my group in the new Faculty of Law. This is true, but it's two hours before we are due to meet. I have begun to arrange my bus journeys so that I have the chance to see Henrik.

On another day we chat about the sights in Uppsala that we haven't yet seen. I haven't been to the cathedral, but Henrik has. And on the weekend he is going again, to a concert. The Royal Academic Orchestra and the university choir—Allmänna sången—will be performing Mozart's "Requiem." He pauses, hesitates, then asks if I'd like to go with him. I am taken back, and delighted, and quickly say that I would love to.

The closer it gets to Sunday, the more nervous I become. My interaction with Henrik on the bus started through a coincidence—maybe the unforced ease between us is because of that? We no longer see each other on the bus almost every morning by chance; maybe it's the same for Henrik, but at least we have so far been able to pretend that that's the case. The question is—can we be equally relaxed on something that resembles a date?

I needn't have worried. My nerves disappear the second we walk in through the cathedral's impressive doors. I love the high vaulted ceilings, the particular smell of wooden furniture and hymn books and candles, the subdued lighting, the ceremonial atmosphere. One look at Henrik tells me that he feels the same. We don't have to say much. We both think this is wonderful, and are happy to have someone to share the occasion with.

The pews gradually fill up, and Henrik and I have to shuffle closer together. The musicians and choristers take their places at the front. I gently lean into him, point out a fellow student I have spotted among the sopranos. He doesn't recognize her, and asks in a whisper what her name is. I can smell his discreet male fragrance, feel the warmth of his body.

As the intense hum of conversation dies down and the bells begin to ring, I have to force myself not to reach for Henrik's hand.

The orchestra and the choir begin their performance. It is magnificent and dignified, mournful and beautiful. The music is as timeless as the cathedral in which we are sitting. There is solace in the knowledge that people sat in these pews and listened to Mozart's "Requiem" long before I was born, and will continue to do so long after I am dead.

After the concert we have a beer and a toasted sandwich at Södermanland-Nerikes Nation, then we stroll through the park in front of the university toward the bus stop. I tell Henrik that I am going to see Melissa Horn in the new concert hall in a few weeks. She has just released a new album and is on tour. I have been listening to the album nonstop since it came out a month ago.

Henrik is not familiar with Melissa Horn. I explain that she is a Swedish singer-songwriter. Henrik doesn't know what a singer-songwriter is. I ask if he has heard of an instrument called *a guitar.* He frowns, searches his memory, says he thinks he might have heard of it. Is it the instrument that is kind of bent and made of brass? I laugh at the fact that he doesn't know who Melissa Horn is, knows next to nothing about pop music in general and is happy to be laughed at. I'm not even nervous when I ask if he'd like to come to the concert with me. He smiles and says he'll check his diary, but it sounds cool. We exchange mobile numbers.

When it is time for him to get off the bus, we hug each other in our seat. "I'm so glad you came," he says in his deep warm voice.

"I'm so glad you asked me," I reply with a smile, giving him a long look as he gets up and heads for the doors.

Back home in my boring, slightly musty room I take off my

jacket and hat and contemplate my reflection in the mirror. I can't stop grinning. I am going to see Melissa Horn, and Henrik is probably going to come with me. And during the concert I might pluck up the courage to take his hand, or maybe he'll be standing behind me in a sea of people and will suddenly put his arms around me, and after the concert he will ask if I'd like to go back to his place for a cup of tea. The evening will end with us sitting on the sofa in his cozy living room, kissing each other. I can even picture his sofa—it's made of leather and quite ugly.

I can't stop thinking about Henrik. I like him so much. And I think he likes me too.

Interview with Milena Tankovic 871121-01410, September 17, 2019, Gällivare hospital, conducted by Detective Inspector Anders Suhonen.

"So you've known Henrik as long as Anna? Longer, in fact?"

"Yes."

"Okay… And Jacob Tessin, he's your boyfriend?"

Silence.

"Yes."

"Do you know where Henrik and Jacob are now?"

Silence. Sobbing.

"They're dead."

"Henrik and Jacob are dead?"

"Yes."

"You're sure about that?"

"Oh, God…"

Sobbing.

"He jumped."

"Who jumped?"

"Henrik."

I am standing with the abyss before me and Jacob has already started to climb down the almost perpendicular rock face. On both sides of the narrow edge that runs across to the other side, there is a sheer drop of hundreds of meters. My knees go weak and I have to back away; I feel as if I am going to fall over.

"Jacob…seriously…" I begin.

I can't see him, but I hear his answer from below. "What's wrong, sweetheart?" His tone is warm, loving. Maybe I'm the only one who picks up on the irony; there is definitely a reproach behind those words.

This is what you wanted, so now you have to take the consequences.

Had he forgotten about this section? Perhaps it's many years since he took this route. Or is it that he's so used to heights that he can't see how horrible the prospect of crossing this part of the ridge is for the rest of us?

Probably not for Anna, but definitely for Henrik and me.

Jacob has already reached the other side. He looks across at me with an expression and a gesture that says *easy as pie—what are you waiting for?*

Anna speaks quietly to me.

"He's insane. This is absolutely crazy. We need to rope up if we're going to cross here."

"Come on, Milena!" Jacob shouts, waving his hand.

"We need to rope up!" Anna shouts back.

"We'll just end up wasting time for no reason! Honestly, it's not difficult!"

"He's insane," Anna murmurs to me again. It's as if she's trying to convince me, get me on her side.

Jacob leaves his rucksack on the other side and begins to climb back along the edge.

"We need to get down to the valley before dark," he calls out. "Otherwise this really will be dangerous."

There is something in what he says. Walking along this ridge in the dark, even where it is a couple of meters wide, would be very unpleasant.

He's reached our side and heaves himself up with a single movement, powerful and athletic.

"We can do this, Milena," he says quietly as he comes over to me. "I'll help you every step of the way." He smiles and gently takes my arm, passing on something of his calmness and self-confidence to me. It's almost as if this is no longer my decision, and that feels good. Perhaps I would rather suppress my fear of heights than stand up to Jacob.

He leads the way to the edge, turns and begins his descent.

"Don't look down. Keep your eyes on the rock face, and focus on what I say to you. I will tell you exactly where to put your foot, where to put your hand."

I also turn around, kneel down, then lie on my stomach. I press myself to the ground and feel my way with my feet, seeking purchase. Jacob guides me, and soon my left foot is on a protruding piece of rock. Then my right foot, left hand, right hand. My body is tense, and my grip on each crevice is viselike.

However the rock face isn't quite as sheer as I first thought. I can easily keep my center of gravity tilted inward, I never feel as if I am about to fall backward into thin air. My knees are like jelly though, and there is a tingling sensation in my shins. It's as if I want to kick out as hard as I can. I force myself not to do that. In a steady, gentle voice, Jacob gives me instructions for every single step.

Focus. One step at a time. Don't look down.

Now I am moving sideways along the edge, right foot first, then left, then right again. Like a crawling grub. It's not fast, but it's safe. It's not difficult to find secure places to put my feet. I can feel myself relaxing a little. My grip is slightly looser.

Jacob has already reached the other side. He beams at me, reaches down with one hand. I take it and he pulls me up—I've done it! I am so relieved, and so proud of myself. We hug each other.

"Fantastic—well done, sweetheart!"

Anna is watching me. Her expression is grim and her arms are folded. I know I am smiling foolishly as I call out to her: "It wasn't too bad, actually!" I think I even give her a thumbs-up. Seriously annoying.

Henrik gets to his feet behind Anna and joins her. He leans forward cautiously, keeping his center of gravity on his back foot, and looks down into the abyss. Then he staggers backward. It looks as if he is about to lose his balance, but he stretches out his arms and sinks to his knees, then onto his bottom. He lies down flat on the grass. Anna crouches down next to him and feels his forehead. Henrik says something, Anna says something, but I can't make out the words.

Oh, God, he's afraid of heights. Henrik!

My instinct is to return across the edge. My own fear of heights has vanished now. I want to sit down beside him on the ground and stroke his forehead and tell him that everything will be all right.

Jacob and I stand there watching. "What's he doing?" Jacob asks.

I don't reply. Henrik isn't moving. He looks as if he's sleeping on the ground. I call out to Anna: "What's going on?"

"Fear of heights. This could take a while."

Jacob runs his fingers through his hair. He is clearly frustrated, but he doesn't say anything.

"It's probably best if we rope up," I say.

"I'm not doing that. It'll take fucking hours."

Now I am irritated too. "And how long do you think this is going to take?"

"Do you even know what roping up means? What it involves?"

"Well no, not in detail, but—"

"No, exactly."

"I assume it means that you're somehow secured by a rope, so that even if you fall, you won't die. Am I right?"

I can see the muscles in Jacob's cheeks working, but I keep going: "We could be stuck here for hours. We have to get Henrik across."

"You managed it—why the fuck can't he?"

"Because he suffers from a fear of heights—surely you can see that?"

Henrik is still lying flat out with Anna beside him. "I'm sorry, Jacob, I realize this isn't…"

"Shut the fuck up—I'll do it!" he snaps at me.

He strides over to his rucksack, tugs and pulls at the straps, yanks things out and hurls them onto the ground in order to find ropes and carabineers and belays. Like an angry child.

I say nothing. I just let him seethe. This is about Henrik now.

"I'm so sick of your useless fucking friends. This whole trip was one big mistake. They're a fucking waste of space. They don't belong in Sarek."

Jacob is ranting, then mumbling to himself, then ranting again. It was his idea to come to Sarek, so his anger should be directed at himself, but obviously I don't point that out. Instead

I look over at Anna and Henrik again and see that Henrik is moving. Good. Maybe he's feeling better.

But what is Anna doing? She turns away from him with an odd expression on her face. Is she crying? No, it doesn't look… It looks as if…

Surely that's not possible.

At that moment the laughter that Anna is trying to suppress comes bursting out. She guffaws so loudly that we can hear it clearly. Jacob stops emptying his rucksack and straightens up.

"What's she doing? Is she laughing?"

I don't know what to say. Anna is laughing so that she can hardly breathe. She is doubled over now, making weird rasping noises. It's a long time since I heard her laugh so uninhibitedly, but I remember that this is how it sounds.

Henrik slowly sits up. He says something I can't hear. Anna covers her mouth with her hand, but carries on laughing. Without turning my head, I can tell that Jacob is staring at me.

"Has she lost the plot completely?" His question sounds sincere; he really can't work out what is going on over there. I shake my head.

Anna is still gasping for breath. I see Henrik's expression as he gazes at her, and it breaks my heart. It's not often possible to read his feelings in his face, but right now he looks utterly defenseless. I see embarrassment, sorrow, resignation.

I actually think I hate Anna at that moment. She is strong and cruel and has no empathy.

She places her hand on Henrik's arm. I assume the gesture is meant to be apologetic, but it is too late. Henrik gets to his feet, goes over and picks up his rucksack. Anna follows him, they exchange words but I can't hear what they are saying. She has stopped laughing and touches him again. She realizes she went too far and is trying to apologize. He won't look at her. He puts on his rucksack with resolute movements.

What is he going to do? Is he intending to head back on his own? "Henrik!" I call out. "How are you feeling?"

But he doesn't set off back the way they came. Instead he walks over to the abyss. And there is something about his determined gait that terrifies me. I have known him for such a long time, and it is clear that something is very wrong. He begins to climb down the slope toward the edge. He is moving much too fast; he's not in control. He is going to fall. Oh, my God, he is going to fall.

"Jacob, please..." I say. "I think he's going to... Can you help him?" He can hear the fear in my voice. I beg him. "Please, Jacob?"

He doesn't answer, but he moves quickly, begins to climb down. "Hang on—let me help you!"

I am relieved, and grateful to Jacob, but I am still terrified.

Henrik is descending the rock face rapidly from one direction, while Jacob is moving even faster from the other. They are heading toward each other, while Anna and I stand on either side of the abyss and watch.

Henrik pauses and looks up at Anna. They exchange a few words, but once again I can't hear. Anna smiles at him. I can't see if Henrik smiles back.

Jacob has almost reached Henrik. "Here, take my hand!"

Henrik isn't moving. He is looking down. Why is he looking down?

"Henrik!" I scream, petrified. I have a really bad feeling.

Jacob is still holding out his hand. Henrik seems to be considering whether to take it, but Jacob's hand remains hanging in the air. They stand there for a moment, frozen in time.

Then Henrik falls backward, straight out into the void.

Interview with Milena Tankovic 871121-01410, September 18, 2019, Gällivare hospital, conducted by Detective Inspector Anders Suhonen.

"I'd just like to go back to something you said yesterday—that Henrik jumped."

"Mm."

"Are you absolutely certain of that? He definitely jumped?"

"Yes."

"Jacob didn't touch him?"

"No… Well yes, he did touch him, but that was because he was trying to grab hold of him."

"So he tried to stop him from falling?"

"Yes… I think his fingertips touched Henrik's sleeve, but…"

Silence.

"Okay, but as far as you're concerned, Henrik jumped of his own accord."

"Yes."

"Another possibility is that he fell, or stumbled, or lost his grip…"

"No. It was… No."

"You mean that's out of the question?"

"It certainly didn't look that way."

"Okay."

"It was no accident."

"There is a third possibility that I'd like to bring up."

Silence.

"That Jacob made Henrik fall."

Silence.

"Is that what Anna's saying?"

"I want to hear what you think."

"That's not what happened. Absolutely not."

"I'd just like you to consider the possibility."

"That's not what happened."

"You said that Jacob touched Henrik?"

"Yes."

"And you can't have misinterpreted it? Could Jacob have pulled Henrik off balance, made him fall?"

"No."

"But you were some distance away, and I assume that Henrik was at least partly hidden by Jacob."

Silence. Inaudible.

"Could you repeat that? A little louder?"

"Why would Jacob want to kill Henrik?"

"Mm."

Silence.

"Are you tired, Milena? Would you like to stop now?"

"I think Anna saw what she needed to see."

"Right... But you believe that Henrik jumped. That he took his own life."

"I do."

"So... I'm not sure I understand the chain of events. It sounds as if Henrik killed himself because Anna had laughed at him. Basically."

"No..."

"Let me simplify. I realize that he was exhausted and so on, but...people don't usually take their own lives for such minor reasons."

Silence.

"That wasn't why."

"Why he killed himself? Is that what you mean?"

"Henrik was depressed."

“Sometimes I try to work out, what do I really want to do? What am I looking forward to? And I can’t think of a single thing. There’s nothing that fills me with enthusiasm. Nothing in my diary that makes me think *that will be fun*.”

It was the second day of our trip. The sun shone from a cloudless sky, the air was fresh and clear. We were walking from Alggavagge to Sarvesvagge, quite a steep climb, and Anna and Jacob were way ahead of us. We could still see them, little dots several hundred meters farther up the mountainside, but soon the terrain would level out for them and they would disappear from view.

Henrik and I set our own pace. He talked and I listened. During the spring he had finally discovered that he was never going to become a professor, at least not in Uppsala. Even though he had been a lecturer for many years, and a tutor for even longer, he still hadn’t been allowed to supervise any PhD students, which was a requirement in order to be considered for a chair. When he asked the dean what the problem might be, he was told that it was his relationship with Anna. Not the relationship itself, but the fact that he had embarked on a liaison with one of his students, then tried to hide it for several years. This made him unsuitable as a supervisor, and therefore he could never become a professor.

I was shocked.

"Surely they know you're not the kind of person who comes on to your students? You're not like that at all!"

Henrik gave a bitter smile. "There are some who think I had it too easy in the beginning. But they're right about one thing—I did break the rules, and I tried to hide it."

He had been beset by self-doubt for a long time, but had managed to keep it together pretty well. When he was finally appointed to a chair, he thought, that would prove to him that his doubts were all in his mind. When it became clear that this was never going to happen, he was sucked down into a vicious circle of negative thoughts and self-loathing. He tortured himself, imagining what people were saying behind his back.

So the child prodigy didn't amount to much after all.

His lectures are pretty mediocre these days, the students find him boring.

Henrik, who was such a superstar! Who would have thought it?

Just going to work, walking through the corridors with the risk of bumping into a colleague before he found refuge in his own little office, took an enormous amount of effort. He felt like a sloth; everything was so slow and took forever. The world became gray and dark, even though spring was turning to summer. He was always tired and only wanted to sleep.

"I've felt like this all summer," he said. "I haven't been able to summon up the energy to do anything. It's like...wading through mud."

I was so upset by what he was telling me; I felt so sad on his behalf. "Henrik, that sounds terrible."

I gently touched his arm and suggested that we should take a coffee break. Soon we were each sitting on a rock with a mug in our hands, enjoying the view.

Alggavagge extended toward the middle of Sarek, a long way away. The majestic bulk of Härrabakte watched over the valley floor, which burned bright with the colors of autumn. There was warmth in the sun now, shining down from an intensely blue sky.

"I hadn't realized things were so bad," I said, blowing on my hot coffee. "You need to get out of there. You're the smartest person I know, Henrik. The smartest person I've ever met. You can become a professor somewhere else."

He didn't answer at first. He simply stared blankly at the magnificent scene before us as he sipped his coffee. Then he sighed. "I don't know. Academia is a small world. Rumors spread."

"What about overseas then?"

"Maybe. But it's tricky with constitutional law."

We sat in silence for a while. That's how it was with me and Henrik; neither of us was bothered by silence when we were together. It was actually something I valued—a sign of the closeness between us, and I think he felt the same.

"What does Anna say?" I asked eventually.

Henrik looked away. "The thing is…" He stopped.

I didn't say anything either. I had an idea of what was going on, but realized it was painful for him to speak about, so I gave him time.

"I haven't told her," he said at last, his voice rough and dull.

"But… Wouldn't it be better if she knew why you're feeling down?"

"To be honest, I don't want to look like more of a failure in her eyes than I already do."

"Stop, Henrik. You're not a failure. Enough."

"Yes, I am," he insisted, raising his voice. "I am, Milena. You don't have to try and console me."

"Please—" I began, but he interrupted me.

"If we rewind ten years to when we met, my hopes for the future, Anna's hopes for the future… She's achieved everything she dreamed of. I've achieved nothing."

"Have you spoken to a professional about this? About how you feel?"

Henrik didn't seem to have heard my question. He went on: "We've been engaged for ages, but I've stopped asking if we can get married soon. I know I won't get an answer… And children, I can't bring that up either. She just gets angry." He sighed deeply. "She wants to break up. I've known it for a long time."

"I really don't think that's true, Henrik."

What do I know?

"It is."

"But how can you be sure, if you don't discuss it? Maybe the two of you should go and talk to someone together? Couples therapy, or…" I fell silent.

"There's only been one occasion during our relationship when I really, really felt as if she needed me. And that was nine years ago, when Erik… I was already in love with her, but the fact that she needed me… I was hooked. But it was an extreme situation, and since then I've never felt needed."

"Oh, Henrik," I said softly.

"I suppose it's because… Anna thought she'd picked a winner, but she backed the wrong horse. I'm… I'm definitely not a winner."

His voice trembled. He bit his lower lip to fight back the tears, but his face contorted and a single tear rolled slowly down his cheek. He turned away so that I wouldn't see, but it was too late, I was crying as well. I went over and put my arms around him. He wept silently, leaned against me, and after a moment he put his arms around me too.

We held each other for quite some time, me standing and Henrik sitting, with Sarek at our feet. It struck me that we cried in the same way—without any grand gestures. We sniveled together, discreetly.

I stroked his hair, and he let me do it.

"Sorry," he said after a while. He took a deep breath and let go of me.

I sat down on the rock beside him. "Shuffle up."

He smiled and made room for me, then wiped his eyes.

"Sorry," he said again. "I've been talking about myself for two hours nonstop."

"It was something you needed to do."

"You know… I said before that I couldn't think of a single thing that I was looking forward to. But I have been looking forward to this—walking in the mountains and talking to you."

I felt a burst of pure joy. Deep down I knew that I didn't come on this trip every year in order to keep my friendship with Anna alive—it was because of Henrik. The hours we spent wandering through a magnificent landscape at our own pace with Anna far ahead of us. A conversation that meandered this way and that like a reindeer track through heather. Or a silence that felt comfortable and familiar.

But I didn't tell him I'd also been looking forward to our time alone together. It was on the tip of my tongue, but I didn't say it. I had Jacob with me this year, and I didn't want to come across as disloyal.

As if Henrik would have thought less of me if I'd told him what our closeness meant to me. It's so idiotic it almost makes me laugh.

I said nothing, I simply smiled. After a while he got to his feet and the moment was gone.

"Shall we make a move?"

"Mm."

We packed up the stove and continued our progress uphill. Soon the ground leveled out and eventually we reached a snowfield. We knew we were nearing the highest point of this pass.

I told him about my job, which was the same as the last time we met up, and my apartment, which was the same as the last time we met up, and my friends, who were more or less the same as the last time we met up. I'd started playing badminton once a week with my friend Jennie on Saturday mornings. I mentioned a couple of new bands I thought he ought to listen to. It was a running joke between us: I recommended various obscure bands and he would try to impress his students with them, but without listening to them first. He often pronounced the names wrong.

Nothing revolutionary had happened in my life. Apart from Jacob.

We had to get to Jacob sooner or later, but I was hesitant—it felt awkward. So it was Henrik who made the first move.

"Listen, I want to apologize for the way I behaved in the restaurant car."

"Mm."

"I'm so embarrassed—I don't know what came over me."

"It's fine," I said feebly. I was glad that the effort of trudging across the snowfield meant I was already red in the face; Henrik couldn't tell that my cheeks were burning.

"He must think I'm a complete nutcase."

"He doesn't bear grudges."

"How did you two meet?"

"Online." I knew it was up to me to carry on, explain, but I didn't.

Eventually Henrik said: "Right. So now I know the whole story."

"What can I say? He's my boyfriend."

"I'd kind of worked that out."

We carried on bantering for a while—Henrik asked questions. I took evasive action.

Because what was I supposed to tell him? Everything? That I'd been online dating like crazy for years, not because I thought I would meet "the one" that way, but because I wanted to "get back on the horse"? That when I saw Jacob on our first date, I thought he was so handsome that there must have been some mistake, that he was there to meet someone else? That he looked irresistible in tight chinos and a tight white shirt, perfectly ironed and unbuttoned just enough to reveal his tanned chest?

We found it easy to chat, he seemed interested and considerate, but even on that first date I had a tiny, tiny feeling that he was acting, that the real Jacob wasn't on show. There was something about the way his eyes glittered at me.

His phone buzzed three times during the evening; he apologized, said it was work-related and he had to take the call. After the third time he switched it to silent and promised to focus on me. I asked him where he worked.

"I'm a consultant with BCG," he said. "My clients expect me to be available 24/7."

I am a hundred percent certain that he said BCG. One hundred percent.

Jacob came home with me that night and we had sex. He was a good lover, sensitive and accommodating, fierce and powerful when I allowed it, when I wanted it. He didn't stay over, and we didn't see each other again until the middle of the following week. I spend most of my time in the intervening days fantasizing about him.

When I told him that I was due to go walking in the mountains soon with two old friends, he was so enthusiastic. He said he loved the mountains and had spent a lot of time there, both in winter and summer. He suggested that he should come with us. I promised to ask my friends, but I didn't mention it to Anna for a while. It just didn't feel right.

One evening we were at a cozy restaurant in the Old Town. In the middle of our starter Jacob's phone buzzed. He excused himself, "Work, have to take this, back in a minute," and went outside. I stood up to go to the toilet, which was by the entrance. The door to the street hadn't closed properly, and I overheard his conversation. "No, I can't tonight. I have to work late." I stopped, held my breath, wanted to hear what came next. "Ha ha.... Listen, is it okay if I come along when I finish?"

I locked myself into a cubicle, gathered my thoughts as tears of disappointment filled my eyes. I'd had a feeling about him, but even so... I took a deep breath. Now all I had to do was get through this evening.

I went back to the table and Jacob, who assured me that he had switched off his phone. I nodded and smiled. He didn't notice a thing.

After dinner he said he was tired and had to be at work by seven in the morning, was it okay if he didn't come home with me? We parted with a kiss outside the restaurant. It was a dark summer's evening with the heat of the day still emanating from the walls of the narrow streets. The sky was deep blue far, far above, and as I walked to the tube station, I thought that I never wanted to see Jacob again.

But a few days passed, and it occurred to me that I had never expected to meet my Prince Charming online, so why was I disappointed? Hadn't we had a pleasant time together? Yes. Wasn't he the best lover I'd ever had? Yes. Couldn't we continue with this charade for a while longer? Yes. We absolutely could.

Jacob kept asking me about the mountains—what had my friends said about him coming along? I answered evasively, but then I began to think that it might be a good idea. I needed to challenge myself and my fear of socially uncomfortable situations. I needed to practice not being embarrassed by what other people did, even if they were close to me. My relationship with Anna had got stuck in an immutable pattern, where she was always a dynamic Pippi Longstocking while I was a submissive Annika. It would do us good to shake things up—maybe she would begin to see me in a different light.

I wanted to shake things up with Henrik too. Wanted him to see me in a different light, not just as an old friend who had always been single.

So a week before we were due to go away, I told Anna that I had met someone, and wondered if he could come with us to the mountains. I half-hoped that she would say no, but she didn't. Which meant it was down to me—should I tell Jacob that Anna had said it was okay, or should I lie?

I thought about it for a day or so, then I told Jacob. He immediately started planning for us all to go to Sarek instead, and I stupidly said that Anna had dreamed of going there for years, which made him even more enthusiastic. Obviously.

Jacob's eyes, glittering at Anna from the moment we met at the station, all the time we were on the train and in the restaurant car. Anna with that direct, slightly bold approach that seems to be so irresistible to virtually every male on the planet. The jealousy—I didn't want to acknowledge it, but it was there anyway. I'd been here before. Did she have to?

And then there was the scene in the restaurant car—so embarrassing, so unpleasant. The business card, BCV, Jacob staring at me. *Why do you tell people I work at BCG?*

He had told me, and no doubt many others, that he worked at BCG, one of the world's most prestigious consultancies. However he was smart enough to realize that someone might find out he was lying, so he had business cards printed with BCV on them to use as a deflection.

I already knew he was dishonest, but the planning that had gone into this, the lie and the ready-made explanation, that was what left me speechless.

Henrik had unmasked Jacob, he just didn't realize it at the time. And I didn't help him. However that night as we lay in our bunks, I made up my mind that as soon as we got back to Stockholm, I would finish with Jacob.

Should I tell Henrik all this, put my cards on the table, expose myself, be completely honest about what I really thought, what I really wanted?

No. I didn't dare. I thought there was still time. So instead I asked: "What do you think of him?"

"Of Jacob?"

"Yes."

He didn't answer immediately. We had gone through the pass, with high mountains on both sides, and the snowfield had begun to slope gently downward. We could just see Sarvesvagge far below.

"He seems nice. He knows a lot about the mountains."

"He knows a lot about the mountains? Is that all you can find to say about Jacob?"

Henrik gave an awkward laugh, and paused again. "I can understand why you're attracted to him."

"Oh? Why am I attracted to him?"

"Well, he's handsome, stylish, a real man..."

"A real man? Do you think that's what I'm after? A real man?"

Henrik gave a sad little smile. "I don't know what you're after," he murmured.

I could see the end of the snowfield now. A little farther on, Anna and Jacob were waiting for us. They looked as if they were in the middle of a discussion. I slowed down.

Another opportunity to tell Henrik what I thought of Jacob, and everything else. The last opportunity for a while, because in a few minutes the four of us would be reunited.

"It's still pretty new," I said vaguely. "We'll have to see how it goes."

"By the way," Henrik said, stopping beside me. His voice was rough, as if his throat was very dry. "I've been listening to Melissa Horn a lot this summer. I'm sorry I didn't get to see her in Uppsala when I had the chance. Maybe everything would have been different if I had."

He glanced at me before he set off to join Anna and Jacob. I stayed where I was for a moment, my eyes filling with tears.

Interview with Anna Samuelsson 880216-3382, September 20, 2019, Gällivare hospital, conducted by Detective Inspector Anders Suhonen.

"Okay, Anna, let's carry on from where we broke off yesterday."

Silence.

"I'd like to go back over a few points in your story, make sure I've understood you correctly."

"I have some questions for you first."

"Right..."

"You've lied to me."

"No, I haven't."

"You let me believe that Milena was dead."

"No—you were the one who told me she was dead."

"You didn't contradict me."

"No, but—"

"So you kept the truth from me. Which in practice is the same as lying."

"No, I—"

"I don't remember exactly which regulations apply to police interviews, but I'm going to check. And I'm pretty sure that anything a witness has said while under a false impression is inadmissible."

"Anna, this is the—"

"Which means you're an incredibly incompetent interviewer."

"First of all, I have questioned you for the purpose of acquiring information. You have not been issued with a summons on suspicion of having committed a crime."

Silence.

"Secondly, when I first spoke to you, we hadn't found Milena. Therefore I assumed she was dead—as you told me."

"When did you find her?"

"We found her… Let me think, make sure I get this right… We found Milena alive on the sixteenth."

Silence.

"And when you told me yesterday, that was the nineteenth."

"It was."

"So you waited three days to tell me that one of my best friends is alive?"

"Correct."

"Aren't you ashamed of yourself? Aren't you?"

Sobbing.

"I understand, Anna… I understand your feelings."

Sobbing.

"The thing is… I realized very early on that you and Milena had different versions of the course of events. And we are investigating a potential murder. A very serious crime. That's why we felt it was justified to let you give your version through to the end."

Silence.

"I know several highly competent criminal lawyers in Stockholm. I will be speaking to them about how you have conducted these interviews."

"Feel free."

"You can't do this."

"I have cleared my handling of the investigation with my superiors in Luleå, but of course you're welcome to take legal advice if you want to check whether any errors have been made."

"Don't worry, I will."

"It's also worth mentioning that what you've told me isn't actually affected by whether Milena is alive or not."

Silence.

"Isn't that true, Anna? Apart from the last bit, when you believed Milena was dead.

"And there is no suspicion of a crime in that element, so it's of no interest."

Silence.

"Therefore, you haven't given me information while under a false impression—that's simply not true. However I would still like to give you the chance to adjust or add to your witness statement. As I said, I can understand that given the trauma you have experienced, memories can change or become clearer as time goes on."

Silence.

"I want to go back to Jacob's death."

"I have nothing more to say. I told you exactly what happened."

"There are one or two points that are unclear."

"What does Milena say?"

"We're focusing on your account, Anna."

Silence.

"Mm... Okay, I just want to reiterate that Milena was heavily influenced by Jacob."

"Go on."

"She kind of saw the world through his eyes. So whatever she's told you, that's Jacob's version of what happened. And it's lies, from start to finish."

Interview with Milena Tankovic 871121-01410, September 19, 2019, Gällivare hospital, conducted by Detective Inspector Anders Suhonen.

"I just want to get the timeline straight, Milena. So what we were talking about yesterday, when you and Henrik were walking together, that was September ninth."

"I don't know."

"It was… And the day after, September tenth, the four of you split up?"

"Yes."

"You and Jacob carried on into Sarek, while Anna and Henrik turned back."

"Yes."

"Why?"

Silence.

"There had been a bad atmosphere. The previous evening. We were playing a game, and we fell out."

"Was everyone there?"

"No, Anna had already gone to bed."

"What did you fall out about?"

Silence.

"It… Jacob lost his temper. Things were going badly for him."

"I understand."

"He got angry, raised his voice, then Anna woke up and came out, and everything just got worse."

"Did Jacob get physical?"

"What do you mean, physical?"

"Did he push Henrik over, for example?"

"No. Is that what Anna said?"

"What was your perception of the situation?"

"Jacob was furious, but he never touched Henrik."

"You're sure about that?"

"Yes. And later that evening he apologized."

"I see."

"So I thought we were done with that."

"Okay. So you had this big row, and the following morning you decided to go your separate ways?"

"Yes. Anna and Henrik wanted to go back to Staloluokta."

"Did you and Anna have a conversation in the morning?"

"Yes, we did."

Silence.

"And…we fell out."

Silence.

"What did you fall out about?"

Silence.

"Among other things, Anna said that Jacob had come on to her. The previous day, when they were walking on their own."

"And how did you react?"

"I was angry and upset."

"Because you thought Anna was lying?"

"No."

Silence.

"I knew it could be true."

Silence.

"By that stage I knew that Jacob had…an unreliable side."

"Mm. I've also beem told that…during the night, Jacob assaulted you in the tent."

"What?"

"He allegedly had sex with you against your will."

"That's not true."

"Anna claims she heard you crying."

"She heard me crying?"

"Yes. She also says that she saw strangulation marks on your throat the following morning."

Silence.

"Seriously?"

"Do you have any comment on these allegations?"

"They're not true. That's all I can say."

"Nothing else?"

"No. Jacob and I had sex, but it was completely… It was with my full consent."

"Mm."

"Anna has no idea what I sound like when I have sex."

"No."

Silence.

"As for strangulation marks… I haven't a clue how she's come up with that. Not a clue. My throat might have been red because I'd been wearing a new polo-neck and sweating the previous day. I don't know."

"Okay—but it's important that you have the opportunity to comment on what Anna has said."

"I understand that, but as I've said, none of it is true."

Silence.

"So… In the morning you split up."

"Yes."

"You and Jacob continued farther into Sarek."

"Yes. We camped by a mountain for two nights. Jacob did

some climbing, and I rested in the tent. The next day we carried on to Rovdjurstorget."

"And you crossed the river?"

"Yes. Jacob spent a long time looking for a suitable place, then when we'd gone a short distance on the other side, I saw Anna down by the water."

"So they'd turned back."

"Yes. They were both in pretty poor shape, Henrik above all. He was absolutely worn out. Jacob and Anna had to go back and look for him. I thought...*we have to get out of here as quickly as possible.*"

"And what was Jacob's response?"

"He was furious. He said that Anna and Henrik had left us, so they could sort themselves out. But I stuck to my guns."

"And he changed the route?"

"He changed the route, and there was a big discussion about that too. Anna was incredibly negative, and I began to realize that..."

Silence.

"Sorry, I just need a drink of water."

"No problem—we can take a break if you like."

Silence.

"I hadn't realized how exhausted Anna was. Mentally, I mean. It was almost as if she was paranoid when we talked about the new route. And then she accused Jacob of having stolen an LPG cylinder. It was as if she wasn't quite there, somehow...she was kind of inside her own head."

"So even then you could tell that Anna wasn't herself?"

"Yes. And I thought about something that happened a long time ago, when we were students in Uppsala. I'd seen it before."

UPPSALA, JUNE 2010

It is early June, the leaves on the trees are still the fresh green of spring, but for several days cold rain has been pouring down on the city. Little streams are running down the hill known as Carolinabacken. All the manholes are gurgling away. This morning the temperature was eight degrees; summer is keeping us waiting.

Not that it matters to me. In three days we have the last major exam before the summer break, so I am sitting in the reading room at Carolina Rediviva from morning till night, studying hard. You have to get there early in order to bag a seat. By nine o'clock it begins to fill up, and by nine thirty there is no space left. Fortunately I am a morning person, and am usually settled by eight thirty. I generally arrive before Anna and save the place next to me for her, even though that's not really allowed. She turns up about nine.

But today is different. It is almost quarter to ten, and there is still no sign of her.

This is stressing me out, because the seat I have saved by draping my sweater over the chair is the only unoccupied one in the entire room, and several people have asked if it's free. "Sorry, no," I have whispered in response. The last time it happened a girl sitting diagonally in front of me turned around and gave me a dirty look. She didn't say anything, but I know what she was thinking. *You don't do that, especially at exam time. Let someone else sit there.*

I am embarrassed, and can't concentrate. Where is Anna?

I take out my phone to text her, ask if I can let her seat go, but at that moment I hear rapid footsteps approaching, and I immediately know it's her. I turn and smile at her, feeling very relieved.

"Hi—everything okay?" I whisper. I don't want to disturb my neighbors. I remove my sweater from the chair.

"Er...yes," Anna replies, without looking at me or making any effort to keep her voice down. Her hair and face are soaking wet; she clearly walked here without an umbrella. Her sweater looks dry, so presumably it was protected by her jacket. You're not allowed to bring outdoor clothes or bags into the reading rooms. Her trousers however are also wet. She puts her books and pencil case down on the table. Her hands are dripping. She doesn't sit down. Instead she paces back and forth, spins around as if she can't decide what to do.

This is so unlike her—walking all the way to Carolina in the rain without an umbrella?

"Has something happened?" I whisper.

"No, no—but thanks for asking," she replies once again more loudly than is normal in this silent reading room. The girl in front of me turns around again, looking even more annoyed this time.

"Do you mind?"

"Sorry." I'm actually glad she said something. It gave me the chance to show that I don't think this is okay either.

Anna doesn't respond. She pulls out her chair, the legs scraping across the floor. She slumps down, spreads her books and papers all over the table. Everything is a bit frenetic, a bit noisy. It is insensitive, almost provocative, given that she has just been spoken to; it would be easy to do all this more quietly. But I don't think she's trying to prove that she doesn't give a shit what the girl thinks—Anna's not like that.

She's just not quite…present; that's the impression I get. It's so unlike her.

I try to concentrate on my revision, but it's impossible to get into it.

I glance at Anna. She has a book open in front of her and she looks as if she's reading, but she's flicking through the pages too quickly—no one can read that fast. She is sitting up very straight and I can hear her breathing, short and shallow, as if she is out of breath.

Suddenly she leaps to her feet, the chair legs scraping across the floor again. She gathers up her things, and I give her an enquiring look.

"Are you leaving?"

"Yes, I'm going for a walk," she announces loudly.

"Anna, what's wrong?" I whisper, but she is already on her way to the exit. She has left wet patches on the table.

Something definitely isn't right. I hesitate—should I go after her? I've asked her several times if something has happened, and she hasn't replied; there's no guarantee that she would answer if I asked again. And I've already missed an hour of valuable studying because of her. I'm stressed about this exam, so I stay where I am.

It's not long before another student, a guy I recognize from our lectures but have never spoken to, sits down beside me. He looks at the table, then goes off to the toilet and returns with a handful of paper towels. He wipes the table, sits down again. Peace and quiet at last. I am finally able to focus.

For maybe ten minutes. Then I hear those rapid footsteps. Anna is back.

Please, no. I have to study!

She marches straight up to the table and addresses the guy next to me in a loud, clear voice:

"That's my seat."

He looks up at Anna, standing there with dripping hair and wet clothes. He is taken aback to say the least.

The girl in front of me has had enough. She swings around and glares at Anna; this time she doesn't bother whispering. "What the fuck is wrong with you?"

I stand up, grab Anna's arm. "Come on, let's go."

"But that's my seat. I was sitting there just now."

"Yes, but you left. Come on, let's go."

To my relief she doesn't resist. We go into the foyer.

"I can tell you're not feeling too good," I say. "Has something happened? Or are you sick?"

"You could say that, you could definitely say that," Anna replies in a clipped, febrile tone. I place a hand on her forehead. It is cold and wet, no sign of a temperature.

"So tell me."

"Erik is dead."

"Erik? Your…"

"Yes, my brother Erik, he's dead, yes. And I was the one who took the bike but I didn't say anything, and I bitterly regret that, and now he's dead and there's nothing I can do about it. I have to study. I have to study."

I persuade her to sit down on a bench, then I call Henrik. Fortunately he isn't in a lecture or seminar at the moment and answers right away.

Henrik and Anna have been together for about six months, and it still hurts, but I'm not thinking about that right now.

"You have to come," I say. "Anna's being really weird—she's saying that her brother Erik is dead."

"What?"

"Yes. She's not doing too well."

"I'm on my way."

He is there in ten minutes, looking both worried and focused; he understands that this is serious. His voice is gentle and calm and reassuring. He sits down close to Anna and puts his arm around her.

"Anna? What's happened?"

"Erik is dead."

Henrik doesn't say anything for a long time. He simply takes her hand, squeezes it.

Eventually he asks: "When?"

"Last night. Mum called."

Another lengthy silence. Henrik's presence has already calmed Anna. Her breathing has slowed, her shoulders have dropped and she seems less eager to take off somewhere.

She has never looked more like a little girl than now with her wet hair and her wet trousers and her slightly confused expression. Henrik with his arm around her shoulders, her hand in his. She needs his proximity, and he is giving her what she needs.

He strokes her cheek.

"Shall we go back to my place?"

"I have to study. We've got an exam on Thursday."

"You can study at mine. It will be nice and peaceful."

Anna thinks for a moment, then nods. "Maybe that's a good idea."

Henrik glances at me, and I nod in mutual understanding. Anna won't be studying anything for quite some time, I'm pretty sure of that, but the important thing now is to get her to Henrik's apartment. It goes without saying that I will accompany her.

Henrik has a two-room apartment in Eriksberg, in a 1950s three-story block. A small kitchen with the original cupboard doors, herringbone parquet flooring in the living room. A modest balcony. The place is still sparsely furnished, even though he has lived there for almost a year. He has bought a sofa, a table, a television and a bookcase that isn't big enough for all his books. They are piled up on the floor. In the window there are pelargoniums with healthy leaves and lots of flowers; it seems as if he takes good care of them.

When Anna goes to the bathroom, he says quietly to me: "I'm going to call 1177."

"Good idea."

While he contacts the health-care helpline, I go into the kitchen and start making coffee. When I hear the bathroom door open, I shout to Anna, tell her what I'm doing. She joins me, frowning.

"Where's Henrik?" The fact that he's out of sight is making her anxious.

"He had to make a call—he'll be back in a minute."

He has gone into the bedroom and closed the door behind him; the murmur of his voice can be heard through the walls.

The coffee machine clicks and bubbles and hisses. Anna sits down at the table. I get out mugs and milk, then I sit down too.

"Do you want to tell me how it happened?" I ask gently.

"What?"

"Erik. We don't have to talk about it if you don't want to."

Anna doesn't answer. She just gazes blankly out the window. For a long time.

The coffee machine falls silent, then gives a little hiss. Or is it a sigh? Silence again. The only sound is the cold rain hammering on the window ledge.

Then she says, in a toneless voice: "He drove into a rock face. In Dad's Ferrari."

We drink coffee, and soon Henrik joins us. He sits down close to Anna, asks how she's feeling.

"Weird."

"I think you need to rest."

"I have to study."

"Absolutely, but maybe you need a little rest first."

"Mm."

Henrik stands up, beckons to me.

"Where are you going?" Anna asks.

"I just want a word with Milena—we'll be in the living room. Would you like some more coffee? Shall I top you up?"

We go into the living room and stand by the balcony door, as far from the kitchen as possible.

"I spoke to a nurse. She doesn't think we need to go to the hospital, but Anna mustn't be left alone."

"No."

"And then I rang a friend who's a doctor and he's written a prescription for sedatives, so that's ready to be collected."

"Would you like me to do that?"

Henrik gazes deep into my eyes, sighs. "Do you have time?"

"Of course," I say. "Of course I have."

He looks grateful, gently strokes my arm. He is there for Anna, and I am there for him.

I take Anna's driving license and hurry to the pharmacy on Västertorg. It is still pouring with rain; it feels more like chilly April than June. I pick up the prescription, a combination of a sedative and an antianxiety medication, and run back to Henrik's apartment. As I walk through the door I can hear Anna's voice from the bedroom. She is sobbing, howling, a sound that horrifies me. Her familiar voice, but with a totally alien tone. Henrik is with her, trying to console and calm her.

I picture him holding her, rocking her slowly, whispering into her ear.

I don't want to disturb them, and I assume that Henrik has heard the front door open and close—he knows I'm back. So I go into the kitchen and wipe down the table just for something to do. It's pointless; there are no marks or crumbs to clean up.

I am ashamed of the way I am feeling.

Wouldn't a normal person be filled with empathy for her close friend, who has just lost a beloved brother?

Yes. And I'm almost there. My predominant feeling is grief on Anna's behalf—her pain is my pain.

But a tiny, tiny part of me thinks that it should be me sitting there on the bed with Henrik's arms around me.

Jealousy. Even at this moment.

You should be ashamed of yourself.

I stay in the kitchen, and after about an hour Henrik emerges from the bedroom. He fills a glass with water, picks up a couple of the tablets I collected and returns to Anna. A few minutes later he's back. He takes a deep breath, then exhales slowly.

"I think she'll sleep for a while."

He sinks down onto a chair. Suddenly he looks bone-weary. I ask if I should go and get a couple of pizzas for lunch, but Henrik finds a packet of fish cakes in the freezer. We cook them in the oven and boil some potatoes to go with them. We have a can of low-alcohol beer each.

I tell him that according to Anna, Erik drove into a rock face. He nods slowly. "She's convinced he took his own life. There was a huge row between Erik and their father over dinner on Sunday."

"Oh, God..."

"Their father thought Erik had taken his bike."

"She mentioned that at Carolina too—something about a bike."

"I didn't understand what she was talking about at first, it was all so disjointed—but I think I've got it now. Erik borrowed the bike on Friday, and put it back in the garage, but then Anna borrowed it on Saturday without anyone noticing. She forgot to put it away, and it disappeared. Presumably someone had stolen it."

"No..."

"And she didn't dare own up to the fact that it was her fault." Henrik sighs, shakes his head.

"Her father is... He's out of his fucking mind. Anna isn't herself when she's with her family. It's as if she's a little girl again."

"God..."

"So their father blamed Erik. And now Erik is dead."

Anna's feelings of guilt. I can't even begin to imagine the extent of them.

We have a cup of coffee after we've eaten, and Henrik produces a bar of dark chocolate. Then he suggests that I should leave. I've already done more than anyone could ask, and he doesn't want to take up all my time. Anna is asleep. He's going to phone the department, call in sick. The fact that he and Anna are a couple is still a well-kept secret.

At the front door he gives me a big hug. I feel the warmth of his body, inhale his familiar smell.

"You're the best friend anyone could have," he says. His words make me warm inside. And sad.

Out on the street in the cold rain I long to be back inside the apartment. I already miss the coziness and companionship born out of tragedy. The subdued voices, the exchange of glances, the gentle touches. And I think vaguely that this will bring the three of us closer together. Anna and Henrik, Henrik and me, me and Anna. Maybe it already has.

Against all odds I find a spare seat at Carolina. I stay there and study until it closes. On the way home I call Henrik, who tells me that Anna has slept all afternoon. He's going to try and wake her now, see if she wants something to eat.

The following morning I am back at Carolina as soon as it opens. I study hard all day, even though my thoughts keep turning to Henrik's apartment, how things are with Anna—and with him. I call him in the morning and we talk for a long time. The situation hasn't changed; Anna is mostly sleeping, although she did get up and have some breakfast. Her brother Gustaf called, but she couldn't face speaking to him. I ask if Henrik needs help with anything—does he have enough food for example?

Shall I go shopping for him? No, he already has everything he needs, but thank you anyway.

In the evening he sends me a sit rep by text. Anna is still mainly taking her tablets and sleeping, but she did have a short conversation on the phone with a psychiatrist. Henrik's feeling is that the most acute phase is over.

The next morning he calls me at seven thirty. I am in the middle of my breakfast. I can immediately tell that he is agitated.

"Do you know where Anna is? Is she with you?"

"What? No."

"She's gone."

Interview with Milena Tankovic 871121-01410, September 19, 2019, Gällivare hospital, conducted by Detective Inspector Anders Suhonen.

"She'd crept out during the night, while Henrik was asleep."

"Right."

"She went to her parents' house in Stocksund, in Stockholm, and threatened her father with a knife. So they called… Actually, I don't know who they called. The police or the emergency psychiatric service."

"Mm."

"Anyway, Anna was taken away."

"Anna threatened her father with a knife?"

"Yes. That's what her mother told Henrik."

"Did they report it to the police?"

"I don't think so. She was their daughter, after all. She was admitted to a psychiatric unit for a few weeks—something like that. When she came out she stayed with Henrik for a while. He looked after her, but she also saw a psychologist on a regular basis. And she was on medication for quite some time."

"I understand."

"By the autumn she was more or less back to normal."

"And what you saw in her behavior on that occasion, when she got sick—that's what you thought you saw again recently?"

"Yes. She became kind of…inaccessible."

"Okay…if we move forward in time, after Henrik had fallen—you said you went back across the edge."

"Yes. Anna started to run away, and Jacob ran after her."

"Why did he do that?"

"Why?"

"Yes."

"Because there was a risk that Anna might hurt herself. We were still up on the ridge—it was dangerous."

"I see."

Silence.

"Somehow I went back across the edge—I'm not really sure how I did it."

"Mm."

"Anna ran, and then she fell, so we caught up with her, but she tore herself free and ran again… She was completely…"

Silence.

"But we caught her in the end, then we went a bit lower down and erected the tent. We put her in our tent, because it was drier. She slept for a few hours, but at some point in the evening she and I were on our own—she asked me to help her with a gash on her leg. She told me we had to stick together, because Jacob wanted to kill us."

"And what did you think?"

"I was scared. I could tell she was psychotic."

"Mm."

"Late at night Jacob woke me up—he was in the other tent…"

Silence.

"You were in the same tent as Anna?"

"Yes—but she'd disappeared. Jacob was soaking wet. And furious."

"Oh?"

"He'd been woken by the sound of someone leaving our tent, so he got up as well to check who it was. He saw that I was still sleeping, so it had to be Anna."

"Jacob told you this?"

"Yes, when he came back. Later. He was worried about what she might do. He thought she could easily hurt herself. Or us."

"Mm."

"So he called after her, but then she ran toward a river. Straight out into the water.

She was drowning, and Jacob waded in to try and drag her out, but Anna fought against him and knocked him over. He thought he was going to drown too."

"I see."

"And then he was like, *I don't give a shit about her, if she dies tonight it's not my fault*. Something along those lines."

"Mm."

"So I went down to the river to look for her, but I couldn't find her. It was pitch-dark—I had a head torch, but I could only see what was in the beam. I followed the river downstream for quite a long way, but there was no sign of her."

"No."

"So in the end I went back to the tent. Jacob had changed into dry clothes and gone to bed in our tent. I went to bed as well—I was exhausted. I fell asleep. And then Anna came back."

At first I don't know if I am awake or dreaming, but I hear the sound of a zip opening, and someone messing around over by the other tent.

Jacob has his arm around me; I move it and try to wake him.

"Jacob! Jacob!" I hiss, but he doesn't react at all. He is clearly even more worn out than me after the previous day and night.

It can only be Anna out there.

I wriggle out of my sleeping bag, open the tent flap and creep out into the chilly air.

Dawn is breaking.

I spot her in the half-light and my heart almost stops.

Her clothes are ripped to shreds. She has cuts and bruises and grazes all over her face and body. Her hair is matted with dirt and dried blood. One arm is dangling in an odd way. She has a knife in her other hand, raised to strike.

She stares at me, and her expression is almost indescribable—terrified and aggressive at the same time, like a wild animal ready to fight for its life. She comes toward me, the knife still raised, and I stand there rooted to the spot, paralyzed, I can't move.

"Where's Jacob?" she asks, looking around. "Has he come back? Is he still alive?" Slowly I shake my head.

"He tried to kill me last night," Anna goes on in a voice that is not her own, a deep, hoarse, rasping voice. "We have to… We have to get away from here, Milena, we have to gather up everything we need and leave before he…"

At that moment I hear something from the tent behind me. Maybe I did manage to wake Jacob when I shook him, because now he is on his way out, and I want to call out to him but I am struck dumb by fear and no words pass over my lips. It is like a nightmare. Jacob almost pulls down the whole tent as he tries to shuffle his big body through the small openings, but he emerges on all fours and stares at me and Anna. She is standing in front of me, still clutching the knife. Jacob leaps to his feet with a roar and rushes toward us.

"Get away from her!" he yells, and I don't know if it's aimed at Anna or me, but the meaning is the same—he thinks that Anna is threatening me with the knife. Is she? Am I the one who has misunderstood the situation? I quickly move backward and Jacob hurls himself at Anna.

They both crash to the ground. There is a horrible sound when Anna lands with Jacob on top of her. She lets out a scream and I see the knife in his side, high up by his rib cage, the blade has gone all the way in. Anna grabs hold of it again, tries to pull it out but with no success, meanwhile Jacob is twisting and turning. The knife is stuck fast.

I stare down at them, transfixed with horror, still paralyzed.

There is an expression on Anna's face that I have never seen before, she looks murderous and determined. A couple of sharp tugs and the knife is out. Jacob attempts to defend himself, waves one hand in the air, hoping to seize the knife, but in vain. His other hand has found its way to her throat.

It is a desperate struggle, silent and intense. Technically Anna shouldn't stand a chance, but she has already inflicted a deep wound. Now she is trying to stab him in the back of the neck.

And at last the shock loosens its grip on me.

I race forward, get hold of Anna's arm just before she stabs again. It breaks her momentum and she only manages to scratch Jacob's skin. She tries to yank her arm free. Her crazed eyes are focused on me now and she aims a blow at my throat that I am not ready for. Instinctively I jerk my head to the side and I think that saves my life, because the knife slashes the side of my neck. Five centimeters to the right and it would have penetrated the middle of my throat. I lose my balance and fall backward, onto my bottom. Anna is trying to stab Jacob in the back of the neck again, and in order to escape he rolls over onto his side.

I touch my neck and my fingers come away red. Clearly I am bleeding but the wound doesn't feel deep.

Anna and Jacob are still engaged in their fight for life or death. Anna is now crawling away from him, but he gets hold of her leg and pulls her down again. She drops the knife. He scrambles on top of her, grabs her hair and bangs her head on the ground, over and over again. I yell: "Jacob! Stop!"

But it's as if he can't hear me. Anna is trying to kill him and he is both terrified and enraged. He turns her over and puts his hands around her throat. I get to my feet.

"STOP! JACOB!"

I push him away from Anna, or maybe I fall into him and knock him over. Anyway he loses his grip and we are lying in a coughing, groaning, bleeding heap.

"You can't... You can't..." I say, but I can't finish the sentence. I am sobbing, out of breath. Jacob lies on his back and feels at his side, where the knife went in. He is also on the verge of tears.

His lower lip is trembling when he says: "She's trying to kill me, for fuck's sake... She's trying to kill me..."

Blood pours over his fingers and he twists his head to see the wound. I see it too.

With every beat of his heart, fresh blood is pumped out of his body.

"Put your hand over it and press hard," I say. I realize it's urgent. We have to stop the flow of blood. I manage to get up and stagger over to Anna's rucksack. I dig and dig, flinging stuff onto the ground until I find compresses and surgical tape, the same things I used to dress Anna's knee.

Jacob comes limping after me, his face ashen, panic in his eyes. He is clutching the wound with both hands.

"There's so much blood…"

"You can't move around, Jacob. Lie down."

"I don't want to die."

"Lie down."

"I don't want to die."

"You're not going to die. Lie down. On your side."

He does as I say. He lies down on his side and pulls up his top, presses his hand on the wound again; the blood wells up between his fingers. I lift his hand, lay a compress on the wound, replace his hand. Unroll a strip of tape, tear it off with my teeth, lift his hand, lay the tape diagonally across the compress. Another strip of tape and the dressing is secure—but it is already sodden with blood. Is this any use at all?

"You have to keep pressing hard with your hand, Jacob." I am almost in tears. The compress doesn't seem to be stemming the bleeding, but I don't have a better plan, so I add another compress beneath Jacob's hand, rip off more tape, and at that moment I hear shuffling steps behind me. I turn around and there is Anna with the ice ax raised, and now she strikes.

A scream of fear, my scream, and I crawl and stumble away from Jacob. I didn't see whether Anna's blow found its target, but I heard the sound. God, I heard the sound.

Interview with Milena Tankovic 871121-01410, September 19, 2019, Gällivare hospital, conducted by Detective Inspector Anders Suhonen.

Sobbing.

"Can you cope with a few more questions?"

Sobbing. Silence.

"Milena?"

"Yes."

"So Anna killed Jacob."

"Yes."

"And what happened next?"

Silence.

"We set off again."

"You and Anna?"

"For a bit. I didn't dare…"

"Did she threaten you?"

Silence.

"Not directly. But she'd… I was in shock after she'd killed Jacob."

"Of course."

"And she'd slashed me with the knife."

"Yes."

"So I was scared. Really scared. She was psychotic."

"But then you split up—obviously, because Anna was found the day before yesterday, near Nammasj. And we found you today, almost ten kilometers from there. In the tent."

"We took a break after a while, and I fell asleep. When I woke up, Anna was doing CPR, what's it called…"

"Mouth-to-mouth resuscitation."

"That's it."

Silence.

"I realized she thought I was dead. She tried to check my pulse, and I decided to carry on playing dead."

"She didn't find your pulse?"

"No."

"Mm."

"Eventually she gave up and left."

"And you stayed where you were?"

"Yes. I was too tired to… I had no idea where I was, or which way to go. So I put up the tent and went to bed."

"And then we found you, two days later. Listen, I'd like to go back and talk a little bit more about Henrik jumping from the ridge."

"Okay."

"You believe he took his own life?"

"Yes."

"The thing is, Milena, I'm sitting here wondering about a pattern I see in all this."

Silence.

"Oh?"

"You say that Jacob wasn't trying to drown Anna in the river that night—he was trying to rescue her."

"I can't say for certain—I wasn't there."

"No, but you believe what Jacob told you."

"Yes."

"And you say it wasn't Jacob who caused Henrik to fall."

"It wasn't."

"But you were standing a short distance away, and you admit that Jacob touched Henrik, and yet you're absolutely sure that he didn't cause Henrik to fall."

"Yes."

"My point is that in all these situations, you have taken Jacob's part and believed what he told you. And I'm wondering whether you might be heavily influenced by him. From what both you and Anna have said, Jacob comes across as a pretty dominant and intense individual."

"No."

"If that is the case, it's not surprising. You were in a very vulnerable position in Sarek, basically at his mercy, whatever he chose to do. It's comparable with a hostage situation—you were dependent on one person for your survival. It's perfectly normal under those circumstances to fit in with the way that person perceives and describes events. It's not necessarily a conscious decision. It's something you do intuitively, so to speak, in order to survive."

"No."

"So I'd like to ask you to reconsider what we've discussed. Is there any possibility of interpreting what happened in a different way?"

"I know there is. I'm sure Anna has her own version."

"But what do you think?"

"I think that… Anna saw what she needed to see so that she can go on living."

"What do you mean?"

Silence.

"She couldn't accept that Henrik was depressed."

"No."

"And when he killed himself, he was the second person who was very close to her who had done that."

"Mm."

"I know she felt guilty when her brother committed suicide. Very guilty. So taken altogether, it's just too much for her. As it probably would be for just about anyone."

"Yes."

"She needs someone to blame, and Jacob fits the bill perfectly. She takes some of his less positive qualities and ramps them up as much as she can…then she adds other stuff that is pure fantasy, or maybe stuff she's got from her father. And suddenly Jacob is a psychopath. He's killed Henrik, and Anna is fighting for her life."

Interview with Anna Samuelsson 880216-3382, September 20, 2019, Gällivare hospital, conducted by Detective Inspector Anders Suhonen.

"I have to tell you that we've looked into a couple of matters."

Silence.

"First of all, we have checked out Stefan Jakob Johansson against the criminal records database. He has no record. His name doesn't appear anywhere."

Silence.

"And the suspected offenders' database?"

"Same result."

Silence.

"What about Jacob Tessin then?"

"There is no person with that name—it's just what he chooses to call himself. He doesn't feature on either database."

Silence.

"How long does a person remain on the suspected offenders' database?"

"That depends on the degree of suspicion."

"Maybe it's so long ago that his name has been removed."

"Although the case you said you remembered Jacob from went to court, and the perpetrator was convicted—according to you."

"Yes, but I told you I made a mistake. It wasn't the case I thought it was. So I can't say exactly which case I remembered him from."

"Right…"

"It could… I mean this is a few years ago, so it could be that I remember him from a case where there was no conviction."

"I see."

"So that doesn't prove or disprove anything."

"No… We've also looked into his life, at least to a certain extent. His employment record, among other things. It turns out that for a short period, I think it was four months, he worked at a place called Klätterverket—a climbing gym—on Telefonplan in Stockholm. On the reception desk, mainly. Five years ago."

Silence.

"Are you familiar with Klätterverket?"

"Yes."

"Yes. And I was curious, because I knew you were also into your climbing. So I checked to see whether they knew who you were, and they did. You've been a member for many years."

Silence.

"Which means it's possible that that's where you recognize Jacob from. The reception desk at Klätterverket. And not from the courtroom."

Silence.

"What do you think, Anna?"

"I have nothing to say about that. It might be true, or it might not."

"Okay…"

"It's not important anyway. I thought I recognized Jacob from my time as a notary, but maybe I was wrong. It doesn't affect the rest of my statement in any way."

"No."

"And I'm a little surprised that you've put so much effort into such an irrelevant detail."

"I just thought it was interesting."

"I realize that."

"And you did say the other day that you thought I should check it out."

"If he had a conviction, yes. Not whether I'm a member of a particular climbing gym or not."

"I can assure you it took very little time to find that out."

Silence.

"We've also discovered that in early June 2010—the third to the eleventh, in fact—you were admitted to the emergency psychiatric unit at St. Göran's Hospital in Stockholm."

Silence.

"According to the medical record of your admission, you had behaved in a confused manner at your parents' house, and had threatened your father with a kitchen knife."

Silence.

"The notes also state: *patient has no recollection of this alleged event.* Do you have any comment on that?"

"No."

"No?"

"And I don't understand why it would be of any interest now. It was nine years ago."

Silence.

"We've also checked the ice ax that was used to kill Jacob for fingerprints. We found only your prints and Jacob's."

Silence.

"This means that we have reasonable grounds to suspect you of the murder or manslaughter of Stefan Jakob Johansson. Do you understand what you are accused of?"

Silence.

"Is there anything you wish to say about the fact that your

fingerprints were found on the ice ax that was used to kill Stefan Jakob Johansson?"

Silence.

"Anna? Do you have anything to say?"

"I want a lawyer."

"We'll arrange that for you."

"And I want to make a phone call. To Jan Samuelsson."

"I'm afraid that's not possible, but obviously we will contact a lawyer for you."

Silence. Sobbing.

"I want to talk to Daddy."

UPPSALA, NOVEMBER 2009

After the concert in the cathedral I don't see Henrik again until the following week, but I think about him almost all the time. I fantasize about what will happen when we go to Melissa Horn's gig together. Uppsala is cold and rainy and dark, each day seems shorter than the previous one. But everything is bathed in a pink glow as far as I am concerned.

At last the day arrives when Henrik is due to give another lecture in the Faculty of Economics. While we are waiting for it to start, I tell Anna that Henrik and I have been to a concert in the cathedral. I wasn't sure whether to say anything; it seems as if I am hinting that we're a couple, as if I'm boasting about it. But Anna is my best friend in Uppsala. It feels odd not to mention it, given that she knows who Henrik is. Besides, I really want to talk to someone about Henrik. I want to talk about him all the time.

"Cool," she says with a distracted smile. Her lack of reaction is a little disappointing. "Actually I was thinking of asking him if he'd like to be one of our Thursday speakers—will you come with me?"

After the lecture she pushes her way down to the podium, against the stream of students leaving the lecture hall, and I follow her. Henrik is busy gathering up his papers and his laptop, and looks slightly confused when Anna accosts him.

"What a brilliant lecture! I was wondering if you'd like to come and speak at Stockholm's Nation. On a Thursday. Hi, by the way. Anna."

She holds out her hand and Henrik shakes it, still looking none the wiser. Then he catches sight of me behind Anna, and his face softens into a smile.

"Okay…er…" he says indecisively. It is a mistake to be indecisive when Anna is around.

"Shall we have lunch so I can fill you in? Milena, you'll come too, won't you?"

I am embarrassed by her presumptuousness; if I know Henrik, he will find it awkward to turn down lunch if he doesn't have something else planned. And I am right—he mumbles his acceptance.

We go to the faculty's crowded, noisy canteen, get ourselves a tray of food each and sit down at a round table. Anna explains what an enormous honor it is to be a Thursday speaker at Stockholm's Nation. Henrik eats his lunch, makes the odd remark to show that he is listening and glances across the table at me from time to time. He is keeping his expression neutral, but occasionally I think I see a glimmer of amusement when he looks at me, as if to show that he isn't taking Anna's pitch entirely seriously. He and I have a mutual understanding. I feel a warm glow around my heart.

When lunch is over, Anna has extracted a half-promise, or maybe slightly more, that Henrik will speak at Stockholm's Nation the week after next. They part with a handshake, while Henrik and I end up somewhere between a handshake and a clumsy hug. The last thing he says before we go our separate ways is that he hasn't had time to check his diary yet regarding Melissa Horn, but he will.

"Be in touch," he says with a smile. I smile back.

I try to control my fantasies, but I am so looking forward

to the gig. I think that's when it will happen. My whole body longs for Henrik. My fingertips long to touch his hair, his face, my throat longs for his lips, my legs long to wrap themselves around his.

The hall at Stockholm's Nation is full to bursting on the Thursday when Henrik is due to speak. It is a beautiful but slightly shabby old room with a high ceiling, crystal chandeliers, and portraits of the Nation's former inspectors hanging on the walls. The oak parquet flooring shows the inevitable signs of wear and tear from many years of student dinners and spring balls. Girls and boys from the Nation are buzzing all around me, all slim and attractive and smartly dressed as if they were at Harvard, or perhaps according to a Swedish perception of what you look like if you're at Harvard, I suspect. There are air kisses and hugs and laughter. Judging by the accents, they all seem to come from Lidingö or Djursholm. I feel ridiculously out of place, but Anna assumed I would want to come and hear Henrik speak, and of course she was right. I sit down near the back and stare at the screen of my phone while I wait for the evening to begin.

Anna steps up onto the stage and gives Henrik a short, zingy introduction. Amid deafening cheers and applause, Henrik takes his place. The talk lasts for just under an hour, and is about the Freedom of the Press Act and its roots in the 18th century. Henrik touched on this topic in his lecture at the Faculty of Economics, but now he goes into more detail and gives a number of amusing examples of what satire looked like in Stockholm during Bellman's time. Then there is a lengthy question-and-answer session. Henrik is interesting, entertaining and relaxed; as usual, he has his audience in the palm of his hand.

When it is all over, pea soup and Swedish punsch are served in a smaller room next door. I am hoping to have a few words with Henrik, thank him for the wonderful talk, but there is no sign of him and Anna. Meanwhile I stand and wait on my own, nervously fiddling with my phone. I'm only there for a few minutes, but it feels like an eternity. More than one of the pretty Stockholm girls glance at me, clearly wondering what I'm doing there.

Eventually Henrik and Anna appear, and everyone sits down at a long table set for about fifteen people. The two of them are seated side by side in the middle. I sit down too, and by this stage I am so self-conscious and uncomfortable that I don't notice that there is a place card next to each wineglass. My neighbor, a guy in a white shirt and club blazer with a razor-sharp side parting in his hair, gives me an enquiring look, then glances at the card by my glass. Which is when I see it too. It says *Sofia D.* I apologize, my cheeks burning. My neighbor gently touches my arm and politely says it's absolutely fine. I walk all the way around the table, searching for a card with my name on it, but I can't find one. Anna and Henrik are deep in conversation when I pass by; Henrik glances at me, then turns his attention back to Anna.

Eventually I realize that this is the top table, designated for the evening's speaker, the Nation's officers, honorary members and so on. Obviously I don't belong there. Other guests who wish to eat are accommodated at three long tables farther down the room.

God, what an idiot I am.

I would like to sink through the floor, or at least go home right now. But that would look as if I were sulking because I didn't have a seat at the top table, and I haven't completely given up hope of a chat with Henrik. So I find a place right at the corner of one of the other tables. I eat my pea soup and drink my punsch, and the other guests turn to me politely and exchange a few words before disappearing back into their world of mutual acquaintances and gossip.

I glance over at the top table. Anna and Henrik are still deep in conversation. Anna touches his arm. Henrik is beaming, looking young and boyish again. I feel an intense stab of jealousy.

A few minutes later I leave without saying goodbye to Henrik and Anna. I'm not feeling too good, and I'm worried that Anna might try to persuade me to stay.

I can't get to sleep that night. Everything was so awful, so different from the way I had hoped it would be. I am ashamed of my jealousy. I have no claim on Henrik, yet there it is. I tell myself that his long conversation with Anna doesn't mean anything at all. He was the guest speaker, she was the host; the fact that they were seated together and had a lot to talk about is the most natural thing in the world.

That's what my head says. My heart suspects something else.

The following day I text Henrik: You were brilliant yesterday! As always. It is a couple of hours before I receive a smiling emoji in response.

I go and book for the Melissa Horn gig. The woman in the box office tells me tickets are selling fast, and the event is expected to be sold out. I haven't heard anything from Henrik yet, but to be on the safe side I buy two tickets.

I don't see Anna again until the following week. We mention Thursday in passing, but it seems to be right at the back of her mind already. She doesn't ask why I went home so early without saying goodbye. I would have liked to know more about the evening, but then the two other students in our group arrive, and we start work.

One morning I catch the bus to the Faculty of Economics. There has been an overnight frost, and the puddles have been transformed into ice mirrors. The cold nips my cheeks like a premonition of winter, and you can see people's breath in the air. The sky is lovely, shades of pale pink and blue. It's going to be a beautiful, chilly day.

Fortunately it is warm on the bus. I choose the same seat as on that first morning when I met Henrik. It's a bit like an invocation, and it works, because there he is at the stop in Eriksberg. He peers down the aisle and I think he's looking for me. I wave and smile. His face lights up. In seconds he is sitting beside me.

We chat about all kinds of things. About how my first exam went, the fact that Henrik is woken by builders at seven o'clock every morning because his apartment block is undergoing a major renovation, a new film I saw recently. The warmth and intimacy between us is there once more; everything feels right, the way it did before that evening at Stockholm's Nation.

I'm in love with you, Henrik. Do you realize that? I think I love you.

I tell him I have two tickets for Melissa Horn, if he's still interested.

His face shuts down and he falls silent. He stares straight ahead, searching for the right words. He is clearly very uncomfortable.

"It's… The thing is… I've been invited to the St. Lucia dinner at Stockholm's Nation… I expect it's because I was the Thursday speaker."

"Oh, right, yes."

"So…unfortunately it's the same date."

"I understand, it's fine. Of course you must go to the dinner."

"Maybe…maybe we can go to something else. In the spring."

"Definitely."

There is a brief silence, but then I ask the question. I have to know. "Is it Anna who's invited you?"

"Er…yes."

I nod, and we sit in silence again, until we dutifully return to our small talk. I have no doubt that Henrik has a good idea of how I am feeling, and he is helping me to keep the mask in place. His kindness merely makes a bad situation worse.

We go our separate ways at Slottsbacken. I had intended to go to the Faculty of Economics, but I don't want to spend any more time with him than necessary. I don't know how long I'll be able to keep it together. When he gets up from his seat, he touches my arm and gives me a look that is full of affection and sympathy.

I get off the bus and walk all the way back to my room in Norby; it takes half an hour and I can't stop crying. The tears are warm on my cold cheeks.

The following day the first snow falls.

★★★★★

ACKNOWLEDGMENTS

I would like to thank my friends Mattias Konnebäck and Johan Norberg, who accompanied me to Sarek in order to carry out research for this book. Thank you for your patience with my overoptimistic planning and my substandard tent. After the trip we concluded that we entered Sarek as fifty-year-olds and came out a few days later as seventy-year-olds.

On the subject of Sarek: the topography has had to adapt to the dramatic needs of the narrative to a certain extent. Parts of the route that the characters follow do not exist in reality.

Overall I would advise against going to Sarek unless you have considerable experience of the mountains. My friends and I have gone hiking every year for twenty years, but we were still surprised by the difference between walking in marked and unmarked terrain (okay, I was surprised, I can't blame anyone else).

It is difficult to get to Sarek. You will need to devote a couple of days of your holiday to the journey there and back. In order to make the trip both safe and comfortable, you will also need to acquire equipment that you might not already have, for example a tracker.

So what will this investment of time and money give you?

Well, there's the privilege of squatting behind a rock three times a day. If you think that sounds like the high life, then Sarek is the right destination for you. (As a bonus you can count on doing it in the pouring rain with the temperature close to freezing on several occasions.) If not: go to Abisko instead, or Jotunheimen in Norway. There are plenty of places in the mountains where you will find equally dramatic views served up on a silver platter—comparatively speaking.

I would like to thank Anders de la Motte, Sofia Schmidt, Janis Gotsis and Torbjörn Andersson for insights that have made the book better.

Thanks also to Federico Ambrosini, my agent at Salomonsson Agency, for your guidance in the literary world and your many valuable comments on the manuscript. And for lots of enjoyable breakfasts at Delselius in Enskede.

A huge thank you to my publisher Helene Atterling and my editor Katarina Ehnmark Lundquist at Albert Bonniers. Your enthusiasm, your wise opinions on both major and minor issues, along with your meticulousness, have elevated the novel by several levels.

Thanks to everyone at Albert Bonniers who has worked on bringing this book to its readers. I am certain that it could not have ended up in better hands.

Finally: thank you to Pia, my beloved wife, my first and most important reader, for your support and your love.

Ulf Kvensler
March 2022